BROKEN

THE VIGILANTES, BOOK FIVE

STONI ALEXANDER

SILVERSTONE PUBLISHING

This book is a work of fiction. All names, characters, locations, brands, media and incidents are either products of the author's imagination, or have been used fictitiously. Any resemblance to actual persons living or dead, locales, or events is entirely coincidental. The author acknowledges the trademarked status and trademark owners of various products referenced in this work of fiction, which have been used without permission. The publication/use of these trademarks is not authorized, associated with, or sponsored by the trademark owners.

Copyright © 2023 Stoni Alexander LLC
Cover Design by Better Together

All rights reserved.

In accordance with the U.S. Copyright Act of 1976, the scanning, uploading, and electronic sharing of any part of this book without the permission of the publisher is unlawful piracy and theft of the author's intellectual property. Without limiting the rights under copyright reserved above, no part of this publication may be reproduced, stored in or reproduced into a retrieval system, or transmitted, in any form, or by any means (electronic, mechanical, photocopying, recording or otherwise) without the prior written permission of the above copyright owner of this book.

Criminal copyright infringement, including infringement without monetary gain, is investigated by the FBI and is punishable by up to five years in federal prison and a fine of $250,000.

Published in the U.S. by SilverStone Publishing, 2023
ISBN 978-1-946534-26-2 (Print Paperback)
ISBN 978-1-946534-27-9 (Kindle eBook)

Respect the author's work. Don't steal it.

To My Amazing Son

You're living an adventure. You are pushing your body, mind, and spirit to their ultimate limits. You are pushing a machine to do what many would consider the impossible.

I am in awe of you. Total awe. Talk about a badass. You. Are. It.

ABOUT BROKEN
FROM BESTSELLING AUTHOR STONI ALEXANDER

Hearts Like Mine Don't Love... They Destroy

I keep a tight lid on my emotions, so when my dream job got ripped away from me, I vowed I wouldn't look back. But the deaths of those innocent souls haunt me, every single day.

I'm broken.

Broken over a mission gone horribly wrong. Broken when the truth got buried under a mountain of lies.

Now, I'm angry... scorched-earth angry.

Offered a chance to unleash my rage, I accept the job without hesitation.
Lone-wolf assassin.
But no matter how many monsters I take out, I can't escape the damning memories.

Then, I'm forced to partner with the person who took me down.
Turns out, that mission broke her too.
Too bad she can't stand me. I used to make her purr like a kitten.

Being around her breathes life into my tormented soul. She's fiery and strong-willed, brilliant and beautiful. And she hates me almost as much as I hate myself. At least, that's what she wants me to believe. I see the way she looks at me, how my touch turns her inside out.

When the unthinkable happens, I step up and do the right thing.
That means, no more flying solo.
It's time to confront my past, man up in the present, and ensure she's the most important part of my future.

Without her... I'm just another broken man.

1

THE AMBUSH

Prescott

Prescott Armstrong killed the headlights before turning into a neighborhood where older waterfront homes stood dark in a moonless night. If anything went wrong, he had no one to bail his ass out. He couldn't shoot up a flare, couldn't call for back up. He wasn't just point man for the mission, he was the *only* man.

Three o'clock in the morning gave him the element of surprise.

He drove onto the target's street, stopped at the curb, and cut the engine. April in Virginia brought a shift in the weather. Residents might have left their windows open, so he had to be stealth, he had to be wicked fast, and he had to take the SOB out before anyone heard him.

I got this.

He pulled on his helmet, flipped up the night goggles, and opened the door of the SUV. The interior light was off, ensuring he stayed hidden in shadow. After quietly closing the door, he opened the back door and clipped the tactical belt around his waist. Next, he slipped the knife into its sheath and tucked both Glocks into their holsters. He pulled a third Glock from the floor of the vehicle, closed that door without making a sound, and made his way down the street, cutting between two homes.

He was fully armed, and he was ready.

After lowering the goggles, he strode from one backyard to the next. Silent, laser-focused, and determined to locate his prey.

Despite his slow-beating heart, his senses were on high alert. Twigs crunched beneath his feet on freshly mowed grass. An energetic fox scurried across his path in search of its next meal.

According to the listing agent, the for-sale property was filled with staged furniture that made the house looked lived in, but not cluttered. The owners had moved away, which gave Maul the perfect nighttime hideaway.

Prescott's blood ran cold.

Terrence Maul had jumped to the top of Z's list the second he found out that Maul had staged a riot, then shot his way out of the maximum-security prison. There was the FBI's Most Wanted, and then there was Z's Most Wanted. If you made it onto Z's list, you got a bullet between your eyes.

The end.

And since this kill had *not* been sanctioned by ALPHA—for reasons Z hadn't revealed—that meant the off-the-books hit would be handled by Prescott. And *only* Prescott.

I can't fuckin' wait.

As he approached the large home at the end of the street, he slowed. Like the others, it stood dark. The back door was locked. Seconds passed while he slid the pick into the keyhole in search of the pins.

Nice and easy.

The lock released.

Inside, he was met with silence. After a quick sweep of the finished basement, he made his way up the stairs. No Maul on the first floor, so he strode to the upper level.

While his controlled breathing remained slow and steady, adrenaline pumped through him. This mission had to be executed without error.

One mistake, and he was a dead man.

With a Glock in each hand, he cleared all four bedrooms. No fugitive. He entered the master bathroom and his stomach dropped. A woman lay on the floor, her body surrounded in a thick pool of blood.

Fuck, he took out the realtor.

Fury thundered through him. Maul had killed her, then bolted.

Back in the basement, he made his way toward the door. With his gaze sweeping left and right, movement caught his eye.

Someone jumped out of the shadows, his eyes wild, a knife in his hand.

POP! POP! POP!

The guy dropped as two armed men emerged from a back room. *BANG! BANG! BANG! BANG!*

Prescott grabbed a second Glock and returned fire with both guns. *POP! POP! POP! POP! POP! POP!*

Both men hit the floor as a fourth darted out the exit. Prescott whipped his head toward the runner.

It's Maul.

He ran outside as Maul scrambled toward the river.

Prescott took aim.

POP! POP! POP!

Maul plunged face-first into the murky waters of the Rappahannock. Prescott bolted over, staring into the blackness as the current raced past him. He flicked his attention downstream, but Maul must have gone under. Determined to get a visual on his mark, he strode along the river bank.

The blast of gunfire woke neighbors because lights flicked on in the house next door. One more earnest glance into the dark river before Prescott took off.

Despite wearing black and covering his face in camouflage paint, he needed to be gone before anyone ventured outside.

He hightailed it to the SUV, set his helmet and tactical belt on the back seat, then jumped behind the wheel.

After turning onto the main road, he flipped on the lights and floored it. Though soaked with perspiration, he'd remove his Kevlar when he got home. Only he wasn't going home. He was headed to Z's Arlington condo where he'd stay until morning.

Philip Skye—known to most everyone only as Z—worked in a shithole, basement office at the J. Edgar Hoover building in DC. Though he *should* be barking orders from a corner office on the top floor, he worked alone.

One of the many reasons why he and Prescott got along so well.

Z had moved to DC years ago, but he kept the furnished condo in case an ALPHA Operative needed a place to stay. Turned out, that someone was him.

Even though Prescott lived alone, he needed a buffer after a mission. And Z's condo was it.

What a clusterfuck.

From the intel he'd read on Maul, the scumbag had been traveling alone. Clearly, that information was wrong. *He was having a goddamn sleepover.*

A growl rumbled out of him.

Prescott hated—fucking hated—surprises.

As he drove north on I-95, he unearthed his phone from the center console. A sharp pain shot up his arm and he rolled up his sleeve. A bullet had grazed his forearm, his black shirt sleeve now blood soaked. He reached behind the passenger seat, grabbed a T-shirt, and wrapped it around his wound. Ignoring the discomfort, he turned on his phone.

Z had sent a text. "Four, not one."

"No fucking kidding," Prescott bit out.

He recognized all three of them from the prison break that Maul had orchestrated, but he'd been assured that the men had split up after the escape.

He tapped Z's number and the call connected.

"How'd it go?" Z answered.

"I got them."

"Confirmed?"

"No."

"What happened?"

"Nothing I couldn't handle."

"You got ambushed, didn't you?"

"I got out. They didn't."

"I'll send local PD in for the bodies."

"There's four in the house, one in the river."

Silence.

"I need details," Z said.

"There's a woman—probably the realtor—in the master bathroom. Maul's guys kept me busy while he ran. I hit him, and he fell in the river."

"Fuck," Z spat out. "Were you hit?"

"A bullet grazed my arm."

"Stop at the safe house."

"I got this."

"Why are you so difficult?" Z pushed back. "The doc can swing by and patch you up in minutes."

"I'm staying at your condo," Prescott said, changing the subject.

"Make sure the security guard doesn't see you."

"He never does."

"Nice job tonight," Z said before killing the call.

Prescott opened the sunroof and drove toward the nation's capital listening to the wind whipping into the vehicle. He thought about that poor realtor who'd simply been doing her job, then his thoughts jumped to Maul.

He was confident he'd wasted him. Prescott was a trained killer who did not miss.

Maul's bloated body would wash up on the banks of the Rappahannock River and ALPHA could close the case on the only ALPHA Operative who'd gone to prison for killing innocents.

"Rot in hell, motherfucker," Prescott ground out as the miles ticked by.

2

THE BREAKUP

Jacqueline

Jacqueline Hartley entered the busy San Francisco restaurant and glanced around. When she didn't spot him, she checked her phone. Nothing. As she waited near the hostess stand, her attention was hijacked by someone waving their arms.

It was Jeff.

Flailing is one way to get my attention.

Forcing a smile, Jacqueline made her way over to the booth. Jeff sat back down, lifted his glass. "I started without you. A mimosa."

As she slid in across from him, her guts churned. "I can't stay long."

His expression dropped. "Why not?"

"I've got to get to the airport," she replied as the server appeared. "Nothing for me, thanks."

The waiter jumped his gaze to Jeff. "Are you ready to order?"

"She'll order something," Jeff said. "We need a minute."

After the server left, Jeff continued, "I thought I was taking you to the airport."

That had been the plan.

She cleared her throat. "Jeff—"

"I wanted to ask you something before you left for your long weekend," he interrupted.

"Uh-huh."

He leaned forward. "I know things have been super chill with us, but I'm ready to take this to the next level. I want you to be my girlfriend."

Jacqueline's eyebrows shot into her forehead. *This is going in the absolute wrong direction.*

He set a key on the table. "The key to my heart." He chuckled. "And my apartment."

Her hands went clammy. *Here goes.* "We've actually been spending *less* time together."

"That's because you've been so busy at work."

While she *had* been putting in long hours, she would have made time for him if he'd been important to her.

"I'm sorry, Jeff, but I don't think it's going to work out for us."

His brows pinched together. "Wait, what? Are you breaking up with me?"

She stared into his deep brown eyes and studied his cute face. There was absolutely nothing wrong with him, except he wasn't The One. She'd known that from the beginning, which is why she'd kept things chill between them.

"Yeah, I just don't think—"

"Take this—" he slid the key toward her— "and think about it over the weekend. Maybe mention me to your family. Mom's love me." He tossed her a cheesy smile. "Let's go. I'll follow you back to your place. You can leave your car—"

The server moseyed over and Jacqueline jumped at the

opportunity. Grabbing her small handbag, she pushed out of the booth. "I'm gonna take off."

She did *not* look back as she hurried toward the exit.

Outside, the sun burst out from behind a thick cloud. Jacqueline slid on her shades and tilted her face toward the bright light. A few months ago, Jeff had told her he didn't want anything serious, so she'd gone out with him. He was cute, had a good job, but the spark had never erupted into anything. Jeff was a nice guy who would make someone happy.

She just wasn't that someone.

An hour later, she was checked in at the airport and waiting at her gate.

As she eyed the people walking past or sitting nearby, her thoughts wandered to dark places. Was he another stranger in the crowd? Had he stayed on the east coast or was he living in another country far, far away? Was he stalking his next victim or had he stopped killing altogether? As a federal agent, she'd spent countless hours trying to find him, but all her efforts had led nowhere.

She hated having to look over her shoulder. Hated that for ten long years she'd been living a lie. Pretending like she was okay when she wasn't. Living in fear wasn't really living. And living with the guilt was starting to take its toll.

She would never truly be free until he was behind bars, but finding him was like chasing the wind. Impossible.

Her phone buzzed with an incoming text.

"I'm kinda in shock," Jeff texted. "What am I missing? I thought things were great between us."

With her thumbs poised over the phone, she stared at his text. Rather than reply, she pulled out her laptop and started working.

She hadn't been home since she'd been transferred—*exiled*—out west, and she couldn't wait to spend the next few days with family and friends.

The flight to Dulles International Airport in the DMV—District, Maryland, Virginia—was uneventful. She worked, half-watched the in-flight movie, and opened an app she hadn't used in months.

Eight. Long. Months.

I wouldn't mind hooking up with him again. He was a good time.

Ding! The fasten seatbelt sign popped on.

"Ladies and gentlemen, it's your captain. We're passing through some storm clouds, so please return to your seats and buckle up."

Already buckled, Jacqueline stared out the window as the blue sky got gobbled up by a sea of angry clouds. She closed the Asylum app and refocused her attention on work.

At just past nine, the jet touched down at Dulles. After collecting her suitcase at baggage claim, she headed toward the exit to grab a taxi.

Her brother and sister-in-law loomed into view, and Jacqueline grinned. Keith looked exactly the same. Tall and lanky, he wore his brown hair clipped short, and he was starting to sport a golfer's tan. Naomi was Jacqueline's height—five seven—with a big smile and light brown eyes.

"I can't believe you're here," Jaqueline exclaimed.

Naomi threw her arms around her. "Of course."

Jacqueline hugged her. "You look amazing. When did you stop wearing wigs?" Naomi's beautiful Afro, resting softly on her shoulders, framed her pretty face.

"A couple of weeks ago," Naomi replied. "I've gotta throw some love to the hubs. He's been begging me to go natural for—"

"Forever," Keith replied before hugging his sister. He took Jacqueline's rolling suitcase. "You got everything, Jack?"

"All set," she replied.

They headed outside.

"Talk about looking good," Naomi said, "*you* look fantastic."

Jacqueline playfully tossed back her long auburn hair.
"Really? You think?"

"Absolutely," Naomi replied.

"Go on," Jacqueline urged, while she and Naomi followed Keith into the airport parking lot.

Keith laughed. "You two are hilarious."

"Your hair grew so much," Naomi said. "And the color is richer."

"I only got one trim in eight months," Jacqueline continued, as they pulled to a stop at Keith's vehicle. "You've seen my hair. We video chatted a bunch of times since I left."

"Your hair was always in a ponytail or piled on top of your head."

"I found this amazing shampoo and conditioner. You have *got* to try it."

"For Black hair too?"

"Absolutely," Jacqueline replied. "It's so good."

After loading Jacqueline's bag, Keith said, "Honey, why don't you sit in back so you don't get a crick in your neck."

Naomi leaned up, kissed her husband. "You are the best."

The ride back to Keith and Naomi's house zoomed by while Jacqueline got caught up with her family. She was close with her brother, even closer with her sister-in-law.

As Keith street parked in front of their older, two-story townhome in Alexandria, Jacqueline asked about her sister, Leslie.

"You haven't talked to her?" Naomi asked.

"Just a few texts, but no video chats like with you guys, and Mom and Dad," Jaqueline said.

"Don't get Naomi started," Keith replied, after pulling out the suitcase.

"What?" Jacqueline asked as they went inside.

"She changed up her looks," Naomi explained.

"A lot," Keith added.

Jacqueline set her handbag on the sofa as their German Shepherd, Cleopatra, barked once from down the hallway. "Why is Cleo stuck in your office?"

With a smile, Naomi clasped Jacqueline's hand. "We'll show you."

Keith opened the door, and Jacqueline stared at the mayhem. Adorable, fluffy, black puppies romped in what had been Naomi's office, now a doggie nursery.

Cleo hurried over, her tail wagging back and forth. Once inside, Keith shut the door behind them.

Jacqueline knelt to greet the dog. "Hi, Mama Cleo."

"Turns out, we *thought* we were busy, but now, it's kinda outta control." Keith rolled his eyes playfully.

Six frenetic bundles of energy crashed into Jacqueline. She ran her fingers through their silky, soft fur. "These are the cutest puppies I have *ever* seen. If this isn't love at first sight—"

"Speaking of that..." Naomi sat on the floor and the babes rushed over to climb on her. "How's your special guy?"

"Not that special. I broke up with him."

"What happened?" Naomi lifted one of the pups to give it a once-over.

"It wasn't love at first sight... or love at all." Jacqueline stroked one of the puppies and he started licking her hand. "He wanted to be exclusive, but I didn't even know we were a 'we'. Anyway, it's over." She set the pup in her lap. "Who's this?"

"That's Loki," Keith said, sitting next to Naomi. "His forever family is coming by next week. We're keeping his brother."

"We tell them apart by the different-colored Velcro collars," Naomi explained. "We're keeping the purple pup."

"They just turned eight weeks old, so their new families are eager to pick them up," Keith said. "We're gonna miss them, but not the craziness."

Jacqueline held Loki up and stared at his face. "He's adorable." She cuddled the small creature and he licked her chin, then barked. Laughing, she set him on the floor, and he scampered off to wrestle his siblings.

"They stay in here when we're gone, but otherwise we let them run around the first floor," Keith continued.

"Are you hungry?" Naomi asked. "It's not even seven, your time."

"Starving, but I'm good with cheese and crackers." Jacqueline petted the puppies before standing.

"We baked a lasagna," Keith replied. "Let's let these little ones out and we'll get you something to eat."

Back in the kitchen, Jacqueline sent her mom and dad a text in their group thread. "I'm home! Still on for golf tomorrow?"

Dots appeared, then a text from her dad. "Absolutely! We can't wait to see you."

Before setting down her phone, Jacqueline homed in on the Asylum app again. Feeling bold, she tapped it, then clicked her way over to Members. Mac's profile was still active, so she sent him a PM.

"Hey Mac, I'm thinking about swinging by the club Friday night. Any chance I'll see you?"

She hit send, set her phone down on the kitchen island. When her gaze met Naomi's, her sister-in-law was smiling. "You've got that look in your eyes."

Jacqueline pointed at herself. "Who? Me?"

Both women laughed as Naomi pulled a small salad from the refrigerator and Keith set the just-heated piece of lasagna on the island.

"Water?" her brother asked. "Wine?"

Jacqueline pulled a glass from the cupboard. "Water's good. You guys are so sweet, but you don't have to wait on me. I'm not company."

The puppies had been frolicking in the kitchen, but when Cleo lay on her side, all six of them descended on her.

"Sorry to bail, but I've got to get up at five." Keith gave his wife a kiss. "Honey, you've got a super-busy day tomorrow. Try not to stay up too late."

She offered him a sweet smile. "Can you let the babies out before you head up, please?"

On a nod, he redirected his attention to the mound of dogs on the kitchen floor. "Who wants to go out?"

Cleo rose, the puppies scurried to their feet, and everyone headed toward the door leading to their small backyard. Minutes later, the dogs rushed back inside. Keith grabbed Jacqueline's suitcase, climbed over the gate in the kitchen, and headed upstairs.

As Naomi poured herself a half glass of wine, she sat beside Jacqueline at the island. "We put you in the guest room."

"Thank you for letting me crash here."

"Of course," Naomi replied. "I've missed you a lot."

"Me too." Jacqueline slid a forkful of lasagna into her mouth. "Mmmmm, so good."

As the two women continued chatting away, Jacqueline's phone buzzed, but she didn't check it. After she finished eating, she helped Naomi bring the puppies into the playroom for the night.

A tired Cleo plopped down, along with four of the puppies, but two started rough-housing in the middle of the room.

"I'm gonna head up," Naomi said. "By the way, I'm working from home tomorrow, if you need my car."

"That would be great," Jacqueline replied. "I was planning on renting one or taking an Uber around."

"You can use it over the weekend too. Keith and I use his."

"Thank you... for everything."

Naomi's face split into a smile. "It's good to have you home."

After Naomi shut the door, Jacqueline watched while Loki roughhoused with a sibling. Seconds later, Naomi returned, Jacqueline's cell phone in hand. "I hope that text is something good."

"What text?" Jacqueline asked as she took her phone.

"You eyed your phone like a zillion times. It's gotta be a guy." With a smirk, Naomi closed the door behind her.

A message waited in the Asylum app. She re-read the message she sent. "Hey Mac, I'm thinking about swinging by the club Friday night. Any chance I'll see you?"

"Probably not," Mac replied.

Damn.

It had been eight months since she'd seen him. She wasn't surprised a guy—no, check that—a *man* like Mac was no longer available.

Loki wandered over and climbed into her lap. She ran her fingers over his fluffy coat. When he peered up at her, her heart melted.

"You evil, little devil," Jacqueline said with a smile. "You just cast a spell on me and I'm in love. Wow, that was easy."

Loki laid his head on her thigh, let out a breath, and closed his eyes.

"Oh, boy," she whispered, as she stroked his puppy fur. "I'm a goner."

Her phone buzzed and she flicked her gaze to the screen.

Another message from Mac waited in the app. "You ghosted on me, then, months later, you expect me to show?"

Jacqueline hit the reply button. "I didn't expect anything," she typed. Then, to herself, she mumbled, "What a jerk."

He had a point, though. She had been so wrecked over what happened, she hadn't divulged her epic, career fail. Instead, she told everyone she had an out-of-town work assignment, which was true, and she bolted.

After staring at their messages, she typed out another text. "I got transferred to San Fran for work, but I'm back for the weekend. If you want to meet up for a drink, great. If not, I get that. We had fun, but it was NO big deal."

She sent it, then carefully lifted little Loki. Sleepy brown eyes fluttered open and she cradled the dog against her chest. After a few seconds of puppy cuddling, she set him down next to Cleo. Mama lifted her head, then relaxed back down, all six of her babies by her side.

Jacqueline stared at them for the longest time. Cleo knew exactly what to do. No instruction needed. Would she be that kind of mom? She wasn't even sure she wanted kids. She wasn't against having a family, but it wasn't on her radar either.

As she turned out the light and quietly closed the door behind her, her phone buzzed again with a message from Mac.

"I'm pissed, but I'll meet you."

"Can't wait," she replied. "You fuck the BEST when you're angry."

"Fuck you? NEVER GONNA HAPPEN, HONEY."

As Jacqueline made her way upstairs and into the guest room, she couldn't help but crack a smile.

Then, why in the hell are you meeting me? You wanna catch up over a cup of tea? I don't think so. Fucking is the only thing we did, and we did it soooo good. I'm asking you for a booty call, baby, and you just accepted.

3

JACQUELINE'S SISTER

Prescott

Early Friday morning, Prescott stopped at the guard station, held his badge in front of the scanner, and the gate rose. As he drove through Armstrong Enterprise's nine-building complex, he thought about Jack.

Sure, he was pissed, but he wasn't stupid.

He was so confident he was getting laid that evening, he reserved a private room at Asylum. Why else would she have contacted him?

He'd never met anyone like her. She was sexy, wild, and so damn beautiful. His cock twitched as he exited his truck.

He'd been putting in too many hours at Armstrong, and doubling up on missions from Z. He needed an escape, and the fiery, auburn-haired clubber with the insatiable appetite was the perfect way to unwind.

After parking at his building, he strode through the lot toward the front door.

Eight months ago—when his life had gone off the rails—he took his rightful place at the company that bore his name.

Beyond his seat on the board, he never envisioned a life in corporate America, but here he was... Armstrong Enterprise's Chief Operating Officer.

As COO, he oversaw every department. While it was a huge undertaking, he threw himself into the new position when his dream job had evaporated into thin air.

Unfortunately, some employees didn't like that the rightful heir had waltzed in at the top, instead of starting at the bottom, like everyone else. Fortunately for him, he didn't give a fuck what anyone thought of him. They could stew in their own piss while he managed the family's thriving business.

He said good morning to the crew of receptionists before entering an elevator. As the doors were closing, his VP of Marketing hurried over. Prescott shoved his foot between them, and they slid back open.

"Thanks," Lorenzo said. "How's it going?"

Prescott tossed him a nod. "Busy day?"

"Always," Lorenzo replied.

The elevator ascended, stopping for both on the top floor. The doors opened and Prescott gestured for Lorenzo.

As they headed down the hall toward their offices, Lorenzo said, "I need to talk to you about something, so I'll schedule time with your assistant—"

"Let's talk now before the day gets away from us." Prescott unlocked his office door and the two men stepped inside.

After dropping his computer satchel on his desk, he said, "Walk and talk? I'm grabbing a coffee."

"Probably better to stay in here." Lorenzo shut the door, but he didn't move toward a chair. Instead, he folded his arms and just stared up at Prescott.

Prescott was short on time... and patience, but he raised his eyebrows and waited. After several seconds, he asked, "Did you want to sit? Do we need HR or something?"

"I... um... so..." Lorenzo ran his hand through his short,

graying hair. "Dios mio." He sighed. "I'm concerned that the messenger is going to get shot."

Prescott chuffed out a laugh. "Are you the messenger?"

Lorenzo nodded.

Prescott gestured to his sofa, slipped off his suit jacket. "Have a seat, Lorenzo." Prescott waited for the VP to sit before he eased into the nearby leather chair. "Take a second and relax, then tell me what's on your mind. We'll figure it out, together."

"Artemis hired a consulting company to rebrand a skincare line that's in need of a new look."

While it wasn't unusual for a multi-billion-dollar company to hire a marketing firm to launch a new brand or re-image a dying one, Armstrong Enterprises had a very competent in-house team.

"Do we normally outsource?" Prescott asked.

"No," Lorenzo replied.

"Are you concerned your department is being squeezed out?" Prescott asked.

"Not exactly," Lorenzo's hands were clasped in his lap and he was twiddling his thumbs.

Prescott needed to move this impromptu meeting along or he'd never get out of there. A very sultry Jack popped into his head.

No way in hell am I working late tonight.

"My department has been focused on a multi-million-dollar rebranding campaign for the past several months," Lorenzo explained. "It's been our primary focus. I know you've only been here a short time, but we're close to presenting it to the board. I'm not sure why your uncle would hire a consultant at this late stage." He exhaled a frustrated breath. "I know family dynamics are complicated, but I report to you, so there it is." Lorenzo rose. "I probably shouldn't have said anything."

As he stood, Prescott offered a reassuring smile. "I can't

imagine this consulting company being any kind of a threat to what you and your team have been working on. I have a meeting with Artemis later this morning. I'll ask him about the consultant."

"Please don't—"

"I won't bring you or your team up." Prescott extended his hand. "No worries. I got this."

Lorenzo offered a tight smile, a firm handshake, and he was gone.

Prescott followed, but was stopped by his assistant, Francis. "We've got a problem."

"What is it?"

"A number of people in Atlanta, Topeka, and Boise have had an adverse reaction to our top-selling painkiller."

"Fuck," he bit out.

"Dana called for you. Her team is concerned that someone at the manufacturing facility tampered with the medication."

That got Prescott's full attention. "Anyone hospitalized or die?"

"Someone needed to get their stomach pumped."

"Get Dana on the phone."

Francis whizzed into her office, called Dana, and put her on speaker.

The head of their Product Safety Division explained the situation, along with the reasons her team suspected internal tampering. At the end of their conversation, Prescott couldn't see a safer option than recalling the product while the manufacturing plant was scrubbed, and team members questioned. He told Dana he'd get back to her and ended the call.

"Let's loop in Artemis," Prescott said to his assistant.

Prescott and Francis left her office as his uncle was hurrying down the hall toward the elevator.

"Artemis?" Prescott called.

His uncle turned, but didn't stop walking. "I'm on my way out."

Already? It's not even eight in the damn morning. Over the past few months, his uncle had been out of the office more than he'd been there.

"Wait," Prescott growled.

At the elevator, Artemis glared at Prescott. Each time Prescott saw him, he looked tanner than the previous time.

"Did you hear about the painkiller?" Prescott asked.

"I did," Artemis replied. "Are you handling it?"

"Your office should put out a press release," Prescott said. "Dana's team thinks an employee at the plant might have tampered with production."

Artemis glanced at his watch. "We can have the product pulled in each of the affected cities—"

Prescott needed to take control of this situation. "We've gotta pull product across the country. That plant ships it to every state, except Alaska and Hawaii."

"Are you crazy?" Artemis's voice raised to a squeaky pitch.

Several employees stared in their direction. "Let's meet in my office."

"Like I said, I'm leaving."

"To do what?" Prescott shouldn't push back. Artemis Armstrong had been the company's CEO for decades. But Prescott didn't give a damn about professional hierarchy, not when the CEO wasn't acting like a damn CEO.

If consumers, who trusted this popular brand, were getting sick from it—and there was even a hint of tampering at the manufacturing level—it had to be pulled from shelves.

Artemis glared at him. "Last I checked, I do *not* report to you."

Holding his ground, Prescott narrowed his gaze. "We've got a major fucking health risk."

"No one's died," his uncle retorted.

Frustration billowed through him. Would his uncle have given more of a shit if someone *had* died? What the hell would it take to get this man to do his job?

"The *only* way we can ensure no one dies is to pull product," Prescott bit out.

Prescott would handle this *his* way. Total recall, factory wash-down, out the guilty party, follow-up with customers who reported adverse reactions, and eat the loss, which would cost them millions.

"Just get it done," his uncle said. "I've got a meeting with TopCon."

Prescott raked his hand through his hair. "Who?"

"TopCon, the consulting company I hired to rebrand an outdated product line. You know, spiff things up. Make us look cool and hip." Artemis did a kind of wiggle.

If that wiggle was an indication of his uncle's interpretation of *hip*, he needed to focus on his *own* rebranding.

"TopCon's ideas are *sensational*." Artemis grinned. "You'll see." He tapped the elevator button, the doors opened, his uncle stepped in. "I'll be back later if you need to get my approval on anything."

After the doors closed, Prescott growled. "What a useless piece of—"

"Crap," Francis muttered under her breath.

"There goes my Friday," Prescott said. "It's gonna take me all day to get a handle on this."

"I'll push your meetings to next week," Francis replied.

Jacqueline

JACQUELINE HURRIED up the walkway of her parents' Northern Virginia home in Potomac Falls. While she'd talked and video chatted with them over the past eight months, she hadn't been home to visit. As she stepped onto the porch, the front door swung open and her mom rushed outside.

"Hey, baby," her mom enveloped her into a warm hug, and Jacqueline melted.

When her mom wouldn't let go, Jacqueline started laughing. "Okay, Mom, it's time to separate."

Her mom broke away and swiped a tear. "How are you? I missed you so much." Her mom wrapped her fingers around Jacqueline's long hair. "Wow, California air must really agree with you. Look how long your hair is."

Arms around each other, mother and daughter went inside. "It's almost to your bum. So pretty, honey."

Her dad walked down the stairs and into the foyer. "There's my baby girl."

After another never-letting-go hug from her dad, they made their way into the kitchen.

"What time are we teeing off?" Jacqueline asked.

"Not for another hour," her dad replied. "But we'll leave in twenty so we can hit the range first."

Jacqueline loved golfing with her mom and dad, especially when they walked the course. "Are we doing eighteen, and are we walking or riding?"

"Eighteen," her mom replied, "and I bought a motorized golf caddy, so I can walk or ride."

"It's a beautiful morning," her dad said. "Let's walk the course."

"Did you fall in love with Cleo's puppies or what?" her mom asked.

"That little Loki was a real heart stealer," she replied.

"Did Keith and Naomi tell you we're taking one of them?" her dad asked.

"No." Jacqueline filled a glass with water. "You haven't had a dog in years."

"We fell in love with the runt," her mom explained. "She's the one with the yellow collar."

Being with family made Jacqueline happy, but she had several more months with the task force before she could start the process of requesting a transfer back east.

"We'll take two cars," her mom said. "We don't have enough room for us *and* the golf bags."

Jacqueline smiled when she saw her clubs in the garage. While she could have taken them with her to California, golfing with her parents was their thing.

After hoisting the bag into her mom's SUV, she got in the passenger seat.

On the short ride to the golf course, her mom asked, "How's Jeff?"

"I broke up with him. He wasn't for me. Plus, his life is out there, and I'm hoping I can transfer back here, after my banishment has been lifted." She sighed.

"We hope so too." After a pause, her mom asked, "Have you seen Leslie yet?"

"No, but that reminds me, I need to send her a text." Jacqueline pulled out her phone and shot one off to her sister. "Hey, Les, can I swing by later today and say hey?"

No dots appeared, so she slid the phone back into her handbag.

"Naomi said she's gone through some kind of change," Jacqueline continued. "I have no idea what that means, but I'm excited to see her."

Her mom grew silent, and Jacqueline glanced over. Worry lines around her eyes were etched deep and her mom was pursing her lips. A dead giveaway that she wasn't going to say anything about her other daughter. Not wanting to get into it, she asked her mom about work... and the conversation resumed.

A few minutes later, they drove into the parking lot. As she was pulling out her clubs, her dad said hello to another golfer.

"Ted, good to see you," her dad said. "You remember, my wife, Gail, and this is our daughter, Jacqueline. Ted works for me."

Ted had a medium build with light brown hair and graying sideburns. He looked like a normal guy, but, then again, so did serial killers.

Stop being paranoid. He's not him.

After a quick hello, Jacqueline grabbed her bag and started walking toward the driving range.

Her mom caught up with her, the electric golf caddy by her side. "Your dad thought you two would hit it off," her mom whispered. "Ted's a nice guy."

Ted might be nice but he was *not* her type. "How old is he?" Jacqueline whispered.

"I don't know. Forties, maybe fifty."

A shiver flitted through her. *Same as the Campus Killer.*

Tamping down the anxiety, Jacqueline forced a chuckle. "I'm home for three days and Dad's trying to fix me up?"

All she wanted to do was play a round of golf with her mom and dad. Was that too much to ask?

Looks that way.

They warmed up at the range, then her dad left to check in at the clubhouse. While they waited, Ted asked about her job.

"I'm with the FBI," she replied.

"Your dad said you're in California."

"I'm there, on assignment, with a task force."

If Jacqueline had been interested, she might have smiled a little more, maybe suggested they pair off and play teams, so she could get to know him.

Mac's tall, ripped body popped into her thoughts and she swallowed down a moan. Her pulse kicked up at the image of his rock-hard body on hers. Wasn't the first time she thought about him since moving west. Wouldn't be the last.

She checked the time. It was just after eleven Friday morning.

She'd planned on getting to Asylum by nine, latest. Though she didn't want to appear overly eager, she didn't want him to think she wasn't showing.

Her dad returned to the group. "We're all set. Let's play teams."

And there it was.

Dammit, Dad. Why are you doing this to me?

Jacqueline narrowed her gaze at her father. His sheepish smile diffused the frustration. She might not see them again during her visit, so she wanted to make the most of it.

"I'll golf with Mom for the first nine, then you for the second," she said. "I haven't seen you guys in months. I'm sure Ted won't mind."

Disappointment flashed in his eyes. "Okaaaay."

She kissed his cheek. "Love you, Daddy."

The next four hours turned out to be a lot of fun. Focusing on hitting a small, white ball was the perfect distraction from the constant frustration that hounded her on a daily basis.

After the game, she rode home with her dad.

"Thanks for trying to fix me up," she said. "I—"

"It was all Ted." Her dad pulled onto the main road. "He saw your picture in my office and asked about you. I've golfed with him, so I figured it would be okay to include him as our fourth. Do you remember that time it was just the three of us and the starter added that guy? I still see him around the club. What was his name?"

"Frank. His golf horror stories are permanently inked on my brain."

Her dad laughed. "I don't remember them."

Jacqueline stared at him. "Seriously? The story about the

spectator at a tournament who got hit in the head with a golf ball. Then he followed up with the story about the golfer who decided that stopping the cart with his *leg* was a smart move."

"Right, and his leg tore... or did it become dislocated at the hip?"

Jacqueline shuddered. "It pretty much got ripped out or something, but I couldn't stop thinking about the woman who got hit in the head—"

"Wasn't there more to that story?"

"Yes!" Jacqueline exclaimed. "Her eyeball popped out of the socket!"

"Ew, that's right." After a brief pause, he said, "So, maybe Ted wasn't such a bad choice after all."

"For golfing, Dad. Not for dating."

"Have you gotten settled into your job?" he asked.

"It's okay. I loved working in Winchester. Being able to pop home on the weekends and see everyone was perfect. Then, everything went to hell... and here we are."

He offered a fatherly smile as he pulled into the garage. "It'll all work out. You'll see." He cut the engine.

She thought of Janey, and her heart stuttered. "You always say that, Dad, but sometimes it doesn't."

"I know, dear, but it's good to be positive, right?"

The guilt swirled around her, but she forced a smile. "Absolutely."

After pulling her golf bag from her mom's SUV, she hugged them both.

"You aren't coming in?" her mom asked.

"I heard back from Leslie and I want to spend some time with her before I have dinner with Keith and Naomi, plus I kinda need my puppy fix. Talk about addictive."

"Your brother or the dogs?" her dad asked.

She laughed while her mom shook her head at him. "So corny, honey."

Jacqueline hugged them, again. "Love you guys. Thanks for golf. It's the best therapy."

"I love you," her mom replied. "I've missed you a lot, Jaqueline."

Her heart ached. Maybe coming home had been a bad idea. It only churned up how much they'd missed each other.

"Why don't you visit me?" she asked as she headed toward Naomi's Jeep.

"We'll check our schedule," her dad replied.

She hopped in, blew them a kiss, and drove away.

Next stop, her older sister's new digs in Reston.

Ten minutes later, she pulled into a beautiful neighborhood with large homes, pristine lawns, and tree-lined streets.

Since she'd been gone, she hadn't heard from Leslie, unless she initiated a text. The sisters had been close, so she was excited to see what had been happening in her life. When Jacqueline left for San Francisco, Leslie had been working retail and had a second job as a server at a high-end DC restaurant.

The nav app announced she'd arrived, so she parked at the top of the driveway.

Wow, this is seriously nice.

The modern-looking structure boasted two stories, but the distinctive angles and bright white paint paired with brown trim looked like something she'd see on the front of an architectural magazine.

As he made her way down the driveway, her phone pinged with an incoming message on the Asylum app.

The message was from Mac. "Drinks at nine. Don't be late."

A charge of adrenaline had her fingers flying as she typed out her response. "If I am late, are you going to punish me?" She added a wink emoji, then sent the message.

As she continued up the walkway, the front door flew open.

"Darling, hello!" Leslie threw her arms into the air with

dramatic flair. Rather than step outside to hug her, or move out of the way to let her in, she stood there like a mannequin.

Oh, wow.

In that instant, Jacqueline knew exactly what her family had been talking about. Her sister's startling new look, paired with the heavy makeup and extravagant jumpsuit, made Jacqueline's jaw drop.

"Look at you!" Jacqueline exclaimed. "I would have walked right past you."

Older by two years, thirty-three-year-old Leslie Hartley twirled slowly. "Do you love the new me or what?"

Jacqueline did *not*, but she wasn't about to go there. Gone was her sister's beautiful brown hair with natural chestnut highlights and pretty hazel eyes. Gone was the girl-next-door figure. She was telling the truth when she said she would have walked right by her.

"You're glowing," Jaqueline said. "You look so happy."

Leslie moved out of the way. As Jacqueline stepped inside, she couldn't take her eyes off her sister.

"Do you want to know my secret?" Leslie asked.

"Absolutely."

Leslie stepped close and Jacqueline went to hug her. Instead, Leslie gave her an air kiss, her new and super-sized breasts bumping Jacqueline.

"Let's start with the obvious." Leslie turned sideways and gestured to her bustline. "Are they the best? I'm a triple D. These babies get me some serious IG likes."

"Instagram?"

"I'm an InstaModel." Leslie threw her shoulders back, accentuating her breasts. "And my girls are what sells products."

"Okay."

"I make buckets of money every time I post," Leslie continued. "The more followers I have, the more money I make. And I get paid by companies who want me to help move their products." She threw her arms into the air, again. "I'm a huge success!"

"That's great, sis."

Wow, she's different.

"Hmmm, so what else about me?" Leslie continued. "I have fillers in my face—so no more wrinkles—plus cheek implants, *and* ass implants." Leslie modeled her backside for Jacqueline. "Touch. It's uh-mazing."

Jacqueline bit back a laugh. "I'm okay." She grabbed her own butt cheeks. "I've got my own ass to hang on to."

Leslie rolled her eyes. "Still with the sarcasm, huh?"

Jacqueline wanted to tell her sister that she looked absurd. Instead, she said, "You changed your hair."

"Extensions and a new color. It's called Endless Sunlight. I love it. It's flashy and the color really pops on my page. I've gotta grab my fans' attention... and keep it."

What is happening here?

"Oh, and I have different contact lenses so I can switch up the color." She pointed. "These are Angelic Blue."

What struck Jacqueline as bizarre, beyond her sister's obvious and extreme changes, was that they were still standing in the foyer, the front door wide open.

Jacqueline eyed her sister's four-inch fingernails. "Those are like weapons."

Leslie wiggled her fingers. "Thanks. What else? Oh, I had a tummy tuck and I'm thinking about doing my breasts again, just a teensy bit bigger."

"Well," Jacqueline said, ready to change the subject, "your career must be going *great*. Your home is beautiful."

Leslie glanced around. "One point three mil for this baby. I need new furniture, but it's good for now. I'll give you a tour."

After shutting the front door, her sister led her through the first floor. In the family room, Jaqueline eyed the treed backyard through the floor-to-ceiling windows.

"There's a golf course on the other side of the trees," Leslie said.

"Did you start playing? Have you invited Mom and Dad over to play a round?"

Leslie scowled. "Play golf? Seriously? I don't have time with all these gigs and trying to promote my brand and my image. I have no idea if mom and dad play over here. They're kinda pissed at me."

"Why?"

"I used the money they gave me on my modeling career."

"What did you do with the money *I* loaned you for college courses?"

"Not take college courses!" Leslie chirped out a laugh. "I needed ten grand for my boobs, so I used the money from Keith and Naomi. I put your five toward cheek implants. No worries. The gifts were put to good use."

"Gifts? Are you for real? Mine was a loan."

"Look," Leslie snapped. "I wasn't happy. Not with my life, or where I lived, or the way I looked. Now, I am, so don't judge me."

Rather than get into it, Jacqueline let it go, but she couldn't help but feel a little sad over the changes in her sister.

Leslie led her through the spacious black and white kitchen with stainless appliances. Jacqueline loved to cook and would have had a blast in a kitchen this large. She didn't bother asking if her sister used the kitchen. Her gut told her she didn't have the time, what with her super-successful modeling career.

What did catch her eye were the two modeling portfolios sitting open on the kitchen island.

As Leslie continued parading through her home, she stood in the doorway of an empty room. "This is going to be my home office, as soon as I have furniture."

Up the steel stairs they went in the ultra-modern structure. Leslie led her past four closed doors as she strode toward the master bedroom. It was fully furnished, the unmade king bed a rumpled mess.

Leslie continued chatting about herself as they made their way back down the stairs. In the kitchen, she pulled out two small bottles of sparkling water from the refrigerator, and set them on the counter.

"Is that for me?" Jacqueline asked, half seriously, half sarcastically.

"If you want it, it's for you." Leslie opened one of the bottles, poured the water into a champagne flute, struck a pose, and sipped.

Jacqueline unscrewed the bottle and took a mouthful, letting the bubbles tickle her tongue before swallowing it down. Leslie fished her phone from her jumpsuit pocket.

"Can you take a few pics of me?"

"Of course." Jacqueline took another swig before snapping a few shots.

When she stopped, Leslie unbuttoned the sleeveless jumpsuit and slipped it off her shoulders, revealing a see-through bra. Behind it sat the largest breasts Jacqueline had ever seen.

She understood the whole "bigger is better" thing, but there was a point when something good goes bad. In this case, Leslie's boobs needed their own zip code. They were that big.

Jacqueline glanced down at her own chest. Her breasts weren't large, but they weren't small either. She'd always liked the size and shape of her girls. She'd never heard any complaints from her lovers either, but if she had, she would have booted them to the curb.

As she returned her gaze to her well-endowed sister, she wondered if maybe she was missing out on a new and sexier life.

Leslie struck several provocative poses, using the champagne glass and the long neck of the sparkling water bottle as props. Jacqueline had to hand it to her sister. She definitely knew how to work the camera.

When Leslie finished with the impromptu photo shoot, she didn't even bother to cover herself up. While Jacqueline had a wild streak of her own, she played things more conservatively when not at her club. Clearly, Leslie was proud of her enhancement.

"What do you think?" Leslie asked, hefting her boobs.

"They're definitely much bigger. Why are you thinking of going larger?"

"For my career, duh."

"You don't need bigger boobs. You're a success. Did you ditch the waitress gig and the retail job?"

Leslie rolled her eyes. "I'm soooo done with those. They sucked. I'm all about my modeling career."

"I get that. I've been focusing on my career too."

Ignoring Jacqueline's comment, Leslie opened her modeling book. "Check out my look books."

Clearly, her sister wasn't interested in hearing what was going on in Jacqueline's life. Another flicker of sadness settled into her bones. Leslie had been a talker *and* a listener.

Not anymore.

Maybe the pendulum would swing back. She hoped that for her sister.

As Leslie flipped through the pages of her modeling portfolio, Jacqueline felt sorry for her. Each pose was more provocative than the one before. While they were definitely sexy, several were super slutty. She was seeing more of her sister than she needed to.

Since Jacqueline had done a lot more than pose for pics, she had no business saying anything judgy to Leslie, so she stayed silent.

"Ooo, you're in LA," Leslie blurted. "I should definitely visit you. I'll have to make some calls, see if I can set up some meetings."

"I'm in San Francisco."

"How close is that to LA?"

"Six hours if you drive, but you could fly—"

"Well, of course I'd fly, but what's the point. I thought you were in LA."

Jacqueline needed to leave. She'd heard enough, seen *more* than enough. "I've gotta take off."

Surprise flashed in Leslie's eyes. "You haven't seen the photos in *this* portfolio." She tapped the cover of the other book with her pointy fingernail.

"I've got plans." Jacqueline set down the bottle and headed toward the front door.

Leslie's stilettos clacked on the shiny floor as she hurried after her. "I've got plans too."

A man traipsed up the steel stairs from the basement. When he and Jacqueline locked eyes, he startled, then his lips split into a smile.

"Hey," Leslie said to him.

As he joined them at the front door, he slid on his shades. "Who's your friend?" he asked Leslie.

"This is my sister, Jacqueline."

The man tossed her a nod. "How ya doin'?"

He was average height, maybe a little taller, with a gut that stretched against his T-shirt. A black knit cap sat on his head, his long dark hair flowed down his back. He had no facial hair and no visible tats.

Jacqueline was surprised to see her flashy sister with someone so ordinary, even underwhelming.

Jacqueline slid her gaze to her sister. "I didn't know you had a... boyfriend."

"He's a friend," Leslie replied.

"I'm in a band and we just got back from touring," he said.

"What's the name of your band?" Jacqueline asked.

"Nothin' you've heard of," Leslie interjected.

Adjusting his sunglasses, he continued staring at Jacqueline. "You two don't look anything alike."

Jacqueline *wanted* to blurt out, "Thank God." Instead, she said, "I've gotta run." She opened the door, stepped outside, and the tightness in her shoulders released.

"Follow me on social media," Leslie called out. "I post something new every day."

Jacqueline slid into the Jeep and backed out of the driveway. The sister she knew was gone, replaced by a plastic replica. But, if Leslie was happy and successful, Jacqueline was happy for her.

As she drove back to her brother's house, she realized that Leslie hadn't even asked how she was. While her sister definitely looked different, it was the change in her personality that disappointed her the most.

People do change, but not always for the better.

4

ASYLUM

Prescott

Prescott spent the day getting a handle on the product recall. The processing facility that made the medication had halted production, the shipping centers stopped sending it out, a press release had been released. A company-wide email had been sent to employees alerting them of the problem. Their major suppliers had been contacted by the VP of consumer relations, and the legal team was all over managing this before scammers caught on to the problem and took advantage of the situation.

Next steps had been delegated to the appropriate department directors and Prescott's entire itinerary had been shifted to Monday, except that the two hundred unread emails would have to be tackled over the weekend.

"I can't fucking wait to work this weekend," he muttered under his breath.

He'd been hoping to get out on the water or hit the links, but this work emergency had taken top priority.

There were, however, two events he was *not* missing. The

first was his late-night hookup, and the second was his brother's Jack and Jill wedding shower.

It was quarter 'til nine, and he needed to bolt. With his computer bag slung over his shoulder, Prescott left his office. The hallway was quiet, the employees long gone, their weekends well underway.

In the parking lot, his phone rang with a blocked caller.

"Hello."

"I've got good news and bad," Z began.

"Go."

"The three men you took out were the men who'd escaped with Maul."

"And the woman?"

"Unfortunately, you were right. She was the realtor."

Anger slithered down his spine. That innocent woman did *not* deserve to die. Hadn't Maul done enough fucking damage?

"Police are calling off the search for Maul," Z explained.

Fuck. Fuck me.

"No body?"

"Not yet. The currents are strong and the search team assured me he'd wash up on shore, but it might take a while. I don't like *not* having a body."

Prescott got into his truck, tapped the start button. The engine kicked on and the Bluetooth connected. "Neither do I," he bit out.

"You sure you hit him?"

"Yes. You want me to return to the area—"

"I'm going to ignore that stupid comment," Z said, frustration tinging his words. "Criminals typically go back to the crime scene."

"I'm the assassin, Philip, *not* the criminal."

Silence.

"I saw the shitstorm you had to deal with today," Z said. "How are the people who got sick?"

"They'll be okay." Prescott drove out of the parking lot. "Are you going to the shower tomorrow?"

"Yeah, I'm making an appearance. Don't talk to me."

Prescott chuffed out a laugh. "We play poker together. You gotta relax, Philip. Tomorrow, you're the father of the bride, that's it. Only a handful of us know what you *really* do, and we won't be talking shop. You tell everyone you're retired, so act like it. Be chill."

A tight chuckle rolled out of Z. "Yeah, chilling isn't something I'm good at."

"Try golf. That relaxes me." Prescott wanted to add "Get laid," but he wasn't going there, not with his *real* boss.

After a pause, Z said, "I'm concerned Maul isn't dead."

"You found him once. Do it again and, this time, I'll put a bullet between his eyes."

"It took me months to find him the first time."

Prescott accelerated on the toll road toward DC. "Better get started. See you tomorrow." Prescott killed the call, the ever-present frustration morphing into agitation.

Another epic fucking fail.

Heat pounded through him. He cracked open the window and sucked down the chilly April air. He'd spent the last few days beating himself up for not being able to confirm Maul was dead. With any luck, the fugitive's decomposing body would wash up on shore.

I don't fucking believe in luck.

He hit the gas and took off toward Asylum. For the next few hours, he was going to calm his raging, angry soul by fucking. Hopefully with Jack, but if she no-showed, he'd find someone else. Anyone to take his mind off his failed mission.

Prescott entered the shadowy Georgetown club, the dim lighting and sultry music setting the sexy tone.

"Hey, Mac, I haven't seen you in a while," said the line manager. "You just missed Rebel, man."

Asylum was owned by his close friend, Rebel. From the swarms of bodies filling the space, he was doing alright.

"Is he coming back?" Prescott held his phone under the scanner and the light turned green.

"He didn't say. I'll let him know you stopped by. It's been a while. Where you been?"

"Working too damn much."

Black walls, red lighting. Prescott loved the vibe. It was like he was entering the gates of hell itself.

And he could not fucking wait.

Prescott made his way through the crowded bar, the chatter dwarfing the jazz quartet playing nearby. Pausing, he swept the room in search of his target. Unless Jack had changed up her look, she hadn't arrived. He checked his phone. It was ten past nine, no Jack, and no message waiting in the club app.

A slow growl rolled out of him. *Dammit. She stood me up.*

A year and a half ago, he first spotted her in one of the exhibition rooms. Dressed as a school girl in uniform, she was doing a scene with a man and a woman. She was riding some guy, skirt on, shirt off, her phenomenal tits bouncing with each thrust.

Her eyes had been closed, but when she opened them, she'd glanced around. When she locked on Prescott, she hadn't looked away. While screwing some stranger, she'd been eye fucking the hell out of him.

She was wild, uninhibited, and a very dirty girl. He could not wait to meet her... and fuck her himself.

After her scene had ended, a group of women descended on him while the clubbers filed out. When the crowd cleared, she stood there, fully dressed, her fiery gaze drilling into him.

With a wild gleam in her eyes, she'd walked over, pressed through the throng of women, took his hand, and led him to a private room where they hooked up for hours.

It was raw, feral, and over-the-top intense.

That had led to a weekly thing of hard fucking where her slutty costumes and wild imagination had gone off the rails while he screwed her to the moon. Beyond her name, which he doubted was real, he knew nothing about her.

He'd never met anyone like her, never been so drawn to another person like he had been to her. They never talked much, not because he wasn't curious or hadn't grown interested, but because she was all about getting down to dirty business.

When she'd ghosted on him, he hadn't tried to find her. He was confident another woman would come along and snag his attention.

Only that hadn't happened. He'd hook up with someone else, but think about Jack. Over time, he just stopped going to Asylum. Tonight, he was ready to cut loose with the one woman who could slay him simply by showing up.

The line manager walked over. "Mac, I forgot to tell you, Jack said she'll be waiting in the exhibition room. Sorry about that."

"Which one?"

"She said you'd know." After a nod from Prescott, the employee retreated back to the entrance.

Fueled by that news, Prescott took off through the crowded room toward the closed door in the back. The retina scanner cleared him to enter. Now, in the inner sanctum, the music pulsed through him, the intense beat pounding in his chest while the faint smell of sex and pungent cologne hovered in the air.

Prescott's cock twitched as he made his way past the exhibition rooms on either side of the hall toward the last room on the right.

He stood in the doorway, taking in the sights in the Threesome Playroom.

A man and two women were playing out a scene. One of the

women was going down on the other, while the guy took the first one from behind. A small crowd had gathered to watch the X-rated scene go down.

Prescott wasn't there to watch, so he scanned the room for his target.

Jack waited, not twenty feet away, her smoldering gaze drilling into his. Heat pressed his chest while his pent-up need jumped to the forefront.

She was intoxicatingly beautiful... more beautiful now than when he'd last seen her, eight, long months ago.

He wanted her greedy mouth on his, her hard, plumped nipples pushing into his welcoming mouth, and he wanted to bury himself so deep inside her he couldn't remember his own fucking name.

Three shirtless guys in leather pants hovered next to her. Two stood too fucking close, and the third knelt at her feet caressing her thigh-high boots. These men were window dressing who were seconds away from getting swapped out for the main act.

Me.

They'd scatter like dust when he stepped in to claim what was his.

Her.

Raking his gaze over her, he soaked up the spectacular view. Her auburn hair was pulled into a high ponytail, leaving her neck exposed. She'd worn a black leather bra and matching shortie shorts, her thigh-high boots revealing a hint of ivory skin where the boots ended and the shorts began. The swell of her tits made his cock stir while streaks of desire pounded through him.

He'd missed her hot little body. She was rocking out her skimpy outfit, but she was much, much better stripped naked, her body on his while she rode him for her own pleasure.

Jesus, she looks phenomenal.

She raked her gaze down his chest, pausing at his crotch, stopping at his dress shoes. Then, she eye-fucked him all the way back to his mussed hair on the top of his head. A sliver of a smile tugged at the corners of her luscious mouth. A mouth he wanted wrapped around his firming cock.

Without breaking eye contact, she spoke to the men. All three guys jerked their heads in his direction.

His feet firmly in place, he slipped his hand into his pants pocket and waited. If she wanted to spend the evening with him, she needed to make amends.

One sultry step at a time, she skulked toward him, the sway of her hips only adding to her appeal.

She tilted her head up. "You're late."

He'd forgotten how much he loved her voice—a little deeper than most women—and how she spoke with a controlled confidence.

"You're fucking lucky I showed at all," he growled. "Ditch your tagalongs."

"They just wanted to admire me up close," she murmured. "I'm here for you." As she caressed his lower lip with her fingertip, her breath hitched. "You wanna play in an exhibition room or a private one?"

She'd played on stage, but he never did. It was one thing to be a member of a kink club and play in private, but a very different thing for the COO of Armstrong Enterprises to get dirty in a room where anyone could video him and post the scene, or blackmail him *not* to post it.

"Private."

Reaching up, she sunk her fingers into his hair, raking her fingernails across his scalp. The intensity in her touch skyrocketed his desire.

"You let your hair grow," she said. "Very sexy. Now, I'll have something to hang on to when you fuck me senseless."

Adrenaline powered through him, and he inhaled a slow,

deep breath. She had this way of undoing him with just her words.

"Room," he hissed. "Now."

"No small talk first?"

"We just had it."

Her lips twitched. "Still mad at me, huh? I can't wait for you to show me how angry you really are."

Unable to resist her any longer, he snaked his hand around her waist, pulled her close and kissed her hard. Their tongues met in an explosion of energy, the desire ripping out of him in an ardent groan.

He broke away, and she sucked down a jagged breath.

"Wow," she whispered. "Fuck, I missed that."

"Show me," he rasped.

Rather than grasp his hand and take off, she moseyed toward the corner to collect a leather duster, then, at the exit, she turned back.

One deliberate step at a time, he made his way over. Claiming what was his, he took her hand. Her fingers entwined his, and she stepped close enough that her shoulder brushed his, sending another spike of energy shooting through him and landing in the hardened rod between his legs.

At the end of the hallway, they stood in front of the wall-mounted retina scanner. The light turned green for them both, he opened the door, and she sashayed through. When the door banged shut behind them, they were met with silence.

In one simple move, he pinned her against the stairwell wall, her arms over her head, held together with one hand while he grabbed her ass with the other. "Ready to get fucked?" he bit out.

She leaned up, bit his lip, and released a low growl. "Are *you* ready?" She pressed her breasts against him and kissed his scruffy chin, then the corner of his mouth. She nibbled his lower lip before kissing him full-on.

If they kept this up, they'd be dry humping in the stairwell.

On a growl, she broke away, and chugged down a jagged breath. Her half-lidded eyes were black with lust. In silence, they walked up the stairs to the second floor. Desperate to touch her, he ran his hand down her back and grabbed her rounded ass.

On the second floor, he pulled her to a stop in front of their reserved room. They'd never played there before.

Virgins Are The Best

He stood in front of the scanner, but the light stayed red. He opened the app on his phone, confirmed he was standing in front of the right room.

He called Rebel.

"Hey, babe," Rebel answered. "My line manager said you're here. Where are you?"

"I'm outside the Virgin suite. Can you give me access?"

"You with Jack?"

"Yeah."

A few seconds later, Rebel said, "You're all set. Stop by later and see me." The line went dead and Prescott slid his phone back into his pocket.

"Try it now," he said to her.

She stood in front of the scanner, the light turned green. He opened the door and waited for her to enter before he followed. The second he shut the door, she was on him.

"Ohgod, I need you," she bleated. "Hard and fast and rough. Over and over." Her breathing was erratic, and she sucked in air.

He'd forgotten how riled she was, at first. Then, after her first orgasm, she'd calm down and he'd help her gain some control. Not tonight. If she was in town for one weekend, he didn't give a fuck about breath control or any other kind of control.

She raked her teeth over his tongue while digging her fingers into his shoulders. The sharp sting of pain only fueled him to want to take her that much sooner.

He bit her lip. A groan ripped from her throat while she pressed her knee against his hardened cock. Then, she replaced her knee with her hand and massaged his shaft. He slowed their rabid kissing, appreciating the talented way her tongue tangled with his, how her breathing always fell in line with his. Was that on purpose or were they communicating on a primal level?

Didn't know. Didn't care.

"Look at me," she murmured between kisses.

He opened his eyes. The lamp on the table bathed the room in a shadowy light.

"I need you inside me," she whispered. "So badly."

"No role playing?" he asked. "We're in the virgin suite."

"No, I'm desperate for you."

"Hard and fast, just like you like it." He toed off his shoes.

"Yes," she hissed as she stripped off her shorts, revealing that sexy swatch of dark, pussy hair.

"Boots stay on," he ground out, while maddening desire thrummed through him.

Unable to resist, he went to her and wrapped his large hand around the back of her neck while he cupped her pussy.

"Touch me," she begged.

He ran his fingers over her soaking wet snatch. Trembling with anticipation, she stared into his eyes.

"I brought you a favorite toy." He slipped his other hand into his pocket and withdrew a small container.

Her face lit up with joy and he couldn't help but crack a smile. Most women liked flowers, Jack liked the cock ring.

"I wish I never had to move away," she whispered. "Time to get you naked."

With her gaze cemented on his, she worked quickly to help him out of his pants as he loosened his tie, pulled it over his head, and tugged off his dress shirt. Then, he unzipped her leather bra and tugged it away from her breasts.

He paused long enough to admire her beautiful tits and firm nipples. When he dipped down to suck, she grabbed his ass.

Her hard nibs plumped as he sucked on her tender flesh. One, then the other while her moans turned raspy.

"Fuck me," she commanded. "And punish me for ghosting on you without saying goodbye. Punish me real good."

Instead of getting on the bed, she knelt on the hard floor, raised her ass, and craned around.

He tugged off his boxer briefs, pulled a condom from his pants pocket, rolled it over his long, hard shaft, and knelt behind her. Then, he positioned himself at her opening.

"Here we go, baby."

He tunneled inside her, the pleasure exploding through him while her throaty groan thundered in his ears. She was nice and tight, just the way he liked her. As he worked his way inside her, she urged him on.

"So, so good. Oh, Mac, yes, all the way in."

He thrust and retreated again and again while she bucked against him. The friction, paired with her sexy ass, and cries of arousal, had him sprinting toward a release.

He grabbed her ponytail and tugged. She cried out. "Oh, fuck, I'm gonna come. Harder. Fuck me harder."

She started shuddering and crying out. "Yesssss, fuck, yessssss." Her insides tightened around his cock as she cried out through her orgasm.

He thrust hard and fast as the ecstasy shot out of him. "Fuck, Jack, I'm coming so hard."

Euphoria rushed through him, the orgasm sending glorious ecstasy racing through his sex-starved body.

She had given him a brief respite from the demons that haunted him night and day. He didn't deserve it—he knew that—but for the few hours they'd spend together, he would cut himself a break from the mayhem that tormented his broken, angry soul.

∼

Jacqueline

Being with Mac turned her into a savage beast. It had been like that from the moment they met. He was beautiful, attentive, and so damn controlling. And the man fucked like a god. Being around him left her buzzing for days. She called it her "Mac high" and she craved him like a drug.

Tugging on her ponytail, he yanked her back to the moment. Then, he withdrew, and she hated that he'd pulled out. They always went fast and hard the first time, but then he'd slow things down and take care of her, as if she were his, as if he actually cared about her. But she wasn't a fool. This was a kink club and they were sex partners, hooking up for a few hours. And tonight was like a one-off, a reunion, of sorts.

Her heart fell and she shoved out the thought. Turning to face him, she said, "More. I need more."

Even in the dim light, his piercing blue-green eyes popped against his tanned face.

I could get lost in those eyes... so lost for days and days.

But Jacqueline was a realist, not a dreamer. They had one night together, and she was going to make the absolute most of it.

He stood, offered helping hands. Pausing, she admired his outstretched fingers, like a lifeline she didn't realize she needed. When she placed her hands in his, another jolt of electricity powered through her. He pulled her up, then snaked his hands around her, anchoring one on her ass, the other on her back.

"What is it about you?" he murmured.

"I like to fuck. You like to fuck." She was lying. Not to herself, but to him. She'd always kept the vibe chill. No point changing things up now. But he was right, there was something magnetic about their chemistry that fed off each other.

"You know what I've missed most about our hookups?" she asked as she pulled out the hair scrunchie.

"You let your hair grow," he murmured. "It's beautiful."

Before she could re-tie her hair, he sunk his fingers into her scalp and ran them through her waves. "You've got a mane, like a lioness."

She shot him a quick smile. "More to yank on."

Desperate to feel his hard body against hers, she stepped close and caressed his striated shoulders. Sparks flew through her. Staring into his eyes turned her crazy with need. His lids were hooded, the frustration between his eyebrows was gone... a thing of the past.

Even in her four-inch stiletto boots, she had to push up on her toes. Mac had to be six three or four. She pressed her cheek against his scruffy beard, closed her eyes, and breathed him in.

A delicious mix of sex and shampoo and Mac.

My calming aphrodisiac.

He broke away, and her heart dipped. Her silly, stupid heart had no business being in the Virgin suite. She was no virgin and they weren't about to role play a scene. Tonight, was all about sex, sex, and more sex.

"What have you missed the most?" he asked, parroting her question back to her.

"Your cock deep inside me," she whispered.

His gritty groan rumbled through her, setting off a series of mini-explosions that travelled to the tight spot between her legs.

"Get on the bed," he commanded. "I'm gonna fuck you with my mouth."

Ohgod, yes.

"We've never done that before," she replied. "You sure you want—"

"Yes," he hissed.

His eyes drilled into hers, the growl in his voice had her sucking down another breath.

"You fucked up when you skipped town. Payback time."

"Eating me feels more like a reward than a punishment, but hey, not gonna argue."

After she lay on her back, he stood there peering down at her. The intensity in his eyes had her swallowing down another moan. He took his time, letting his gaze roam over every inch of her naked body. Being under Mac's microscope was a little overwhelming. He was a large man—and all muscle. His massive size made him an intimidating beast, but she never felt that way around him. She felt safe, like she could trust him with her life, and he would protect her from harm.

When he finished eye-fucking her, he fished something from his pants pocket. She wanted to ask him if he liked what he saw, but when he turned back, he dangled nipple clamps in the air.

"I brought you another present," he said matter-of-factly.

A smile tugged at the corners of her mouth while her heart kicked up speed. "Now, you're just spoiling me."

His smile melted her.

Gorgeous.

No one man should be *that* ruggedly handsome. He had the kind of bone structure that could sell magazines, with high cheekbones and a strong jawline. A beautiful smile, piercing eyes, and a granite body that did not quit. Mac was an Adonis, and for one perfect night, he was all hers.

He sat on the edge of the bed and started to place a clamp on her nipple.

"Whoa, cowboy," she said pushing his hand away. "Don't you want to adjust those first?"

"I never changed them from the last time we played."

Her eyes grew large, and she wished she had more of a poker face.

"These are only for you," he replied.

Translation. That meant that each of his kink partners had their own stash of toys, *not* that she was his only kink partner. She was so high on being with him, she was delirious.

"You want me to ratchet them back some?" he asked as he fiddled with one of them.

She hadn't used nipple clamps with anyone but him... and it had been eight months since she'd used *any* toys.

"No, I like the pain." Discomfort kept things real, reminded her that she didn't deserve to feel good without also feeling bad.

On went the first clamp, and she flinched.

"Too much?" he asked as he dipped down to kiss and lick the tip of her erect nipple.

"It's good."

Before attaching the second clamp, he said, "Breathe, Jack."

Her gaze was cemented on his as she filled her lungs with air. She loved how he took care of her.

He tucked a pillow under her head. "Watch me."

She shuddered in another breath, her insides pulsing with desire.

He kissed her, then kissed her again. She wrapped her arms around him, caressing his heated skin with her fingertips. His kiss turned ravenous while she started moving beneath him. He was careful not to bang the clamps as he kissed her breasts, then ran his tongue around her areolas, moving down her tummy. He licked the inside of her thigh, tongued her opening, and swirled around her clit while hit after hit of pleasure streaked through her.

"Yesss," she hissed. "Mmm, so good."

She couldn't stop moaning, couldn't stop writhing either. His face between her legs was the dirtiest, sexiest thing she'd ever seen. Her breathing labored, her insides on fire, she arched up, pushing her wet pussy into his face.

Each time she released a moan, he applied more pressure. The build was fast, her senses overwhelmed with the onslaught of euphoria.

"Mac, you're gonna make me come."

Crying out, she started bucking on the bed, and he unleashed a torrent of energy, all focused on her sex. The orgasm exploded out of her, the ecstasy slamming through her like an earthquake.

When finished, she lay boneless on the bed.

"That's a good girl," he murmured as he removed the nipple clamps.

"Wow, I... that was—"

"Been a while?" he asked, a cocky smile touching his eyes.

"No actually, it hasn't been that long," she deadpanned.

In truth, her orgasms had all been forgettable. No one did it for her like Mac did.

No one.

He pushed off the bed, rolled a condom onto his saluting shaft, then slid on the cock ring. "I'm a giver... and then I take."

"Ohgod." She shuddered in a shaky breath, while another burst of energy powered through her.

She tossed the pillow aside, spread her legs for him. With his massive cock in hand, he positioned himself over her. He tunneled inside, their gritty groans filling her ears.

Streams of pleasure pounded through her. She raked her

nails down his shoulders. His kiss was hard and his tongue thrust into her mouth. The rush of pleasure had her undulating beneath him while his lustful gaze stayed cemented on hers.

The cock ring, along with the intensity of their connection, had her hurtling toward another orgasm, but she needed to slow them down and appreciate him while she had him.

She broke the kiss. "Girl on top."

Still rooted inside her, he rolled them over. Now, she was in the driver's seat.

She sat up and stared down at him. The fire in his eyes turned her inside out. He was all man, and for the next few hours, he was her perfect escape.

He massaged her tits, teased her sensitive nipples. She started gliding on his shaft, the euphoria spiraling through her with every thrust, the cock ring stimulating her clit.

Though she wanted to stare into his eyes, fucking him felt too good, and her eyes fluttered closed. She started moving faster, exhilaration sending her higher and higher.

"Fuck, Jack, you feel good."

She opened her eyes to find him waiting. Lips parted, breathing jagged, hooded eyes. She'd missed being able to bring him the ultimate pleasure, having that kind of absolute power over him when they played.

She raised her arms over her head as his cock firmed to steel inside her slicked pussy. His groans turned to grunts and his eyes closed. His orgasm shot out of him, the force making him grunt her name through gritted teeth.

"Fuck, Jack. I'm coming."

She nursed him through his orgasm, until he stilled beneath her. Seconds passed. He opened his heavy-lidded eyes, but he seemed far, far away.

She wondered if he'd been thinking about someone else. An unexpected sadness curled around her heart. Pushing off him, she shoved away the melancholy. This was a hook up with a former sex partner. She knew nothing about him and she planned on keeping it that way.

One night of guilt-free pleasure until the club closed and they parted ways... this time for good.

5
THE PARTY

Prescott

Prescott didn't like that she'd pulled off him, especially since she hadn't come. "Not so fast."

Jack leaned down and kissed him. "That was for you."

"Cock ring's for you."

Knock-knock.

"Closing in thirty," said a woman.

"I'm gonna head out," Jack replied.

"We're not finished."

"Maybe we can pick up where we left off, tomorrow night, around eleven."

He leaned up on his elbows as she threw on her leather outfit. He loved how she slid into those hot little shorts and how she rocked that leather bra, but he hated that she was bolting.

"Why so late?"

"I'm in town for a thing."

Pushing off the bed, he pulled off the cock ring. "I'll walk you out."

"I got this."

He laid his hand on her shoulder. "Do *not* leave without me. It's late. Guys have been drinking. Idiots who've been drinking can be dangerous."

Her gaze softened. "Thank you."

Pausing, he studied her face. She was beautiful, especially after he'd sexed her up good. "I owe you an orgasm."

"That fuck was my apology for ghosting on you."

He wanted to kiss her, then ask her to have a drink with him at the bar. But she was his *former* kink partner who was in town for a few days.

Let her go.

An unexpected feeling of loss stayed with him as he entered the bathroom. Shaking off the emotion, he cleaned up and returned to get dressed. She slipped past him and shut the bathroom door.

On went his boxers, pants, and shirt.

As he was buttoning up, she sidled close. "If you want to get together tomorrow night, lemme know. If not, tonight was fun."

To his surprise, she leaned up and kissed his cheek.

His chest warmed.

After stepping into his shoes, he collected her leather duster, held it out for her. After she slipped into it, he pulled out her long hair, collected a handful and tugged. "You look good, Jack."

Truth was, she was a gorgeous woman. Beyond her looks, there was a strength and a vulnerability to her that captivated him. He was just as intrigued now as he had been all those months ago.

They left the suite, made their way to the first floor. He wanted to ask her what she was doing tomorrow, but he didn't.

They'd never shared anything about themselves. Why ruin a good thing? Better to stay strangers.

The crowded bar had thinned out. Before he could check himself, he asked, "Can I buy you a drink?"

Her eyebrows crowded into her forehead as her eyes grew large. "Uh, no. I don't want to find out you're married with three kids and your wife thinks you're out of town on business."

"I wouldn't talk about my wife with you… and I have six kids."

Her laugh touched a part of him that had died, months ago. *C'mon, man, get it together.*

"If I was married and hanging out here without her, then I shouldn't be married."

She turned toward him. "Exactly. Should I assume you're not married, not that it matters."

"Not married," he replied. "How 'bout you and your new life?"

"I was seeing someone casually," she said as she pushed open the front door and sailed into the night.

"What happened?"

"He wanted to take things to the next level, but I ended it."

"Cut him at the knees," he replied.

Her smile sent energy traversing through him.

She said nothing more about it, and they walked in silence to her Jeep. After opening the door, she turned back. "You fuck good. Thanks for meeting me."

He leaned in and kissed her. One brief peck on her mouth. "Maybe I'll see you tomorrow night."

"Yeah, maybe." Leaning up, she laid a searing kiss on his lips, lingering an extra beat before breaking away. After climbing in, she shut the door.

Damn.

He didn't want to let her go, but he had to. *Better this way*, he told himself, as she started the vehicle.

She winked and drove away. He'd never been *that* attracted to anyone.

She lives three thousand miles away. Move on.

Back inside Asylum, he paused at the scanner before making his way down the hall to Rebel's office.

Knock-knock.

Prescott opened the door, stepped into Rebel's office. "Yo—" His brain skidded to a halt.

Leaning back in his executive chair, Rebel was getting a hummer. A woman knelt in front of him, her head bobbing over his cock, her long hair obscuring her face.

"Don't you lock your fucking door?" As Prescott pulled the door closed, he said, "I'll be at the bar."

Back in the front room, Prescott pulled up a stool at the bar.

One of the bartenders moseyed over. "Hey, Mac, we had last call," he said.

"I got this," said Rebel's GM. After taking his order, she made him a dry martini.

"Thanks." Prescott sipped the cocktail.

"I haven't seen you in a while," she said. "How've you been?"

"Busy," he replied. "You?"

The small talk continued until Rebel slid onto a barstool next to him.

"Yo, babe," Rebel said.

"I don't need to ask how you're doing," Prescott replied.

Rebel shot him a grin. "I'm feeling no pain." After instructing his GM to pour him a whiskey, neat, he turned back to Prescott. "How long has Jack been back?"

"Weekend only. She moved to California." After sipping the martini, he said, "You gotta lock your office door."

"That member swung by to bitch about something. Next thing I know, my dick is in her mouth."

Prescott laughed. "There've gotta be parts of that story you're leaving out."

"She was pissed, I let her rant. She was grateful." Rebel grinned.

"Will I see you tomorrow?"

"Wouldn't miss it." Rebel pulled out the hair tie and raked his fingers through his wild, blond hair. "I heard they gave up looking for Maul," he murmured. "You shoulda let me come with you."

Prescott shook his head. "No fucking way."

"Why the hell not?"

"I work alone."

"We would've gotten that job done."

Prescott glared at him. "I *did* get that job done. Drop it, will ya?" That sex high that had brightened Prescott's normally dark mood evaporated, replaced by the constant agitation that hounded him all the damn time.

Prescott drained the martini glass. "I love you, brother, but you piss me off. If I wanted to work with you—or anyone else—I'd say something."

"Don't get your hackles up. We were a great team."

"Yeah, *were*." Prescott pulled out his wallet.

"I got this." Rebel pushed off the barstool. "I'll walk you out."

The two men made their way outside and Prescott pulled his friend in for a bro hug. "I gotta take things down a few notches, don't I?"

"You just got laid." Rebel squeezed his shoulder. "Enjoy the high. Reserve a room for tomorrow night and get wild with her."

"What's the point?"

"What's the point of any of this?" With a smile, Rebel opened the front door. "See you tomorrow."

On the way to his truck, Prescott opened the Asylum app and checked for a room, but the club was totally booked.

Dammit.

Even if they couldn't hookup in a private room, he'd buy her that drink, so he sent the invitation for Saturday at ten.
Ding!
He glanced down at the private message from Jack. "The club is booked. What did you have in mind?"
"A drink," he replied.
"We need a private suite. Make it happen."
"Fuck," he bit out as he jumped into his truck.
On the way home, he called Rebel.
"Yeah, babe," Rebel answered.
"I need a room for tomorrow night."
"I'm not a magician, brother. Hold on." After a few seconds, he said, "I got you one at midnight. You owe me."
"Thank you." Prescott hung up and sent Jack a message. "Midnight."
He set down his phone and drove toward the large house that *should* have been filled with a wife and six kids. But he lived alone.
As he pulled into his three-car garage, his phone dinged with a reply. "I can't wait," Jack messaged.
Neither can I.

THE FOLLOWING AFTERNOON, Prescott opened the front door to the Savage's McLean home and stepped inside. Jericho and Liv were hosting a Jack and Jill wedding shower for his younger brother, Nicholas Hawk, and Nicky's fiancée, Addison Skye.
In one hand he held a bottle of Hennessy Paradis Imperial Cognac, in his other, a wrapped gift.
As he made his way toward the spacious living room, he spied servers prepping platters in the kitchen. Once in the main room, he set his wrapped present on the gift table.
"Armstrong," Jericho called.

In a sea of guests, his band of brothers—Stryker, Cooper, Jericho, and Hawk—were huddled in a corner. With the bottle of luxury cognac in hand, Prescott made his way over.

After the guys greeted him, Prescott hugged his brother. "I'm happy for you, Nicky."

"Glad you're here, Scotty," Hawk replied. "Did you hear what happened?"

Prescott flicked his gaze from one man to the next. "No, but I'm going with something bad."

"An Op was killed," Hawk replied.

"Wrong place, wrong time," Stryker added. "Happened last night, during an attempted carjacking at a gas station."

"Who was it?" Prescott asked.

"Gloria Whelan," Hawk replied.

"Former Special Agent with the Bureau," Cooper said. "She'd been with us for a decade."

The guys shouldn't have been talking shop in the middle of a party, but he wasn't about to lecture them. Instead he asked, "How's everyone holding up?"

"It's rough when we lose one of our own." Jericho said. "But today's all about Hawk and Addison, right?" He slapped Hawk on the back. "Who woulda figured this guy would have a Jack and Jill wedding shower?"

Hawk grinned. "I know, babe, but when Addison asked me, I—"

"Pussy-whipped," Stryker murmured, and the guys laughed.

"Abso-fucking-lutely," Hawk said puffing out his chest. "My woman's got me *exactly* where she wants me, and I got no prob with that."

Rebel joined the group and they brought him up to speed.

"I knew Gloria," Rebel said. "Worked a coupla gigs with her. She was good."

Hawk had been staring at Prescott.

"What?" Prescott asked.

Hawk broke into a grin. "You got laid."

The guys started laughing and Prescott flicked his gaze to Rebel. "Did you tell them?"

"No, dummy, but you just did," Rebel replied.

"Good for you," Stryker said. "You work too much."

"Leave the man alone," Cooper said. "But I gotta say... you needed that, Prescott. You look less pissed than usual."

The guys cracked up again while Prescott bit back a smile. "You guys are idiots."

"We're definitely that," Jericho said.

Determined to get them off his sex life, Prescott held up the bottle of Hennessy. "Let's toast the groom."

"Hell, yeah," Hawk replied.

Jericho raised his arm, and a dutiful server hurried over.

"Yes, Mr. Jericho."

"I'm gonna need six cognac glasses."

"Be right back with those." The server scurried toward the kitchen.

"Where're your women?" Prescott asked.

Jericho pointed outside, where several women were huddled in a tight circle.

The server returned, poured their drinks, then left.

All six men raised their glasses.

"Nicky, congratulations on finding your forever person," Prescott said. "We love you, brother. To you and Addison."

The men clinked glasses and tossed back the top-shelf liquor as the women joined their group.

Addison hugged Prescott. "I was worried you'd be out of town. You've been away so much for work."

"No way was I missing this," he replied. "Is your dad here?"

"He said he'd stop by later," Addison said. "When I told him Livy and Jericho had some lawn games, he got cold feet."

"Sounds like him," Prescott replied.

"Where's Liam?" Stryker asked. Liam Savage was Jericho and Liv's baby.

"He's with his Auntie Georgia," Jericho replied. "Me and Livy need a night out."

Liv wrapped her arm around Jericho. "Date night."

"We're headed to Jericho Road tonight, right?" Danielle, Cooper's fiancée, asked.

"We better," Addison replied. "I need to get my line-dancing on with my man." Clasping Hawk's hand, she led him away to welcome their other guests.

Jericho and Liv headed toward the kitchen to check on the caterers.

When Stryker and his wife, Emerson—along with Cooper and Danielle—left to mingle with other ALPHA Ops, Rebel said, "I rearranged the schedule at Asylum and moved your res from midnight to ten."

"Now, *that's* what I'm talking about," Prescott said with a smile. "I owe you, brother."

"You work all the damn time. You gotta have a little fun."

Guilt slithered through him. "No, I don't."

Rebel squeezed his shoulder. "Don't be so hard on yourself. Isn't it time to let that one go?"

"Would you, if you were me?"

Rebel broke eye contact for a second. "Yeah, if I'd done what you did, I probably would."

"Well, lucky for you, you're not me," Prescott replied.

~

Jacqueline

WITH A GIFT-WRAPPED box in her arms, Jacqueline entered the beautiful estate home.

Wow, this is stunning. I'd get lost living in a house this big.

Liv, and a muscular man with long hair, greeted her.

"Jacqueline, it's good to meet you in person," Liv Savage said. "This is my husband, Jericho. Babe, this is Jaqueline Hartley. She and Addison were close friends in college."

"Lemme help you out." Jericho took the oversized box from her.

"Your home is beautiful."

"Thank you," Liv said. "Addison's excited to see you. I can take you to her."

"That's okay. I want to surprise her."

"We'll put your gift on the table," Jericho said, as a server appeared with a push cart filled with various beverages.

"Make yourself at home," Liv said before she and Jericho left.

With a glass of champagne in hand, Jaqueline walked through the two-story foyer. In the living room, she glanced around.

While the invitation had said, "dress comfortably", she was glad she'd worn a bright orange dress, cinched at the waste with a shawl draped over her shoulders. On her feet she'd worn her favorite four-inch stilettos. At five seven, she considered herself average height, until she slipped into those shoes. Now, she towered over most everyone. And she loved it.

As she made her way around the throng of guests in search of her close friend, she admired the layout of the home. It was open, with perfectly placed sofas and coffee tables. While the rooms were large, each felt cozy and comfortable. Various-sized vases with beautifully arranged bouquets of tulips had been set around the room.

There had to be seventy people chatting in small groups. Most were inside, but some were clustered by the covered swimming pool. A few played horseshoes on the lawn.

Excitement coursed through her. Addison was one more reason why Jacqueline was so happy to be back in the area.

A small table, near the sliding glass doors, was filled with framed photos of Addison and Hawk over the years. They'd been friends first, but Jacqueline knew Addison had it bad for him, though she denied, denied, denied.

While she admired the pictures, someone slid open the glass door and stepped inside. She glanced over at him and a hit of adrenaline spiked through her.

Ohmygod, it's him.

Her heart took off in her chest.

Mac looked even more handsome in the light of day. His tailored sport coat clung to his perfectly sculpted shoulders while his bright white shirt accentuated his tanned face and made his blue-green eyes pop. Oozing wealth and power, he was the epitome of sophistication and class.

He glanced over, then did a double take. "Jack, what are you doing here?"

She froze. No words.

Her chest heated, the warmth spreading up her neck to her cheeks.

Say something, anything.

"I saw a bunch of cars and thought I'd crash the party."

His laugh sent a bolt of lightning charging through her.

In the bright afternoon light, it was so much easier to appreciate his tousled hair with its sun-kissed ends. But it was the fire in his eyes that kept her cemented in place, like a mannequin. All she could do was stand there and drink him in. She made a mental note of the light dusting of freckles on his nose, his full, perfectly sculpted lips and chiseled jawline. She wanted to press her mouth to his, her cheek to his, her body on his.

Wow, just wow.

For all the gawking as she was doing, he was doing plenty of his own. He devoured her with his hungry gaze while a shiver of desire skirted through her.

His massive body blocked the doorway, and a man with

long, blond hair had been waiting to come in. She curled her fingers around Mac's bulging bicep—because she *had* to touch him—and tugged him toward her.

He mistook that for an embrace and leaned down to drop a lingering kiss her cheek. Her eyes fluttered closed while a whoosh of heat burned through her like a raging forest fire.

"Babe, you're blocking traffic," said the man who'd been standing behind him.

Mac flashed him a smile. "Sorry, brother. Come on in." With a wink, he continued into the house.

Still standing close, Mac peered down at her. His stunning male beauty mesmerized her.

"Fuck, I want to kiss you," he murmured.

"Are you insane?" she whispered. "I'm not even supposed to know you. What are you doing here?"

"My brother's getting married. What are *you* doing here, party crasher?"

"My—"

"There you are!" Addison pulled her in for a hug. "It's so good to see you!"

As Jacqueline embraced one of her closest friends in the world, she smiled. That's what Addison always did for her. She made her smile.

"Congratulations!" Jacqueline said as she pulled away.

Addison clasped Jacqueline's hand. "I am not letting go of you the entire day." And just like that, it was as if no time had passed between them at all.

"I missed you." Jacqueline squeezed her hand.

"Me too," Addison replied.

Jacqueline slid her gaze to Prescott. The fire in his eyes, and that hitched eyebrow, had her biting back a moan. His penetrating gaze was turning her inside out.

Breathe. Just breathe.

Addison flicked her gaze from her to Prescott, then back to her. "Do you two know each other?"

"No," Jacqueline replied, biting back a smile.

"We haven't met... yet," Mac said.

"This is Jacqueline, my Big from college. Jack, this is my future brother-in-law, Prescott."

Prescott extended his hand and she slipped hers into his. Electricity traveled up her arm sending another surge of energy whizzing through her. It was powerful, intense, and absolutely fantastic.

She couldn't stop the feeling, and she didn't want to either. Mac... er... Prescott... was doing it for her in the best of ways. Their chemistry was just as strong today as it had been in their private room at the club.

With his eyes locked on hers, he asked, "What the hell is a Big?"

Addison's laugh made Prescott smile.

Ohmygod, ohmygod.

Hard to imagine he could look any better than he had stripped down, but his killer smile sent heat from her chest to her cheeks.

He's gorgeous.

Jacqueline sipped the champagne, hoping the chilled liquid would tamp down the inferno running rampant through her. Prescott wrapped his fingers around her arm.

"You okay?" he asked.

"Uh-huh," she bleated. "Why wouldn't I be?"

"You kinda swayed, or something," Addison said. "Have you eaten?"

"I'm good."

"What's a Big?" Prescott repeated.

"We were sorority sisters in college," Addison explained. "I'm a year behind Jack, and the second we met, we just clicked. It was crazy." Addison put a comforting arm around her. "She's one of my besties. After I pledged, I asked Jack if she'd be my *Big*, as in Big Sister. She said yes, and, from that moment on, we were pretty inseparable, until she graduated and broke my heart."

Jacqueline laughed.

Hawk joined them. "Hey, baby."

"Hello, honey," Prescott replied.

The three of them cracked up.

This was definitely a side of Mac Jacqueline had never seen before.

"Jericho is corralling everyone outside for games," Hawk explained.

"Babe," Addison began, "you remember my friend, Jack."

"Oh, hey," Hawk replied. "It's been a while."

Jacqueline nodded, her attention jumping back to Prescott.

He was waiting, his hypnotic gaze drilling into hers. The thrill of staring into his eyes sent a frisson through her.

"We should head outside," Addison said. "We paired you two up for the wedding. My cousin, Livy Savage, is my matron of honor and she'll be walking down the aisle with her husband, so Prescott, you're paired with Jack. Your only job is to make sure this amazing woman has a good time."

"I can do that," Prescott replied.

"Ohgod," Jacqueline murmured.

Everyone stared at her.

"Did you hear my stomach growl?" Jacqueline lied, hoping to cover her slip up.

Prescott placed his hand on the small of her back. Her skin tingled from his touch. A touch she was now craving.

Lower. Drop your hand to my ass.

"We'll get you something to eat before we head outside," Prescott said.

"Go into the photo booth," Addison said. "Nicholas and I want memories of *everything*."

This time, Jacqueline bit back a smile. They could take some very spicy pics in that photo booth to document their *real* relationship.

Hawk and Addison vanished out the sliding glass doors. Now, alone, again, with Mac, Jacqueline squared her shoulders. She had to get a handle on her emotions... not to mention her libido.

"Let's get you some food," he said, but he hadn't removed his large hand from her back.

"I don't think I can stomach anything."

Leaning close, he murmured, "Do I need to take you upstairs and relax you?"

She swallowed. That was a phenomenal idea that would never, ever happen. "I... um... that's not—"

"Deep breath," he murmured. "I've been asked to keep you company, which I'm gonna do."

"Ohgod, sorry. Addison is one of my closest friends in the world. Being Big and Little Sisters, we have a special bond. My kink is something she *doesn't* know about."

"I got you. You gotta trust me."

Trust him? She hardly knew the man. She could absolutely trust him to take care of her sexually, but that was all she knew. Up until several hours ago, that was all she wanted to know.

I can do this.

Hanging with him would be no big deal, *except* that she wanted him in the absolute worst way. But, she could pretend they were strangers for an hour or two, couldn't she? They'd hook up later, never speak of today, and she'd be back on a plane by the end of the weekend.

End of story.

"So, no wife and six kids?" she asked.

"No wife, no kids, and you're no party crasher."

"Nope."

Guests started moseying outside. Rather than follow,

Prescott stood there, gazing down at her. The more she peered back, the more she liked what she saw. How could she not? The air became charged with energy while the chatter of guests melted into white noise.

Then, she made a fatal error and inched closer. Her shoulder brushed against his chest. His massive, ripped chest with those perfectly sculpted pecs.

A low, rumbling growl erupted from his throat. "I gotta kiss you."

He dipped down, stopping millimeters away, the warmth of his breath heating her lips.

On a moan, she pressed her lips to his, and kissed him. The glorious sensation of his mouth on hers revved her engine and quieted her tormented soul. He could do for her what no one else could. Chase away the demons that had haunted her for the past ten years.

She ran her fingertips down his sculpted cheek and over his jawline. He was a feast for her senses. His tanned skin felt like silk, his familiar scent settled her nerves, but it was the way he kissed her that stole her heart.

One, tender kiss that made her feel like she was his.

Then, he broke away, stood tall. She inhaled a calming breath, but his cocky smile had her glaring at him.

"Wow, you think you know me just 'cause we hooked up a few times," she whispered.

"I do know you," he murmured. "And we've hooked up *more* than a few times. It was good, real good, and you know it."

He was right. It *was* good.

"Meh," she said, and he chuffed out a laugh while opening the slider.

She set her flute on a nearby tray, shot him a passing glance, and stepped outside. Seconds later, he was by her side, his large, steady hand taking up a lot of real estate on the small of her back.

Her skin tingled, every part of her hyperaware that he was touching her, his talented fingers inches above her ass.

When she glanced over at him, he returned her gaze. "You're tight. You want me to take my hand off you?"

"It's fine," she said.

In truth, she loved it.

Jericho was making a speech, but Prescott guided her in the direction of the photo booth. Once there, he pulled back the curtain, and gazed into her eyes.

If she stepped inside that small space with him, she would not be able to keep her hands off him.

Do it...

6

I KNOW YOU

Prescott

Prescott loved that he'd been asked to take care of Jack. He couldn't stop staring at her, couldn't soak up her beauty long enough. She'd captivated the hell out of him at Asylum, but she was driving him wild now.

Jack—Jacqueline—in that snug dress with those stilettos had snagged his attention before he'd seen her face. She looked just as stunning in street clothes as she did in her sexy club outfits. She'd left her hair down, but curled the ends so they wound around each other in chunks. At Asylum, the smell of sex hung heavy in the air, but here, at this party, her flowery scent wafted in his direction, and he couldn't get enough of her.

Rather than overthink things, he was going with it. She was his assignment for the afternoon and his naughty pleasure that evening.

She hadn't moved, so he entered the photo booth and sat on the small bench. She flicked her gaze from him to the bench, then back to him. The seat was small. His frame, large. The easiest place for her to sit was on his lap.

He patted his thigh, her lips twitched. Instead of taking him up on his invitation, she pushed in beside him.

"This is for Addison and Hawk," she murmured, "so we need to act like we just met."

Not happening.

He pulled her onto his lap and she let out a yelp. "What are you doing?"

"Having fun so that my brother and his future wife will have some good memories of their bridal shower. You ready?"

"I can fake it if you can," she bit out.

"There's no faking when it comes to us. I know how to push *all* your buttons, Jack."

He tapped the start button and stared at the lens. As the camera began flashing and clicking, he switched up his expression. She smiled, then peered at him. He looked in her direction. The attraction was pulling him closer. Unable—and unwilling—to resist, he leaned over.

Her smile was fucking killing him. She was a total hottie anyway, but that smile catapulted him to the stratosphere.

Then, they kissed. Only this time, she wrapped her arms around his neck and smothered him with her mouth. His insides roared to life, their kiss turned explosive. He snaked his arm around her back and planted his other hand on her thigh.

They had one speed.

Full throttle.

But they weren't in a sexy club. They were in a photo booth at a damn party in the middle of the freakin' day. And they *still* could not keep their hands or their mouths off each other.

Fucking hell.

He boned in his pants, but he ignored his trapped erection, focusing on the stunning auburn-haired woman in his arms.

The camera stopped clicking and they slowed their kiss down.

The string of photos dropped into the receptacle and she pulled it out.

Knock-knock.

"You guys done in there?" asked a familiar voice.

Before Jack had gotten off his lap, Stryker and Emerson pulled back the curtain and peered inside. When the men locked eyes, Stryker chuffed out a laugh.

"I think they need more time," Emerson said with a gleam in her eyes.

"We'll stand guard," Stryker deadpanned.

Jack moved off him, ran her fingers through her long hair, and straightened her dress. Gazing over at him, she said, "Let's take some actual photos, you know, with goofy faces."

She tapped the start button, the camera started clicking away. She stuck a pose, then craned her head toward him. He stuck out his tongue, then crossed his eyes.

But the pull was too strong to ignore, and he found himself peering over at her. She'd moved to the edge of the seat and started flexing her biceps. He reached over and felt the hardened muscle.

"Nice," he said.

"I eat my spinach," she whispered, then laughed.

Her melodious laugh was like medicine for his raging soul. Again, he stared at her as the camera continued clicking away. When she returned his gaze, he leaned over and dropped a soft kiss on the end of her nose.

She cradled his head, angled it down, and kissed his forehead.

The camera stopped. The whirring continued while the photos quick-processed. Out slid another string of photos. This time, he collected them.

"That was intense," she said before pushing off the bench.

She slid open the curtain and stepped outside. He followed and introduced her to his close friends.

"Stryker and Emerson are also in the wedding party," Prescott explained. "This is Addison's friend, Jack—Jacqueline."

"I met Jacqueline during a bridesmaid video chat," Emerson said. "Good to see you."

"You, too," Jack replied.

"How do you two know each other?" Emerson asked.

"Addison asked me to host her," Prescott replied.

Stryker's eyebrows jumped into his forehead. "You just met?"

"Uh-huh," Jack replied. "Yup, that's us. We just met."

Stryker laughed. "It didn't *sound* like you just met."

Prescott bit back a smile.

"Get in there, wife," Stryker said. "There's something in that booth that's got my boy all jazzed up."

Emerson laughed. "Jacqueline, how's your assignment working out?"

"It's okay," Jack replied.

"What do you do?" Stryker asked.

"I'm with the FBI," Jack said.

Prescott flicked his attention in her direction. "You're with the Bureau?"

"Are you guys in line?" asked a guest behind them.

The line for the photo booth was ten couples deep. "We'll come find you," Emerson said before she and Stryker disappeared inside.

After he and Jack stepped away from the entrance, she said, "Let's go play a game."

As they made their way across the lawn, she came to abrupt stop.

"My heel's stuck in the grass." After tugging out her stiletto, she wrapped her fingers around his arm. "This is for support."

"You are the only person here who can grab *any* body part of mine." He flashed her a smile. "In fact, I encourage it."

"You think that's actually gonna happen?"

"Not ruling it out."

The flirty banter continued while they played the giant lawn version of Connect Four. Being around her was addictive. As intense as she was at the club, she was super chill now. She didn't say much, didn't ask any questions either. She seemed to like hanging with him, and he was good with that.

Damn good.

Liv and Jericho were calling guests over to play the Wheel of Fun. A six-foot game wheel that could land on: Bride and Groom Kiss, Kiss Your Date, Pick a Couple to Kiss, Show Us Your Best Dance Move, and several more.

He and Jack pulled up alongside Hawk and Addison as Stryker and Emerson, and Cooper and Danielle, joined the group.

As more partygoers gathered around, Liv spun the wheel.

It landed on the Bride and Groom Kiss. The crowd hooted while Hawk pulled his fiancée into his arms and kissed her. The lingering kiss had a guest shout, "Save something for the honeymoon."

Everyone started laughing.

Liv spun the dial again and it landed on Kiss Your Date.

Prescott leaned down and kissed Jack before she had a chance to object. When she kissed him back, he murmured, "You're so greedy."

A whisper of a smile touched her eyes.

This time, Jericho stepped over and gave the wheel a big spin. It landed on Pick a Couple to Kiss.

Liv whispered in Jericho's ear and his gaze jumped to Prescott. "My wife thinks Prescott should kiss his date. What do you think?"

"I think they've already been going at it pretty good," Stryker called out.

"Scotty," Hawk exclaimed. "We asked you to show Jacqueline a good time, not maul her to death."

The group started laughing.

Prescott slid his gaze to Jack.

She turned toward the group and announced, "Prescott's making sure I'm having a *real* good time."

The crowd cracked up again.

"Go 'head, brother," Hawk said. "Show her what you got."

Prescott pulled her into his arms, dipped her back, and kissed her. Someone whistled while others were clapping and making cat calls. He stood her back up, and kissed her again.

"Who's next?" Liv tugged the wheel and everyone followed the spinning dial, but not Prescott. He couldn't take his eyes off Jack... and she hadn't let go of him either.

"I'm gonna take a break," Jack murmured.

"I'll go with you." Offering his arm, he waited for her to take hold. "Your feet have got to hurt in those stilts."

"The shoes are great, but I'm sinking into the soft soil."

"I can help with that." He whisked her into his arms and strode toward the house.

After he set her down on the patio, she said, "I'm gonna have that drink now. Want to join me?"

He sure as hell did.

After opening the slider, they went inside. The smell of flame-grilled steaks wafted in his direction, and his stomach growled in response.

A server appeared. "Can I bring you both something?"

"I'll have a sparkling water," Jack said.

"Whiskey, neat," Prescott replied.

As the server headed toward the kitchen, Prescott asked, "What do you do at the Bureau?"

"Temporary assignment with a task force."

"What *were* you doing?" he asked.

"I was the RAC—Resident Agent in Charge—of a smaller office. It's like a—"

"SAC," he replied.

She nodded. "Right. Special Agent in Charge. I got transferred out west."

The server returned with their drinks. After taking several sips, she asked, "What do you do?"

"Corporate America." Prescott's phone rang with a call from Dana, the head of his Product Safety Division. "Sorry," he said to Jack. "Gotta take this."

She nodded.

Prescott answered. "Hey, Dana, what's going on?"

"A plant employee confided that a coworker had tampered with a large batch of the painkiller. Turns out, the employee who came forward is the one who did it. The two had some kind of ongoing dispute and the one who poisoned the batch was hoping the other one would get fired."

"Nice job," Prescott replied. "You get eyes on this?"

"We've got video surveillance of him dumping a liquid into the vat."

"Jesus, what the hell was it?"

"Antifreeze."

"We're lucky no one died."

"The police are at his house now, and I've looped in Lorenzo from Marketing to put together another press release. I'm sorry, Prescott. This is gonna cost us."

"It's only money." He thanked Dana and hung up.

"That sounded serious," Jacqueline said.

"Someone in our manufacturing plant tampered with a popular painkiller and several people around the country got sick." He told her the name of the painkiller. "Do you have any?"

"I'm sure I do, but it's from a while ago," she replied. "So, how are you involved with that?"

"I'm the COO of Armstrong Enterprises."

Jacqueline

JACQUELINE STARED at him for several seconds. *It can't be. There's no way.*

A wave of nausea swept through her and she swallowed down the bitter bile. "Are you Prescott Armstrong?"

"Yes," he replied. "Addison introduced us hours ago."

She fisted her hand on her hip. "Addison introduced you as her future brother-in-law, Prescott. Isn't your last name Hawk, like your brother, Nicholas?"

"No, it's Armstrong."

Her entire world flipped on its axis. The air got sucked from her lungs while months of seething anger jumped to the surface. As reality took hold, she stared at him in disbelief. For months, she'd been addicted to his touch, craved him like no other man she'd ever met. Being around him was fire and all-consuming.

And now?

She wanted to throw up.

Prescott—*Prescott Armstrong*—shot her a smile. "You want to go back outside and play another game?"

She wanted to scream at him for what he did, storm out, and never, *ever* get within fifty feet of him, ever again.

Fury—and an overwhelming sadness—enveloped her.

She needed to put distance—like three thousand miles of it —between herself and him as soon as possible.

"It's you," she murmured. "I can't believe it's you."

"Right, it's me, Mac."

She stepped close. "How long have you worked at your family's company?

"I've been on the board since I was eighteen."

Standing tall, she glared at him. "How long have you

worked there full-time?"

"Eight months."

"Were you with HRT before that?"

He glanced over his shoulder. "That's classified. Very few people—"

"Were you at the Winchester cult standoff last year?"

Please say no. Please don't be that Prescott Armstrong.

"Yes," he replied. "How do you know about that?"

Ignoring his question, she forged on. "You shot the cult leader."

Anger flashed in his eyes, then a shadow darkened them. Muscles ticked in his chiseled jawline, but Jacqueline didn't care about any of that. Now, she just needed confirmation.

"I took him out," he said.

A growl shot out of her as she accepted the God-awful truth.

"Do you remember what happened after that?" she asked, trying to keep her emotions in check.

"Look," he rasped, "I know all those cult members died."

"Three hundred and ninety-four," she spat out. "I had been on the phone negotiating with the leader. I'd convinced him to let them all go. And then, you—" she narrowed her gaze at him — "*you* took him out and everything went to hell. That mission was considered an epic fucking fail."

As they glared at each other, a seething silence engulfed them.

She blew out an exasperated breath. "You decided to go rogue and take him out. I got demoted because of you."

Realization flashed in Prescott's eyes. "You were the woman who called and reamed me a new one after it all went down."

"Bingo. Before that, I'd never lost my shit at work. Never. The fallout from that was catastrophic. If you were the last man on earth, I wouldn't want a thing to do with you."

"You don't know the whole story."

She hitched a brow, crossed her arms over her chest. "Go ahead, enlighten me."

The sliding glass door opened and Addison walked into the room. "There you are." She pressed her hand on her heart. "It's great that you're getting to know each other. The waitstaff are about to serve dinner."

"I was just saying goodbye to Prescott. I have a work emergency. This was lovely and I'm really happy for you, Addison." Jacqueline hugged her very surprised friend.

"I'm so bummed you have to leave," Addison said. "We'll video chat next week. Thank you so much for being here today."

After Addison closed the slider behind her, Jacqueline turned to Prescott. Her heart ached, her head was pounding so damn hard. In addition to their crazy sexual chemistry, she'd been having the best time with him. He checked *all* her boxes, even the ones she didn't know needed checking.

"I'll walk you to your car," Prescott said.

"No," she bit out. "And in case there's any confusion, I *won't* be at the club tonight."

Once outside, she walked on rubbery legs up the long driveway toward her sister-in-law's Jeep, parked on the street.

The Winchester cult standoff had been intense from the beginning, but she'd had every confidence the leader would free his followers. She hadn't been able to save Janey, but she'd been hellbent on keeping those people alive.

And I would have, if Armstrong hadn't gone rogue.

Three weeks into the standoff, the cult leader had called in the middle of the night. The negotiator had stepped out, so Jacqueline got on the phone with him. He liked talking with her, so she'd continued their conversations over the next seven days. Then, in the dead of night, she'd been on the phone with him, encouraging him to let everyone leave the compound. When he moved to a backlit window, Prescott took his kill shot.

One minute, he was on the phone, the next, he was gone. Within minutes, mass suicide.

She'd worked her ass off to get to where she was—and that one bullet had sent her on a very different trajectory.

As she got to the Jeep, Addison's dad, Philip Skye— Z— loomed into view.

"Hello, Mr. Skye, it's good to see you."

He pulled to a stop at the Jeep. "Jacqueline, how are you?"

"Doing great. You?"

"Did I miss the party?"

"They're just about to have dinner."

"Why are you leaving?"

"I've got a work—"

His expression made her laugh.

"I can't BS you, can I?" she asked.

Z shook his head. "No, you can't. What's going on?"

"The HRT agent who took out the cult leader was my assigned host for the party, only I didn't know who he was. But you did, didn't you, Z?"

Z nodded. "Gut it out, if you can. I know Addison was looking forward to seeing you."

"Normally, I would, but..."

"You aren't happy out west, are you?"

She shook her head. "I miss my family and close friends. I loved running the Winchester office. I loved my job so much." Fighting the emotion, she gave him a quick hug. "I'll see you, next month, at the wedding."

Without waiting for him to reply, she jumped into the vehicle and pulled onto the quiet residential street. She would spend the evening playing with the puppies and trying to forget she ever met Prescott Armstrong.

Too bad he turned out to be my worst fucking nightmare. He could have been the man of my dreams.

7
ANOTHER DEAD OP

Prescott

Prescott managed to get through the Jack and Jill shower by hiding his emotions. He'd mastered that skill during his early days at the Bureau, then perfected it when he'd moved to the Hostage Rescue Team, known as HRT.

He loved that job with every fiber of his being, but when it got ripped away from him, he moved on. Then, when an unexpected door had opened, he marched through it.

Despite soldiering on, he carried the mass suicide with him. Those trusting, brainwashed individuals haunted his dreams while the mishandled event fueled him ever-forward. That epic, fucking fail was the reason he refused to join ALPHA, and more recently, BLACK OPS.

If Jack knew the truth, she might not be so quick to persecute him for his actions. Life isn't always as it seems, and sometimes situations are much more complicated than they appear.

That evening, when the group headed to Jericho Road, he canceled the private room at Asylum and drove home. There was always work to do, so he stayed up until three, grinding through Armstrong emails.

He wanted to reach out to Jack, but he had to let her go.

Just because he kept his emotions on lockdown didn't mean he didn't have them. He'd felt plenty for the feisty, auburn-haired beauty. But that, too, had led to another epic fail. So, he'd put her in his past.

Monday brought the beginning of a new week *and* a new month. May meant warmer weather and a chance for him to escape reality on his yacht. Maybe even get in a few rounds of golf.

The morning flew by without incident.

Later that afternoon, his desk phone buzzed. "Sally Sagall is waiting in the lobby," said one of the receptionists.

As he powered down the hall toward the elevator, his uncle stepped out of his office. Prescott stopped short of crashing into him. A woman with bright blond hair stood in the doorway.

"Prescott, I was just on my way to see you," said Artemis. "This is the consultant from TopCon. Leslie, my nephew, Prescott."

While giving him a quick once over, Leslie pulled her hair around to one side, and stuck out her chest. Her oversized breasts were spilling out of her tight, low-scooped shirt, but Prescott wasn't interested in the peep show, so he shifted his focus to his uncle.

"What's TopCon working on?" Prescott asked.

"Re-imaging some of our outdated brands," Artemis said. "Giving them an updated look." His uncle smiled warmly at Leslie.

"That's right," Leslie agreed. "I've been busy, busy making that happen."

"I've got someone waiting in the lobby," Prescott said. "I look forward to seeing the final product."

The three of them rode downstairs in the elevator.

"What do you do?" Leslie asked him.

"I'm the COO," Prescott replied.

Leslie slid her gaze to Artemis.

"Chief Operating Officer," Artemis explained.

After they exited the elevator, Artemis pulled Leslie aside to speak with her.

Prescott spied his sister outside on the phone. While waiting, he checked in with his team of receptionists at the front desk. A moment later, Sally made her way over.

Prescott greeted her with a warm embrace. "Good to see you."

"Thanks so much for this opportunity," she replied.

A few months ago, Sally had reached out and introduced herself. She had reason to believe they were half siblings. Despite Prescott's skepticism, he'd spoken with her, then video chatted. After they'd both submitted their DNA, the results had provided them with the truth.

They were related through their biological father, a man neither of them had met. He died when Prescott was an infant.

His thirty-five-year-old sister was older by a year. Her mom had been in a relationship with their dad, but had broken up with him before she found out she was pregnant. According to Sally, her mom never told their dad about her. When Sally's mom passed away, she found a box revealing Sally's dad's true identity. After several internet searches, Sally found her way to Prescott.

Not long ago, she'd moved to the area with her young son, Ethan. She had a strong financial background and had expressed interest in working at the family business. Prescott had mentioned her to his HR director, who agreed to meet with her. It was the least Prescott could do for a sister who had no family beyond her son and him.

His uncle was heading back toward the elevator bank when Prescott intercepted him. "Artemis, this is my sister, Sally."

"Sister?"

"Yeah, I mentioned—" Prescott began.

"Welcome to the family," Artemis replied, cutting him off.

"Thank you," Sally said. "Do you have a family?"

"I've been married over forty years. I've got two grown children and seven grandchildren. I guess that makes me the patriarch." Artemis chuckled.

"Arty!" Leslie called from the entrance.

"My consultant needs me." Artemis hurried off.

"I'd love to meet his family, one day," Sally said. "It was just me and my mom, then I got married and we had Ethan. My husband passed, then my mom. My family has always been so small. I would love to be a part of a big, extended family."

"Welcome to the mayhem," Prescott said before suggesting they head upstairs.

On the elevator ride, he told her she'd be meeting with the HR director.

"Not gonna lie," she replied. "I'm super excited. Armstrong is a fantastic company to work for, plus with daycare in the next building, I would feel so relieved knowing Ethan is nearby."

"Where is he now?"

The elevator doors opened, and they stepped out.

"He's in daycare twice a week." On the way down the hallway, she said, "Ethan's such a social, energetic little boy. He loves making friends, plus I've got two days to get everything done, so I can focus on him the rest of the week."

"You're a good mom."

His sister smiled. "I try. Ethan is my entire world and I want to balance having a career with being a single mom."

He escorted her to the director's office, made the introduction, and left.

Jacqueline

EVEN THE THREE-THOUSAND miles that separated her from Prescott couldn't shake him from her thoughts.

Monday morning had her back in California and working at her desk, but her mind kept wandering to the mountain of a man who turned her inside out with a single glance and ignited her need with his passionate touch.

She wasn't sure she believed him when he told her, "You don't know the whole story", but she wasn't going to obsess over it. The damage had been done. She would put the debacle known as Prescott Armstrong behind her and focus on her current situation—busting her ass on this task force so she could get another shot at putting her career back on track, and snag a job back east.

At the end of the day, she packed up her laptop. Once home, she changed, and went for a good, long run.

When finished, she walked the last block to her apartment building and punched in her passcode. As soon as she entered the lobby, she eyed Jeff waiting on a nearby sofa.

Ah, crap.

He jumped up. Smiling big, he hurried over, arms outstretched.

"Hey, I'm glad I caught you," he said.

Rather than allow him to hug her, she stopped a few feet away. "What are you doing here?"

"I went to the airport yesterday to pick you up, but I forgot your arrival time, so I waited around forever." He rolled his eyes. "I shoulda put it in my phone. You know me. I never remember the deets."

She furrowed her brow. "You didn't answer my question. What are you doing here?"

"I thought we could hang out."

A chill slithered down her spine. "We broke up."

He laughed. "Ah, c'mon, you didn't mean that. I think you just freaked because I was giving you a key, you know, to the kingdom." He gestured to himself.

"How did you get in?"

"I know your building code, duh."

"You need to go."

His eyebrows jutted into his forehead. "What? You can't be for real."

She pointed toward the entrance. "Out. Now."

He raised his hands in surrender. "And here I was all ready to chillax with my girl."

Jacqueline stormed to the front door and shoved it open at the same time she pulled her phone from the strap around her arm. "If you don't get the hell out, I'm calling the police."

As he moseyed close, he chuckled. "What are they gonna do?"

"I'll get a restraining order."

As he passed her, he banged his shoulder against her.

On a shudder, she exited the building and waited while he meandered down the sidewalk. Once he was gone, she re-set her code, and retreated inside.

She might have overreacted, but she wasn't comfortable with him showing up and getting into her building. The last thing she needed was a stalker.

Her blood ran cold while dread had her hurrying up the stairs to her apartment.

Once inside, she bolted the door. She hated that she lived in fear, hated that she overreacted to an ex showing up. Just because he showed up didn't mean he was going to harm her.

I'm okay, she told herself as she set her Glock on the bathroom counter. After stripping down, she stepped into the shower.

I'm safe. She repeated the mantra over and over.

After the trembling subsided and she regained her composure, she rinsed off the soap and dried off.

While eating dinner, she hopped online in search of a ruthless killer who had gotten away with murder for far too long. She'd been looking for a decade, and she'd continue looking until she found him.

Even if it took her the rest of her life.

Prescott

AT JUST AFTER eleven that evening, Prescott walked into his home office, set down his mug, and opened his laptop. Though he wasn't an ALPHA Operative, he had full access to ALPHA's secure system, thanks to Z.

After plugging in his sixteen-digit password, he opened the video chat window and dialed in. He had time before the call started, so he opened a different ALPHA window and typed in Jacqueline Hartley.

While waiting for the report, he sipped his coffee.

Seconds later, the report was completed. Thirty-one-year-old Hartley was single with no children. She'd graduated from Virginia Tech with a degree in criminology, then earned a Master's in psychology at Maryland two years later. Her career with the Bureau had begun when she was in high school where she spent every summer and winter break working at HQ in DC. From what he could tell, the Bureau had been fast-tracking her.

Since graduating, she'd worked her way up to RAC at the Winchester office. A few weeks after the cult standoff ended, she was transferred to San Francisco to work on a task force.

Over the years, she'd received numerous honorary citations for her exemplary work and her contribution to helping the

Bureau apprehend several known serial killers and serial rapists. Her superiors considered her a team player and a natural leader.

A myriad of emotions—disappointment, anger, guilt—started to take hold.

Things could have gone so differently, for everyone.

His attention was diverted when Dakota Luck appeared on the screen. Dakota's current position with ALPHA was running BLACK OPS—an elite group of ALPHA agents.

"Hey," Prescott said.

"Sorry we didn't get a chance to chat at the shower yesterday," Dakota said.

"Probably a good thing. We would have ended up huddled away in a corner, talking shop."

"Speaking of huddled away, I saw you hanging with someone. Who was she?"

"A friend of Addison's from college," Prescott replied.

Bert Grimes appeared on the screen. "Hey, guys, how it going?"

"Hey, Bert, good to see you," Dakota said. "Do you know Prescott Armstrong?"

"How's it going?" Prescott asked.

"I didn't know you're with ALPHA," Bert said to Prescott.

"I've been trying to get him to join my group," Dakota interjected. "More like begging, but Armstrong is a stubborn man."

Prescott chuckled. "I work missions alone."

"Gotcha," Bert replied.

"Okay, guys," Dakota said, "I need confirmation you're on the secure network."

Both Prescott and Bert affirmed that they were.

"Are you both in a private setting?" Dakota asked.

"On my ALPHA laptop in my kitchen," Bert said. "My wife is visiting her sister in Florida, so I'm home alone."

"Home office," Prescott replied.

"I'm in my home office, and in about ten minutes, my toddler's going to realize that I've left the room," Dakota said. "Expect some persistent knocking."

Both men laughed.

"My son is grown," Bert said, "but we went through that when he was little. One minute he was daddy's boy, the next, he wouldn't leave my wife's side. Enjoy those days, Dakota. They go by too fast."

"I love every second of it," Dakota replied. "Okay, let's get started. Bert, I'm building an elite team of Ops for assignments that will take us out of the country. You've been with ALPHA for years, so I wanted to see if this would be something you'd be interested in."

Bert smiled. "Might be. Can you tell me—" Bert glanced over the top of his laptop. His eyes widened. "What the hell are *you* doing here?"

BANG!

A bullet pierced Bert's forehead between his eyes and he slumped back in his chair.

"What the fuck," Dakota exclaimed.

"I'm on it." Prescott grabbed his phone and called Cooper, co-lead of ALPHA.

"Mute your laptop," Dakota said.

Prescott muted his computer as Cooper answered. "Hey, brother."

"Dakota and I are on a video chat with Bert Grimes," Prescott explained. "Someone broke into his house and shot him execution style—"

The killer slammed Bert's laptop shut, but the video chat between Prescott and Dakota was still active.

"I'm calling you and Coop." Dakota dropped off.

"The killer is in Bert's house," Prescott said to Cooper. "He just shut Bert's laptop."

"Jesus," Cooper exclaimed.

"Dakota's calling us," Prescott said, and hung up.

Prescott accepted the invitation, punched in his code, and Dakota's face popped onto the screen again. Seconds later, Cooper joined them.

"I called the police," Dakota said. "Told the operator Bert's with the Bureau."

In order to keep their ALPHA identity concealed, Ops were assigned IDs from several federal law enforcement agencies, one being the FBI.

"Walk me through what happened," Cooper said.

After Dakota did, he added, "One minute he's sitting at his kitchen table, the next he's got a bullet in his brain."

"Could have been a B&E that went bad," Cooper said.

"It wasn't," Prescott said. "He knew his killer."

"I'm getting word out to the team," Cooper said. "Once police find Bert in the system, they'll contact me."

Prescott remembered that an ALPHA Op had recently been killed during a carjacking. "Do you think Gloria Whelan's murder is connected to this one?"

"Doubtful," Cooper replied.

"Two Ops killed within days of each other isn't a coincidence," Prescott pushed back.

"I'll check with the detective assigned to Gloria's case." Cooper's phone started ringing. "It's the police."

They ended the call, and Prescott shoved out of his chair and started pacing. Bert Grimes's death had all the markings of a revenge kill. The killer entered his home and made sure Bert saw him before he got a bullet between the eyes.

Who the hell wanted Bert dead?

FRIDAY EVENING, PRESCOTT raised his glass. "Congratulations."

When Prescott found out that Sally's interview with his

company had gone well, he asked his finance veep to interview her ASAP. She had the skills, along with a great attitude, so she was offered a position on the team. To celebrate her job offer at Armstrong Enterprises, Prescott had put together a last-minute dinner party.

His sister Kerri and her husband Lamar couldn't make it, but his mom and dad, along with Hawk and Addison were there to support Sally and her son, Ethan.

Seated around his kitchen table, the family raised their glasses and toasted his sister.

Sally's eyes filled with tears. "Thank you so much for welcoming Ethan and me into your family. I'm so grateful."

"We're happy you're here," Prescott's mom said.

Sally choked back a sob. "Sorry, it's just that everyone is so nice."

"We're all drunk," Hawk replied. "We don't know *what's* going on."

Everyone laughed.

Platters of food from Jericho Road—burgers and ribs—were passed around, along with a large bowl of fries. His mom served the salad, and everyone dug in.

Sally cut up a hamburger for Ethan, but he was too busy devouring fries to notice.

"Addison and Hawk, thank you so much for including me at your wedding," Sally said. "I sent the RSVP back today, and no worries, I'll find a sitter for Ethan."

"Bring him," Addison replied. "We're having a fun, family-oriented wedding at the farmhouse."

"With over a hundred of our closest friends," Hawk added.

"Are you sure?" Sally asked.

"Absolutely," Addison replied. "In fact, close friends of ours have a toddler. How old is Dakota and Providence Luck's son, Graham?"

"Three or four," Hawk replied.

"I'm free!" Ethan exclaimed.

"Yes, you are," Sally said. "When will you be four?"

Ethan grinned. "August."

"Do you know what day?" Sally asked.

"Fourteen," the tyke replied.

"That's right, Ethan." Sally held up her hand and Ethan high-fived her.

"I'm not sure if I'm more excited over the job or that Ethan will be at daycare a few buildings away in the compound," she said. "Thank you again, Prescott."

"I just got you in the door," he replied. "You did all the heavy lifting."

"When do you start?" Prescott's dad asked.

"Monday, which is crazy, but doable, right Ethan?"

Ethan was reaching for more fries, paying his mom no attention at all.

"Lemme help you with that." Prescott spooned a handful of French fries onto his nephew's plate. "You want some ketchup with that?"

"Ew, yucky," Ethan replied.

"Ethan, what's a polite answer?" Sally asked.

"No, fank you." Ethan tipped his sippy cup into his mouth. "Mommy, it's empty. More, please."

"I'll get it for you, buddy." Prescott filled the cup with filtered water from his refrigerator, and handed it to the child.

Ethan grinned at him, "Fank you." After taking a few sips, he grimaced and set down the cup. "I don't like water. Juice please."

"You don't like water?" Hawk asked. "It's the best drink on the planet."

"I thought whiskey was the best," Prescott replied, and the adults laughed.

Sally took Ethan's spill-proof cup and changed out the

water for apple juice, then added a splash of water. She handed him the cup and he drank down the sweet drink.

"He's a sugar addict," Sally explained. "I'm to blame, but now I'm having the hardest time weening him off it."

Conversation came easily, and Prescott was grateful to his family for being so welcoming of his sister and her son. He wasn't sure how his mom would react, but she wasn't fazed in the least. Her response had been, "Your first dad had a girlfriend before we met and he didn't know she was pregnant. Your sister seems like a lovely woman who's got a hard job raising a child on her own. That could have been me, if I hadn't met your second dad."

He adored his mom. She was rock solid and kind to everyone she met. He wondered how his parents would feel if they knew the truth about their sons. Both were trained assassins who took out the worst of the worst with no regret.

"This food is super good," Sally said. "Where is Jericho Road?"

"It's in Alexandria," Addison answered. "It's owned by a close friend of ours and it's our go-to place for ribs and fries."

"Yummy fries," Ethan added.

Prescott was never around children, so he was interested in getting to know his young nephew. "Ethan, what are you learning in daycare?"

"Counting and letters. We do story time and we play outside. And we have nappy time." He scrunched up his nose. "I don't like nappy time."

"Why not?" Prescott asked.

"I want to play!" He giggled.

Prescott and his sister didn't look anything alike. She had an olive complexion with shoulder-length dark, brown hair and deep brown eyes. Ethan was fairer with light brown eyes and wavy hair that touched his shoulders.

Prescott was happy to be in a position to help, just like he did for everyone in his family.

Years ago, when his brother's life had gone off the rails, he'd made Hawk his top priority. Whatever it took to help get him back on track. And he would do the same for his sister.

After dinner, Prescott made a pot of coffee, and everyone moved to the sunroom. Sally grabbed a tote bag and sat on the floor with Ethan. Together, they started building a small racetrack and unearthed some plastic trucks.

"You come prepared," Prescott said.

Sally smiled. "If I don't, Ethan will find your pots and pans, a large metal spoon, and he'll make a lot of noise."

Prescott's mom and dad laughed.

"That sounds like you, Prescott," his mom said.

"I did that?" he asked.

"All the time," his dad replied, "but I changed out the metal spoon for a plastic one."

"What about me?" Hawk asked.

"You liked building blocks, you loved airplanes, and you stole one of Kerri's dolls. She became your constant companion for a while."

Addison laughed. "That does not surprise me... at all."

"I was just practicing for you, babe," Hawk said.

"I hate to run," Addison said, "but I need to swing by the mall, real quick, and grab a few things."

"Why don't you order online?" Prescott asked.

"It's wedding stuff from the bridal store," she said. "I'll be back in thirty, forty max."

Hawk had been sitting on the floor, playing with Ethan. "I'll go."

"Oh, no!" Ethan said. "Stay and play wif me, pleeeeease." Then, he looked at his Mom. "Is he my uncle too?"

"I sure am, buddy," Hawk said. "I'm your uncle Nicky."

Ethan handed Hawk a truck. "Here."

"Hey, what if I go with Addison?" Sally asked.

"I'd love that," Addison replied. "But I'm not doing any shopping. Just a quick pick-up."

"I haven't made any friends since I moved here, so I'd love a little girl company," Sally said.

When Addison excused herself into the bathroom, Prescott pulled his brother aside. "You gotta go with her," he whispered.

"That's why I told her I'd go with her," Hawk said.

"You got a weapon?" Prescott asked.

"In the SUV," Hawk whispered.

Addison exited the bathroom and bumped into Hawk. "I heard you guys. I don't have my weapon with me."

Hawk shook his head at her. "Then, you shouldn't go to the mall, baby."

"You'll have yours," she said.

"You got body armor?" Prescott whispered and they both stared at him.

"No," Hawk replied.

"I saw Bert get shot between the eyes at close range," Prescott murmured. "You gotta watch your backs."

"We got this," Hawk insisted.

Sally told Ethan she was running to the store. He stopped playing to look at her. "Okay, Mommy. Who will stay with me?"

"I will, buddy." Prescott sat on the floor next to the child. "Maybe my dad will play with us too."

As they were leaving, Prescott's mom called out. "Sally, does Ethan have any food allergies?"

Sally returned to the living room. "None that we know of, but he's such a picky eater that he doesn't eat much beyond chicken nuggets and mac-n-cheese. He will eat a PB&J though, so no peanut allergy." She knelt in front of Ethan. "I love you, honey."

"Love you, Mommy."

She kissed his forehead and hurried after Hawk and Addison.

Prescott's dad let out a groan as he eased onto the floor.

"Dad," Prescott said, "you're too young to be making old man sounds."

His dad laughed as he picked up one of the child's trucks. "This is a great truck, Ethan. What kind of track are you building?"

"A circle," the child replied.

"Can I play with you?" his dad asked.

"Okay."

While they finished building the track, Prescott's mind wandered to Jacqueline. He wanted to make it up to her, wanted to apologize for derailing her career. During the week, he thought about her numerous times, wondering what she was doing. Would she even return for Hawk and Addison's wedding, knowing he'd be there?

"I'm firsty, please," Ethan said.

Prescott collected the sippy cup from the kitchen table. He added juice, then diluted it with water. Returning to the sunroom, he handed it to Ethan.

After sipping, he grimaced. "This is yucky."

"I added a little water so we don't use up all the juice your mom brought," Prescott explained.

The child stared at him. "I don't like water."

Prescott smiled. "I don't like juice."

The toddler laughed. "I have to go poopy."

Prescott glanced at his mom.

"Don't look at me Prescott McCafferty Armstrong. He's *your* nephew."

"Do you use the potty?"

"I pee pee in the potty and poopy in my pull-on, then Mommy, she puts me in a new one." Ethan wandered over to the corner where he spent a few minutes in a squat, grunting.

Prescott had to purse his lips to keep from laughing. It was bizarre and adorably weird at the same time.

"I'm done!" Ethan exclaimed. "Can you help me?"

Prescott went in search of Sally's tote bag. He rummaged through for a diaper and wipes. Then, he laid out an old towel on the floor of the family room.

"Hey, Ethan, I've got your diaper."

The tyke walked over. "Diapers are for babies. I wear big-boy pull-ons."

"Okay, so do you lay down and I take this off you or what?"

"Uh-huh."

Ethan laid down, and Prescott pulled off his shorts, then the disposable. "Whew, you got some stinkos, kid."

Ethan giggled. "Poopy smells."

Prescott cleaned up his nephew, tugged up the pull-on, then the shorts. "How does that feel?"

"Good," Ethan replied before running back into the sunroom to play.

While Prescott was taking the kitchen trash to the garage, his phone rang. It was Hawk. "Yo," he answered.

"Addison and Sally were shot," Hawk said, his breath coming fast.

"*What?*"

"Addison was shot in the shoulder. Sally, in the back. Meet me at the hospital, but wear body armor and bring one for me. I called Z and he's on his way. Don't bring the kid."

"Got it." Prescott hung up and strode into the house.

Back in the sunroom, he pulled his mom aside while his dad played with Ethan. "I need to leave."

She furrowed her brows at him. "Why?"

"Addison and Sally were shot."

"Ohmygod!"

"We gotta keep things chill and not let Ethan find out. Addison was shot in the shoulder, Sally, in the back. I'm going to the hospital so I can be there when they get out of surgery. Can you and Dad stay here with Ethan tonight?"

"Of course. Call us when you know more."

"I'm gonna tell Ethan that he gets to have a sleepover with you guys before I take off."

In times like these, Prescott appreciated that he was a master at controlling his emotions. He was able to focus on taking care of tasks without letting his nerves get in the way. He could see the fear in his mom's eyes, but he needed to push forward.

He and his mom returned to the sunroom to find his dad reading Ethan a children's book. The small child sat on his dad's lap, his tiny thumb in his mouth, staring at the pictures in the book. The sight tugged at Prescott's heart strings.

The child saw him and smiled, his thumb still in his mouth. Prescott knelt close by. "I have to go out for a little while, but I'll be back very soon. The child nodded. "My mom and dad—"

"We thought it would be easier if Ethan calls us Nana and Papa," his dad explained.

Prescott offered a grateful smile. "Ethan, Nana and Papa are going to have a sleepover with you until everyone gets back."

"Where's my mommy?"

"She's at the store with Addison and Uncle Nicky," Prescott lied.

"Is she coming back soon?"

"Hopefully not too soon," his mom interjected with a smile. "We're having too much fun and we don't want you to leave yet."

"I've got blankets and pillows in the upstairs hall closet," Prescott said. "I've gotta grab a few things before I take off."

"Bye," Ethan called.

Prescott tousled the boy's wild head of hair. "You're a good boy, Ethan."

In his first-floor home office, Prescott attached his ankle

holster, opened his safe, and slid one of his Glocks inside it. Next, he yanked off his shirt and armored up. As he was pulling his shirt back on, his mom walked in. Her eyes widened when she saw the bullet-proof vest.

"You're scaring me," she said. "What is going on?"

"It's gonna be okay, Mom." He didn't have time to explain and he wasn't sure what he'd say. He needed to get to the hospital and get a vest on his brother. Not knowing the extent of the women's injuries, he grabbed the other two vests, then kissed his mom on her forehead. "I'll call as soon as I know anything."

He bolted through the kitchen and into his three-car garage. Rather than take his truck, he jumped in his ALPHA SUV, tapped the garage door, waited for it to rise, then drove out. After the door closed, he backed out of his driveway, hit the gas, and sped off in the direction of the hospital.

As he pulled into the parking lot, he was convinced a predator was out there, hunting down and killing ALPHA Operatives, one at a time.

8
THE UNTHINKABLE

Prescott

With a Kevlar vest in hand, Prescott sprinted into the busy ER waiting room. *Too damn crowded.*

His brother stood near the entrance to triage, talking to a nurse. Prescott strode over as the nurse hurried back inside.

"Thanks for getting here so fast," Hawk said.

Prescott held out the body armor. He expected a full-on argument, but his brother yanked off his blood-stained T-shirt, pulled on the vest, then tugged the shirt back on.

"I didn't think to bring you a clean shirt," Prescott said.

Two nurses standing behind the reception desk eyed them. "You're gonna give us a heart attack," one of them said. "What's with the vest?"

"I liked him better without his shirt," said the other nurse. "That sent my heart into an arrhythmia."

Hawk shot them a smile. "It's all good. I've just got an overprotective brother."

The women slid their gaze to Prescott. "You're brothers?"

"Yeah," Prescott replied.

"It's nice to have some eye candy for a change," said one of the women. "We've seen it all and most of it ain't pretty. You guys police?"

"Nope," Hawk replied.

"You boys be good," said the other nurse.

After the brothers moved to a quiet corner of the busy waiting room, Prescott asked, "How are they?"

"They're in surgery. They got hit from behind, so I didn't see a thing. When I realized they'd been shot, I was too concerned about them to go after the shooter. Addison took a bullet to her back, up by her shoulder. She was a beast. I gave her my shirt and she held it against the wound until paramedics arrived. Sally took a bullet to the middle of her back and she might've banged her head on a car as she hit the ground. She'd passed out, so I focused on her."

"How you holding up?" Prescott asked.

"Me? I'm fine, but seeing them both take a bullet got to me. Do Mom and Dad have Ethan?"

"Yeah, they're gonna stay at the house. When I left, Dad was reading him a bedtime story." Prescott unearthed his phone. "I gotta call them." He dialed, put the phone on speaker.

His mom answered on the first ring. "What's happening. Is Nicky with you?"

"I'm here, Mom," Hawk said. "I'm fine. Addison and Sally are in surgery. They're gonna be okay."

Prescott raised his eyebrows. His brother had no way of knowing that. Neither had even come out of surgery, but he knew Hawk didn't want them to worry.

"I'm relieved to hear that," she said. "Ethan fell asleep on Dad's lap. He's such a sweet little boy. We're having a slumber party in the family room."

"Thanks for taking care of him," Prescott said.

Z entered the ER and beelined over.

"Mom, Addison's dad just got here," Prescott said. "I'll call you when they're out of surgery." He ended the call.

"How are they?" Z asked.

After they updated him, Z's phone rang. "It's Dakota." He answered, put phone to ear. "Did you get the word out?" He listened, then said, "I'm with Prescott and Nicholas now. Both women are in surgery." Z glanced at Hawk's shirt. "He's covered in blood, but I think he's okay."

"I'm fine," Hawk said.

Z hung up and eyed both men. "ALPHA is on official lockdown. Nicholas, you'll be hearing from Cooper."

"Isn't that extreme?" Hawk bit out. "When the hell do Ops go into hiding? It's our job to chase down the criminals, not hide from them."

"The second you see Addison, you won't want to leave her side," Z said. "Knowing you, you'd probably impose your own lockdown. ALPHA's just saving you from fighting with your strong-willed fiancée, who won't want to stay locked up either."

"He's right," Prescott said. "We don't know who's after you, or why."

"Nicholas Hawk," a physician called out.

They made their way over. "I'm Hawk."

"Addison is out of surgery and asking for you," said the attending physician. "She's in a recovery room on the fourth floor."

"What about my sister, Sally Sagall?" Prescott asked.

The doctor checked with the front desk. "She's still in surgery, but tell someone at the nurses' station that you're waiting to see her. They'll let you know when she's been moved to a recovery room."

They made their way upstairs, stopping at the nurses' station for Addison's room number.

Hawk blew out a sigh when he saw that Addison was awake and resting comfortably in bed.

Addison's gaze floated from Hawk to her dad to Prescott, then back to Hawk. "My three favorite guys." Her relaxed smile had tight muscles running along Prescott's shoulders loosen a little.

Hawk kissed her before sitting beside her, while Z pulled up a chair bedside. Prescott stood at the foot.

"How's Sally?" Addison asked.

Hawk clasped her hand. "Still in surgery."

"Is she going to be okay?" Addison asked.

"Yup, all good, baby," Hawk replied.

She flicked her gaze to her father. "I'm okay, really. Minimum pain. The doctor told me that I'm going to make a full recovery and I can leave in a few hours. They're giving me some antibiotics to take with me so I don't get an infection."

"My woman's a beast," Hawk said with a proud smile.

"ALPHA's going on lockdown," her dad said.

Addison furrowed her brow. "That's insane."

"I'm gonna grab a vest for you," Prescott said. "Z, you wearing one?"

"Always," Z replied.

Once outside, Prescott did a sweep in the parking lot. Was the killer lurking in the shadows, waiting to finish the job? How many other ALPHA Ops would die before the killer was stopped?

Anger ran rampant through him and he curled his hands into fists. He grabbed a vest and strode toward the hospital entrance.

His phone rang. It was Cooper. "Hey," he answered.

"I just talked to Hawk and Addison," Cooper said. "How's your sister?"

"Still in surgery."

"ALPHA is going on lockdown," he explained. "That doesn't include BLACK OPS, but it does include Hawk and Addison, since they're crossovers."

"Got it."

"Who do you think was the target tonight?" Prescott asked.

"Both of them," Cooper replied. "I spoke to the detective assigned to Gloria Whelan's case. I agree with you. I don't think it was a random carjacking. I think she was the killer's first hit."

"What a clusterfuck." Prescott hung up and returned to the nurses' station to ask about his sister.

Sally was out of surgery but hadn't been moved to a room. Prescott breathed a little easier. It was bad enough that Ops were being gunned down, but Sally was an innocent bystander in all of this.

In Addison's room, he laid the vest on the bed. "Wear this."

"Any word on Sally?" she asked.

"She's in recovery."

Addison couldn't raise her arm to put on the vest, so Hawk laid it over her.

Ten minutes passed, then thirty.

Addison dozed, still groggy from the anesthesia. Hawk and Z spoke quietly while Prescott paced the hallway outside her room. Pent-up agitation had his trigger finger itching to take the killer out.

As he was passing the nurses' station for the fourth or fifth time, one of the attendants told him his sister was asking for him.

Sally was pale, her eyes glassy. Though she was propped up in bed, she'd slid down. Her crooked smile gave him hope.

"How you doin'?" he asked.

"Sleepy, pretty drugged up. Where's Ethan?"

He sat in the chair, held her hand. "He's totally fine. My mom and dad—now being called Nana and Papa—are having a sleepover with him in my living room. He doesn't know what happened to you, so he's not worried."

She sighed. "Thank you so much. The doctor said my injury

is going to heal, but it's going to take a while, so I've gotta go easy. I don't know if I can start work—"

"No worries. I'm going to make sure you've got food, your rent gets paid, and Ethan can continue with daycare. You won't be able to lift him, so I can hire someone to help you around the house."

She choked back a sob. "You don't have to do that. Really. I've got money."

"I'm sorry you got shot, Sally."

Her brows knitted together. "It wasn't your fault. Things happen, right? Are Addison and Hawk okay? Did police catch the person?"

"Addison got shot, but she'll be okay," Prescott replied. "No one was caught."

A physician entered the room. "How are you feeling?"

"Meh," Sally replied. "My head hurts."

"That's the concussion." She slid her gaze to Prescott. "Are you family?"

"Her brother."

"We're keeping Sally overnight. The surgery went well, but I'm concerned because she hit her head pretty good. I want to make sure there's no swelling."

"Understood," he replied.

"Do you live alone, Sally?" asked the doctor.

"My young son is with me."

"Is there someone who can help you—"

"Sally and her son will stay with me until she recovers," Prescott blurted.

In a matter of seconds, he'd gone from hiring someone to help her, to opening up his home to her. He worked from home a lot, everything on his computer was deemed top-secret. Didn't matter. She was family. That's what his parents had taught him. They looked out for one another.

The doctor nodded. "Sounds like a plan. You should get some rest."

"I thought concussion patients needed to stay awake," Prescott interjected.

"That's outdated," explained the doc. "Sally can sleep, but the nurses will wake her every few hours and check her vitals." She offered Sally a warm smile. "Do you have any questions for me?"

Sally didn't, so the doctor wished her a speedy recovery and left.

"I'm sorry to be such a burden," Sally said.

"You just need to get better," Prescott said. "I'll make sure Ethan is okay. For now, get some rest." He kissed her forehead and left.

He would hire someone to help Sally during the day and he'd do his best in the evenings to assist with Ethan. He knew absolutely nothing about kids, but how difficult could it be?

He exited her room to find Z waiting in the hallway.

"I need your help catching a killer," Z murmured.

A smile lifted Prescott's lips. "I'm all in, and when I find him, I'm gonna rip his fucking heart out."

"I was hoping you'd say that," Z replied.

Jaqueline

JACQUELINE HEADED inside her government office building, set her computer bag and handbag on the conveyer belt, flashed her badge at a guard, then stepped through the metal detector. She paused while a second guard waved a wand over her.

Cleared to enter, she collected her bags. As she squeezed into the packed elevator, her phone buzzed in her handbag.

Once at her desk, she pulled out her laptop and fired it up. She grabbed her mug and yesterday's coffee splashed against her bright pink shirt. She flinched from the chill, then glanced down.

That's just great.

Her phone, still tucked inside her handbag, rang. *You're just gonna have to wait.*

She hurried into the bathroom, looked in the mirror, and laughed at the huge splotch. With a wad of paper towels, she soaked up the liquid as best she could, buttoned the suit jacket—which only hid part of the ugly stain—and hightailed it back to her desk.

Her phone buzzed with another incoming text. She'd missed a call and two texts from Z.

"Call me," he texted.

Then, the missed call.

His second text said, "It's important."

Experience had taught her that *everything* with Philip Skye was urgent. Every single time he'd contacted her, she done whatever he'd needed. She'd worked late or given up a weekend to put together an "emergency" profile. She burned the midnight oil because he always needed it, like, ten minutes ago.

But she had deadlines of her own. Plus, when she'd been exiled so that the Winchester mission could fade into the background, where was he then?

It was probably Z who exiled me.

The head of the task force popped her head into Jacqueline's cubicle. "You've got a call in my office."

No way.

Jacqueline left her cubicle, her boss by her side. "Who is it?"

"The call came from The Director's office, but the caller only identified himself as—"

"Z," Jacqueline said.

"How did you know?"

The women entered the office and her boss lifted the phone cradle. "Here she is, sir." She handed Jaqueline the phone.

"Hello, Z."

"I'm not in the mood to be kept waiting," Z snapped.

"Yes, sir."

"Call me back." The line went dead.

Jacqueline hung up. "I need to call him back."

"Who's Z?" her boss asked.

Only one of the most powerful men in the free world. "No one important," she lied.

On her way back to her cubicle, she called him on his private line.

"That's better," Z answered. "I wanted you to know that Addison was shot."

"Ohgod, is she okay?"

"I don't call for foolish reasons."

"Of course not. What happened?"

"She and Prescott's sister were shot in a mall parking garage, last night. They both needed surgery to remove the bullets. Addison was released. Sally will be today. Nicholas was with them, but he wasn't hit. We think he and Addison were the targets. That makes four in my elite team down in a week—"

"You're what? What *elite* team?"

"I need you to work up a psychological profile of our killer."

"Of course, but you'll have to clear my schedule. I've got a several deliverables—"

"Done."

Silence.

"I need you to come back to the DC area."

Her heart kicked up speed. "Winchester?"

"No, you'll work in the DMV."

"Understood."

"I don't want you flying commercial," Z explained. "Your supervisor is being briefed. Go home and pack your bags. Two

Secret Service agents will be by in two hours. Once they arrive, call me to confirm they're the agents I assigned you. They'll be escorting you back to DC."

Secret Service?

Anxiety flitted through her. "Got it. Anything else?"

"Safe travels." The line went dead.

Prescott

IT HAD BEEN ALMOST two in the morning when Prescott got home. He updated his mom and dad while Ethan slept on the family room floor beneath a blanket. After sending his parents upstairs to a guest room, he slept on the nearby sofa so Ethan wouldn't be alone.

That morning, he woke to giant eyes on a small face staring at him. It was a little after six.

"I have to go potty."

Prescott brought the tyke into the guest bathroom. Ethan lifted the lid and urinated like a pro.

"Good job, buddy." Prescott turned on the faucet, made sure the water wasn't too hot, and held him up so he could wash his hands.

"I don't have to wash my hands."

"You gotta wash your hands after you use the toilet."

"I only touch my wee wee."

"Let's wash now and argue later."

Strangely, that made Ethan giggle. He washed his hands, somehow managing to get water all over the vanity *and* the floor.

Next stop, finding him a toothbrush. Upstairs they traipsed, where Prescott found a new, soft-bristled one from his dentist and helped Ethan brush his teeth.

Ethan's wild hair needed to be tamed. Using a hair brush, Prescott did his best, but Ethan kept saying, "Ouch," so Prescott gave up.

Back in the kitchen, Ethan climbed into the booster chair Sally had brought with them. "Where's Mommy?"

"She wasn't feeling well, so she went to the doctor," he replied, then added, "Ethan, do you like eggs?"

Prescott's mom and dad entered the room. His dad went straight to the coffee machine, but Prescott hadn't made any yet. His mom made coffee while his dad started opening cupboards.

"Whatcha need, Dad?" Prescott asked.

"I'll make eggs. Where's your bread so Mom can make toast?"

Prescott wasn't used to so many people cooking in his kitchen.

His phone buzzed with a text from his brother. "We got home late last night. Addison's sleeping. I'm watching her sleep."

Prescott chuckled. "Addison's home," he told his parents.

"That's a relief," his mom replied. "How's she doing?"

"Nicky said she's sleeping."

"I want cereal," Ethan blurted.

Prescott pulled out all the cereal boxes from his pantry and set them on the table. Ethan examined all of them. "I don't like."

"This is all I've got," Prescott said.

"Nooooooo!" Ethan wailed. "I want my yummy bites."

Prescott filled the sippy cup with fresh juice, added a little water. "This is sweet. Drink this, then take a bite of cereal. You won't know the difference."

"No!"

The back and forth continued until his dad appeared with a

bowl of scrambled eggs. His mom had several slices of toast piled on a plate.

"What about honey?" she asked. "That's sweet."

"You can't give a child honey," Prescott said.

"You can't give an *infant* honey," his dad corrected him.

Prescott was at a loss. He knew absolutely nothing about children. On top of that, he'd hardly slept wondering how the hell he'd find the ALPHA Killer.

After Prescott phoned his assistant at Armstrong and let her know he was taking a personal day, he returned to the table.

Ethan hadn't eaten any eggs, he hadn't chosen a cereal, and he refused to eat the, now-cold toast, slathered in honey. Prescott needed him to eat, so he could move on with his day.

"Lemme see your muscle," Prescott said to him.

Instead, his dad flexed like Hercules, and Ethan giggled.

"Looking good, Dad."

"Okay, Ethan, what kind of muscles do *you* have?" Prescott asked.

The tyke mimicked Prescott's dad. Prescott gave his arm a gentle squeeze, then set his arm on the table and pointed to his bicep. "Grab that."

The child pushed with tiny fingers.

"Okay, Ethan, you ready for a big muscle."

"Uh-huh."

Prescott flexed, his biceps bulged, and Ethan said, "Big muskels."

"You know how I got these?" Prescott felt like he was throwing a hail Mary to get him to eat something.

"I can't know."

Prescott scooped eggs onto his fork. "Eggs." He ate the forkful, then, bit into a piece of toast.

Ethan picked up a handful of scrambled eggs with his chubby fingers, grimaced, and dropped them. "They're yucky."

Prescott scooped them onto a fork and offered them to him. Ethan shook his head.

That was all the patience Prescott had. He was plum out, and it wasn't even seven in the morning.

After wolfing down the eggs, Prescott said, "I'm going to the H to check on things." Then, he leaned close to Ethan. "I'll be back as soon as I can with your mommy, okay?"

To his surprise, Ethan threw his arms around Prescott's neck. "Bye, Uncle Res... Cres."

"Pres-cott," he said slowly, then repeated his name. "Can you say that?"

"Prescott," Ethan mimicked.

"Good job." Prescott addressed his parents. "Be back soon. Lock yourselves in."

His mom and dad exchanged glances.

Once at the hospital, Prescott stopped at reception for Sally's room number, then rode the elevator upstairs. As he strode down the hallway, medical staff rushed into the last room on the right. He entered that room, and froze. A team hovered around his sister.

"Clear," one of them called out.

Defibrillator pads were pressed against Sally's chest. Electricity surged through her, then silence.

"Nothing," said one of the attendants staring at the monitor by her bedside.

"Again," said a physician.

Prescott stood there in shocked disbelief as they placed the pads on her lifeless body.

"Clear," the technician said.

Another jolt was administered. Again, nothing from Sally. His sister lay still on the bed. Prescott bowed his head.

Lord, don't take her from us. We just met her. She deserves to live, to watch her little boy grow up.

"How many is that?" asked the doctor.

"Seven."

"We've gotta call it."

"One more," Prescott blurted.

All eyes whipped toward him.

"You can't be in here," said an attendant.

"One more," Prescott bit out. "She has a young son. Do. One. More."

After a nod from the physician, the attendant placed the pads on Sally's chest. After several seconds, he said, "Clear."

"Come on, come on," Prescott ground out.

Nothing.

Silence fell over the group.

Prescott's heart shattered into a million pieces as a nurse pulled the sheet over Sally's exposed chest.

The doctor stepped forward. "I'm so sorry. We couldn't bring her back."

Forcing down the loss, Prescott asked, "What happened? I thought the gunshot wound wasn't fatal."

"We'll need an autopsy to know for sure, but sometimes a blood clot can form during surgery. Did your—"

"Sister," Prescott replied.

"Did your sister smoke? Was she on the pill?"

"I never saw her smoke and I have no idea about her birth control. How can I get the results of her autopsy?"

"A nurse can take your contact info at the station," said the doctor. "Why don't you come with me—"

"I'd like a minute with her," Prescott said.

As the medical personnel began to clear away, he added, "Thank you for doing everything you could."

They expressed their condolences as they filed out.

Alone with a sister he'd only known for a few months, Prescott dragged a chair over and held her hand.

Dropping his head, he sat there in silence. Minutes passed. Then, the anger took hold. Some career criminal had gunned down an innocent woman. As he raised his head and let his gaze fall upon Sally's lifeless face, he vowed to avenge her.

"I will find the monster who did this to you. There will be no sanctuary for him. There will be no place he can hide that I won't find him. I won't rest until I've ended his life and watched him take his last fucking breath."

He set her lifeless hand on the mattress and pushed out of the chair. His heart ached, his soul burned with unspeakable rage.

How the hell was he going to tell Ethan that his mom was gone... and never, ever coming back?

∼

Jacqueline

JACQUELINE BOARDED THE UNMARKED, twelve-passenger jet. In addition to the two Secret Service agents who'd escorted her to the airport, two more waited in the plane.

Her head was spinning. *Why do I need this much protection?*

She had no idea what elite group Z was referring to. She had no idea what they did or for whom.

One of the agents made a call. "Hello, sir. Yes, Ms. Hartley is on board. Yes, sir, there are four agents." More listening. "We can drive her to that location. So, just for confirmation, we are not bringing her to you." Silence while the agent listened. "Who are we handing her over to? Understood. I'll call you as soon as we land."

The agent hung up and sat across from her. "Ms. Hartley, that was Z."

She nodded.

"Do you know someone named Prescott Armstrong?"

Her stomach dropped. "Yes, why?"

"We've been instructed to take you to him. Will you be able to identify him?"

Jacqueline unbuckled her seat belt. "Unfortunately, I can, but I won't be working with him, so I won't have to." She pushed out of her seat. "Please take me home."

9

GROVELING

Prescott

As soon as Prescott entered his house, Ethan charged over. Prescott set the hospital bag of Sally's things in the corner.

His expression fell. "Where's Mommy?"

His mom and dad made their way in from the family room. The second he met their gazes, they knew.

"Oh, no," his mom whispered.

"Ethan, let's show Uncle Prescott what we've been doing?" his dad urged.

Ethan didn't budge, his large eyes peering up at Prescott. Emotion had him biting back the loss as he picked his nephew up.

"Mommy isn't feeling very good, so the doctors want her to stay at the hospital."

"Can I see her?" Ethan asked.

Prescott stared at the toddler's small face. "Not today. She has to rest." Unsure how to proceed, he flicked his attention to his parents. "What have you guys been doing?"

Ethan pointed toward the family room. "Papa, he got sooooo many toys for me." That elicited an adorable smile.

"Show me." Prescott carried him into the family room and stared at the array of toys on the floor.

"I ran to the store," his dad said.

Prescott set Ethan down, then sat on the sofa while Ethan walked him through everything, one at a time. There was a large, transforming firetruck, a few books on dinosaurs, a light-up crayon board, a race track with oversized vehicles, three board games, two coloring books and a large pack of crayons.

"Wow, it looks like Christmas," Prescott said to his parents. "Thank you."

"You don't have a lot of food in the house, so, Ethan and I placed a grocery order," his mom said. "The food'll be ready for pick-up soon." She smiled at the tyke. "Ethan, why don't you tell Uncle Prescott what you got?"

"I got my favorite cereal! Yay! And hot dogs."

Prescott forced a smile, for Ethan's sake. "That sounds yummy. I should go grab those." He pushed off the floor. "I've got Sally's handbag, so if you want to pull Ethan's car seat while I'm gone—"

"Why don't I come with you?" his dad suggested. "We can move the car seat over when we get back."

"Ethan," Prescott began, "how 'bout you and Nana color a picture? Can you do that?"

"Uh-huh." The child popped up and went to the table.

"Back in twenty," Prescott said.

On the way to the store, his dad asked what happened.

"When I got there, she was already gone. There was a team working on her, but they couldn't bring her back."

"I'm sorry, son."

"Probably a blood clot in her lung. They'll know once the autopsy comes back."

"Mom and I will do whatever we can to help you."

"I have no idea how to tell Ethan."

"The truth is painful, plus he's so young. Problem is, if you lie to him, that's not the right way to start a relationship with him."

"Whoa, what do you mean, 'start a relationship with him'?"

"Well, you're keeping him, aren't you?" his dad asked.

"For now, until I can figure out where he can be placed."

"Placed? Like in foster care?"

"Well, I can't take care of him. He's not a pair of shoes that I can store in my closet and rotate out every few days."

"He's a baby, and he's family. What other choice do you have?"

"Besides foster care, there's adoption. I can't take care of —*raise*—a child. I just changed a poopy diaper for the first time in my life."

"Congratulations." His dad smiled. "You haven't really lived until you've smelled your child's feces."

"That's just it, Dad, he's not even my child."

"I adopted you."

"So?"

"You're just as much my child as Nicky and Kerri. I have three children who equally drive me crazy." His dad smiled, and Prescott appreciated his levity during such a painful time.

"You're an amazing dad, but I don't know the first thing about children." He pulled into the grocery store parking lot and drove toward the entrance.

"Neither did Mom and me. Parents figure it out as they go. Just keep an open mind, that's all, Scotty. That little boy is all alone in the world. He has no one." His dad choked back a sob and turned away. "Sorry," he murmured.

A stabbing pain sliced through him. His dad was right. He couldn't abandon his nephew.

In silence, they loaded the groceries and headed toward home. As he pulled down his street, his phone rang. It was Z.

Prescott answered, put the phone to his ear. "I can't talk."

"Did you bring your sister home from the hospital?"

"She died this morning."

Z gasped. "Ohgod, I'm so sorry to hear that."

"My dad's with me. I'll call you back."

"This is important." Z pushed back. "I spoke with Addison. She and Nicholas are leaving at midnight."

"Why?"

"ALPHA Ops *were* on lockdown, but that decision has been upgraded. They've been told to leave the area, until we can get a handle on things. We've got two dead Ops and the attempted murder of Nicholas and Addison."

Silence.

"You there?" Z asked.

"Haven't gone anywhere."

"I'm gonna need you to take down the killer."

"Yeah, so I know I'm your go-to guy, but I got my hands full."

"You're not in ALPHA and there's no documentation *anywhere* that BLACK OPS even exists. You're my only hope."

"Thank you, Obi-wan. I'll keep that in mind *after* I figure out how I tell a three-year-old his mommy is never coming home."

"I'm so sorry for your loss. We'll talk later." Z hung up.

"Was that work?" his dad asked as Prescott pulled into the garage.

"Yeah." Prescott cut the engine, got out, and grabbed several grocery bags.

In the house, his mom and Ethan were busy coloring at the kitchen table. After setting the bags on the center island, Prescott admired their artwork. "Wow, look at you two. Ethan, that's cool."

Ethan continued coloring a dinosaur. "It's for Mommy to help her get better."

He flicked his gaze to his mom before tousling the tyke's long hair. "That's a great present."

After putting away the food, he decided to grill chicken breasts. It was that or fix Ethan chicken nuggets or a hotdog. Twenty minutes later, he served the chicken with a side of peas. He was flying without a net. He wasn't even supposed to be at home, and he rarely ate lunch there.

His stomach was in knots and he had no appetite, but he fixed himself a serving as well. His mom put together plates for herself and his dad, then they sat at the kitchen table.

Prescott started cutting up Ethan's chicken.

"Ew, what's that?" Ethan asked.

"Chicken."

"I like nuggets."

"These are the same thing, only good for you."

The child shook his head. "No, fank you."

The doorbell rang and the child perked up. "It's Mommy!" He unbuckled and was sliding out of the booster seat when Prescott went to answer the door.

To his surprise, Z was standing there. "Can I come in?"

Prescott opened the front door as Ethan came crashing into him. Peeking from behind Prescott, he said, "You're not my mommy."

Prescott picked him up. "This is Addison's daddy. Do you remember her?"

Z extended his hand and Ethan shook it. To Prescott's surprise, Z smiled. A rare occurrence. "I've got a funny name," he told the child. "Wanna know what it is?"

"Okay."

"It's Z."

"You want some chicken?" Prescott asked.

"I can't stay," Z replied. "I need to talk to you."

Prescott brought Z into the kitchen. "You remember Addison's dad, Philip."

Prescott's dad rose and shook his hand. "You're welcome to join us."

"Thanks, but I can't," Z replied. "Sorry to interrupt your lunch, but I need to borrow Prescott for a minute."

Prescott's mom set a plate of chicken nuggets in front of Ethan.

Grinning, he said, "I loooooove nuggets. Fank you, Nana."

"We have to ease into healthy food," his mom whispered before buckling Ethan back into his seat. Then, she handed him a sippy cup. After several slurps, he smiled.

"We'll be right back." Prescott led Z into his home office and shut the glass-paneled French doors.

"I can't help you, Philip."

"Yesterday, you couldn't wait. Today, you're unavailable."

"A lot has changed."

"I've got an entire organization going into hiding and a killer on the loose. A killer who murdered your sister. You're a ruthless man driven by revenge and anger. Where's all that determination and fury when I need it? When *she* needs it?"

"Did you see that child out there?" Prescott asked. "I told him his mom isn't feeling well because I have no idea how to break it to him. No freakin' idea." Prescott gritted his teeth. "I'm his closest living relative, and now I'm responsible for someone I met three months ago."

"He's lucky to have you and your family."

"Even if I agree to help you, then what? I'm an assassin, not a detective."

"I lined up someone to partner with you to find the perp. Unfortunately, she refused the assignment, and I need you to persuade her to take it."

Ethan toddled his way toward the office, his little fingers clutching a nugget. He pressed his face against one of the glass panes. "I give you a chicken."

Prescott opened the door, knelt down, and bit into the nugget. Ethan giggled.

"You eat *all* of it," Ethan explained.

"What about the chicken I made you?"

Ethan shook his head. "I like this."

Prescott stood, then placed his hand on Ethan's head. "If you couldn't convince her, why should I? You know I'm not a team player."

"Dammit, Prescott. It's Jacqueline Hartley. She's one of the best—and you know it. You weren't the only one who failed on that mission. As RAC, the Bureau held her responsible. This is what she needs to get her career on track."

"Why don't you just bring her back?"

"She has to earn this, and you can help her... by *encouraging* her to work with you. She's excellent at her job. You're excellent at yours. It's a win-win."

"Let's go see my Mommy and bring her my dinosaur picture," Ethan blurted. "Let's go right now!"

Prescott peered down at him, while reality took hold. He would avenge his sister. He would do this for ALPHA. And he needed Jack to learn the truth about what went down the night he took out the cult leader. So, he would grovel, beg, and plead with her to return to DC with him.

"How would you like to take a ride on an airplane" Prescott asked Ethan.

The child peered up at him. "Can Mommy come wif us?"

"We're going today," Prescott said with enthusiasm. "Your mommy needs to stay with the doctors. But we'll have fun, right?"

"I have complete confidence in you," Z said. "You're my rock, Prescott."

. . .

TWO HOURS LATER, Prescott climbed the stairs, Ethan in his arms, and boarded his private jet.

"It's sooo big," Ethan exclaimed.

"Have you even flown on an airplane?" Prescott asked.

"Nuh-uh. Where is the people?"

"This is my plane, so it's just us and two pilots. Do you want to see where they fly the jet?"

Prescott set down the diaper bag and made his way through the cabin toward the cockpit. There, he waited until the pilots finished talking.

"Good to see you, Mr. Armstrong," said the pilot. "Who's this little guy?"

"My nephew, Ethan."

The pilot asked if Ethan wanted to sit on his lap and look out the window.

Ethan wrapped his small arms around Prescott. "No, fank you."

Prescott's heart expanded as he hugged the child back. "Ethan, these two pilots fly the airplane in the sky."

"Okay," Ethan replied.

Prescott tossed them a nod. "Safe flight."

"We'll be taking off shortly," said the female copilot.

Prescott returned to the cabin and set Ethan in a leather chair by the aisle before sitting next to him. He buckled him in, then tightened the strap. There was so much strap leftover... and that's when it hit him. Ethan was small, helpless, and completely dependent on Prescott to look after him. His guts churned.

Z's right. I need to hunt down the monster who stole my sister's life and make him pay for what he's done.

Determination streaked through him. He would do whatever it took to bring Jack back with him.

We will find this killer.

Ethan slipped his thumb into his mouth. "I'm cold."

Prescott pulled a blanket from the overhead bin and covered him. "Better?"

"Can I sit on your lap?"

"Not yet, buddy. You have to stay buckled until that light up there goes off, then you can sit on my lap."

Tears filled Ethan's eyes as the plane taxied toward the runway.

Fuck the rules.

After unbuckling him, Prescott pulled Ethan onto his lap.

"I love flying," Prescott said. "If I had enough time, I'd get my pilot's license and fly the airplane myself. Uncle Nicky's a pilot... one of the best."

Ethan looked out the window as the plane started gaining speed.

"This is my favorite part," Prescott said. "We're gonna fly like a bird, buddy. Fly like a bird."

Craning to look at him, Ethan smiled, then he slipped his thumb back into his mouth and laid against Prescott.

In that moment, Prescott knew he could never send this child away. If he did, it would be the worst thing he could ever do.

Time to man up and do the right thing.

Jacqueline

A SECRET SERVICE agent drove Jacqueline home, where she left her packed suitcase, drove to work, and struggled to focus on her projects. Her thoughts kept drifting to Prescott. Why would Z pair her with him? Why him? Why continue to punish her for something that happened months ago?

Jacqueline could help Z from her desk in the Bay area.

There was absolutely no reason for her to have to partner with Armstrong in order to do her damn job.

As the afternoon ticked on, she was surprised Z hadn't called her to demand she get her ass on that plane.

Her supervisor passed her cubicle, then reappeared. "I thought you were flying to DC. What happened?"

"Change of plans."

"Everything okay?"

"Oh, sure," Jacqueline lied. "It's all biz as usual."

It was after six when she headed out, stopping at the gym. Over an hour later, she grabbed carry-out from her favorite seafood restaurant. Her stomach had been growling during her entire workout, and she couldn't wait to enjoy her dinner with a glass of sauvignon blanc.

Feeling like a pack mule, she entered her apartment building, her computer bag, gym bag, and handbag slung over her shoulders, her take-out bag clutched in her hand.

Like the other day, Jeff waited on a sofa, head down on his phone. Anger slammed through her. She wanted to scream.

How is he not getting the message? She'd never pinned him for a stalker, but he was fast becoming one.

He glanced up, did a double take, and his face split into a grin. "Finally! I was beginning to wonder if you'd left town." He glanced at her take-out bag. "I'm starving. God, I hope you bought enough to share."

She glared at him. "How did you get in?"

"I walked in with one of your neighbors, like, three hours ago." Jeff stood. "Not complaining. You're definitely worth it."

A tenant said hello on her way to the elevator.

Jacqueline set down the bags, fished out her cell phone. "I'm calling the police if you don't leave *now*, then I'm getting a restraining order. I broke up with you. How are you not getting—"

"Jack, everything okay?"

She whipped her head in the direction of the very familiar —and extremely sexy—baritone. *Ohmygod, it's Mac.*

Her heart started thumping hard and fast in her chest, their gazes locked on each other.

"Yo, dude, who you calling Jack?" Jeff asked.

Jacqueline regarded the small child in Mac's arms. When she locked eyes with him, the little one smiled at her.

He's adorable.

"Who's this cutie?" she asked.

"My nephew."

It was thrilling to see Mac standing there, the intensity of his fiery gaze sending ripple after ripple of excitement thrumming through her. Then, reality jumped to the forefront and the excitement turned to exasperation. Her *former* lover was someone she despised with a passion.

She glared at him. "What are you doing here?"

"Groveling," Mac replied.

Wow, okay.

Jeff meandered closer. "Hey, man, whatcha doing with my girl?"

Jacqueline wanted to laugh. One looked like a disgruntled boy, the other, like a man.

A sophisticated, captivating, powerful, and extremely confident man.

Without question, her attention was glued to Mac.

The youngster whispered something in his ear and Mac set him down. With a plastic truck in his hand, he toddled over to her.

"You can ride on a plane. It's Uncle Prescott's plane and it's soooo much fun." He held out his truck. "Do you want to see my truck?"

"This is super cool," she said admiring his toy.

As Mac stalked his way over, a frisson of desire ripped through her. His male beauty halted her breath while his hypnotic eyes drilled into hers. Tall and hard-bodied, his bright blue dress shirt stretched against his sculpted chest and bulging biceps, while his black pants hugged his massive thighs.

Her insides came alive, the pull to be near him had her taking a step in his direction.

"We need to talk," Jeff said.

"You need to go," Jacqueline bit out. "You're not getting the message, so I'm getting a restraining—"

"You don't mean that," Jeff whined.

"Get out!"

Jeff's jaw went slack. "Whoa."

"Jacqueline, please," Mac said.

She flicked her gaze from one man to the other.

Mac had been her lover and she had nothing but good thoughts about him. *Prescott*, on the other hand, was reckless, selfish, and a rogue agent.

"I'll give you ten minutes." She stabbed the elevator button.

Jeff hurried over, but Mac was by her side, his large body dwarfing Jeff. The doors opened, Mac collected her bags, and waited for her to enter. As soon as she did, he joined her.

When Jeff started to get on, Mac stiff-armed him, sending him reeling backward.

"She told you no," Mac ground out, his deep voice reverberating through her. "Get lost."

"Who the hell are you, asswipe?"

"Her bodyguard." Mac's confidence radiated off him. "If you go near her again, you'll have me to deal with, and you'll regret it."

Ohmygod.

She melted. His sheer presence, paired with his protective nature, made her feel safe. Perfect words from a fantastic lover... and a prick of a man. Her head was spinning. How could one man evoke so many conflicting emotions, all at the same time?

She tapped the button, the doors closed, and she gazed up at him. "Thank you."

"Did that buy me any points?"

"No," she deadpanned.

But, it did.

Then, she smiled at the little boy. "I'm Jacqueline, but my friends call me Jack. What's your name?"

"Efan."

"Ethan," Mac translated.

"Ethan, tell me about the airplane ride. Did you get something to drink?"

As he prattled away about the flight, her gaze floated to Mac. Penetrating eyes stared back. Despite being flat-out thrilled to see him, she was also raging angry that she was being forced to work with him.

The elevator doors opened and she led them to her apartment.

Once inside, she said, "I'm starving, so you can grovel while I eat." Then, she eyed Ethan, and the resentment fizzled. "Are you hungry?"

"We had dinner while we waited for you," Mac said.

"I ate nuggets," Ethan offered.

"That's all you eat," Mac said.

"That's because they're yummy!" the child exclaimed.

Watching Mac interact with Ethan was adorable and entertaining, but she wasn't interested in him or his family, no matter how damn compelling she found him.

She set the food in a porcelain bowl, warmed it in the microwave, and set out three forks. She despised him, but her parents had taught her to share.

Prescott sat across from her, putting Ethan on his thigh.

Ethan pointed. "What's that?"

"That's salmon and this is calamari, which is squid." She regarded Mac. "Does he have any food allergies."

Sadness flashed in Mac's eyes. "None that we know of."

"Can you call his mom or dad?" Jacqueline took a bite of salmon. It was delicious and she was famished.

"Mommy is in the hospital."

"I'm sorry to hear that," Jacqueline said.

"I can't call her because she's not well," Mac explained.

"I want to try the crispy chicken," Ethan said. "Are they nuggets?"

"No, buddy, they aren't," Mac replied. "It's a squid from the ocean."

Ethan reached over and pulled one off the plate, then took a bite. "Yummy."

She slid the calamari onto a different plate and set it in front of him. "They're all yours." With a smile, she said, "Good, huh?"

"Uh-huh," Ethan replied.

After a few bites, she pulled a bottle of stilled water from the fridge.

Mac extracted a sippy cup from a diaper bag, but she poured a little water into three glasses. "Ethan, this is my favorite water. It's the best."

Using two hands, he picked up the small glass, and drank it down.

"Oh, sure, for you he drinks water," Mac said. "Good job, Ethan."

"Can I have more?"

She poured more, and Ethan gulped it down.

Jacqueline never thought she'd see Mac in her apartment. It felt surreal, but there he was.

"I'm still waiting on the groveling."

Mac wiped Ethan's mouth with a napkin. "Did you like the calamari?"

"Uh-huh," he replied. "I like Jack's water. It's sooooo good."

"We have water like that in Virginia," Mac said before eyeing Jacqueline. "Can we talk in the living room so Ethan can play?"

Once there, she sat on the floor while Mac opened the oversized tote bag, pulled out some mid-size trucks, and set them on the floor. Ethan rolled them over the carpet, making adorable engine sounds.

"I need your help," Mac began.

"I heard," she replied. "I was on a plane earlier being escorted by four Secret Service agents to track down someone who's taking out a group of elite agents. When I was told I'd have to work with you, I got off the plane."

His laughter made her heart soar. She soaked up the joy on his face, taking a mental picture of the way his eyes crinkled at the corners, the dimple on his chin, the way his bedroom eyes came alive.

Then, his breathtaking expression fell away. "I agreed to do a job, and I can't do it without you. I'm not good at groveling, but here goes."

He sat beside her, collected her hands in his, and gazed into her eyes. Common sense was telling her to pull her hands away, but she couldn't. Being touched by him sent streams of butterflies whizzing through her. Staring into his eyes made her feel safe. A feeling she craved every moment of every day.

"I will do whatever it takes to get your career back on track, even if it means sacrificing my own… and I'm not talking about my job at Armstrong," he began. "I'm talking about my *other* job."

"I'm listening." She loved the tender way he stroked her skin, the sincerity in his eyes. Her traitorous heart leapt… until reality crept back in.

She wouldn't be working on a damn task force, if it wasn't for him. But… maybe this was her chance to get back in the game, prove she could handle the pressure of hunting down a killer, all while teaming with her nemesis.

"On a personal level, where you know me as Mac, we're very compatible," he continued. "As a show of my commitment to you, I'll make you a proposition. I will take care of you. Only you. Nothing for me. I will ensure you're satisfied... all the time."

She hitched a brow at him. "You must be desperate."

"There's a lot at stake, a lot going on, that I can't get into right now." He tossed a nod toward Ethan. "But we have to be able to trust each other completely—"

"Mac is the best l-o-v-e-r I've ever had," she murmured.

Up went his eyebrows. "I love a direct woman."

"But, Prescott, former HRT team lead, is unreliable and untrustworthy. You did whatever the H you wanted, and there were *no* winners in that scenario."

Darkness flashed in his eyes, but he stayed silent.

She studied him for a beat. "There *was* a winner? Seriously? Who won?"

"Jack, I'm begging you to get on that plane with me. You don't have to like me. We don't even have to work well together. I just need you to do your job, so I can do mine."

There was a certain sense of satisfaction watching a powerful man like Prescott Armstrong begging her to help him. She held all the power... and she liked it.

While his offer to satisfy her every sexual desire was tempting on its own, she *needed* to get her career back on track.

On a nod, she said, "You've got yourself a partner, Prescott Armstrong."

10

JACQUELINE'S NEW DIGS

Prescott

Once aboard his private jet, Prescott buckled Ethan into his seat while Jacqueline strapped herself in across from him. For the moment, his motley crew was appeased. He would take any win, no matter how small.

Jacqueline had agreed to work with him in exchange for a permanent case of blue balls. At the moment, it felt like a small price to pay to hunt down a cold-blooded killer, but he knew the ultimate challenge would be seeing her naked and writhing beneath him.

While he *wanted* to breathe a sigh of relief, he couldn't. He needed to have an excruciatingly painful conversation with his three-year-old nephew. He was tasked with taking out the ALPHA Killer while partnering with someone who couldn't stand him. Not the best working situation. To top that, she would need protection. If Z had insisted she fly back with four Secret Service agents, the job of keeping her safe fell to him.

He locked eyes with her, and his determination skyrocketed. He had no idea how he'd juggle all of this, along with his responsibilities at Armstrong, but he would.

Ethan slipped his thumb into his mouth, then stared up at him. "I'm sleepy."

It was one in the morning, east coast time, so Prescott wasn't surprised. "Close your eyes, bud. When we land, we'll be back home."

Ethan's sleepy smile tugged at Prescott's heart. He was grateful Ethan had been so good during their whirlwind day. Prescott removed two blankets from the overhead bin. After covering Ethan, he offered the second one to Jack.

She took it and draped it over her shapely legs.

The copilot made her way into the cabin, explained that they were waiting to taxi. Once the flight got underway, the cabin lights would dim.

"Please stay buckled when seated," she said, before returning to the cockpit.

Shortly after, the plane taxied out, then glided down the runway, gaining speed, until the bird lifted effortlessly into the air.

A few minutes into the flight, Prescott regarded his young companion. For the first time in his life, he understood the phrase "sleeping like a baby", and he exhaled an audible sigh.

Ethan was slumped over, so Prescott reclined him. Rather than sit back down, he moved across the aisle, so he and Jack could talk quietly.

In truth, he wanted to be close to her. The need to be near her hadn't let up from the second he entered her apartment building.

When he peered in her direction, her beauty soothed his demons, but her furrowed brow a constant reminder she couldn't stand him. He wasn't fazed. Anger and hate were strong motivators. He needed her to do her job, so he could do his. It was that simple, except for the one-sided sex. That's where things got messy.

Before they'd headed to the airport, she showered. Her just-washed scent, mixed with her own sweet fragrance, wafted in his direction. She was looking super-hot in a white shirt and tight, black jeans, her wild mane framing her beautiful face.

"Thank you for working with me," he began.

She nodded, once.

"What do you know about this case?" he asked.

"Z told me that Addison and your sister had been shot, but that Addison and Hawk were the targets. Then, he mentioned something about his elite team."

Prescott had to confide in her. Breaking protocol was something he'd never done, but if he wanted her to start trusting him, he had to take that first step.

"Years ago, Z and another man created a top-secret organization. Basically, trained assassins who would eliminate the worst offenders. Serial rapists, serial killers, child molesters whose DNA linked them to multiple crimes. They either got off on a technicality or they escaped prison. The organization is called ALPHA."

"Are you in it?"

"No," he replied.

"What's your connection?"

"After I got fired from HRT, I was wrecked over the epic fail in Winchester and without a job. Working for the Bureau had been a dream of mine since I was a kid. Not long after that, I was contacted by Z who asked me to join ALPHA."

"But you didn't."

"No. Being an Operative means being a team player. The missions are dangerous, and I didn't want to be the reason any of my teammates died."

"I see," she murmured. "So, if you're not with ALPHA..."

"I'm a lone-wolf assassin."

Her eyebrows crowded her forehead while big, green eyes stared at him. "Oh, wow. Okay. I was *not* expecting that."

"I've been on ALPHA missions when other Ops ask for me."

She stared at him for a long beat. "Like Hawk or Addison?"

Crossroads. Prescott was willing to confide information about himself, but he didn't want to loop others in.

Her lips twitched and she bit back the smile. "It's okay, you don't have to answer that."

"Guess I already did, huh?"

"I have a feeling you're not supposed to be telling me as much as you are, so we'll keep everyone else out of it." She tucked her hair behind her ear, the glint of a diamond-stud earring catching his attention.

For a brief few seconds, they stared into each other's eyes, letting the silence hover between them. The energy shifted, the desire to kiss her started to take hold. She was easy to look at, even easier to be around. She was the one, bright spot in a very dark week.

Two ALPHA Ops had been gunned down in cold blood. His sister too. If those deaths weren't bad enough, Addison had been shot, he'd inherited a child he had no business raising, and he'd bribed his former kink partner with sex to get her to work with him. If things went south between them, Z would fire his ass.

"I meant it when I told you I'd take care of you sexually."

She nodded.

"But to be clear, we gotta to separate business from pleasure."

"If that's the case, turn the plane around. Deal's off." Then, she cracked a smile. "I didn't accept this job because of that. That would be highly unethical, but I gotta say, the sex was *fantastic*. I'm here because I want my old job back."

"So, we'll keep Mac and Jack separate from Prescott and Jacqueline."

"Absolutely," she replied. "So, how was the sex for you?"

"Meh," he replied.

"Nice." Then, she leaned close and whispered, "Liar."

He tucked his finger under her chin and tipped her head toward him. "It was good enough for me to show up at Asylum months later, even though I was pissed."

"I'm glad you did," she murmured.

As they stared into each other's eyes, warmth blanketed his chest.

"You're impossible to resist," he said. "Fucking impossible."

He dipped down, brushing his lips against hers. Desire swept through him as she released a sigh and pressed her lips to his. He relished in the fullness of her mouth, her soft skin, the way her breath hitched. His tongue pressed into her mouth and tangled with hers. Rather than deepen the embrace, he kissed her softly again. Her eyes fluttered open and she broke away.

Ethan stirred, and they glanced in his direction.

"Did you bring your adorable nephew to tempt me?"

"Would you have come if I hadn't?"

"I would have, but I gotta hand it to you... it was a smooth move."

He paused. "I brought him because his mom died. My sister didn't make it. She pulled through surgery, but when I got there yesterday morning, she was gone."

Jacqueline placed her hand on his arm, and her soft touch comforted him. "I am so, so sorry." She slid her attention to Ethan. "Does he know?"

"No. He's been asking to go to the hospital to see her. I don't have a clue how to tell a toddler that his mom has died."

"Why doesn't his dad tell him?" She removed her hand leaving him aching for her tender touch.

"He died when Ethan was a baby," Prescott explained. "I just met them a few months ago."

"You gotta fill in the blanks for me."

"My biological father also died when I was a baby. My mom remarried a year later, my second dad adopted me, but he's the only dad I know."

"Got it," she replied.

"My sister, Sally, reached out to me a few months ago, after her mom died. She was going through old boxes and found out who her dad was. That's when she contacted me. We did a DNA test and we were a match. She moved up here and I got her a job at Armstrong. She was supposed to start on Monday."

"Ohgod, that's so sad."

"I'm all the family that little boy has."

She placed her hand over her heart. "When are you going to tell him?"

"My close friend, Jericho, is married to a psychologist."

"I met them. They hosted the wedding shower."

"Right. I'm going to see if Liv can help me navigate this."

Her gaze hadn't wavered from his. For the first time since she'd learned who he really was, compassion sprang from her eyes.

"That's a lot for you to deal with." A little smile tugged at the corners of her mouth. "I'm glad I agreed to help you." She held up a hand. "Not for you, but for him."

Ethan started crying. He was balling his little eyes out and trying to get out of the chair, but the seatbelt restrained him.

Prescott was by his side in a flash. He knelt down, unbuckled him, and pulled him into his arms.

"Hey, Ethan, it's Uncle Prescott. You okay?"

"I want my mommy," he said, between sobs.

Prescott's heart broke. He would never be able to give this child what he wanted... what he truly needed.

"Ethan," Jacqueline said. "I brought the water that you like." She searched the tote bag, pulled out an empty sippy cup, and filled it with water. Then, she offered him the cup.

He wiped his eyes and shook his head. "No, go away. I want my mommy." His eyes filled with more tears that spilled down his little cheeks.

Prescott sat in the chair and put the tot on his lap. "I know you do." He regarded him. "Did you have a bad dream?"

"Uh-huh," Ethan replied.

"Sometimes when we talk about them, it helps make them go away," Prescott urged. "Do you remember your dream?"

"I don't like Mommy's friend."

"Well, how 'bout I protect you from her friend. How's that?"

"Okay. Are we there yet?"

"Not yet," Prescott replied. "How 'bout some water before you go back to sleep?"

Jack held out the cup and, this time, Ethan accepted it from her. After a few sips, he handed it back. "Fank you."

Her sweet smile might not assuage his young nephew, but it was sure as hell helping him.

"Feel better?" she asked.

"Uh-huh," he replied.

Within minutes, Ethan had fallen back to sleep. Jacqueline was staring out the window at the city lights below.

He'd said enough—too much really. "I'm gonna grab a little shut-eye."

She offered a nod before returning her gaze out the window.

Prescott closed his eyes, but sleep wouldn't come. Too many thoughts occupied his headspace.

Prescott wasn't a man of words. He was a man of action.

As the miles flew by, he needed to let this small child beside him know that he would be there for him, day in and day out.

Being a parent—a father—wasn't something he thought about. Going forward, it would become a priority. He'd step up like his dad had. Fortunately for him, he had a damn good role model.

Jacqueline

At seven in the morning, the plane touched down. Despite the tense situation, Jacqueline was happy to be back in the DC region.

Prescott had Ethan in his arms, her computer bag slung over his shoulder, and her large rolling suitcase in hand, leaving her with the smaller one, along with her carry-on and handbag.

They looked like a family back from vacation. Only they weren't a family and this was no vacation. She had a job to do and a deadline of yesterday by which to do it.

"I need to rent a car," she said.

"I got you," he replied.

They proceeded to short-term parking and he pulled to a stop in front of a black SUV.

After opening the doors to air out the vehicle, Prescott set Ethan down. "Do. Not. Move."

Jacqueline eyed the small child. "Ethan, will you hold my hand?"

When he slipped his small one into hers, she melted. He was so sweet, so trusting of her. "How 'bout we load you into your car seat? Can you help me with that?"

"Okay," he replied.

She guided him to the back door, he climbed in, and then clamored into his seat. She buckled him in while he stared at her. Once finished, she smiled at him. "We'll have to make sure your Uncle Prescott buys you some of that delicious water I drink, don't you think?"

"It's yummy," Ethan replied.

"It is yummy," she agreed.

After loading everything into the back, Prescott got behind

the wheel as Jacqueline buckled herself into the passenger seat.

"Can I see my mommy?" Ethan asked.

"Not yet, buddy," Prescott replied, as he backed out of the spot. "I have to check with her doctor, first."

Jacqueline's heart squeezed.

As they headed out, Prescott murmured, "I was going to ask Liv what to do, but you've got a Master's in psychology—"

"Classwork only," she replied. "I would hate to give you the wrong guidance. Wait. How do you know I've got a degree—"

"I read your file," he replied before eyeing Ethan in the rearview mirror. "Ethan, do you like music?"

"Uh-huh, Mommy has songs on her phone that I know all the words to."

"You want me to help?" Jacqueline asked, not wanting to overstep.

"Thanks," Prescott replied.

Jacqueline opened an app and searched for popular children's music. Looking back at Ethan, she said, "I'm going to play some songs. Will you let Uncle Prescott know if you like them?"

"Okay."

She tried one. Ethan didn't know it. She tried a second. He didn't like that one. She continued until he said, "I know this." She added it to a playlist while he started singing along.

The sweet sound of his young voice touched her soul, yet it made her profoundly sad. He was happily singing away, unaware of the loss he would have to face.

He's too young to have to face one of life's worst hardships.

She continued searching for tunes, slowly building a playlist for him. She'd been so focused on helping Ethan, she hadn't been paying attention to where they were going.

Prescott had pulled off a street tucked in some residential area, then driven down a dirt road, passing a "No Trespassing" sign. He continued until the woodsy area cleared and a warehouse loomed into view. He drove around back, tapped a button on the visor, and the hangar-like door started to rise. He pulled in and cut the engine.

"You can use one of these SUVs." Prescott got out, then pulled Ethan out and set him on the treated hangar floor. "Hey, buddy, we're going to find a truck for Jack to drive. You wanna help me?"

She got out and stared at the fleet of identical black vehicles in the oversized garage.

"I like that one." Ethan pointed.

Prescott laughed. "That was easy. Why that one?"

"It's soooo shiny."

Prescott opened the driver's side door, pulled the keys from the visor, and pushed the start button. "It's got gas, so I think picked you a winner, Ethan."

Jacqueline stood there, staring at the SUVs.

"What is this place?" she asked.

He stepped so close she had to tilt her head up. "It's ALPHA's black site that doubles as a safe house."

He smelled delicious... and so damn familiar. It was a mix of him and whatever soap he rubbed all over his Adonis-like body.

It had to be the lack of sleep and the three-hour time difference. While she could blame jet lag all she wanted, she could breathe him in and stare at those piercing eyes for hours.

Snap out of it.

He stepped away. "The vehicle is bullet proof, so you'll be safe driving around."

"Do you need to let someone know?" she asked.

"Already did." He held out the key fob.

Once she took it, she asked, "Can I grab my bags?"

"Later," he replied.

"I've gotta find a place to stay."

"Let's get this guy something to eat, then we can figure out logistics."

"Where are you going?"

"Home," he replied.

She walked over to Ethan who'd been staring at all the identical SUVs. "Ethan, I'll see you back at Uncle Prescott's house, 'kay?"

He hurried over and hugged her legs. "Bye, Jack."

Love washed over her. "I had fun riding in Prescott's airplane with you. You did a great job." She laid her hand on his small head.

He let go and walked over to Prescott, then tucked his small hand into the larger one. Prescott helped him into the truck, then got in himself.

Jacqueline started up the vehicle, adjusted the seat and mirrors, then backed out after him. She tapped the remote built into the visor and the giant door closed. Once it touched down, Prescott drove away, Jacqueline on his tail.

As she followed him onto the main road, she thought about who she could stay with. She had three options.

First, her brother Keith and sister-in-law Naomi. Staying in their small house, along with their puppies, might be a lot for them, especially since she had no idea how long this assignment would last.

Next option? Her sister, Leslie. She lived in a large house with ample room. Then, she remembered Leslie's musician friend. She had no idea if he was staying there or had just stopped by. Her challenge would be dealing with her social-media-obsessed sister.

Her third option was renting an Airbnb.

While her mom and dad had room for her, staying with them was *not* an option. She adored them, but she couldn't live with them. She just needed a place to crash, so she'd check with Leslie first.

Prescott turned into a neighborhood. Her brain skidded to a stop at the size of the estate homes lining both sides of the tree-lined street. A few more short turns and he pulled into the long driveway of a massive, two-story estate.

Wow, that's impressive.

The light gray stucco front had a double-wide front door with a roof overhang supported by two columns. Instead of driving around to the side and parking in the three-car garage, he stopped out front and cut the engine. She sat there staring at the magnificent structure that had over a dozen front-facing windows. While the grounds were perfectly manicured, she couldn't stop gawking at the house.

This is idyllic.

For a split second, she wondered what life would be like if she lived there with him. Would they get along? Would she fit into his life? Would he fit into hers? Sexually, they were a great match. Professionally, their one encounter had been a complete disaster.

She was about to put their professional lives to the test again.

Here we go.

As she approached Prescott, she checked him out. He was easy on the eyes... too easy. When he turned in her direction, she spied a vulnerability she'd never seen before. He took a few steps in her direction before Ethan plowed into him.

"We need to buy you a football, Ethan. Do you have one at your house?"

"Nuh-uh. I have a soccer ball."

"Let's have breakfast, we'll help Jack get situated, then we're gonna grab some toys from your house."

Ethan stared up at him. "Is my mommy there?"

His shoulders dropped, his smile fell away. He squatted. "No, she's not."

"But I want to see her!"

"I know. I wish I could make that happen, but I can't."

"When I have a tummy ache, she gives me magic medicine and it makes me all better. Can we do that to her?"

Prescott's gaze jumped to Jacqueline and her heart broke. This was a very difficult, very sensitive moment that involved family only. She needed to get out of there so Prescott could give Ethan his undivided attention.

"I'm gonna take off," Jacqueline said. "Sounds like you guys have a busy afternoon."

"No, don't—"

"I'll let you know where I end up staying." She opened the liftgate, extracted a bag, and brought it over to her vehicle.

He was by her side in seconds. "You're welcome to stay with us."

"Seriously?" Before she could stop herself, she curled her fingers around his triceps. "That's not a good idea."

Stop touching him!

But she couldn't get her hand off his arm.

"I live alone," he said. "Well, I did. I've got three floors if you include the finished basement. You'd have all the privacy you need."

"We're already going to be working together. I don't think we should push our luck."

After loading up her bags, he handed her his phone. "I need your number."

She sent herself a text from his phone. "Done." Then, she shifted her sights to Ethan. "I'll pick up some of that water you like and bring it by soon, okay?"

"Bye, Jack."

"Have fun with Uncle Prescott." Her gaze jumped to Prescott and a rush of heat warmed her chest.

"We'll talk later," he said.

She climbed into the SUV, plugged in Leslie's address, and headed out.

On the drive over, her phone rang from a number she didn't recognize. She answered, put the call on speaker. "Hello."

"I'm so glad you picked up," Addison said. "I heard you're back in town."

"Did you change your phone number?" Jack asked.

"I'll be using different burners for a while," Addison said.

Jacqueline didn't want to betray Prescott's confidence, so she wasn't about to comment on what she knew.

"Hawk just called Prescott," Addison continued, "and told us you're working with him to find the killer."

"That's the plan. How are you doing?"

"I'm okay," Addison replied. "Prescott said you need a place to stay, and I have the perfect solution."

"If you're going to tell me to stay with Prescott—"

"No, but his house is gorgeous and so huge."

Jacqueline bit back a smile. It sounded like Addison was describing Prescott and his very impressive junk.

"That would be weird," Addison continued. "You just met him at our shower."

Not exactly.

"Anyway, my dad has a furnished condo in Arlington that he doesn't use because he lives in DC. It's super nice. There's a guard at the front desk, plus the views are fantastic. You're welcome to stay there."

"Can you check with him?"

"I don't have to. It's sitting unused since Liv moved out."

"Are you sure?"

"Absolutely." Addison texted her the address along with the six-digit code to his condo. "I have complete confidence you and Prescott will find the killer."

"Thank you," Jacqueline replied. "A lot is riding on this."

She wanted to ask Addison about her job at ALPHA, but burners could be monitored like any other cell phone, so she closed with, "Thank you for offering me a place to stay."

The line went dead as Jacqueline drove down her sister's street. After parking in the driveway, she cut the engine, and sat there mulling Addison's offer. While it would be great to stay in a furnished condo, Z had arranged for her to work this case.

I should probably ask him directly.

On the other hand, she had money.

I can afford to rent a place. But if I go that route, I'll need to look for something. That'll take time I don't have.

She wanted to start working first thing tomorrow, so finding a place today would help her achieve that goal. She could live at her boss's spare condo or stay at her lover's house.

Or I can check with Leslie. We were close once. It could be fun.

Jacqueline made her way to the front door, rang the bell, and waited.

When Leslie didn't answer, Jacqueline started typing out a text. "Hey sis, I'm back in town and wanted to see—"

The door opened. Leslie's musician friend stood there, the black knit cap on his head, his long dark hair resting on his chest. Dressed in jeans and a T-shirt, he stood there staring at her.

A few seconds passed before he broke into a grin. "Hey, you're the sister, right? How you doin'?

"Is Leslie here?"

"She's on a modeling gig. You wanna come in and wait?"

"Will she be home soon?"

"Sure." He swung the door wide.

Jacqueline stepped inside and he shut the door.

"I was hanging on the back deck." He headed toward the kitchen. "Can I getcha something to drink?"

Jacqueline followed. He opened the fridge, pulled out a can of soda, and offered it to her.

"I'm good, thanks."

He popped the top, drank some down, and gestured to the deck.

Once outside, she eyed the thick layer of yellowy-green pollen covering the white patio chairs and white table. He left the glass slider open, and sat.

"Pull up a chair," he said.

"I'm fine."

"Sorry, the furniture could use a wipe down," he said.

Rather than do anything about it, he tossed back more soda.

"I didn't get your name," Jacqueline said.

"I'm Luam," he replied. "I go by Lou."

"You mentioned being in a band. Do you play an instrument?"

"Lead singer, and I play bass."

"Do you get together with your band and practice a lot?"

He furrowed his brow, said nothing.

"The last time I was here you said you were between tours," she continued.

"The guys have been talking about going their separate ways." He chugged down more soda, then stifled a belch. "Excuse me."

"So, are you staying here?" Jacqueline asked.

"For now, yeah."

I can't stay here. He's here all the time.

"How do you know my sister?"

"Met her a while ago," Lou replied.

"Are you two—"

The front door opened, then slammed shut. The clacking of heels on the hard flooring got louder and louder.

"Did you buy me a SUV?" Leslie's voice pierced the quiet afternoon. Her sister stepped onto the deck, slid her gaze to Jacqueline. "Oh, hey, is that your SUV in my driveway?"

"Well, I didn't fly over on a broomstick, so yeah," Jacqueline replied.

Lou chuckled, but her sister didn't. "You could of gotten an Uber, yeah?"

"I wanted—" Jacqueline began.

"My photo shoot was *the* bomb." Leslie struck a pose, then grinned. "I did so good. They totally want me back for more gigs." She sniffed her underarms. "I'm gonna go take me a bubble bath." Then, she regarded Jacqueline "Whatcha doing here?"

Jacqueline pushed out of the chair. "Stopped by for a second, but you're super busy, plus I gotta—"

"Hang here. I won't be longer than thirty."

Who am I kidding? I can't stay here one more second.

"I'm gonna take off." Jacqueline wanted to go inside, but her sister was still striking a pose in the doorway. "Can I sneak by?"

On a huff, Leslie meandered into the kitchen. "I'm starving. Hey, sis, order us some food, will ya?"

Jacqueline followed, her gaze trained on the front door. *This was a total time suck.*

"Stop by anytime," Lou called out from the back deck.

"See ya." Jacqueline showed herself out and made her way to the vehicle. As she started the SUV, Lou meandered outside and waved.

After sliding on her sunglasses, she backed out of the driveway, and headed out of the neighborhood.

She was angry she'd wasted her time, sad that the Leslie she knew and adored was gone. Her sister didn't look the same, she didn't act the same either. Jacqueline had no idea if her sister and Lou were friends, friends with benefits, or more. They didn't give off any kind of vibe at all. As she drove away, she realized they hadn't even spoken to each other. Leslie had become so self-obsessed, she hadn't even said hello to him.

I'll stay at Z's condo.

She plugged the address into the nav app, then made her way to the main road. As she headed east toward Arlington, she opened the sunroof and punched up tunes. She'd find a way to work with Prescott, despite her distrust of him.

Of one thing she was certain, she would be taking *total* advantage of Mac every chance she got.

Forty minutes later, she pulled up to the condo building, got out, and stopped short at the entrance. Addison had given her the code to Z's condo, but would it work on the building keypad? She tried it.

As she suspected, Z's code didn't give her access to the building. She called Addison's burner but Addison didn't answer.

After she waved at the guard, he cracked open the front door. "Can I help you?"

Jacqueline gave him the condo number and told him she'd be staying there.

"I'm sorry, but I can't let you in without permission from the owner. Can you call him?"

"I will," she replied.

He returned to the security desk.

She called Addison again. This time, she answered. "Do you know the condo building code? The front desk guard won't let me in."

"It's not the same code as my dad's condo?"

"No."

"Can you put the guard on?" Addison asked.

Jacqueline knocked on the glass door, offered a friendly smile, and showed him her phone. The guard returned. She put the call on speaker. "I've got the guard here."

"Hello," Hawk said. "This is Philip Skye." He rattled off the condo number. "Please let Jacqueline Hartley into the building. She can stay at my condo for as long as she needs."

"Thank you, Mr. Skye," said the guard.

"Thank you," Jacqueline said and hung up.

The guard keyed in several numbers, then told her to set a passcode. After she did, she thanked him, then fetched her suitcases. Shortly after, she stood inside her temporary living space, staring out the floor-to-ceiling windows across the Potomac River into DC.

While she loved her new place, she wasn't feeling so good about how easy it was to fool the security guard. If Nicholas Hawk could imitate Philip Skye and get her access into the building, how safe was she, really?

11

HEARTBREAK

Prescott

Prescott made mac and cheese, then cut up carrots and celery.

"Hey, bud, I made us lunch."

Ethan scrambled off the family room floor, where he'd been playing, and made his way into the kitchen.

Prescott braced for an argument, but a quiet Ethan climbed into the booster seat. "Yummy. Mac and cheese."

Prescott smiled. "I'll consider this a win. You like carrots?"

"I can't know."

Prescott pulled up a chair beside him, then held out a cut-up carrot stick. Using his bicuspids, he bit into it. "Mmm, carrots are good."

Ethan mimicked him. A few chews in, Ethan's expression fell. "Yucky."

A sigh escaped Prescott. Children were a challenge. He had no clue what he was going to do, but for the moment, he had more pressing matters than getting him to eat a damn carrot.

"How 'bout celery?" Prescott bit off a piece.

Ethan mimicked him. This time, his eyes lit up. "This is good."

"A win."

They grew quiet while they ate. When finished, Prescott colored with Ethan.

While they worked in silence, Prescott studied him for a minute. "You color good, Ethan."

"Fanks."

"We're going to your house, so we can bring your toys and clothes back here."

"Are me and Mommy staying here?"

A jolt of pain sliced through him. "Yeah." The truth got stuck in his throat.

Prescott pulled out his phone, dialed.

Jericho answered. "Yo, what's happening?"

After pushing away from the table, Prescott walked into the family room. "Thanks for the texts," he said while staring into his screened porch.

"I'm sorry, brother. How you holdin' up?"

"I need to tell my nephew his mom died and that he's gonna live with me."

"Whoa."

"I don't have a clue how to do this. I need to talk to a therapist. Is Liv there?"

"Hold on. She's putting Liam down for a nap."

"Tell her to call—"

"I got you," Jericho said. "Hold two seconds. Hey, babe, Prescott needs you."

"Hi," Liv said. "I'm so sorry about your sister. How can I help?"

Prescott explained his situation.

"Be honest with Ethan," Liv began. "It's impossible to predict how anyone will react, and that includes a young child. Based on his age, he won't fully understand the finality of it. He might be scared because his mom isn't coming back, so you have to reassure him that you and your entire family are *his* family. In fact, I would start the conversation with that. Let him know how much you love having him in your life and how special he is."

"That's good."

"The timing is going to be tricky," she continued. "Don't tell him at bedtime."

"Hell, no. That would freak anyone out."

"Exactly. Is he in daycare?"

"He'll be going to daycare at Armstrong."

"If you can, keep him with you for a few days, maybe a week. He needs to feel safe, that you're not going to abandon him. What's the story about his dad?"

"Passed away when he was a baby."

"Okay, so it's just been him and his mom, right?"

"Uncle Prescott," Ethan said.

Prescott peered down. "Hold on, Liv. Yeah, buddy."

"I have to poopy."

"You want to try pooping in the toilet?"

"No, fank you."

"Once you finish, we'll change your pull-on."

Ethan walked away to do his business.

"Sorry about that," Prescott said.

"Potty training, huh? You got thrown into the deep end. I admire you so much for what you're doing. You've taken on a huge responsibility. I know you must feel overwhelmed, especially with the Ops going into hiding. Jericho and I are at an undisclosed location, but we're a call away."

"I appreciate that."

"Call me for anything," she said. "Oh, if you can find a picture book on death, that'll help."

He ended the call as Ethan was finishing with his pooping.

Since he didn't have a changing table, he laid Ethan on the towel, sat on the floor, and started to change him.

Ethan stared up at him.

Talk to him. "Ethan, I love that we get to spend so much time together."

"Can we get a football?"

"Absolutely, but we're gonna swing by your house and pack up your things."

"This is a biiiiiig house."

Prescott smiled at him as he pulled him to his feet. "And I live here all alone. It's gonna be a lot of fun having you live here with me. I won't be so lonely."

"Okay, let's go get a football."

Prescott grabbed two empty suitcases, checked the tote bag, added more diapers, filled the sippy cup, and guided Ethan toward the door leading into the garage. Once everything was loaded, and Ethan was secured in his seat, Prescott got behind the wheel.

"Okay, Ethan, let's go pack you up."

As he was heading toward his sister's apartment, he made a call.

"Hey, brother," Rebel answered.

"Thanks for the texts and calls," Prescott said. "Sorry I haven't called you back."

"No worries," Rebel replied. "I wanted you to know I'm here for whatever you need."

"I'm gonna take you up on that."

"Name it."

"Can you meet me at my sister's apartment and help me pack up my nephew?"

"You got it."

Prescott gave him the address and hung up.

He wanted to put on tunes for Ethan, but the playlist was on Jacqueline's phone, so they drove over in silence.

When he got to Sally's apartment building, he glanced in the rearview mirror. Ethan was out cold. Moving as carefully as he could, he unbuckled him, lifted him into his arms, and made his way toward the entrance.

They took the elevator to her floor, walked down the hallway, the smell of grilled meat filling his nostrils. Once inside, Ethan woke up.

He struggled to be put down. "Is Mommy home?"

Prescott set him on the floor and Ethan ran down the short hallway, Prescott close on his heels. Sally's room was neat, her bed made.

Anger cut through him like a thousand knives to his heart. Someone was living in the shadows, taking out Operatives, and Sally had been collateral damage. Determination would fuel him to find the killer. But, in this moment, his only concern was Ethan.

"Hey, bud, can you show me your bedroom?"

Ethan ran across the hall. "This is my room."

"Super cool. I'm going to bring your things home with us."

As he was packing Ethan's clothing into one of the suitcases, there was a knock on the front door.

Ethan bolted from the room and had opened the front door before Prescott could get there. He stared up at Rebel.

"Ethan," Prescott said, "you gotta wait for me before you open the front door."

"Who's he?" Ethan asked.

"That's my friend, Rebel. He's gonna help pack you up so we can get to the store and buy you that football."

Rebel extended his hand. "How you doin'? You're Ethan, right?"

Ethan smiled at him. "Uh-huh. Do you like football?"

"Love it." Rebel stepped inside and shut the door. After eyeing the toys scattered around the family room, he tied his long hair into a man bun. "I'll load up the toys."

"I have long hair," Ethan said.

Rebel pulled out a second hair tie. "You want me to pull your hair outta your face?"

Ethan scrunched up his nose. "No, fank you." Then, he shook his head and his long, wild hair whipped back and forth. The guys laughed.

"You're funny," Prescott said before addressing Rebel. "I'm packing up his clothes and taking the crib apart."

"Lemme get this stuff loaded, then I'll help you."

Forty minutes later, everything Ethan owned had been loaded into Prescott's truck.

"Do you want to talk to the manager before you take off?" Rebel asked in the parking lot.

"I'll see if someone's in the office."

"I'll stay here with the wild one," Rebel replied before he started tickling Ethan.

Ethan's giggle followed Prescott inside. The manager's office was locked, so he snapped a pic of the contact info and left.

Rebel had Ethan on his shoulders and was walking around on the grass pointing out different things. Gratitude had him taking a breath. He wasn't alone, and he could do this.

"Thanks for your help," Prescott said.

"I'll follow you to the toy store. Then, we'll teach Ethan how to play backyard ball."

"Hurray!" Ethan exclaimed from Rebel's shoulders.

"How are you making this look so easy?" Prescott asked as Rebel set Ethan down.

Ethan ran toward the parking lot. Prescott bolted after him, grabbing him before he got to the street.

Ethan started crying. "No! I want to run!"

"You can't run into a parking lot. Cars are driving fast and we have to stop and look both ways."

Ethan stared at him. "Mommy says look before running."

"She's right." Prescott clasped his hand.

They stopped at a toy store where Ethan took full advantage of Prescott, but Prescott was happy to buy him a few presents. In the book section, he spotted an age-appropriate book about a dinosaur that dies and a different one about the death of a parent. That book was written for ages six and older, but Prescott needed help, so he grabbed them both.

As they waited in line, Prescott stared at the boatload of toys in the cart. "Is this bribery?" he asked Rebel.

Rebel chuckled. "You're just doing something nice for him. Moving is stressful enough. Have you told him?"

"No," Prescott replied.

"Hi, there," the cashier said to Ethan. "You're a cutie." Then, she shifted her gaze at the men. "Your son is adorable." She started scanning the toys.

"He's my nephew," Prescott said.

This was going to be his child... forever. This was the beginning of a lifelong relationship. He would be Ethan's role model. Ethan would look to him on how to behave, how to speak, how to treat others.

I'm gonna mess this kid up.

"Sir, you can swipe or tap your card," the cashier said.

I'm not qualified to be a parent.

"I got this." Rebel held up his watch and the purchase got approved.

Prescott snapped back to reality. "You didn't have to pay for that."

"I wanna get outside and play some football before it's tomorrow," Rebel replied.

They left the store and Prescott murmured, "It's one thing to be his uncle, but another to be his father-figure. I can't raise a child. I'm an assassin."

"If I were you—and it's just me talkin'—I'd play up your exec job at Armstrong." Rebel loaded the toys into the SUV. "One day at a time, brother. And right now, it's more like hour by hour. He's—" he flicked his gaze to Ethan, still in the cart—"How old are you, Ethan?"

"Free," Ethan replied.

"Three?" Rebel confirmed.

"Uh-huh," Ethan said.

"You got this," Rebel said to Prescott. "He's like a block of clay. You get to shape him, little by little. You get to help him navigate life."

"You make it sound easy."

Rebel chuffed out a laugh. "It's the hardest job on earth, but I still wanna do it."

Forty minutes later, Prescott had put the crib together in the bedroom closest to his, while Rebel took Ethan out back to play with his new football.

Next, Prescott unpacked Ethan's clothes, skimmed both books he'd bought on death, then went outside.

Ethan was running, the Nerf football clutched in his small hands while Rebel chased after him. Prescott had planned to uncover his built-in swimming pool but there was no way in hell he was gonna do that now. If Ethan darted into parking lots, he might also wander out back and fall into the water.

A chill slid down his spine.

"How are you so good with kids?" Prescott asked Rebel.

"I *am* one, plus I got six nieces and nephews. It's like my brother and sister are completing for who can have the most children. All their kids are young, so it's still fun."

They played catch with Ethan, who loved running around the yard more than he loved catching the football.

"Thanks for helping," Prescott said. "I'm gonna grill. You wanna stick around?"

"I gotta take off," Rebel replied.

Rebel lifted Ethan. "I had fun with you, Ethan. I'll come back sometime and play more football with you."

"Okay. I like running."

With a smile, Rebel set him down. "I'll talk to you," he said to Prescott.

After Rebel left, Prescott suggested they go inside. "I bought you a dinosaur book," Prescott began. "How 'bout I read it to you?"

After giving Ethan a drink, they sat together on the sofa, and Prescott read it to him. "Dinosaurs are cool, huh?" he asked. "They lived a long time ago."

"This one died."

He inhaled deep. "He did."

"That's sad."

"It is sad, bud."

Dread crept into his soul. While he'd planned on reading him the second book, he just needed to tell him, straight out, that his mom had died.

He set the book down. "Ethan, do you remember that I told you your mommy wasn't feeling good and she had to stay in the hospital?"

Large, innocent eyes stared up at him. "Uh-huh. Is she better?"

"No, she isn't better. I'm very sad to tell you that she died." Prescott's heart exploded into a million pieces. He wasn't sad for his loss, he was wrecked for Ethan.

"Like the dinosaur?" Ethan asked.

He nodded. "Just like the dinosaur."

"Is she coming back?"

"No, Ethan, she isn't."

"Can I see her?"

His heart broke. "Ethan, I'm sorry, but you can't."

This was much harder than he'd anticipated. He had to balance being honest with saying too much, or worse, scaring the child.

Tears filled Ethan's eyes. "I want my mommy."

"I know you do. I want her, too, buddy."

Ethan started crying, giant tears sliding down his small cheeks. Prescott picked him up and stood. Then, he held him in his arms and hugged him. Life had dealt this child another horrific blow, but as he held him close, he silently vowed that he would be there for him, no matter what, for the rest of his life.

THAT EVENING, rather than put Ethan in his crib and leave him alone, Prescott set up a sleepover in the family room. He laid out two sleeping bags, a bunch of pillows, and several board games.

After Ethan had calmed down, he asked Prescott to read him the dinosaur book again, but he didn't ask any questions. Prescott wasn't hungry, but he wanted to make sure Ethan got something to eat.

Somehow, he'd managed to pull together a decent dinner. He breaded chicken breasts, cut them up, and told Ethan that they were homemade chicken nuggets. To his relief, Ethan ate them.

After Ethan had fallen asleep, he stood on his back deck, staring up at the stars. Going forward, Ethan would be his priority, all while finding the ALPHA killer, putting in the hours at Armstrong, and taking care of Jack's sexual needs.

That last one made him chuckle. Without question, that would be the most frustrating of all. Being around her turned him into a beast. From the beginning, their physical connection had been intense. There was something about her, beyond her looks, that drew him to her.

Now, however, he had to help Ethan reacclimate to his new life, his new home, and most importantly, his new family.

Prescott had always been up for a challenge, so he'd confront these head on. Only this time, he wasn't just responsible for himself. He had to ensure Ethan and Jack stayed safe.

With a killer out there, he had to watch his six... and, more so, he had to watch theirs.

∼

Jacqueline

By eight o'clock Monday morning, Jacqueline was ready to work, so she texted Prescott. "Where should we meet?"

No dots appeared.

Assuming he had his hands full with Ethan, she shouldered her laptop satchel, grabbed her handbag, and left the condo.

On the way to his house, she stopped at a grocery store, loaded up with some non-perishables, including bottled water for herself and Ethan. As she headed toward the front of the store, she walked down the pet isle.

Her thoughts drifted to the puppies. After grabbing a handful of dog toys, she spotted giant bounce balls near the registers. She fished out a large blue one, then proceeded to a cashier.

After loading her car, she texted her sister-in-law, Naomi.

"I'm back in the area and would love to see you guys... and get my puppy fix. What's your after-work sched this week?"

Within seconds, dots appeared. "THAT IS THE BEST NEWS!!!" Naomi texted back. "Keith is out of town for a convention. How 'bout girls' night tonight? We can cook and play with the pups."

"I love it," Jacqueline replied. "Six-thirty?"

Naomi replied with a thumbs-up emoji.

Her phone rang. It was Prescott and her heart skipped a beat. *Settle down, woman.*

"Good morning," she answered. "How's it going?"

"We've gotta work at my place, but I'm not sure how much we're gonna get done today."

"I'm at the grocery store getting the water Ethan likes. Need anything?"

"The playlist you made for him."

"You got it."

She drove to Prescott's palatial estate in McLean. After parking on his circular driveway, she knocked on the front door.

No answer.

She rang the doorbell.

A moment later, the door opened. Ethan stood there wearing nothing but a pull-on diaper. Sad eyes stared up at her.

"My mommy died."

Pain slashed through her. "That's so sad, Ethan. I'm sorry."

He left her standing there and toddled away. Her heart broke for him.

She pushed open the door to see Prescott coming down the stairs. His T-shirt was stretched to its limit over his muscular torso, while his worn and tattered blue jeans hung low on his hips. Prescott, casual, had her biting back a gasp.

Wow, just wow.

She stepped inside, shut the door. "You told him."

"Yesterday."

He stopped inches away, the anguish in his eyes impossible to ignore. She might dislike him—and *not* want to work with him—but her heart still ached for him and his family. She wrapped her arms around him and hugged him. "I'm sorry."

He pulled her flush against him. The seconds ticked by while they clung to each other. Then, he took a deep breath, his chest expanding against hers. She loved being in his arms, but she also loved being a refuge for him.

A heady mix of empathy and passion, dislike and determination washed over her. Drowning in the feelings, she broke away, severing their connection. She was there to work, not be his friend, and certainly not his lover.

Yet, when she stared into his eyes, the pain had been replaced with the confidence she'd become so addicted to.

"How's Ethan doing?" she asked.

"Last night was rough."

She stroked his shoulders. "What can I do?"

"Find the SOB who did this."

That, she could do, but not alone.

"Let me grab the water," she said.

He followed her out front, pulled the waters from the back, then eyed the large, bouncy ball. "Is that for him?"

"No, that's for you," she replied. "A blue ball for the man who's going to have them. It's a fun reminder of your promise to me."

His deep, sexy laugh rumbled through her. She liked his laugh… but she liked *making* him laugh even more. They brought the items inside and she followed him to the kitchen.

Ethan was coloring, but not in the book, he was drawing on Prescott's very expensive-looking kitchen table.

Ignoring that, she said, "Ethan, I brought you the water you like."

He stopped coloring. "I don't want water." The belligerence in his voice didn't surprise her. He was grieving, yet not old enough to fully comprehend what had happened.

She set the large bouncy ball on a chair, poured two waters, and sat. He stopped marking up the table to eye the water. "I don't like your water."

Jacqueline sipped, set the glass down. "It's just as delicious as the water at my house." She offered a little smile. "Can I color with you?"

Prescott sat next to him and eyed the markings on his table. "I think it would be nice to let Jack color with us."

A stack of printer paper, along with a large crayon box, sat on the table.

Prescott slid a few pieces of paper in front of her. She

started to draw the three of them playing with the new blue ball in Prescott's yard. Prescott joined her, drawing a bunch of geometric designs. Ethan watched them, then picked up a piece of paper and started scribbling.

Jacqueline thought Prescott did the right thing by not scolding him for coloring the furniture. Today was a hard day for Ethan.

After they finished their masterpieces, she said, "This is us playing with the new ball I brought." She slid the piece of paper into the center of the table, pulled another and started drawing a picture of the puppies, along with their mom.

"What are those?" Ethan asked.

"My brother's dog had puppies," she explained. "I got to see them and they're little and cute. Do you like dogs?"

"My mommy said maybe we can have a dog when I'm bigger, but they're too much work now."

"Do you like dogs?" Jacqueline repeated her question.

"Uh-huh." As he colored, he stuck his tongue out. It was adorable and something she'd seen other children do. "Are you Uncle Prescott's special friend?" Ethan asked.

She glanced at Prescott.

"I'm his work friend," she replied. "What do you know about special friends?"

"Mommy has a special friend, but he makes scary faces at me. I don't like him."

She jumped her gaze to Prescott, then back to Ethan. "I don't like scary faces either."

"Did you tell him to stop?" Prescott asked.

"Yes, but he didn't."

"I don't make scary faces, ever," Jacqueline added. "What's your mommy's friend's name?"

"Mr. Man."

"Well, I'll keep him away from you," she said, "And I'm sure Uncle Prescott will too."

"Absolutely," Prescott replied.

Ethan eyed the blue bouncy ball. "Is that your ball?"

"It's for you." Jacqueline sipped more water. "Maybe we can go outside and play with it."

Ethan set down the crayon and picked up the small glass with both hands. He drank down the water. "Can I have more?"

Relief had her smiling. "Absolutely."

She filled their glasses. Together, they colored and sipped water. While she normally worked long hours and pushed hard for results, she knew she had to tread lightly until they could find solid footing.

Next, they went outside and played with the new ball. Ethan was an energetic, naturally athletic, little boy. The physical activity seemed to lift his spirits, or maybe give him a respite from thinking about his loss.

When Prescott took Ethan upstairs for his afternoon nap, Jacqueline retrieved her laptop and waited at the four-chair kitchen island.

A moment later, Prescott returned, his laptop in hand. "Thanks for hanging in. Ethan's registered for daycare at Armstrong, but it's too soon for him to go."

"You're his anchor and he needs to know you aren't leaving him," Jacqueline said. "How are you holding up?"

He fastened his gaze on her. "Me? I have no fuckin' idea. My priority is him, but I feel the pressure of helping you get started on our case."

"We'll get there," she said. "What are you doing about your job at Armstrong?"

"I took leave. My assistant will delegate or reschedule anything not urgent. Where'd you end up staying?"

"A friend's condo in Arlington."

"Are you safe?"

She thought about how Hawk had fooled the guard, but

opted not to share that with him. He had enough going on without having to worry about her.

"Jack, you there?" he asked.

She blinked several times, returning to the moment.

"*Jacqueline*, are you safe?" he repeated.

All she heard was him calling her Jacqueline. The sensual way her name rolled off his tongue, the way his luscious mouth moved over the letters.

Her cheeks warmed.

"Yeah, I'm good." She opened her laptop. "If you want to get started, let's do it."

He hitched an eyebrow and his gaze darkened.

"Doing it" would be the perfect escape. They'd steal away and bring each other the ultimate pleasure. Nothing but feels to balance out the mayhem.

"We *should* do it," he murmured.

He sat beside her. His size dwarfed her, his achingly beautiful face mesmerized her. Prescott Armstrong was a powerful aphrodisiac.

Heaving down a breath, she pulled out her phone. "Let me share Ethan's playlist with you."

"I'm glad you're here," he said. "To everyone else, we're two strangers working together." He raked his gaze across her face. "But I know that if I touch you here—" he ran his long finger down the nape of her neck, and a moan escaped from the back of her throat— "you like that."

"And I know if I caress your thigh, you'll harden." She sat tall, leaned close. "But I'm not. There's a killer out there hunting down his next target. If we get something done in the next few days, I'll let you take very good care of me."

His lips parted, a groan ripping from his throat.

She had to put space between them or she'd maul him. Pushing out of the chair, she grabbed a bottle of water and filled their glasses.

"You didn't say anything to Ethan about coloring on the table. I was wondering how you'd handle that."

"I'm pretty sure it comes off." Prescott pressed the glass against his lip and sipped. Cool, clear water slid into his mouth, and his Adam's apple bobbed as he drank it down.

She had never met anyone who captured her attention so completely, but they were losing precious time, something they had very little of.

After squaring her shoulders, she said, "I need to take what appear to be random facts or information about four different people and find commonalities."

"Understood."

She asked basic information like the victim's names, years with ALPHA, prior professional experience. Although Hawk and Addison weren't killed, she had to include them in her profile to determine what they had in common with the first two Operatives.

Both Gloria and Bert had been with ALPHA for over a decade. Gloria had prior law enforcement experience. She'd been a detective. Bert had military experience.

"Can you show me their files?"

"It would be easier if I gave you access," Prescott replied.

"That would be great. I can work at night."

"Too bad you don't have anything better to do in the evenings."

Her lips tugged up at the corners. "I will, soon enough. And if you're lucky—*very lucky*—maybe you will too."

12

PRESCOTT'S NEW NORMAL

Prescott

Though Prescott's life was forever changed, having Jacqueline in his home brought him a sense of calm he never anticipated. All these months later, they were going to be together every single day.

How the hell am I going to keep my hands off her?

"Who knows about ALPHA?" she asked.

"Current and former employees, and a handful of people at the White House, FBI, CIA, and Homeland Security."

"Outside of law enforcement, who knows the Operatives exist?"

"No one is *supposed* to know, but spouses or partners might."

"Are all ALPHA employees full time?"

"No, some are brought in for mission-only work."

"Are the criminals always taken out?"

"No. Sometimes, they're arrested."

"So, Ops testify in court?"

"Their testimony is recorded, their identities concealed, and their voices altered."

"How could the ALPHA Killer have found his targeted Ops—Gloria, Bert, Hawk, and Addison?"

"He shouldn't have been able to," he replied.

"Well, he did. So, he either had access to ALPHA files or he paid someone who had access to those files. In Bert's case, he knew his killer."

Ethan's voice floated through the baby monitor perched on the counter. "Mommy." Then, he said something Prescott couldn't understand.

The crib creaked.

"Your athletic nephew is escaping his prison."

Seconds later, Ethan padded downstairs. Instead of heading in their direction, he walked into the bathroom.

"It's the craziest thing to see him here," Prescott murmured.

After Ethan peed, he called out, "Uncle Prescott, I can't reach to wash."

Prescott pushed out of the chair. "I gotta get some kid-friendly stools." As he left the room, he muttered, "I need a damn parenting manual."

Jacqueline

JACQUELINE SMILED. Despite the sadness that hung in the air, Ethan was in good hands with Prescott. He didn't know it, but she did.

She was ready to examine the ALPHA missions of the four targeted Ops. Unsure how much work she'd get done with Ethan underfoot, she slid her laptop into her bag.

The boys made their way into the kitchen as she shouldered it.

"Do you live wif us?" Ethan asked.

"No," she replied. "I live by myself in a different house."

Ethan toddled into the family room, picked up the bouncy ball she'd bought for him, then flung it toward them.

"How about we throw that ball in the basement or outside?" Prescott suggested.

Ethan ran after the ball and threw it again. This time, Prescott intercepted it. "Basement or outside? What'll it be?"

Ethan glared at him. Prescott didn't budge.

Jacqueline bit back a smile. She had a front-row seat to a power struggle.

"No," Ethan pushed back.

"You can play with something else then." Prescott set the ball on top of the counter.

"I want to play with my new ball from Jack." Ethan regarded her. "Jack, can I have my ball, please?"

Refusing to get involved, she said, "You have to ask your uncle."

"Why are you leaving?" Prescott asked.

"I'm going to research the missions for overlap, then head to my sister-in-law's for dinner. Good luck with this stand-off. May the best man win." She regarded Ethan. "I'll come back another day, and we can play football or color together. Would that be fun?"

"Okay. Bye, Jack."

"Don't forget to drink some of that delicious water I brought you."

As she made her way toward the front door, Prescott pulled up alongside her. "How'd I do today?"

She opened the front door, turned toward him. "With me or the kid?"

"Both."

"Great with him, and since I didn't end up screaming at you —like the last time we worked together—there's hope for you yet. But there's still plenty of time for you to screw this up." With a wink, she left.

Back at Z's condo, she jumped onto ALPHA's secure site. She was looking for cases where the four targeted Ops had overlap. Starting with Gloria Whelan, she scanned her cases. Then, she opened a new browser and searched for Gloria's home address. It took a little digging, but she found it. If she could find it, so could her killer. Then, all he had to do was tail her until he decided to gun her down.

Next, she started reading through Gloria's missions. There were dozens, so she focused on the ones where the suspects were arrested and jailed for their crimes.

Her phone rang. It was Naomi.

"Hey," she answered.

"What happened?" Naomi asked.

Jacqueline glanced at the time. It was six-forty. "I got absorbed in work. Be there shortly."

She hung up, logged out of ALPHA, and left.

When she arrived at Naomi's, she brought in the dog toys. Her sister-in-law was busy cooking while Cleo lay in the corner. Three pups scampered over to her.

After greeting all the dogs, she hugged Naomi. "Smells so good."

"Tuna steak with seasoned vegetables and wild rice," Naomi gave her a double take. "You look… hmm… happy? Yeah, you look a little glowy."

Prescott.

"Probably just my oily complexion," Jacqueline replied, and they shared a laugh. "Your crew is getting smaller."

"Three of the babies were picked up by their families." She handed Jacqueline a bottle of unopened Chardonnay. "I miss them, but six puppies were a lot."

Jacqueline opened the wine, poured two glasses. "I brought them presents, but I think you should make sure they're age appropriate."

Naomi laughed. "They're dogs, not children, but I'll check

them. That's so sweet of you." After checking the toys, she said, "These are great."

Jacqueline gave the first one to mama Cleo, who, with a wagging tail, hopped the puppy gate and vanished into the living room.

"She loves her babies, but she's definitely not into sharing her presents," Naomi lifted the wine glass. "It's great to have you back."

They clinked and sipped.

Jacqueline sat on the floor and handed out the identical rope toys to the three remaining dogs. "Loki is still here." She picked him up and stared at his face. As soon as she set him down, he went on a tear with his new toy.

Naomi checked the tuna steak. "Turns out, the family who was taking him backed out. Keith and I talked about keeping two puppies, but three German Shepherds in our small townhome is too much."

"I'd love him," Jacqueline said, as Loki returned to play with her.

"Really? That would be awesome."

"How much do dogs cost these days?"

"Depends on the breed and the market. We're asking three thousand."

Jacqueline laughed as she tossed the toy. Loki bounded after it, captured it in his little teeth, and romped back over. "You're not serious, are you?"

"Black Shepherds are less common than the black and tans. We've seen some priced at seven grand."

"*What?*"

"I know. I struggled asking for three, but no one had an issue. Anyway, if you take Loki, we'd gift him to you."

She cuddled him in her lap, but he was much more interested in running wild with his new toy. "I'm short on time and this little guy needs a lot of attention."

"Give it some thought," Naomi said. "We'll hold off posting an ad."

During dinner, Jacqueline raised her glass. "Here's to you."

Naomi smiled. "How sweet."

"I'm grateful for you, and I hope you stay exactly the way you are."

After sipping, Naomi said, "You saw Leslie, didn't you?"

Jacqueline slid a piece of tuna into her mouth. "I felt sad when I saw her, surprised at how self-absorbed she's become, but a little jealous. Those are some big melons she's lugging around."

"Don't be jealous," Naomi said. "You're a beautiful woman with so much going for you. Once you start with implants, you have to trade them out for new ones."

"I didn't know that."

"Yeah, they don't last forever. Do you really want to be seventy and need new implants?" Naomi shook her head. "No, thanks." She scooped rice into her mouth. "You saw the finished product, but we watched Leslie change and we couldn't stop it. First, it was her hair and contact lenses. Then, the surgeries. When her personality began to change, I tapped out. I just didn't have the energy to listen to her anymore."

"Leslie isn't Leslie."

"Keith is angry because she owes us money."

"Yeah, me too." Jacqueline sipped the wine. "Have you seen her new home? It's huge."

Naomi's eyes widened. "When did this happen?"

"No idea, but it's over a million. How much does she owe you?"

"Ten grand. Keith wanted to hire a lawyer to try to get our money back, but I told him we'd probably end up spending ten, and I'm not confident she'd pay us anyway."

"—Enough about Leslie—"

"I agree," Naomi said. "What kind of work are you doing?"

"Targeting a killer."

"It's so great that we like our work, don't you think?"

Hanging with Naomi made her happy. The video chats were great, but they didn't compare to spending quality time together in person.

"Can I confide something?" Jaqueline asked.

"Always."

"There's this guy—actually he's a man—and I've got it *so* bad for him."

Naomi set her fork down. "Do you know how long I've waited for you to say that?"

"I've had boyfriends."

"Operative word, 'boy'. Tell me about this man."

"I hate him."

Naomi laughed. "Nowhere to go but up, then."

"We've known each other for a while, but it's complicated. I don't want you to judge—"

"I would never—"

"We hooked up a bunch of times at a kink club, but we had a bad run-in at work."

"That makes no sense."

"The hookups happened *before* the work thing. Then, after the work thing—where we never actually met in person—I got transferred."

"Got it." Naomi held up the bottle of wine but Jacqueline shook her head.

"Anyway, I'm forced to partner with him on this project. I don't like him, but I'm lusting after him like crazy. He's dealing with some serious family stuff, and, I gotta say, I'm impressed with how he's handling everything."

"See how things go," Naomi suggested. "If you change your opinion of him, put him to the test. Does he golf?"

Jacqueline shrugged.

"If he does, get him on the links. Your dad and Keith will size him up before you hit the back nine."

"Brilliant."

"Let me know how it goes," Naomi replied.

After they finished, Jacqueline helped clean up, spent a few minutes with Loki, and left.

As she headed back to Z's condo, she tried talking herself out of taking the puppy, but by the time she'd gotten home, she'd convinced herself that taking him would be the smartest thing she could do.

Prescott

THURSDAY MORNING, Prescott was going to try something new. The past few days had been critical in helping him and Ethan develop a routine, giving Ethan a glimpse into what his new life would be like. While Ethan had cried every night at bedtime, he had done a remarkable job of adapting to all the changes.

Last night, Prescott's mom and dad had stopped by with dinner, and Ethan was excited to show them his new bedroom and his ever-growing toy collection.

What wasn't working was Jacqueline's decision to work from home. Since they couldn't discuss the case in front of Ethan, that left them limited time to talk. Beyond the slow progress they'd been making, Prescott missed her.

After breakfast, Prescott asked Ethan if he'd liked the daycare he'd been going to.

"Uh-huh," Ethan replied.

Prescott pulled a piece of printer paper off the stack and drew a series of squares that represented buildings. "Check this out," he said sliding the piece of paper in front of him.

Ethan stared at it. "Good job!"

Prescott chuckled. "Thanks, buddy. These are supposed to be buildings." He drew some smaller squares inside the big ones to represent windows. As he stared at the picture, he acknowledged his complete lack of artistic talent.

"This is where I work." Prescott drew an arrow at his building. "We have daycare in this building. Isn't that cool. You'll be right next door."

"I go to *my* daycare."

Ignoring that, "Prescott said, "Let's go to my office so you can see where I work."

"No, fank you. I want to play."

Opting for a different tactic, Prescott explained that he'd gotten *special* permission for Ethan to come to his work. "There's a lady in my office who has a bowl of candy on her desk. Maybe we should see what kind of candy she has today."

Ethan's face lit up. "I like candy."

Prescott hated himself for being a hypocrite. He was bribing Ethan with the very ingredient he'd been trying to ween him off of.

Fifteen minutes later, he buckled Ethan into his car seat, jumped behind the wheel of the ALPHA SUV, and took off for Armstrong Enterprises. On the drive over, he pulled up the playlist, and Ethan started singing along.

Another small win.

With the diaper and computer bags slung over his shoulder, he held Ethan in his arms. First stop, his office. The receptionists in the lobby did double takes as he made his way to the elevator.

"You wanna push the button?" he asked Ethan.

Ethan pushed the up button. Inside the cab, he instructed Ethan to push the sixth floor.

"I can't know."

Prescott pointed. "That's a six."

Ethan tapped the button.

"Nice job," he said.

Up they went, then down the hall he strode. After unlocking his office, he dropped the bags on the sofa, and set Ethan down.

"Where's the candy?" Ethan asked.

"This way." Prescott exited his office, Ethan close on his heels. He stopped at Francis's doorway. She was typing away, glanced up, and smiled. "Good to see you." Her gaze slid to Ethan's as he walked up to her desk and shoved his face against the glass container filled with individually wrapped chocolates.

"Hi," Ethan said.

"You must be Ethan. I'm Miss Francis."

"Are these your candy?"

"Uh-huh." Francis smiled. "Would you like one?"

His ear-to-ear grin made Prescott chuckle. "Yes, please."

She opened the glass lid and pulled out two. Maybe your uncle would like one too."

He snatched them up. "Fank you." Then, he peered up at Prescott. "Can I have one now and one at home?"

Francis laughed. "Wow, you've got your hands full."

"I thought one of those was for me," Prescott said.

Ethan giggled. "Can I have yours?"

"Go for it."

"Fank you!" Ethan exclaimed with a grin.

Prescott chuffed out a laugh. He wanted to say no, but he couldn't. Ethan was dealing with so much. If a bitesize piece of candy made his nephew *that* happy, he'd break his own damn rule.

"How 'bout I show you the playground?" Prescott asked. "There's a slide and a cool maze."

"I've got a few things to run by you," Francis said. "There's a board meeting this morning that you should attend, if you can."

Prescott nodded. "That's the plan."

In the elevator, he let Ethan push the button again. Once

outside, they followed the path to the building next door. As they entered the daycare center, children's laughter and chatter floated into the lobby. The man sitting behind the counter walked around to greet them.

"Good morning, Mr. Armstrong." He smiled at Ethan. "You must be Ethan. We're excited you're here."

Ethan tightened his hold of Prescott's hand.

"Ethan already has a daycare, but we just wanted to see what's going on over here, right Ethan?"

"No, fank you."

"What about the outside maze?" Prescott asked.

"But we're inside!" Ethan exclaimed, raising his small arms as if to question his uncle's knowledge between inside and out.

The daycare staffer laughed. "The three- and four-year-old class is about to start story time. Why don't you sit in and listen?"

"We'd love to," Prescott replied, and they followed the employee down the hallway.

"These classrooms are for our two-year-olds." He pointed left and right, like a flight attendant. "And these six rooms are for our three- and four-year-olds. That's our biggest group of students."

He entered one of the playrooms. There had to be twenty little ones playing in small groups, pairs, and even alone. Four employees were interacting with the children.

"Miss Nancy," called out the front-desk staffer.

A young woman hurried over. When her gaze met Prescott's, her cheeks flushed. "Mr. Armstrong. Hi, I'm Nancy, the head teacher in this pod. Welcome."

"This is my nephew, Ethan."

Nancy smiled at him. "Hi, Ethan, I'm one of the teachers here. You and your uncle are just in time for a story." She left, returning with a large dinosaur picture book. "Join us in the circle while me, Miss Keisha, and Mr. Tim read it."

A boy wandered over. "What's your name?"

"Ethan. What's yours?"

"Dylan. You can sit with me."

Ethan peered up at Prescott.

"You can sit with Dylan, and I'll sit in the chair right there." Prescott pointed to an adult chair nearby.

Prescott's breathed a little easier as Ethan sat beside Dylan, and the teachers took their seats. They didn't just read the story, they acted it out, which made the kids laugh.

Prescott's attention was anchored on Ethan. He turned twice to make sure Prescott hadn't left.

When the story ended, Miss Nancy announced outside play. Ethan bolted over. "Can I play?"

"Absolutely, Prescott replied. "I'll be right in the next building."

"Can you come with me?" Ethan asked.

"Of course."

Once outside, he watched as Ethan started to interact with the other children. He had to give props to the instructors who introduced Ethan to a handful of students. Within ten minutes, Ethan was running and laughing.

Knotted muscles running along Prescott's shoulders released a little.

When playtime ended, Ethan came running back over. "Can I stay for lunch?"

Prescott smiled. "I even packed a lunch for you."

They went inside and Miss Nancy helped get Ethan situated with his cubby. When finished, Prescott said goodbye to him.

Ethan slipped his small hand into Prescott's. "You have to come back."

Prescott picked Ethan up. "I promise I will come back when school is over for the day and we'll go home together."

Ethan threw his arms around Prescott and hugged him, and Prescott's heart grew in his chest.

"Bye."

"I'll see you later, Ethan."

After Prescott set him down, Ethan walked with his new teacher to his table. As Prescott was heading through the lobby, Miss Nancy came rushing out.

"I didn't want to say anything in front of Ethan, but I read the form you sent over. That helps us a lot. I'm sorry about your loss... and for Ethan's."

"Thank you."

"I noticed Ethan has a lunch. Did you bring any diapers?"

"I brought a few but left them in my office. He can pee in the toilet, but he likes to poop in his diaper. I'll bring a box tomorrow."

"No worries. We've got extra. We're all great at helping to potty train the kids."

"Good luck with that," he said, and she laughed.

"If you want to check on him, we've got cameras everywhere, except the adult restrooms. Just download the app, then use your work email address to create an account."

He thanked her and left.

Prescott wasn't sure if he felt free or guilty for leaving him. But he knew Ethan needed to be with other children. And he needed to work.

Back in his building, he rode the elevator to the top floor and stopped in the break room for coffee. His uncle was standing by the window, his cell phone pressed to his ear. He was talking quietly, but Prescott caught, "I can't wait to see you."

As Prescott filled a mug, Artemis said, "I've got to run. Yes, I'll make sure you have it. Yes, today. I promise." He hung up, and the wistful look in his eyes faded.

His cheeks were rosy, like he'd been exercising, but Prescott doubted his uncle had been working out.

"Are you attending the board meeting at eleven?" Artemis asked on his way out.

"I'll be there, but I haven't looked at the agenda." Prescott sipped the hot drink.

In the doorway, Artemis turned back. "I'm pitching TopCon's rebranding proposal."

"Is TopCon the woman I met?"

Artemis's face split into a smile. "Yes, she's the one."

"I wanted to tell you that my sis—"

"Sorry, I'm short on time. We'll talk later." Artemis rushed out.

With mug in hand, Prescott returned to his office and spent the next hour playing catch up. At eleven o'clock, he entered the executive conference room. Not only was the table full, the second row of chairs hugging the wall were filled. Prescott took his place at the head. His uncle was already seated at the other end.

As the meeting began, Prescott's phone buzzed with a call from Z. Prescott left the conference room. "I'm at work and can't talk."

"I've got a job for tonight."

"Tonight? Seriously, there's no way—"

"We've located the Piranha."

The Piranha had been on Z's Most Wanted List for a while.

"Where?" Prescott asked.

"Near Baltimore."

"Send me the deets." He hung up and returned to the conference room.

His uncle was explaining why he was recommending TopCon to rebrand their image on a line of creams, lotions, and gels for sensitive skin. The products had been in the red for so long, another C-level exec had suggested the line be eliminated altogether.

"With the rebranding, along with our three-punch marketing strategy, I'm confident this will give the dying brand new life," Artemis said.

"Artemis, why aren't we using our in-house marketing team for this skincare line?" asked a board member.

"We need a fresh, new perspective when re-branding this image," Artemis explained. "If the same group looks at the same products, we'll get the same results. TopCon's team is offering something different."

"How much?" another board member asked.

"One point five million," Artemis replied.

The board had seven days to review the suggestions before a final decision was required. Artemis closed his presentation, and the meeting moved on to the next agenda item.

Prescott pulled up the daycare app. Once it downloaded, he signed in. After toggling around, he found Miss Nancy's classroom. A few more clicks and he found Ethan. He was sitting with Dylan and three other children at a table. They were all eating lunch. Dylan said something and Ethan started laughing, then Dylan laughed. While Ethan could have been crying thirty seconds ago, Prescott had captured a happy moment.

Gratitude and relief coursed through him. If anyone could manage through a challenge, it was him.

I've got this, one day at a time.

Leaving the app open, he returned his attention to the next presentation. In truth, there were certain aspects of corporate America that drove him insane. Meetings topped that list. While some of them were necessary, he considered most of them a total time suck.

His thoughts jumped to Jacqueline. Was she working? Was she reviewing the case history of the deceased Ops? It had been three days since he'd seen her, in person, and he missed the hell out of her.

The meeting ended, and several stayed in the conference room. Prescott needed the privacy of his office so he could review the Piranha file.

As he was leaving, Artemis called out, "Prescott, what did you think of TopCon's preso?"

"It was fine," he replied. "I'm not sure we need to hire an outside consulting firm when we've got multiple teams of employees doing the same job."

"Read over the materials," Artemis said. "I hope you'll vote to approve my request."

Back in his office, Prescott locked his office door, then signed in to ALPHA remotely.

The Piranha was one of the most wanted serial killers in the country. Known for his ritualistic killings of men and women, forty-six-year-old Stanley Deanson had seven known aliases. For the past decade, he'd left a trail of death and destruction in his wake, starting in Washington state and winding his way down to Miami. His DNA had linked him to eighteen murders, but the federal agents assigned to his case were convinced there were dozens more.

Three days ago, he'd been spotted in a dive bar, eight miles east of Baltimore, then confirmed in the same area by a confidential informant yesterday. If Prescott could find someone to stay with Ethan overnight, he'd take the job. According to a source, he'd been spotted outside an abandoned house frequented by drug addicts.

He hated imposing on his mom and dad, but Ethan seemed comfortable around them. Prescott called his mom.

"Hi, honey," she answered. "How're things?"

"Well, I'm at work and Ethan's at the daycare on Armstrong's campus, so I'd say pretty good."

"That's great. Did you tell him about his mom?"

"Yeah. It's been rough, but he's a resilient little boy."

"How are you doing?"

"Getting used to taking care of him. I had no idea kids were so much work."

His mom laughed. "But they're also a lot of fun. You'll see."

"I was hoping you and dad would be able to help me out tonight. I've got an out-of-town work thing, but I'll be back in the morning. Is there any way you guys could stay with him?"

"We'd love to," his mom replied. "What time are you leaving?"

"Ten."

"Tonight?"

"Right. I'll be back around seven to get him ready for daycare."

"What kind of a trip is this, Scotty?"

"A fast one," he replied.

"Why don't we bring dinner and we'll spend a little time with him before you leave, in case he gets anxious."

He thanked his mom, hung up, and texted Z.

"I'm in."

"Let me know if you have questions," Z replied.

Prescott doubted he would.

When I get the Piranha in my scope, the son of a bitch won't know what hit him.

13

INSATIABLE

Prescott

At eleven that evening, Prescott stood in front of the retina scanner at ALPHA HQ, the light flashed green, and he entered. The place was quiet and dark, exactly how he liked it. Though he wasn't an Operative, he'd been given access to the building so he'd have a top-secret place to prep.

Automatic lights flicked on as he made his way toward the conference room.

There, he unearthed his laptop and got to work. The Piranha changed up his looks by shaving his head or letting his brown hair grow past his shoulders. He grew beards of different lengths or he was clean shaven. He changed up his clothing too and dressed to blend in.

Prescott zoomed in. Looked like he changed his eye color too. He was a master of disguise and, based on the reports in his file, very charming. A real people-person who had no trouble luring his victims into his car or even into a motel room. Over the years, witnesses would come forward with accounts of him showing up at parties and charming his way inside. Law enforcement pieced together a pattern. He'd stay until fewer than ten guests remained, then he'd kill them all.

One thing was certain, Stanley Deanson never lived in one place too long, and he went long stretches of time before going on another violent killing spree.

While Prescott hadn't prepped for a mission at his house, he'd never, ever prep there now. The crime scene photos were brutal. If Ethan were to ever see them—

His stomach clenched.

In a short amount of time, he'd become attached to his nephew. While he loved his family and close circle of friends, Prescott always considered himself a loner. Crazy the power this little boy had on him, and their relationship had only just begun.

Refocusing, he read through the mountain of information that law enforcement had collected. Prepping for these missions included a review of best- and worst-case scenarios. Best was simple. He wasted the guy, didn't get shot himself.

Worst-case scenarios required careful contemplation. Prescott couldn't assume anything. So, he spent the next hour running through a myriad of situations that didn't work in his favor. Not something he liked doing, but it kept him on high alert, reminding him that he—and only he—had his back.

On the other hand, he didn't have to be responsible for another person's safety. He didn't have to live with the burden of a teammate dying because he hadn't done his job. All he had to do was watch his six.

That, I can do.

When finished, he closed his laptop, left his phone and wallet on the table. Already dressed in black pants and a black turtle neck, he entered the men's locker room and strode to his locker. There, he pulled on his body armor, then a double shoulder holster that wrapped around him, like a backpack. He swapped out his shoes for combat boots and covered his face in camouflage paint.

He pulled a burner from the charger, checked to make sure it worked, then turned it off.

Time to weapon up. One gun into his ankle holster, a Glock in each of the shoulder holsters. He slid on black gloves, grabbed his helmet with the built-in night goggles, and left the way he entered, through the employee entrance in the back of the building.

The drive north was filled with the sound of wind rushing through the sun roof. One by one, he ran though all possible outcomes except the one where he *didn't* make it out alive.

No room for error.

It was almost one in the morning when he drove past the abandoned house, continuing on two blocks to a plaza shopping center. He parked farthest from the stores and away from a street lamp. He exited the SUV, fastened on his helmet. With a Glock in hand, he made his way toward the rundown building.

He expected he'd find a user there. Could be several. Sex workers might be turning tricks. A gang could have taken up residence. To assume the house would be empty was dangerous. To assume he was the only one with a gun could get him killed.

Nevertheless, he was willing to risk his life to waste another predator.

Most of the houses sat dark, but a few lights dotted the street. A chain link fence wrapped the house from the sidewalk all the way around to the backyard. He continued past the house, around the corner, and down the next street. His goal? Hug the shadows, enter the house through the back.

Once in the backyard, the two-story structure loomed before him. He lowered his night goggles, approached the house, and tried the slider. It was unlocked.

It squeaked. He stopped, then inched the door open

enough so that he could turn and squeeze in. Leaving the door open, he surveyed the room.

What a dump.

A stained, ripped sofa sat tucked against the back wall, discarded needles tossed in a corner. Empty beer and booze bottles everywhere. With his weapon drawn, he cleared each room.

As he ascended, the stairs creaked. Two men, who'd been hooking up, pulled up their pants and ran out the front door.

The first floor was just as much of a shit hole as the lower level, however more dilapidated furniture filled the living room. After clearing the empty dining room and filthy, moldy kitchen, he made his way upstairs. The stench from the bathroom had him holding his breath as he peered inside to clear. No one, dead or alive.

First bedroom stood empty. No furniture, less trash. The second he entered the master bedroom, the smell hit him.

Dead body. A decomposing body of a man in the bathroom, a syringe sticking out of his arm.

It wasn't the Piranha, so Prescott went downstairs and stood behind the open front door. Now, he waited for his mark to show. If he didn't, Prescott would return the next night, and every fucking night until this dickwad showed his motherfucking face.

According to the Piranha's file, his most recent killing spree happened in a group house on a Pennsylvania university campus where he shot everyone who lived there, then dragged their bodies into the living room, where he'd posed them in a bizarre pagan scenario. Some of the victims had been dismembered. A gruesome scene that defied any logic. But he wasn't there to analyze the Piranha, he was there to take the monster out.

As the minutes ticked by, he focused on his breathing, and on staying vigilant.

A car drove by, then minutes later, another.

While his thoughts kept wandering to Jacqueline, he'd inhale, forcing her from his mind on the exhale. Thinking about her was much more enticing, but staying focused would give him a better chance of making it out alive.

A car drove up, the engine went silent. Prescott steeled his spine. The vehicle door opened, then slammed shut.

Footsteps on the sidewalk, then the chain link gate squeaked on its rusty hinges, as if crying out a warning.

If it was the Piranha, he couldn't wait to take this predator out for good.

"Fuckin' door's open," the man grumbled.

As he walked up the cement steps, his phone's flashlight lit the way.

Prescott flipped up his night goggles, so he wasn't blinded by the light. When the man shut the front door, Prescott got his answer. Stanley Deanson had just stepped into his trap.

"Deanson," Prescott rasped.

The man whirled around.

Prescott grabbed Deanson's phone, shoved it in his pocket. Plunged into darkness, Prescott flipped down the goggles and eyed his target. Deanson had pulled a gun.

"Who the fuck are you?" the Piranha asked.

"Your worst fuckin' nightmare." *POP! POP!*

Prescott shot him in the chest, twice.

Deanson crumpled to the floor, blood pouring from him.

Prescott grabbed Deanson's gun.

"Nice job," Deanson bleated. "Someone finally got me."

"How many?" Prescott bit out.

Gasping for air, his chest rising and falling fast, Deanson murmured, "I'm gonna take that number with me to the great beyond."

"You've been keeping track, like a secret score card. C'mon, Deanson, what's the number?"

"Sixty-one," he whispered.

"That makes sixty-two *my* lucky number."

POP! POP! POP!

Two bullets to the brain, one more to the chest. Prescott wasn't removing his glove and leaving a print on Deanson's carotid, so he waited for his panting to slow.

Then, Deanson stilled.

Only silence filled the dead of night.

The hatred in Prescott's heart dissolved, leaving only pity. Everyone has one life. Just one. This man chose to spend his torturing and killing. Deanson's purpose in life was stealing it from others.

"What a waste of a human." Prescott collected Deanson's gun.

Down the stairs he went, and out through the back slider. His feet ate up the grass, then the cement, as he made his way to the SUV.

He set his helmet on the back seat, got behind the wheel. After storing all weapons and Deanson's phone in the center console, he rolled out. Not until he'd driven onto the main road did he flip on the headlights.

The drive back to Northern Virginia was slow and steady. His face was covered in camouflage paint, he was dressed in black, he was driving an ALPHA vehicle that wasn't registered to anyone. Getting pulled over would likely get him arrested.

Like every other mission, he never went straight home. He needed to clear his head, get rid of the evil that clung to his skin and hovered all around him. He opened the sunroof and drove in silence to Arlington. Once there, he street parked. From the privacy of the vehicle, he turned on the burner and made a call.

Z answered. "Yes?"

"Done," he replied.

"Confirmed?"

"Confirmed." Prescott hung up, turned off the burner, and

exited the SUV. The Kevlar vest and helmet would stay hidden in the vehicle, the weapons locked in the center console.

Instead of entering the building through the front door and having to explain his face paint to the night guard, he entered through the delivery entrance and rode the freight elevator to the penthouse. Down the hall he went, stopping outside Z's condo.

He punched in the code and entered. Usually the condo stood dark, but the light over the stovetop was on, bathing the small foyer in diffused light. He'd stayed there after the Terrence Maul hit. Had he left it on?

As he made his way into the living room, he stopped short.

Jacqueline stood twenty feet away, a Glock in her outstretched hands.

"Down on the ground, now!" she shouted. "Or I'll blow your fucking head off!"

"Jack, it's Prescott Armstrong."

"Now!" She yelled, her feet firmly rooted on the floor.

"Jacqueline Hartley," he said, keeping his voice low and slow. "It's me, Mac. I'm not gonna hurt you."

Jacqueline

"Mac?" Jacqueline's heart was thumping so loudly in her ears, she couldn't hear herself think... and she hadn't heard anything he said until she heard the word Mac.

She flipped on the pole lamp in the living room and gasped. Prescott, dressed in black, his face concealed in camouflage paint, was a terrifying sight.

She lowered her gun, but she didn't put it down. "I need to see ID."

"I don't have it. I'm sorry I scared you. Z's condo has been empty since Liv moved out."

On a quivering breath, she set the gun on the coffee table. Then, she soaked up this beast of a man. Tall, strapping, and built like a slab of granite, she paused to take in every glorious inch of him.

A long minute passed before her heart rate slowed. She walked over, peered at him. "Wow, you look scary as fuck. You're already a formidable man, but holy shit." She put her hand over her heart. "Scary. As. Fuck."

"Thank you for not shooting me." He took a step toward the door. "I can take off."

Don't let him leave.

The second she wrapped her hand around his triceps, her insides came alive, and her heart beat hard and fast, but this time for a very different reason.

She liked this way, much, much better.

"Don't go," she said.

She fought against the desire to jump in his arms and kiss him, then unleash her innermost demons on him. Her hair must've been crazy wild because he pulled a chunk from one side to the other.

"You're sexy and adorable." His deep voice rumbled through her. "Sorry I scared you."

"Next time, knock, will ya?" She offered a little smile. "What's with the SWAT look?" Then, reality sunk in. "You were on a mission."

"Yeah."

"What are you doing here?"

"When no one lives here, I stop by after a mission. I need a few hours to get my head on straight. The jobs are intense."

She hadn't removed her hand from his arm, so she took a step toward the kitchen. "Let's get you a drink, so you can shake off the evil."

In the kitchen, she stepped out of his way. "I just moved in, so I have no idea where the booze is."

Prescott opened a cabinet over the refrigerator and pulled out a bottle of McCallan whiskey. Then, he set out two glasses. "You want to join me?"

"I'll have water."

She filled her glass. "If you need to be alone—"

"No," was all he said.

"Where do you sit?"

"In the chair overlooking the river, but I want you next to me."

Her heart—her traitorous, little heart—leapt for joy. "There's not enough room. I'll sit on the sofa."

"On my lap."

She loved that he wasn't asking. He told her what he wanted. Now, it was up to her.

After flicking off the stove light, he turned off the living room pole lamp.

When he sat, his broad shoulders and thick thighs dwarfed the oversized chair. She eased onto his lap. The connection was immediate, electric, and so damn powerful. She loved being close, her body snuggled against his. She closed her eyes, savoring the way he felt, his familiar smell, the rise and fall of his chest against her.

She'd hated him for so long, she was struggling to make sense of how she felt now. The desire to be close to him, to touch him, to connect with him turned her wild with need, but also filled a place in her heart she'd never known existed. The power and strength and confidence radiating off him was addictive. She'd found her drug of choice in Prescott Armstrong.

Together, they stared out at the sprinkling of lights across the dark water.

Being in his arms soothed her. She couldn't begin to

comprehend what it must be like to take another person's life, to accept a job where the best possible outcome was their death.

As their breathing fell in sync, she wondered if their heartbeats did too. She loved his hard body beneath hers. Loved that he was caressing her arm, slowly. His long, thick digits, stroking her skin.

Dressed in a tank top and panties, she would have been cold, but his warm body wrapped her in an invisible blanket. She had been forcing herself to peer into the night, but she desperately needed to stare into his eyes. Unable to resist, she turned.

Their eyes met.

A low growl rumbled from the depths of his chest. "You shouldn't be here."

"*You* shouldn't be here," she retorted.

"But I am."

"So am I." A tremble skirted through her, lust jumping to the forefront. She set their glasses on the side table.

Her insides were on fire. Had to kiss him, ravage him, lose herself in his angry energy. She had to have him.

There was no other option.

She placed her hand on the side of his greasy, painted face. Electricity scurried up her fingers, and a moan ripped out of her. She ran her tongue over her lower lip while her gaze jumped from his eyes to his mouth, and back to his eyes.

Greedy, undeniable desire sprung forth from the depths of her soul. She leaned close, pressed her mouth to his. Hit after glorious hit of pleasure powered through her. She could get lost in him for hours, and she could not—*would not*—wait one more second.

She pushed off him, but she didn't turn back. There was only one direction they should go, so she would lead. It was up to him whether he would follow.

Maybe she did put a little more sway into her hips as she sashayed down the hallway. She passed the hall bath, continuing into her bedroom. Slowing, she turned on the small bedside lamp before entering the bathroom.

There, she turned on the shower, but not the lights. The bedside table lamp bathed the bathroom in a sexy glow.

As she secured her long hair in a scrunchie, he pulled up behind her. He slid his arms around her waist, kissed the back of her neck, then the sensual spot below her ear.

An ardent moan tore from her throat. He bit her lobe. Streams of desire raced through her, her blood running hot in her veins. His reflection in the mirror was sexy as hell and terrifying as fuck. He towered over her, his achingly handsome face masked by the paint. All that was visible were the whites of his eyes.

She curled shaky fingers around the hem of her shirt and pulled it over her head. Now, topless, she waited. She'd made the first move, and the second. He could take it from there.

He turned her toward him, snaked his arms around her, and pulled her tight against him. They came together in a wild embrace. His unshaven cheek scraped against her skin like sandpaper, and she loved it. His kiss was hard, his tongue spiked against hers, the intensity stealing her breath.

She thrust her fingers into his hair, grabbed handfuls, and tugged. His growl landed in the wet space between her legs. The kiss—*Ohgod, the kiss*—was an explosion of energy, like fireworks on the Fourth of July. She bit his lip, raked her teeth down his tongue. She released her pent-up energy into him, and he devoured it.

"More," he murmured.

She dragged her fingernails across his back. The brutal kiss had her growling his name. "Mac, fuck me," she commanded.

He ended the kiss, yanked off his shirt. Then, he knelt at her feet, slid his strong, sexy hands up her thighs and inside her panties. He pulled them off her, leaned close, and kissed the area above her sex. A moan escaped from her throat.

"You smell good," he rasped, and her insides thrummed with desire.

He untied his combat boots and stood. With his heated gaze drilling into hers, he stripped naked, his jutting erection snagging her complete attention.

All that awaited them was sweet, sweet ecstasy.

When she wrapped her hand around his cock, his smile was her reward.

Brilliant white teeth shone like a beacon on a dark, stormy sea, and her insides hummed with delight. He had the capacity to undo her with nothing more than a smile.

"I don't have a condom," he muttered.

"I would hope not," she replied, and he laughed.

A blast of heat rose from her chest, past her neck, to her cheeks.

I'm a goner.

Grateful, he couldn't see her reaction to his laughter, she left the bathroom, retrieved a condom from her night table, and returned.

She slinked up behind him, pressed her body to his, and caressed his chest. Smooth and defined, she ran her fingers down his pecs to his hard-as-fuck abs.

Then, she curled her fingers around his thick, long shaft.

"I love your touch," he murmured.

She loved touching him, but she was *not* gonna tell him that.

He turned to face her, tilted her face toward his, dipped down and kissed her. "I'm going to give you all the pleasure, Jack. All of it... just for you."

She didn't believe him for a second. Every man she'd ever been with had been all about taking. It wasn't like they didn't take care of her needs, but she wasn't their priority.

He clasped her hand, walked into the doorless shower. It was plenty large for two people with two extra-large faucet heads positioned on two different walls. The first was a standard spray, while the second offered a waterfall experience.

Prescott stood beneath the waterfall, the water drenching him from head to foot. Even soaking wet, he was breathtaking. She felt no shame in gawking, so she stood there, letting the hot water pound her shoulders while she admired the spectacular view.

With sudsy hands, he washed the paint off his face, slowly morphing from the beast back into the man.

Her fingers tingled while electricity powered through her. She pumped shampoo into her hands and reached up to wash his hair. As he peered down at her, he teased her nipples with his thumbs.

Ohgod.

He had this way of knowing exactly what turned her on. Her insides hummed while she trembled from the tender way he caressed her straining nibs.

Seconds passed while she tried to focus on him, but every fiber of her being was captivated by his sensuous touch.

"I love that," she whispered.

She could let go with Mac, let him do all the dirty things to her, then send him away. But, tomorrow, she would have to face Prescott. It was a troubling thought she'd deal with tomorrow. Now, she would let Mac steal her body—and her mind—with his talented hands, and mouth, and cock.

He tilted his head back, letting the shampoo rinse down his back. Then, he wiped the water from his eyes and peered down at her. Despite the dim lighting, she couldn't miss the hunger radiating from his eyes.

Within seconds, they were entwined around each other, their mouths greedy. Like wild animals, they clawed and bit each other. The intensity of their desire had her grinding against him.

His hand found her ass and pulled her against his hardness. The kiss continued, their tongues slow and tender one second, feral and untamed the next. The onslaught of pleasure made her insides throb so hard, she thought she'd pass out from pure want.

"I'm dying for you," she admitted.

"I love making you come," he said on a growl.

He spun her around, pinned her against the shower wall before she realized what had happened.

The real Prescott Armstrong.

She was trapped between the shower wall and his hard body. Trapped and loving every filthy second of it. He reached around, ran his large hand over her tummy then over the swatch of pubic hair, teasing her clit with his talented fingers.

"Mmm," she groaned out as more streaks of desire hummed through her.

He slid his fingers between her folds, taking his time to explore her pussy, to caress her gently before he started finger-fucking her.

She couldn't stop moving, her thoughts hijacked, her body primed for a release. He teased her clit, pumped her with his fingers over and over until her breathing was jagged, her insides on fire, the explosion teetering on the edge.

"You're gonna come for me, baby," he growled in her ear. "And it's gonna be so good when you do."

He brushed his lips against her back, licked her skin and bit her shoulder. She yelped, the excitement coursing through her at a ferocious speed. She was flying out of control, rising higher and higher, the glorious waves overtaking her.

With his hard cock pressed against her ass, he fondled her breast, but when he pinched her nipple with one hand and fucked her with his other, the ecstasy started deep inside her.

"Say my name, Jack."

"Mac," she ground out between clenched teeth. "Fuck, Mac, I'm coming so good."

A volcanic orgasm exploded through her as the waves of euphoria annihilated her. Groaning and crying out, she released into his extremely competent hand. Her knees gave out, but he held her fast against him.

She'd never craved anyone she despised. It was heady, naughty, and so damn good.

Regaining her senses, she turned toward him, wrapped her arms around him, sunk her fingers into his thick, wet hair, and kissed him. One, long, magnificent kiss of gratitude for a man she loathed like no other.

At the end of the day, no one could make her shatter into a million pieces like he could.

No one.

∼

Prescott

NOTHING better than making Jack unravel around him. She'd always been responsive to his touch, but tonight she was different. More eager, maybe even more trusting. It could have been because he was in her home, in the middle of the night. Could have been any number of things. At the moment, he didn't give a fuck.

He loved taking out evil, but it came at a price. His soul. No other way to explain it, but the missions took a toll on him.

Not tonight. Tonight, he felt alive. Being around Jack was exhilarating. He breathed her in and he felt complete.

She ended the kiss, pulled the condom packet off the bench and offered it to him. As badly as he needed to root himself inside her and fuck her good and hard, he was going to honor his promise.

He slipped his arms around her, pulled her close, and kissed her gently. "You came hard."

She nodded. "Now, it's your turn."

He turned off the shower. "I told you that if you agreed to partner with me, I would take care of you. You alone. Not me."

Surprise flashed in her eyes. "You did say that."

"I'm a man of my word." He wrapped her in a bath towel, pulled one off the shelf for himself.

Rather than leave the shower, she stood there, staring up at him. "You're gonna have blue balls bad."

"I get 'em every time I'm around you." He flashed a quick smile. "I'm getting used to it."

In truth, it sucked. He was already spending too much time thinking about her, fantasizing about her too. Being with her and not appreciating her fully was torture, but he wanted her to trust him.

How else could he do that?

They toweled off. She slipped back into her panties and top. He pulled on his clothes, picked up his boots.

"Gotta say, I wasn't expecting that," she said. "Lemme walk you out."

He eyed her bed, the rumpled linens. He hadn't spent the night with a woman in a long time, but if she invited him to stay, he would.

She said nothing as they returned to the main room. He tugged on his combat boots, raked his hands through his damp hair. "I've got a team meeting in the morning. You wanna work together at eleven?"

"Sure." She pulled out the hair tie, her auburn mane framing her face.

Stunningly beautiful.

"How are we going to manage with Ethan?"

"He went to daycare yesterday," Prescott replied. "Turns out, he liked it, so he stayed all day."

Her smile sent a shock of energy through him. "That's great, for both of you. Where do you want to meet?"

"You good working at my place?"

"Sure," she replied. "So, can you do me a favor?"

"I thought I just did you one."

"Yeah, well that was ten minutes ago. I'm already looking for my next one."

He chuffed out a laugh.

"I gotta show you something." She got her phone, toggled through her photos, and tapped on a black German Shepherd puppy.

"He's adorable," Prescott replied.

"My brother and sister-in-law's dog had puppies. I fell in love with him the second I laid eyes on him."

She stilled, as if she'd said too much. Then, she shook her head, as if chasing away a thought.

"The family that was supposed to take him fell through and I'm seriously thinking of getting him. Can you please ask Z what his thoughts are on pets in the condo?"

Prescott admired Jacqueline. She was a feisty, independent, confident and competent woman. He didn't think she was intimidated by Z.

"I'm happy to ask him, but why don't you?"

"He doesn't know I'm staying here," she explained. "Addison called me to let me know she was skipping town and to thank me for taking this case. When I told her I needed a place to stay, she told me the condo was empty and gave me the code."

"I'm still not tracking... why don't you want Z to know you're here?"

"In addition to the condo code, there's a building code, which I didn't have and Addison had forgotten to give it to me, so I called her. Rather than call her dad, she put Hawk on the phone with the security guard. He pretended to be Z and gave the guard permission—"

"The guard bought that?" Prescott asked. "You can't stay here. It's not safe enough."

Hairs on the back of her neck prickled. She hated having to look over her shoulder, hated wondering if the killer was still out there, but she hated living in constant fear too, so she squared her shoulders and forced it out.

"I *was* safe until you barged in at four in the morning and almost got shot," she pushed back. "Please just check with him."

Prescott was at a crossroads. He could talk to Z or he could nudge her in the right direction. If she lived in his house, he could ensure her safety... and see her every single day.

"I don't have to ask him," Prescott began. "He'd never allow a dog, especially one that sheds as much as a shepherd. I'm not sure, but he might be allergic."

"Damn."

"You can't leave a puppy all alone in a condo all day," Prescott said.

"Well, I wouldn't. I'd come home—"

"You and the pup should move in with us."

Her eyes widened. "I can't move into your home. You have Ethan. That would be confusing for him. And what about the puppy? He'd get attached to it. The puppy would get attached to Ethan."

He fully expected her pushback.

"I've got master suites on all three floors. I was sleeping on the first floor, but I moved upstairs to be closer to Ethan. You can take the first floor."

"I'm not sure my moving in, with a puppy who's not potty trained—"

"Ah, hell, you definitely have to move in. If Ethan sees you training the dog, maybe it'll motivate him to do his business in the toilet."

She smiled. "You sound desperate."

"If anyone knows how desperate I am, it's you." He dipped down and kissed her, then dropped another kiss on her bare shoulder.

"I'll give it some thought." She leaned up, kissed him back. "That kiss is from Jack because Jacqueline still can't stand you." Biting back a smile, she opened the front door.

He stepped into the hall. "Gotta say, I love the way you hate me."

So, do I, Prescott Armstrong. So, do I.

Jacqueline

AFTER SHUTTING and bolting the door, she walked into the living room. As she stared through the picture windows into the dark night, she thought about Prescott.

I shouldn't be feeling this way. He derailed my career.

Despite the war raging within, she was falling in love with him. Even if she fought herself every step of the way, she'd still fall.

Jacqueline knew herself well enough to know how she felt. And she couldn't even hate herself for feeling that way. Being with Prescott Armstrong was the absolute *best* thing that had ever happened to her.

14

UNEARTHING THE PAST

Jacqueline

As Jacqueline rang the doorbell, a kaleidoscope of butterflies zoomed around her stomach. She couldn't wait to see Prescott, but she was dreading working with him. Their history was so divergent it was hard to reconcile that Mac and Prescott were the same person.

When he opened the front door, a zing of attraction skittered through her. Dressed in a white dress shirt and dark blue dress pants, he held a tie in his hand.

Swinging the door wide, he said, "C'mon in. I just got back."

She followed him into the kitchen. A handful of toys were scattered across the family room floor, a laundry basket filled with Ethan's clothes sat nearby, and breakfast dishes waited on the kitchen island.

He offered a sheepish smile. "We had a challenge getting out the door today."

She smiled. "Your house looks like a home. Where are we working?"

"My office. Coffee?" He poured himself a mug.

"I'm good."

He led her down the hall and into a large room with a beautiful walnut desk that looked like it had been made for that space. A dark walnut border ran along the edge of the stately furniture. Behind the desk stood a wall of built-ins. Other than a handful of books and several framed photos, the space was bare.

A guest chair sat in the corner.

"It might be easier if I work beside you." She rolled the spare chair next to his. "In case we need to review the same files."

She pulled out her laptop and eased into the chair. The second he sat beside her, his manly scent filled her lungs.

Delicious.

"After you left, I couldn't sleep, so I worked on the case," she said.

"After I left, I couldn't sleep either."

She patted his thigh. "You had your chance." *Stop touching him and concentrate.* "Like I mentioned the other day, I read through Gloria and Bert's ALPHA missions, then Addison and Hawk's."

He nodded.

"Like Hawk and Addison, Gloria and Bert partnered a lot. Is that common in ALPHA?" she asked.

"Operatives develop work relationships that bleed into missions," Prescott explained. "Sometimes they can choose their partners, but most times Cooper puts together the mission teams."

"Gloria and Bert were both married. Neither spouse was in ALPHA. I couldn't find anything that leads me to think they were having an affair." She tucked her hair behind her ear as her phone started ringing in her handbag.

It was Naomi.

"Sorry, I'll just be a sec." She answered, "Hey, what's up?"

"My neighbor asked if any of our puppies are still available," Naomi said. "I wanted to check with you about Loki."

"I'll take him," Jacqueline blurted.

"Oh, that's great! I'm so happy."

"What have I gotten myself into?" Naomi laughed. "It'll be great. He's so smart."

"But I'm paying you guys for him. There's no way you're gifting him to me."

"No, Jacqueline—"

"Text me the food you feed him. I'll swing by tomorrow and pick him up."

"Love you," Naomi said.

"Love you back." Jacqueline hung up and shifted to Prescott.

Intense eyes were drilling into hers and she melted from the heat of his gaze. "Congrats on the pup. When are you moving in?"

She barked out a laugh. "I am *not* living with you."

"Sorry, babe, but you don't have a choice. You can't live in Z's condo with a dog."

"What about Ethan? He just lost his mom. He just moved in here with you. Then, I move in with a puppy? How is that fair to him?"

Prescott pulled up Ethan's new daycare on his laptop. He was sitting in circle time while the teachers read and acted out a story. He pointed. "There he is, and he looks okay to me."

Pausing, she watched Ethan. He was listening intently, then he started giggling.

Her heart warmed, and she smiled. "He's adorable. Okay, I'll think about it." She shifted in the chair. "Let's get back to work. Initially, I wondered if Gloria and Bert's murders were revenge hits, but then I added Hawk and Addison into the mix and reviewed their files. They partnered on missions pretty much right after Addison started, but their missions never included Gloria or Bert, so I kept digging."

He nodded.

"I started looking into missions where they testified against someone," she continued. "There are dozens, so I'm checking if any of those overlap with Addison or Hawk."

"Hawk only does kill missions."

"What about Addison?" she asked.

"I don't know," he replied. "Did I tell you I witnessed Bert's murder?"

What the hell?

"No."

"That's on me. I've been preoccupied."

"What happened?"

"Dakota Luck and I were on a video chat with Bert when someone broke in, shot him, then slammed down the laptop."

"So, Bert saw him."

"And he knew him."

That would have been helpful to know at the beginning of her investigation, but busting his chops now would benefit no one. So, she opted to move on. "How do you know?"

"He said, 'What the hell are *you* doing here?'"

"I looked for video from when Gloria was gunned down, but couldn't find anything."

"I'll see what I can find."

"I also read through ALPHA employee files to see if anyone had filed a complaint against any of them, but I came up empty there too."

"What about a former employee who's got a grudge?" he asked.

Jacqueline made a note.

"Do you need police reports or autopsy results?"

"I already pulled them," she replied.

They grew silent as they worked side by side. At first, she

was having a hard time focusing. The energy rolling off him was both powerful and distracting.

She wanted to touch him from the moment she entered his home. Run her hand down his arm and appreciate his striated triceps or comb her fingers through his windblown hair. She imagined turning, their eyes would meet, and they'd come together in a tender kiss.

She found herself watching him as he navigated his way around ALPHA's secure site in search of the documents she needed.

As if he felt her gaze, he turned. "You need me?"

Ohgod, yes. So badly.

One sexy wink before he shot her a smile. "Daddy loves to take care of his baby."

She burst out laughing. "I cannot believe you brought that up."

"It was crazy and sexy—"

"And kinda weird," she replied.

"Probably because we didn't know what the hell we were doing."

"That was during my experimental phase."

"That was just last year," he pushed back.

"I have a friend who has a daddy fetish, so we tried it."

"The sex was great," he murmured.

"Sex with us is always great," she blurted.

Stop talking about sex.

"You still into threesomes?"

"Just that one time... the night we met."

He hitched a brow. "A night I'll never forget."

"Is this appropriate business conversation?" she asked as she tried tamping down on her growing desire.

"Hell, no."

She tried to stay focused, but the pull was too strong. She

looked over and her pulse kicked up speed. The intensity in his eyes sent a rush of warmth to her cheeks.

He ran the back of his finger down her cheek. "I love when I make you blush."

She swallowed down a moan before it escaped.

"What are you into now, Jack?"

You, I'm so into you, Mac.

She tapped her fingernail on the keyboard. "Catching a killer," she replied.

Prescott

PRESCOTT'S PHONE RANG.

He was seconds from kissing her. Being around Jack was driving him wild with desire. He couldn't stop staring at her, couldn't squelch the need to touch her. And he sure as hell couldn't stop himself from wanting her.

He pulled his phone from his pocket. It was Dakota.

"Hey, what's happening?" he answered.

"I'm checking in," Dakota said. "How're you doing?"

He flicked his gaze to Jack. "I'm working with Jacqueline."

"I'm here if you need anything," Dakota said. "I know it's last minute, but Providence suggested we get the boys together. Can you and Ethan have dinner with us tonight?"

"Sure. Are you in town?"

"We're doing lockdown at home. I've got round-the-clock armed guards protecting us."

For a man who had little interest in children, suddenly toddlers were the center of his universe. "How old is Graham?"

"Almost four, like Ethan. Have you worked out daycare?"

"We've got a center at Armstrong."

"Providence bought me Glenfiddich 30. We'll open the bottle."

"She must love you a lot," Prescott said.

"Babe, Prescott said you must love me a lot since you bought me the Glenfiddich." Dakota listened, then laughed. "She said she loves me a thousand dollars' worth."

"You spoiled, spoiled man," Prescott said, his gaze falling on Jack.

She was peering at him. No, she was checking him out, her bedroom eyes wandering slowly over his face, his hair, then back into his eyes.

"How 'bout seven?" Dakota asked.

"That'll work."

"If the boys hit it off, you're welcome to leave him for a sleepover. If you need a night, it's yours."

"Thanks, brother. What can I bring?"

"Don't go there. Just you and Ethan. See you tonight."

Dakota hung up, and Prescott swung his gaze to Jacqueline.

"What are you doing tonight?" he asked.

"Having dinner with Addison and her sister."

"Where?"

"Carole Jean's."

"How can Addison go out in public?"

"She's great with disguises. In college, we used to throw sorority parties or go to fraternity parties. Even back then, she was into wearing wigs and playing dress up." She wrapped her fingers around his arm and his pulse kicked up speed. "Do not tell her dad she's going out or he'll—"

"Chill, woman. I won't say a word. Plus, Nicky would never, ever let anything happen to her. He'll be at that restaurant, packin' heat, and making sure she's safe."

Jack sighed. "True love. I'm so happy for her. I adore her and not just because she's my sorority Little." She paused for a beat. "As her Big, I was her mentor, but she ended up being there for me, when I needed support."

"Why's that?" he asked.

On a shudder, she flicked her gaze to her laptop.

"I've been staring at all these files all week," she continued, "and I don't see a connection between Gloria and Bert's murders and the attempt on Hawk and Addison."

He wanted to know what had happened to her during college, but she'd ignored his question. Rather than push for an answer, he got busy searching for the police and autopsy reports.

At five o'clock, he broke the silence. "What time will you be done with dinner, tonight?"

"Maybe nine-thirty."

He opened the Asylum app and made a reservation for ten. Her phone pinged with an incoming message, but she continued working.

"You got an invitation."

After she checked her phone, he couldn't miss the gleam in her eyes. "You're a naughty boy, Mac."

"It's all for you, baby. All. For. You."

Her whisper-soft moan sent a hit of adrenaline through him. She could bring him to his knees by simply existing. He was dying for her, but he would wait this one out. For a power-obsessed man, it was ironic that she held all of it.

The energy shifted, the desire to kiss her, take her into his bed and make her purr with delight, roared through him like a tornado.

"I'll be waiting at the bar," she murmured.

Delayed gratification would make the wait so fucking worth it.

~

Jacqueline

JACQUELINE ENTERED THE BUSY, upscale restaurant and stopped at the maître d' stand.

"Good evening, Miss, and welcome to Carole Jean's."

"I'm meeting Addison—"

"Right this way, please."

The maître d' escorted her to a booth in the back of the Michelin-starred restaurant where a blonde waited. "Enjoy your evening. Your attendant will be over shortly." With a slight bow, he left.

Addison pushed out of the booth.

"I would have walked right by you," Jacqueline murmured as she hugged her close friend.

"That's perfect," Addison replied.

Not only was Addison wearing a blonde wig with bangs, black-framed glasses sat perched on her nose. She was also rocking a goth look. Dark eye makeup, black lips, and a black, flowy dress. On her feet were black boots.

Addison slid into the booth and Jacqueline sat across from her.

"Is Hawk here?" Jacqueline asked.

"Two tables away. He's with a friend, and he's got bodyguards scattered through the restaurant."

Secretly hoping Hawk was having dinner with his brother, Jaqueline glanced over. Her heart dipped when she spotted him with a good-looking man with long, blond hair.

"Who's with him?" Jacqueline asked.

"His close friend, Rebel."

"What happened to your sister?" Jacqueline asked.

"She's running late, so she said we should order."

"I thought she lived in Colorado," Jacqueline said.

"She does, but she's here for an art event."

The server appeared. Addison ordered a glass of white wine, but Jacqueline ordered an iced tea.

"No wine?" Addison asked after the server left.

"I'm going to Asylum later and alcohol makes me sleepy."

Addison regarded her for a long minute. "Are you playing with Mac?"

Just thinking about Mac made her smile. "Yeah, he's so sexy."

Conversation came easy with Addison.

"I know you can't talk about work, here, but I'm really hoping you've made some progress," Addison murmured.

Jacqueline sighed. Everyone wanted results and they wanted it yesterday. "I am, but it's slow."

Addison's shoulders fell. "I was hoping the case could get resolved by my wedding."

"I know, honey, me too."

"Sorry, I'm being a baby. We've hired ThunderStrike, so everyone will be safe."

"Is that a security company?"

Addison nodded. "It's owned by Maverick Hott, a close friend of Jericho's."

The server returned with their drinks, told them about the specials, and took their order.

"How are things working out with Prescott?" Addison asked. "Don't you just love him?"

"*What*? Love him? Why would I love him? I just met the man. I mean, he's okay to work with. He's been helpful, but love? I think that's a bit much."

Addison laughed. "What is up with you? I meant, isn't he a great guy? It's crazy that Hawk and I paired you guys up for the wedding and now you're working together."

Heat blasted her chest. Within seconds, her cheeks warmed and she took a long draw of her cold tea. "Pretty crazy," she murmured.

Addison smiled. "You're crushing on him, aren't you?"

"Totally not," Jacqueline protested.

Addison leaned forward. "I get it. He's sick handsome, super-hot body, and very smart. Hawk's recruited him for some of our missions. The man's a freakin' beast."

Jacqueline could keep her feelings to herself... or she could share them with one of her closest friends in the world.

Tell her.

"I've got it *so* bad for him," Jacqueline admitted.

Addison smiled. "Does he know?"

Jacqueline leaned forward. "He's Mac, my kink partner at Asylum."

Addison's mouth dropped open. "You knew him at the wedding shower?"

"Oh, yeah, and there's more. Do you remember the Winchester cult case?"

"Of course. That's the reason you got transferred."

"More like exiled."

Addison reached across the table and squeezed her hand. "But you're back now."

Jacqueline nodded. "And I'm so happy to be here. Anyway, Prescott was working the case too. When everything went to hell, we had a *very* heated conversation."

"But you were playing together at the club?"

"I never met him during the standoff. I only talked to him on the phone." Jacqueline leaned back. "It was more like I screamed at him and hung up."

"Ouch," Addison said. "Prescott never talked about that, but he wasn't the same after."

"It was intense. Anyway, I can't stand him—well, I couldn't, then our worlds collided."

"That's crazy," Addison said. "Are you guys working together okay?"

"We are now, but sometimes I get a little... um... distracted."

Addison laughed. "You two make absolute sense to me, which is why I put you together in the wedding. Have you met his nephew?"

Jacqueline smiled. "He's adorable."

"I love his long hair. He's a very sweet little boy. How's he doing?"

"He's become very attached to Prescott, and Prescott to him."

The server returned with their appetizer, topped off Jacqueline's iced tea, and left.

They dug in.

"So good," Addison said.

The conversation changed to Addison's wedding. Jacqueline was beyond happy that Addison had found her forever person. Addison lit up whenever she mentioned Hawk.

"Speak of the devil," Jacqueline said as Hawk approached the table.

He shot Jacqueline a smile before turning his full attention on Addison. "I couldn't help but notice you sitting back here," he said. "I was curious what you look like, so I thought I'd stop by."

Addison offered a little smile, but her eyes blazed with light. "Like what you see?"

"Hell, yeah. I'd love to see you later, if you don't have plans."

She stared into his eyes for an extra beat, then said, "No plans. In fact, I grabbed a ride here. Maybe I could bum one from you when I leave?"

"I'm all in, baby." He shot her a smile, then headed back to his booth.

A couple was being escorted to a table nearby. Jacqueline glanced over, then did a double take.

"Ohmygod," she murmured. "That's my sister."

Moving slowly, Addison peeked over her shoulder. "The blonde in the full-length fur?"

"Yes." Jacqueline flicked her gaze to Addison, then peered over. Her sister was sitting with her back to her, but the man sat facing in her direction. Tanned, in his fifties or sixties with short, graying hair, he wore a dark suit and bright pink tie.

"That's Leslie?" Addison whispered.

"Yes," Jacqueline murmured. "Who wears a fur coat in May?"

"Someone who wants to show it off," Addison replied.

"When did she go blonde?"

"Since I've been gone." Jacqueline bit into a stuffed mushroom cap. "She just moved into a million-dollar house in Reston."

Addison's eyebrows jumped into her forehead. "I thought she was working retail."

"She's an Instagram model," Jaqueline replied.

"Who's the man she's with?"

"No idea. A different guy is staying at her house."

"Should we go over and say hi?" Addison asked.

"God, no. She's become completely self-obsessed. She's even got the guy she's with taking pictures of her."

Addison glanced over as the server returned with their entrées. "Plates are hot, so be careful," he said. "Can I get you another wine?"

"I'm good, thanks," Addison replied. "There are two men two booths down behind me. One has short, dark hair and the other, long, blond hair."

The server glanced over. "I see 'em."

"Is that one of your tables?" Addison asked.

"Sure is. You want me to send them a drink from you?"

"I'll take their check," Addison said.

"Wow, that's nice," he replied.

After the server left, the women dug into their dinners.

"I want to tell you something," Addison said.

"Okay." Jaqueline pierced the salmon with her fork and slid a small piece into her mouth.

"It's about the Campus Killer."

Jacqueline's stomach dropped.

"But I don't want to upset you."

"I can handle it."

"Janey's remains were found."

Jacqueline's heart broke while a shiver skirted through her. "Tell me what you know."

"Hikers spotted remains off a less-traveled trail at Cascade Falls," Addison explained.

"Aren't the falls, like, ten or twenty miles from campus?"

"Yeah."

"How'd you find out?" Jacqueline stabbed at an asparagus stalk.

Addison leaned forward. "I check for updates."

"I do too, but I didn't see that."

"The results came in yesterday." Addison studied her for a split second. "Are you okay?"

Trembling, she'd broken out in a cold sweat.

Tell her the truth.

"I wonder if he's still out there, and I'm paranoid he'll find me."

Pain flashed in Addison's eyes. "I'm so sorry. She reached across the table and held Jacqueline's hand. "Ohgod, you're shaking. I shouldn't have told you."

"I would have found out on my own. It's better that we're together." Jacqueline wanted to scream, she wanted to curl into a ball and sob for hours, but she had to keep herself together. "How was she murdered?"

"Inconclusive. They found her skull and a few bones."

A shot of adrenaline pounded through her, then a wave of nausea.

Addison slid her water goblet over. "Drink this."

Jacqueline sipped, but her guts were in knots. "Thank you for telling me. I don't want to talk—"

"I know," Addison soothed. "Not another word about it."

Needing a distraction, Jacqueline glanced over at her sister.

Leslie's date set a small box on the table in front of her. After opening it, she pulled out a diamond necklace. Then, she pushed out of the booth, kissed him, and sat back down. As soon as she clasped on the necklace, she started snapping selfies.

Addison glanced over. "What's going on with her?"

"Sorry, my sister is posing for more pics," Jacqueline explained. "She's changed a lot over the past several months and I miss the old Leslie."

"People change, right?" Addison's phone buzzed. "Damn, Brit can't make it."

"I was looking forward to seeing your sister. How's she doing?"

"Good. She's been busy with her art. You guys can catch up at the wedding."

Jacqueline poked at the remainder of her salmon, but she couldn't eat any more. Thinking about Janey unearthed the worst time in her life. While she'd never expected that her sorority sister had survived the kidnapping, she was still devastated by the news.

In Jacqueline's dreams, Janey was alive and happy, and living her best life. Her heart ached for the loss of her close friend, but the anger she kept in check over the monster who killed her burbled to the surface.

When they finished, the server returned and they settled up. Addison paid for Hawk and Rebel's meal, then they made their way toward the front of the restaurant. As they passed Leslie, Jacqueline glanced over. While she should stop and say hello to her sister, she couldn't bring herself to do it.

Her thoughts were too focused on Janey... and on what could have been her own fate.

Outside, darkness surrounded them. Within seconds, Hawk and his friend pulled up alongside them.

After introducing Jacqueline to Rebel, they walked her to her ALPHA SUV.

"Glad to see you're in a fleet vehicle," Hawk said.

"Prescott put me in it," she replied before hugging Addison. "Love you, sis."

"Love you more," Addison replied.

"Hey, I'm just curious," Jacqueline said. "Is your dad allergic to dogs?"

"Not that I know of," Addison replied. "Why?"

"I was thinking of getting one and I was concerned about the shedding."

"Do you want me to ask him?" Addison asked.

"That's okay. I might be moving out anyway."

"Prescott mentioned you're getting a puppy," Hawk offered.

"Do you talk to your brother a lot?" Jacqueline asked.

"Every day." As Hawk clasped Addison's hand, he winked at her.

He knows.

As she drove to Asylum, she thought about Janey. Within seconds, the fear crept back in, then the guilt. Her normal pattern of behavior was to redirect her thoughts to work. When she did that, Prescott's handsome face and rock-hard body jumped to the forefront. If Z found out they'd hooked up, he'd ship her ass back to San Fran.

I'm not going back. I love it here and I want to stay.

Then, prove it by solving the damn case.

15

ASYLUM

Prescott

Prescott tipped the Glenfiddich whiskey into his mouth. After savoring the luxury liquor, he swallowed it down. "This is fantastic."

He and Dakota were relaxing in the Luck's screened-in porch while Ethan and Graham played nearby. The guys had helped them set up a very large track so they could run the toddler-sized vehicles across them. Prescott was relieved that the boys had taken so quickly to each other.

"You can play with that," Graham said. "That's my favorite."

Ethan held it out. "It's okay. I can play with this one." He handed Graham the yellow truck and picked up the red one.

Graham began zooming it around.

"Gray-Gray," Dakota said, "what do you say to Ethan?"

"Thank you!"

Providence entered the room, their daughter, Sammy by her side. "Daddy, can I have a sleepover too?"

Dakota glanced at Providence. "What does Mom say?"

"Mom says the more the merrier," Providence replied with a smile.

"How many friends?" Dakota asked.

"Just one," his daughter answered.

"That's fine, honey."

With a grin, she scampered inside. Providence curled up on the sofa next to Dakota, then eyed the toddlers.

"Fast friends," Providence said.

"They're doing great," Prescott agreed.

"How are you handling insta-parenting?" Dakota asked.

"Minute by minute." Prescott sipped the whiskey.

"Our conversations have always been shop talk," Dakota said. "Tonight, it's been all about the boys."

Providence took Dakota's lowball glass, sipped the whiskey. "There's more to life than work. You've got more in common, now." She handed Dakota back the drink.

"I've got two BLACK OPS missions I want to run by you," Dakota said before tossing back a mouthful of liquor.

Providence chuckled. "And we're back to work."

"You know I *declined* your job offer," Prescott replied.

"This group is *perfect* for you," Dakota pushed.

"I don't want to be responsible—"

"Thank you for *not* talking shop within earshot of the boys." Providence patted her husband's thigh.

"I gotta listen to my *real* boss," Dakota said with a smile. "Have you taken your yacht out this season?"

"A few times," Prescott replied.

"That might be fun for you and Ethan to do together," Dakota added.

"I can't take him boating alone," Prescott said. "For a little thing, he's so damn fast. One minute he's playing in the family room, the next, he's upstairs in his bedroom."

"We've always got eyes on Gray," Dakota said. "Sammy's easier now—"

"My mama-bear radar is always on," Providence added.
Prescott sipped the Glenfiddich. "I wanted to let you know that Ethan isn't fully potty trained. He's got the peeing down, but he likes to do his business in his diaper, then swap it out for a clean one."

"We just finished the pooping phase with Graham," Providence said, "but he wears a pull-on diaper at night."

Prescott started laughing. "I can't believe I'm even having this conversation."

"I admire what you're doing," Providence said. "You had options."

"I considered giving him up for adoption, but I couldn't do it. He lost his dad when he was a baby, now his mom. He was just getting comfortable with me and my family, especially my mom and dad. I couldn't send him away. I'm ruthless enough. I couldn't add abandoning him to my long list of atrocities."

"Mommy," Graham called out, "can me and Ethan watch a movie?"

"Sure," Providence replied. "Do you want to put your jammies on and we'll get out sleeping bags?"

"Hurray!" Graham exclaimed. "A sleepover!"

Ethan beelined over to Prescott. "Are we staying here?"

"You can stay here with Graham tonight and I'll pick you up in the morning."

Graham pulled up alongside Ethan. "We get to watch a movie and sleep in bags. In the morning, we have pancakes with sayrup!"

"I don't know that," Ethan replied.

"Syrup," Providence translated.

"It's sugar, buddy," Prescott said.

"Hurray!" Ethan jumped up and down. "I love sugar!"

Prescott finished his glass of Glenfiddich, thanked Providence and Dakota for a fun evening.

"I'll walk you out," Dakota said.

Prescott hugged Providence, offered a high-five to Graham, then ran a hand across Ethan's back. "Hey, bud, you have fun with Graham, okay. I'll see you in the morning."

Ethan wrapped his arms around Prescott's legs, so Prescott lifted him up and hugged him.

Once outside, Dakota asked, "Where you headed on your night off?"

"Meeting a friend for a drink at Asylum."

"Rebel's club?" Dakota asked.

"Yeah."

Dakota smiled. "I met Providence at Stryker's old club."

"The Dungeon?"

"Yeah, and it was intense." He smiled at the thought. "She was there spying on me. Nothing like sleeping with the enemy."

Prescott chuffed out a laugh. "Looks like it all worked out for you."

"Better than I could've imagined." He slapped Prescott on the back. "Once things get back to normal for you, we'll talk about these missions."

"Thanks for dinner and for keeping Ethan. I'll swing by tomorrow around ten."

"Or later, if you end up having a sleepover of your own," Dakota replied.

As Prescott headed toward his truck, parked at the curb, Ethan came bolting down the driveway.

"No!" he wailed, then burst into tears.

Dakota swept him into his arms. "What's wrong, Ethan?"

Providence and Graham hurried outside.

Prescott strode up the driveway. Ethan held out his arms, and Prescott took him from Dakota.

Ethan flung his small arms around Prescott's neck. "Are you leaving me like Mommy?"

A thousand knives stabbed his heart. "Of course not, Ethan.

We're a team. You're having a sleepover with your new friend, Graham, and I'm going home."

"My mommy went to the store, but she didn't come back." Tears filled his eyes and he started sobbing all over again.

Prescott hugged him. "I'm not leaving you, Ethan. I promise. How 'bout we go home and you can have a sleepover with Graham another time?"

Ethan nodded. "Okay," he said after he stopped crying.

"Why don't you say goodbye to Graham, then we'll grab your bag?"

"I'll get it." Providence said, and retreated into the house.

Prescott put Ethan down.

Graham hugged him. "It's okay that you don't want to stay. We can play at your house next time so you can be with your daddy."

Prescott's eyes blurred with tears. Unexpected and sudden, he couldn't stop the emotion that constricted his throat. Dakota nodded, a silent bond between two savage men whose hearts had been softened by the strong bonds of family.

Prescott cleared his throat. "That's a great idea, Graham."

Providence returned with Ethan's diaper bag.

Graham slipped his hand into Dakota's. "Bye, Ethan. Bye, Uncle Prescott."

Prescott tossed Dakota and Providence a nod. "Thanks again for dinner. I'll talk to you next week."

"Good luck with the case," Providence said. "Work fast. I've got a team on hold until they get cleared to work."

"We're doing our best," Prescott replied.

On the ride home, Ethan was a complete chatterbox, his meltdown long forgotten.

While Prescott gave him a bath, Ethan peered up. "Will you leave me like my mommy did?"

His heart clenched.

"No, Ethan, I'm not leaving you," Prescott said. "I promise. It's you and me, buddy."

"Graham said you're my daddy. Are you my daddy?"

Prescott grew quiet, unsure how to proceed.

In silence, he dried him off, then helped him into his pull-on diaper and jammies, all while ruminating his answer. He set the hair dryer on low and dried Ethan's hair.

Then, he lifted him into his arms and brought him back down to the family room. Together, they sat on the sofa. This was such a big moment. Ethan was looking for safety and security. He wanted to know that Prescott would be there, day in and day out.

An unexpected calmness washed over him.

"Ethan, I'm not going to leave you, but I know it feels like I was going to tonight."

Ethan climbed into his lap and snuggled close.

"Are you my daddy?" he asked again, before slipping his thumb into his mouth.

Prescott's lips tugged up in a smile. Ethan was a smart little boy who wanted an answer to his question. He was also persistent, just like his uncle.

"Right now, I'm your Uncle Prescott. I would have to adopt you in order to become your daddy."

"Okay, we can do that tomorrow."

Prescott's heart was so full. "It takes a while for that to happen. Would you like me to be your daddy?"

"Uh-huh. I never had a daddy."

Prescott kissed the top of Ethan's freshly washed hair. The soft strands tickled his nose, while the smell of baby shampoo wafted in his direction.

"I'll think about it, how's that?" Prescott asked.

"Okay," Ethan replied before slipping his thumb back into his mouth.

Jacqueline

AT TEN-FIFTEEN, Mac hadn't arrived, but Jacqueline was enjoying Asylum's chill vibe while nursing her tonic water at a two-person high top near the bar.

When she first got there, she moseyed around the main floor, pausing in some of the exhibition rooms to watch the scenes. A rope bondage scene played out in one room, a role-playing scene in another, a daddy scene in a third. Room after room was filled with hedonistic delights. Intense scenes that captured her full attention while he body thrummed from the carnal lust.

Jacqueline hadn't always been so open about sex. In college, she'd been somewhat of a prude. Though she did date, and had two boyfriends, neither relationship lasted long.

Then, during fall semester, her junior year, her life had gone off the rails. After that, she'd just tried to stay focused so she could graduate. Instead of applying at the FBI, she went to grad school, living at home with her parents. Being there helped her feel safe, something she desperately needed.

After earning her Master's, she applied at the Bureau. Having worked there as a student intern every summer, she had no trouble getting a job offer. And she threw herself into her new career. Too much downtime sent her mind wandering to terrifying places, and she'd become unhinged.

Tonight, talking with Addison about Janey had ratcheted up the fear and the guilt, but she'd forced herself to go to the club instead of hiding out in Z's condo.

"Excuse me," said a man. "Is this seat taken?"

"Go ahead," she replied.

Rather than drag the chair to a different high top, he joined her. She didn't feel obligated to make small talk and glanced toward the door, hoping a strikingly handsome, hard-muscled man would breeze through.

"You here alone?" the stranger asked.

"I'm meeting someone." She checked her phone.

"Someone special?" he asked.

Very special.

"I'm not available."

"No worries," he replied. "I'm waiting on someone myself. I haven't seen you here before and I've been a member for a while."

Feeling no obligation to answer him, she sipped the tonic water. A few seconds passed and he started up again, only this time, he leaned closer. "Whatcha into?"

"The guy I'm meeting."

"Threesomes are the best, the rope scenes are dope. I like bondage." His lips split into a creepy smile. "When I tie 'em up, I've got all the control—"

"Get lost," she said cutting him off.

"Whoa, honey, you don't need to cop a 'tude. You wanna head back to some of the exhibition rooms and watch with me for a while?"

Jacqueline ignored him.

She hated giving up her table. From her perch, she had a clear line of sight to the front door, but she couldn't take another second of this guy.

"You're really hot," he said.

"You're harassing the hell out of me." She glanced around for a server. She needed to speak with the manager. Enough was enough.

Another man sidled over.

Whoa, what's he doing here?

Her sister's housemate, Lou, tossed her a nod. "Hey, I thought that was you. Jacqueline, right?"

Same black knit cap, his long hair trailing down his back.

Instead of wearing a T-shirt and jeans, he'd dressed in a button-down and black pants.

She wasn't interested in hanging with him either. "Hey, Lou."

"I heard you tell this guy to beat it," Lou said.

"We're good," the stranger said.

"The lady asked you to go. Why are you still here?" The man didn't move.

Lou got in his face. "Leave her alone, or I'll turn your face into dog meat."

The stranger narrowed his eyes, then his shoulders slumped. He abandoned his seat and moved into the crowd.

Lou set down his beer, but he didn't sit. Instead, he stood across the small table. "You okay?"

"Yeah," she replied, glancing over at the door.

Dammit, Prescott, where are you?

"Dudes like that are an embarrassment for the rest of us, who are trying to do the right thing."

"I appreciate the save, but I had this."

"I've got three younger sisters and I was always watching out for them," Lou continued. "You gotta be careful being by yourself. Sorry to be lecturing, but you can never be too safe. That's what I always told my sisters."

"What are you doing here?" she asked.

"Chillin' with my band, but they left."

"Where's Leslie?" she asked, knowing full well that her sister was having dinner with another man.

"She's got a work thing," Lou replied.

Didn't look like work to me.

Her phone buzzed with a text from Prescott. "Ethan had a meltdown and I couldn't leave him. Sorry! Call you later."

She collected her small purse. "I'm outta here."

"Are you by yourself?"

"I was meeting someone."

He chugged the beer. "I'll walk you out."

"I'm good."

"You do *not* want to run into that stalker in the parking lot," he said. "I don't even want to think about what could happen to you."

A shiver flew down her spine.

Outside, the evening breeze cooled her heated skin.

As she walked toward the SUV, he said, "I bummed a ride from my lead singer. Any chance you can drop me at your sister's?"

Her heart slammed against her ribcage. She would never give a stranger a ride.

"I thought *you* sang lead."

"We both do. Depends on the song."

She slowed at the SUV. "See ya."

"Can I grab a ride from you?"

"No." Owing him no explanation, she got behind the wheel, locked the doors, and drove out.

As she headed toward home, she scolded herself for hooking up with Prescott. *Get your career back on track and stop sleeping with him.*

Once she was back at the condo, her phone rang. It was Prescott.

"Hey," she answered.

"I'm sorry," he murmured. "This is the first chance I've had to call you—"

"Don't worry about it. It's probably a good thing. We work together, so we gotta keep things chill."

"Ethan lost it, and it was heartbreaking."

"What happened?"

"We went to Dakota and Providence's for dinner. Ethan and their son, Graham, hit it off great. They were excited for a sleepover, until it was time for me to leave. Ethan was panicked I wasn't coming back, like his mom."

Jacqueline's heart squeezed. She couldn't imagine the fear and uncertainty Ethan must be feeling. "You did the right thing."

"We came home, but he wouldn't even sleep in his crib. He fell asleep on my lap while I was reading to him."

"Where is he now?"

"With me on the sofa. Every time I move, he wakes up. The reality of everything has sunk in, and he's scared."

"I would have felt awful if you'd left him there for me."

"I was looking forward to seeing you tonight, and *not* just because we were getting together at the club."

She melted from his romantic words.

Me, too... so much.

"Addison knows about us, so does Hawk," she said.

"I didn't tell him," Prescott said. "He figured it out."

"Z cannot find out. Being brought back here—being singled out by Z—is my chance to get my career back on track."

"Come over tomorrow and catch me up on your progress with the case."

"I'll have the puppy with me."

"Well, you gotta come over. Ethan would love that."

"What about you? Would you love that?"

"I'm much more interested in the puppy's mama."

She smiled. "See you tomorrow."

"Thanks for not being angry with me, Jack."

"You did the right thing."

"Sweet dreams," he said before the line went dead.

If you're in them, they'll be sweet.

16

COINCIDENCES

Prescott

Late morning, Prescott tossed the blue bouncy ball to Ethan in the front yard. He caught it, then dropped it, and kicked it. Within seconds, they were playing a simple game of soccer, with Prescott making sure that Ethan got a lot of contact with the ball.

"You're fast," Prescott said.

When they finished playing, Prescott asked if Ethan played any sports.

"I can't know," Ethan replied.

Seconds later, Prescott pulled up a video of toddlers playing soccer. "Have you ever played soccer like this?"

"Nuh-uh," Ethan replied. "Can I do that?"

"After lunch, I'll check into soccer clubs for you."

"Do you play too?"

"It's just for kids."

"Do you leave?"

Prescott knelt. "No. I stay and watch you play."

Ethan stared at him for an extra second, then said, "Okay, that looks fun."

They went inside, and Ethan ran into the family room to play. Within minutes, Prescott made two turkey and cheese sandwiches, then he sliced up an apple and cut a carrot into narrow slices.

They ate together on the back porch. "Can I play in the water?" Ethan asked as he eyed the covered swimming pool.

"Only with me," Prescott explained.

"Why?"

"For safety," he replied.

"Why?"

"You ask a lot of questions, you know that?"

"Uh-huh."

"You can *only* get in the swimming pool with me," Prescott reiterated.

"Okay," Ethan quieted down and ate his sandwich.

Prescott's phone rang. Z was calling. "Ethan's with me," he answered. "I'll call you back."

"It's important," Z replied.

"Yeah, I figured that out on my own. I'm smart like that." Prescott hung up.

Ethan finished his sandwich, ate one carrot slice and started to get down.

"Where you going?" Prescott asked.

"To play."

"What do you think about asking if you can be excused?" Prescott asked.

"Why?"

"It's polite."

Ethan peered over at him.

"It's the nice thing to do," Prescott explained.

"Okay, can I pleeeeeeease be accused?"

"Thank you, Ethan. Go for it."

He scampered down and trotted into the family room. Prescott called Z back from the kitchen, where he could keep an eye on Ethan.

"Hey," Z answered. "How's Ethan doing?"

"He's resilient," Prescott replied. "He's concerned I'm going to leave him, but that's understandable."

"I've got two updates," Z began. "A body washed up on the Rappahannock river bank, about twenty miles from where Terrence Maul hit the water."

"And?"

"Vultures got to it pretty good. It was headless, so a dive team will be searching for the skull in the next day or two. The remains are being confirmed by DNA."

"That's Maul."

"You're sure you hit him?"

"For fuck's sake, Philip," Prescott bit out. "I had on my night goggles. I saw him fall in the river."

Ethan appeared with a toy train in his hand. "What is night goggles?"

"Z, hold on," Prescott said. "Ethan, can you remember that question and I'll answer it when I finish talking?"

With the toy in hand, he toddled back into the family room.

"It's like I'm living with a spy," Prescott murmured, while cupping his hand over his mouth to block the sound.

Z chuckled. "He's easy now. Wait until he turns into a teenager and grows horns."

Prescott couldn't jump that far ahead. His current project—soccer for toddlers—was as far into the future as he could go.

"You there?" Z asked.

"I'm here," Prescott replied, returning to the present.

"Until we get DNA confirmation, watch your six."

"Always do," Prescott replied. "As far as I'm concerned, I eliminated my target."

"I'll let you know when the results come back."

"What else?"

"There was an assassination attempt on Luther Warschak."

"Fuck," Prescott bit out. "Is he okay?"

"He wasn't hit, but he was shaken up pretty good."

Years earlier, Luther and Z had started ALPHA. Though Z continued to pluck certain Ops for his own projects, Luther passed the reins of the top-secret organization to Dakota and Providence. When Dakota moved on to BLACK OPS, Cooper Grant stepped up to run ALPHA with Providence.

"Specs?" Prescott asked.

"Luther was getting into his car after a tennis game at his club. This was more of a sniper attempt, like with Addison and Nicholas."

"Any surveillance?"

"Only of Luther ducking into his car as a bullet pierced his ALPHA SUV."

"I'll see if there's video of the shooter." Prescott watched Ethan knock down his tower and start laughing. "Where's Luther now?"

"Secret Service escorted him and his wife out of town in the middle of the night, and I'm about to board a plane myself."

"Are you leaving the country?" Prescott asked.

"I'm going to Bali, or as Addison says, 'Bali baby!'" He chuckled. "But it's no vacation. I'll be working and surrounded by too much security. What progress have you and Jacqueline made?"

"It's slower than we'd like."

"I uploaded the video of the assassination attempt on Luther. Review it with her."

"Speaking of Jacqueline—you had her escorted back here by four Secret Service agents. Why so many?"

"Two escorted her," Z explained. "Two needed to fly back, so they tagged along. Why?"

"Addison gave her permission to stay in your condo, and I'm concerned it's not secure enough."

"It's plenty safe," Z pushed back.

"Well, Nicky impersonated you to get her into the building. The guard gave her access no problem."

"Hmm, okay, that *is* a concern. What are you thinking?"

"She can move in here. She'd have plenty of privacy, plus I've got a shit-ton of security."

"That's up to her," Z said. "I can't enforce where she lives."

"What if I told you she's getting a puppy?"

"So?"

"Aren't you allergic to dogs?"

Z chuckled. "No, I'm not, but that's irrelevant. I don't live there. If she refuses to move out, I'll have Nicholas install a security system in the condo. How's that?"

"Not fucking good enough," Prescott bit out. "I'll handle it."

"I need you two to put together a profile and find that damn killer," Z snapped before the line went dead.

"Dammit," Prescott hissed. Every Op in ALPHA was counting on him to take out a killer. An assassin hiding in the shadows, planning his next attack.

And he would not fail them.

Jacqueline

EXCITEMENT HAD Jacqueline hurrying inside the pet store. She couldn't believe she was getting a dog. It was something she'd wanted to do for years, but the timing had never been right. While she wasn't convinced the timing was right now, she knew that Loki was the perfect dog for her.

After selecting a collar and leash, she walked down the toy isle and stopped. There was so many to choose from. Six toys later, she headed toward the doggie bedding section. More options awaited her. She selected one that gave Loki room to grow, but was still cozy, then continued to the crate area.

Crate training was an option if she were leaving him at home, but she'd planned on taking him with her as often as she could. Skipping them, she found a portable dog carrier to transport him in the car. At some point, he'd be old enough to ride in the back, but for now, she needed to ensure he stayed in one place.

Naomi had suggested she keep Loki on the same food to avoid any gastro issues. Since the store was out, she checked out, then drove to the grocery store, found the refrigerated puppy food she needed, and loaded up.

While waiting in the self-check-out line, she texted Naomi. "Be there shortly!"

"Jacqueline, is that you?" asked a man behind her.

She turned. Lou stood behind her, a case of beer in his cart.

What the hell?

She glanced around for Leslie, but he was alone.

"I thought that was you," he said. "I keep running into you everywhere."

He was dressed in a T-shirt and pants, the knit cap in place. Black sunglasses shadowed his eyes. "Small world, huh?"

"What brings you out here?" she asked. "There are plenty of stores in Reston that sell beer."

"I'm jammin' with my band this afternoon." He leaned over, eyed her cart.

"You got a dog?"

"I'm getting a puppy." She moved up in line.

"That's great," he continued. "Whatcha getting?"

"A German Shepherd."

"Great breed." He rolled his cart forward. "Leslie and I were talking about you this morning. I told her I ran into you last night. She was sorry she missed you."

Yeah, right.

"What college did you go to?" Lou asked.

Hairs on the back of her neck prickled. *Too many questions.* "Why do you ask?"

"Leslie said you went to Virginia Tech, but I remembered seeing you at Madison when Leslie and I were students there."

Jacqueline regarded him for an extra beat. She had him pegged for being in his forties, but maybe he just looked older or he'd gone to college later. "How long were you there?"

"All four years, like Leslie."

He's lying.

"My sister dropped out after her freshman year."

"Right," he replied. "Settle a bet. Were you at Madison or Tech?"

"What's with the interrogation?"

A grocery clerk, directing shoppers, pointed, and said to Jacqueline, "That one's open."

"See ya," she said to Lou and went to check out.

After loading her bags in the SUV, she glanced around for Lou, but didn't see him. As she drove to her brother's, she thought about him showing up at Asylum. That could have been a coincidence. But popping up again at a grocery store nowhere near Leslie's house made the hair on the back of her neck prickle.

Is he stalking me?

She turned off the main road and into Keith and Naomi's neighborhood. As she pulled down their street, she glanced in her rearview mirror. She was alone.

Am I being paranoid?

Lou was the right age, but he looked nothing like the Campus Killer.

In the driveway, she grabbed the dog carrier and hurried up the walkway. Keith swung the door wide. "Hey, sis, c'mon in. You ready to become a doggy mama?"

"I'm excited," she replied, pushing Lou from her thoughts.

"I've never had a pet."

"You'll do great. Loki's such a smart dog." Keith led her to the playroom where Loki and his brother were curled up, sleeping. Naomi was sitting nearby, rubbing Cleo's belly.

With a smile, Naomi rose. "Congratulations, sis."

"Thank you. I'm so glad you're keeping his brother," Jacqueline said.

"We can get them together for playdates," Naomi replied.

"So, is Loki the last pup to go?"

"Yes," Naomi replied. "I loved having them—we both did—but it'll be good to get our house back in order."

"Two dogs will be easier to manager than seven, that's for sure," Keith added. "We played with him so he's pretty worn out. When he's ready to burn energy, he's a wild thing." Keith gently picked him up and gave him a little hug. "I'm happy you're taking him."

Naomi patted his head before Keith told Cleo to say goodbye.

Jacqueline's heart stuttered as Cleo sniffed her baby, then licked his coat. Keith slipped him into the carrier, closed the door.

Jacqueline pulled out a check and set it on Naomi's desk.

"Loki is our gift to you," Naomi said.

"I wrote the check for half," Jacqueline explained.

"Thanks," Keith said. "We appreciate it."

"We'll walk you out," Naomi said.

Outside, Keith placed the carrier in the back seat and secured it with the belt. "He's probably going to whine. He's never been separated, but he'll be fine." Keith gave her a hug. "Love you, Jack."

"I'll email you the shots he's gotten," Naomi said. "He'll need a few boosters. I'll include the vet's contact info if you want to use her. She's really good."

"Is she nearby?"

"Just on the other side of Alexandria. Where are you?"

"Arlington, but I might be moving to McLean. Jacqueline climbed in the SUV and lowered the windows. "I'm a dog mama. Is that crazy or what?"

Rather than go home, she headed toward Prescott's.

For the past ten years, she'd been paranoid, with good reason. After running into Lou again, she didn't want to be alone.

Maybe moving into Prescott's house isn't such a bad idea.

Prescott

PRESCOTT FOUND a local soccer club for tots and filled out the enrollment form, read Ethan his favorite dinosaur book, encouraged his nephew to poop in the toilet—even prepped for dinner. Despite being efficient and productive, his thoughts kept wandering to dark places.

If the killer was going after the former head of ALPHA, no one was safe. He and Jack needed to step up their efforts. The frustration he carried around on a daily basis had morphed into full-blown agitation.

Fucking find him before he kills again.

"Someone is outside," Ethan called out. "The bell rang."

Ethan stood in the foyer, pointing at the front door.

"Ethan, you're very smart for not opening the door." He whisked him into his arms. "Let's check who's outside."

"Computer, who's out front?" Prescott asked.

"Jacqueline Hartley," the computer replied.

Ethan looked around. "Who talks?"

"That's my computer."

Prescott swung open the door and his heart kicked up

speed. Jack stood there looking smokin' hot in a dark, red shirt and torn jeans, her hair in a ponytail. That familiar hit of adrenaline spiked through him, easing his anger.

Her eyes softened. It was subtle, and it was over too soon, but he caught it. Was he having the same intense effect on her that she was having on him?

"Hi," she said. "Am I too early?"

The puppy barked. Prescott eyed the dog carrier at her feet.

Ethan gasped. "Do you have a dog?"

"Are we doing the right thing?" she asked.

"Absolutely," he replied. "Come on in."

Again, the puppy barked.

When Ethan's face exploded in joy, Prescott couldn't help but smile.

"Can I see?" Ethan asked.

She carried the carrier across the threshold, and he shut the front door.

"I got a puppy, Ethan. Would you like to meet him?"

A joyous giggle exploded out of him as Prescott set him down.

Ethan knelt in front of the carrier, and the dog barked again. Though Ethan flinched, he shoved his tiny fingers into the cage. "It's okay," he said. "You can come out and play wif me."

Jack gently pulled his fingers out. "He might be afraid, so let's give him a little space, okay?"

"Why don't we take him out back so he can pee?" Prescott suggested.

"Good idea." Jacqueline held out her hand to Ethan. "Would you like to come with me?"

"Okay." Ethan clasped her hand.

She lifted the carrier, then regarded Prescott. "Would you mind bringing in Loki's food? It needs to be refrigerated."

He tossed her a nod, before she and Ethan walked toward the back deck.

Seeing them holding hands touched his soul. They looked like they belonged there, with him, in this large, way-too-quiet house. In that moment, his mind was made up. He didn't want her to leave. He wanted her, and her puppy, to stay.

He stored the dog food in his second refrigerator, located in the mudroom, then joined them on the back patio.

The dog was still in the carrier. Jacqueline had pulled over a lawn chair and was talking to Ethan.

"Why?" Ethan asked.

"He's a baby so we have to teach him not to bite," she explained.

"Okay."

"Are you ready to meet Loki?"

Ethan started jumping up and down, his excitement contagious. Jacqueline opened the door and the black puffball made a beeline for Ethan.

Ethan ran a hand over his fluffy coat. "He's soooo soft. Can I hold him?"

Prescott laughed. "He's almost as big as you are, bud."

Ethan giggled when Loki licked his hand. Next, Loki went over to Jack.

"Hi, Loki," she said. "You're a good boy."

His tail wagged as he made his way to Prescott and started sniffing his bare feet. Prescott petted him before Loki took off into the grass. Ethan followed while Loki sniffed around, then peed.

Prescott eased into a patio chair beside her. He wanted to pull her onto his lap and kiss her, but he needed to take things slowly so he didn't push her away.

"He went pee pee," Ethan announced.

"Good boy, Loki," Jacqueline said before she flicked her gaze to Prescott. "I have no idea what I'm doing."

"You and me, both," he replied. "We'll figure this out, *together*."

The air crackled with chaotic energy, her gaze locked on his. Unable to resist the constant pull, he slipped his hand around the back of her neck and gently massaged. Her eyes fluttered closed and a sigh floated from her. He loved touching her, loved making her happy. He massaged one shoulder, then her other.

When he finished, she peered at him. "I... you... that was—"

He leaned over, kissed her. "I'm good with my hands."

She bit back a smile. "You're okay, but you can practice on me if you want to get better."

As she returned her attention to Ethan and Loki, she pressed her hand on his thigh. That one act said it all. She had this incredible power to lift him from the depths of hell with her touch.

Ethan shrieked, "No!"

The tot was running around the yard, Loki was chasing him and nipping at his hand.

Pushing out of the chair, Jack yelled, "Loki, no! Ethan, stop running."

In seconds, she was by Ethan's side, pulling him in for a hug. When Loki crashed into her, she lost her balance and fell on her butt.

Her laughter was a godsend. Ethan calmed down.

With one arm around Ethan, she stroked Loki, who was panting so hard, his entire body shook. "Easy, Loki," she said before turning to Ethan. "Are you okay?"

"I was scared."

She smiled. "Did he bite you?"

Ethan showed her his fingers. "Uh-huh."

Prescott joined them while Jack examined his small hand, then she kissed his finger. "No blood. Does it hurt?"

"I'm okay."

"He likes playing with you, but I have to teach him not to bite. I'm sorry I didn't do a good job making sure Loki didn't hurt you."

"He's a baby, so we have to teach him!"

She smiled at him. "You're right, Ethan. Do you want to help me bring in his water bowl?"

With Loki in her arms, they walked around to the front, stopping at the SUV. This was Prescott's chance to transition her from Z's condo to his house, so he collected everything.

"What are you doing?" she asked.

"Saving myself another trip."

Though she hitched a brow, she didn't object.

Nice and easy.

Into the house, they went. He put the doggie bed in the corner of the family room and set the bags on the kitchen table.

"We'll put his water bowl in the laundry room." He led her down the hall and into his combined mudroom-laundry room.

"This is larger than my kitchen," she said as he filled the water bowl and placed it on the floor.

She set Loki down and he started lapping up the water.

Ethan stood too close to Loki, so she gently moved him away. Back in the kitchen, she pulled out a toy from one of the bags.

"I should have bought a gate." She offered Loki a toy, then she ran a gentle hand over Ethan's head. "Ethan, if you take Loki's toy, he might bite you, so we have to teach him about sharing too."

"Okay," Ethan said before he followed Loki into the family room.

She turned to Prescott. "This is too much."

Unable to resist, he slipped his arms around her, pulled her close, and kissed her. "It's a lot, but I wouldn't change a thing. Not one damn thing."

She peered into his eyes, then leaned up and kissed him

back. A light brush of her lips against his. "I thought about taking Loki home, but this is fun for Ethan."

"This is fun for *you*," he murmured, kissing her again.

"Wow, you are cocky."

He kissed her again. "I missed you."

"I missed you too," she whispered. "But it's purely lust. You owe me. I'm just here to collect."

His cock moved. "I can't wait."

She shuddered in a breath as her expanding pupils masked her green eyes.

AFTER DINNER, JACK suggested they take Loki for a walk. Strolling through his neighborhood felt foreign to him. He'd never ventured down his street, never even seen the neighbors who lived in the cul-de-sac. Several were outside, and they offered a friendly wave, or said hello.

Despite the laid-back evening, he couldn't shake Z's news. The killer was targeting present *and* past employees.

No one is fucking safe.

He released another growl. *We gotta find the SOB and find him fast.*

Prescott had managed to get Ethan into the bathtub and wash him in record time. "You might not be the cleanest child on the planet, but you aren't the dirtiest."

Big, brown eyes stared up at him.

"Okay, Ethan, show me your muscles," Prescott said with a smile.

Ethan raised his arms, Hercules style, and Prescott gave each of his biceps a gentle squeeze. "Whoa, those are definitely getting bigger. You're becoming such a good eater. I'm proud of you."

An adorable grin filled his face. "Fank you."

With an assist from Prescott, Ethan brushed his teeth, then

Prescott helped him into his jammies. By the time they returned to the first floor, Jack had cleaned up the kitchen.

"You didn't have to do this," he said.

"Loki's passed out," she said. "I'm hoping Ethan is next."

He hitched a brow. "I'll go faster."

But a shadow fell over her eyes. "I need to talk to you about something."

Prescott grabbed a picture book, and he and Ethan got situated in the oversized chair in the family room. When Jack sat on the floor next to the dog bed, Loki crawled into her lap, rested his head on her thigh, and fell back to sleep.

A peace Prescott had never known before settled into his bones. Then, a sense of duty and a determination fueled him from the depths of his soul.

He would do whatever necessary to protect them from harm.

17

PRESCOTT'S PUNISHMENT

Jacqueline

"Can Loki come upstairs so he can see my bedroom?" Ethan asked after Prescott had finished reading to him.

"Sure," Prescott replied. "What about Jack?"

"She can come too," Ethan replied.

Jacqueline smiled. She was relieved that Loki had done so well on his first day with her. And she loved how happy he'd made Ethan.

Her concern was with the achingly beautiful man she'd spent the last few hours with. He was attentive with Ethan and he played with Loki. Beyond the few romantic kisses, she even found him peering in her direction several times throughout the evening. They'd lock eyes and time would stop.

But the divot between his brows was etched deeper than usual and the muscles ticking in his jawline had only gotten worse as the night wore on. There was an undercurrent of agitation that had been rolling off him the entire evening.

With Loki in her arms, she stood. Prescott hoisted Ethan

into his. Side by side, they walked up the winding staircase, each carrying a precious load.

Heading upstairs with her work partner felt like they were crossing a line, but here she was, at the top of the landing. They passed four bedrooms before ducking into a bedroom nearest to the master suite.

"Ethan, how 'bout one more potty?" Prescott asked.

The guys went into the en-suite bathroom.

Ethan's bedroom was a combination of gray walls with white accents. Very adult. She imagined splashes of color on the walls, a toy box in the corner, and a toddler bed instead of a crib.

Ethan exited the bathroom and beelined right for Loki. "Come back and play wif me, tomorrow." He kissed the dog's forehead. The sleepy pup opened his eyes, offered a wag of his tail, and was done for the day.

Prescott lifted Ethan into his crib.

After he lay down, he regarded Jacqueline. "Can you tuck me in like Mommy did?"

So many emotions washed over her. Sadness, hope, love. She was touched by his invitation.

"I'd love to." She handed Loki to Prescott.

After covering Ethan with his blanket, she kissed his forehead. "I'm happy you and Loki became friends today. You did a *great* job with him."

A relaxed smile touched his sleepy eyes. "Will you and Loki come back tomorrow?"

"If I can," she replied. "Thanks for letting me tuck you in. I hope you have a great sleep."

Ethan rolled over and slipped his thumb into his mouth.

After a gentle caress on Ethan's back, Prescott said, "Goodnight, Ethan. I'll be downstairs with Jack, okay?"

"Uh-huh."

Prescott raised the side of the crib and turned out the overhead light, but the nightlight kept the room plenty lit.

Back in the family room, Prescott set Loki in his bed. Like Ethan, he curled up and fell back to sleep. Being alone with Prescott felt like a luxury. But they weren't together, not even dating. It was time to work. They sat side by side at the kitchen island and opened their laptops, their arms brushing against each other.

Touching him was like breathing. Necessary, unavoidable, and automatic.

Heat shot up her arm. The energy that passed between them was palpable. They'd been alone for seconds and her insides were already pulsing with excitement. This went beyond carnal need. An invisible string tugged her heart closer and closer to his.

But the concern in his eyes hadn't gone away, and the muscles in his cheeks had been ticking for far too long.

"Before we get started, I need to know what's going on with you," she began.

"Boy, can you read me." He paused. "Z called with an update."

As she waited, a shadow fell over his eyes.

"The ALPHA Killer tried to take out the former head of ALPHA, Luther Warschak."

"Oh, no. What happened?"

"He was getting into his car at his country club and a bullet pierced his vehicle."

"Is he okay?"

"Yeah. Secret Service took him and his wife to an undisclosed location. Z is headed out of town as well." A growl shot out of him. "I'm so fucking pissed. We've got nothing more than a guy in a hoodie at a gas station."

His growl sent shock waves running rampant through her. He looked down and she followed his gaze. To her surprise, she was stroking his massive thigh, the heat from his leg radiating through his pants.

She removed her hand. "I'm sorry. That's so unprofessional."

His gaze darkened, he shifted on the chair. "Don't stop. I love your touch."

Her fingers trembled as she caressed his thick leg. "Let's get started."

He arched a brow. "I think you already have."

Pausing, she inhaled a calming breath that did absolutely nothing to quell her desire. Just his sitting beside her had turned her ravenous with lust. Forcing down the burgeoning need, she asked him about Luther.

"He and Z started ALPHA years ago," Prescott explained. "About five years in, Z decided to manage missions that were so far off the grid, they weren't even sanctioned by ALPHA."

"What happened to Luther?"

"He retired. Dakota and Providence took over, but Dakota left to head up a BLACK OPS team, so Cooper Grant stepped in to run ALPHA with her. He manages the missions and she runs the organization."

"Did Luther get called to testify against any of the criminals ALPHA caught?"

"I don't know, but I can find out." He called Z. The number was no longer active, so he sent Z a message through ALPHA's secure system.

She dragged her hand off his leg, opened her laptop. "I reviewed the surveillance video when Gloria was gunned down." She logged into ALPHA. "I watched it enough times to feel confident she knew her assailant. The carjacking was a ploy to throw law enforcement off his trail. And yes, Gloria's killer is a male."

She played the video, pausing it when the killer approached Gloria. "It was just after midnight, but the convenience store is open twenty-four-seven. He wanted it to look like a carjacking gone wrong, but they talked before he pulled out his gun and shot her."

Jacqueline played the video. "His face is hidden by the hoodie, and there weren't any cameras on site where I could see his face. Gloria didn't have a dash cam, and there weren't any other customers."

She paused the video.

"He drove in, parked away from the cameras. After he shot her, he took off."

She started the video again. "That's him driving away. I enlarged the screen shot, but he covered the license plate with a deflector."

"What did the store employees tell police?" Prescott asked.

"There were two, and they followed emergency protocol. They locked the front door, called 9-1-1, but they never checked on Gloria. I doubt she would have survived, even if they had. She was hit between the eyes at close range."

"So, both Bert and Gloria knew their killer."

"Yes," she replied. "Can you find me video from Luther Warschak's hit? I've put together a profile—"

"Run it by me," he interjected.

"I thought we'd compare my profile against my suspect list."

The hard lines around his eyes vanished and his sexy, full lips lifted into a smile. A hit of adrenaline surged through her.

"Nice work," he said.

"I haven't been sleeping well, so I thought I'd make good use of my time."

"Why not?" His brows knitting together.

"Later," she said as she dragged her gaze back to her screen.

His phone rang, he answered. "Armstrong." He listened, tapped his phone. "You're on speaker. Jacqueline and I are working—"

"Any progress?" Z interrupted.

"Z, did Luther testify in court against any of the criminals ALPHA arrested?" Jaqueline asked.

"No, never," Z replied.

"That's all I needed," she said.

"Contact me through ALPHA and I'll call you back." The line went dead.

She'd been staring at Prescott, more like gawking, but when Z hung up, she shifted her attention back to her laptop. While she wanted to get lost in him, she had to keep pushing forward. The killer was winning... by a lot.

"Let me read you my profile," she said. "A male between forty and fifty. College degree, possibly a family. Current or former law enforcement. He knows his victims and his victims know him. Since the killer didn't take out Addison, Hawk, and Luther, he's not a sniper, so I'm ruling out special forces with the military."

Prescott nodded.

"I thought he could be a criminal that ALPHA had testified against, but he wouldn't have known Luther was with ALPHA, so that changes my profile. All his targets have been White. Is Luther?"

"No, he's Black."

She scanned her list. "I had twelve suspects, but I'm eliminating one." She turned her laptop toward him. "Do you recognize any of these names?"

Rather than pull the laptop close, he dragged his barstool flush up against hers. His musky, leather scent jumbled her thoughts as she breathed him in. She wanted to bury her face in his neck and get lost in his touch, his kisses, his everything.

The need to bed him was primal and out of her control. She swung her gaze in his direction. The pull so strong, she glanced at his mouth, then studied his profile.

Prescott was the epitome of wealth. He had an aristocratic look that should be shared with the world. Model-like features so beautiful, it pained her to stare at him, yet looking away would hurt more.

Like they'd been chiseled from stone, his cheekbones sat high on his face. A strong Roman nose without a bump or even a blemish. Dark, thick stubble shadowed his tanned cheeks, chin, and upper lip. He had full lips that, when pressed against hers, made him the perfect kisser. Her sigh floated in the air between them.

His light, almond-shaped eyes slid from the page to her, and a gritty growl filled the silence. "Can I help you?" he ground out.

"Most definitely."

"If I kiss you, I won't stop. You'll end up in my bed, beneath me and over me. I will pleasure you until the light of day reminds us that we're hunting down a killer."

All she heard was "in my bed".

She was shaking—more like vibrating—so hard, she couldn't think. All she could so was stare at his face and imagine them together.

Snap out of it. Someone else will die and it'll be all your fault.

He kissed her, the rush of energy leaving her breathless. He never touched her, never slid his tongue inside her mouth. When it ended, he gazed into her eyes.

"Irresistible," he murmured. "As soon as we finish, you are *mine*."

Fueled by the promise of Prescott and his late-night talents, she turned back to her list of suspects. "Do you know any of these people or recognize their names?"

"I know the first three," he replied. "So, you've narrowed it down to ALPHA only."

"And Gloria and Bert's spouses."

"You can cross off Terrence Maul."

"Why?" she asked.

"I killed him."

"Recently or a while ago?"

"Last month," he replied.

A squeaky toy interrupted her thoughts. Loki was awake and ready to play.

"I'll take him out to pee." She whisked him into her arms, kissed his soft fur. "Loki, let's go outside and empty."

She collected the leash and headed for the front door. Prescott was by her side in seconds. Together, they stepped outside.

She walked Loki around the yard, waiting for him to pee. While he did, she said, "Empty, Loki. Good boy." When he finished, she gave him some love.

Back inside, Prescott said, "Computer, alarm the house."

"House alarmed, Prescott," replied the computer.

Jacqueline collected all the squeaky toys that could wake Ethan and put them out of the dog's reach, then she sat on the floor playing tug with a rope toy.

Prescott put on a pot of coffee, before joining her in the family room. Rather than sit on the floor, he eased onto the sofa.

"With Gloria and Bert, it's personal," she said. "He wanted them to see him before he killed them. But with Addison, Hawk, and Luther, he didn't want to reveal himself. He wanted to kill them from a distance. For them, it wasn't personal. From a profiling perspective, they don't mesh, but maybe he couldn't get near them."

"We can split the list up and do a deeper dive," he said. "Of your list of eleven—now ten because Maul's dead—there are five who are former ALPHA Ops, three who are current employees, and Gloria and Bert's spouses."

They returned to the kitchen. Prescott held up the coffeepot. "Can I fill you up?"

She stifled a moan. *With you.*

"Do you have unsweetened almond milk?" she asked.

"I've got two percent milk for Ethan."

"Black is fine."

He filled two mugs, sat beside her.

She sipped the hot drink. "I'll do a deep dive on Gloria and Bert's spouses."

"I'll take the three current Ops," he offered. "Bert told us his wife was visiting her sister in Florida the night he was killed."

"That'll be easy to confirm," she replied.

The minutes ticked into hours. It was almost three-thirty in the morning when she pushed off the stool. Loki was out cold, on his back, in his doggy bed. *So adorable.* He was going to be a handful, but she was up for the challenge.

She turned toward Prescott. "Bathroom?"

"There's one next to the mudroom and one in the foyer."

On her way toward the mudroom, she admired his beautiful home.

While it was way past her bedtime, she wasn't tired. Being around Prescott energized her. Research was just that. It was time consuming and oftentimes laborious. Yes, she loved her job, but some aspects were a means to an end.

But around Prescott, the mundane was thrilling. Even while working, there was strength in his actions. At one point, she'd stopped working to watch him. Everything he did was purposeful and exacting.

She found Prescott lying on the family room floor. Loki was trotting back to him, a ball in his mouth. He dropped it, Prescott rolled it across the floor, and the pup bounded after it.

"Thanks for riling my dog before I leave."

He chuffed out a laugh. "He's the one who riled *me*, and *you're* not going anywhere."

Prescott

JACK EASED onto the floor across the room from him. If she'd been any farther away, she'd be in the kitchen. While they'd been working together, he had to force himself to concentrate. She smelled so damn good. A mix of coconut and her own baseline scent. She was an unassuming woman he found both intoxicating and addictive.

He was tired, but energized. Being on call with Ethan was something he was getting used to, but being around Jack was all adrenaline.

He rolled the ball to her and Loki bounded after it, then she rolled it back to him. The game of keep-away was fun until Loki started barking. He got the ball out of necessity. If Ethan woke, their adult party for two—that he was determined to launch—would never get off the ground.

Despite his aching balls, he would keep his promise and take good care of her. At least one of them would be satisfied.

"I ruled out the three current Ops," Prescott said breaking the silence.

"Already?" She ran her fingers through her hair and his gaze jumped to her breasts as they lifted inside her shirt.

She bit back a smile. He was so busted.

"ALPHA Ops have tracking chips in their necks," he explained.

"Seriously?" she asked.

"Yeah, it's for their protection. If they're kidnapped—which has happened—those trackers can save their lives. All three Ops were at home on the night Bert was killed. Two were home when Gloria was gunned down. The third was out of town."

"What about pay-for-hire?"

He shook his head. "We can circle back to them, if none of the others you profiled pan out."

Loki dropped the ball in front of Prescott. He pulled the dog into his lap.

"How 'bout you?" She scooted closer toward him. "Do you have a tracker in your neck?"

"No. I'm a lone wolf."

Loki hopped off him and trotted over to her. Her smile touched her eyes, and Prescott paused to soak up her beauty.

"Here comes my boy," she said.

Loki plopped down next to her, lifted his leg, and started cleaning himself.

Prescott chuffed out a laugh.

"Thanks, Loki," she said. "Just what I needed to see."

"He's showing you how comfortable he is around you," Prescott said.

"Well, if you start licking *your* balls, I'll know you're about to propose."

Again, he laughed. "If I start licking my balls, we've got much bigger problems on our hands."

"There would be no *we*," she replied. "I'd be outta here in seconds."

"All that ball licking sounds like something I'd want *you* to do."

"Last I checked, I don't have any balls."

"To me, Jack. Do. That. To. Me."

The energy shifted, her gaze darkened, her lips parted. From across the room, they stared into each other's eyes. Their undeniable connection had him pushing off the floor. With his gaze cemented on her, he made his way over. One step at a time.

He extended his hands. She placed hers into his, and he pulled her to her feet. Then, he circled his arms around her, pulled her close, and kissed her. She pressed herself against him, slipped her fingers into his hair, and moaned into his mouth. He opened his and she dipped her tongue inside.

The kiss turned greedy and feral, the unrelenting need to take her into his arms had him tightening his hold. He wanted to be as close as two people could be, and he wanted her in his bed all night long.

She slowed the kiss down, but she didn't break away. Staring into his eyes, she whispered, "I want to stay, but I don't think we should cross that line."

He wanted to laugh, but the anguish in her eyes had him running his fingers through her long, wavy hair. "We already crossed it."

"That was different. We were kink partners who didn't know anything about each other. Now, we're working together. I'm grateful to Z for this opportunity, but he would ship me back to the task force without a second thought."

"You can sleep in any of the spare bedrooms, including the suite downstairs. But I want you with me."

"What about Ethan? I don't want to confuse him. I mean, he's already attached to Loki. If I return to California and take Loki from him, that won't help him feel safe and secure."

"Then, you won't go back to California."

She sighed. "I want you. I can't stop thinking about how much I want you. I want to pleasure you—"

"What happened to punishing me?"

Her lips tugged up. "I want you in my mouth." Adrenaline coursed through him. "I've never done that with you. But it wouldn't be for you, it would be for me."

"And I'll take my punishment like a man." He whisked her into his arms and headed up the stairs.

"Computer, turn off lights on the first floor."

As he ascended, the lights flicked off. On the second floor, he set his sights for the closed double doors at the end of the hallway, pausing at Ethan's doorway.

The nightlight cast a soft glow on him. He was on his back, sleeping peacefully, his thumb finally out of his mouth. Knowing Ethan was safe let him turn his full attention on the beautiful woman in his arms.

He slid his gaze to her, and she was waiting. Her breathing had shifted, her eyes filled with anticipation. He remembered that look and he couldn't wait to make her unravel around him. Prescott continued down the hallway, his heart picking up speed as he strode toward his bedroom.

Time to act like an adult, with an adult.

He closed and locked his bedroom door, told the computer to set the night table light on low. Then, he set Jacqueline down in the middle of his bedroom. They came together in a whoosh of energy, their bodies pressed tightly against each other, arms locking each other in place.

Despite the lust streaking through him, he wanted to take his time and savor her. Worship her for as long as she would let him. They weren't hooking up at their club. No hiding behind fake names, no sexy scene they were acting out.

Just the two of them, in his bedroom. Suddenly, things got very real and very personal. And he could not fucking wait.

She yanked off her shirt, wiggled out of her jeans. Excitement firmed his cock as she leaned up, dropped a kiss on his lips. Then, she unbuttoned his shirt, helped him out of it. Within seconds, his boxer briefs topped the heap of their discarded clothes. He naked, she still in her bra and panties, the swells of her breasts catching his eye.

Her fingers drifted into his hair, she stood on her toes while he snaked his arms around her, palmed her ass, and pulled her close.

"I have no expectations," she whispered. "I don't want you to think—"

He stopped her with a kiss while he ran his hands up and down the sides of her body, appreciating her hourglass waist.

Her breathing shifted, his too. She jumped into his arms, clinging to him while their tongues explored, teased, stroked, and pleased. She started moving in his arms, writhing against his torso while her moans turned ardent.

The desire to root himself inside her had his rock-hard cock throbbing so hard it felt like a bass drum between his legs.

He pulled off the comforter, sending bed pillows flying. After stripping off her bra and panties, he paused to soak up her naked body.

"Sexy, sexy, Jacqueline."

She laid down sideways across the mattress—*his* mattress.

Laying on top of her, he stared into her eyes. "I'm glad you're here," he murmured.

"This feels personal," she whispered.

"It *is* personal."

"We're not at Asylum. I'm Jacqueline, not Jack, and you're Prescott, not Mac. I've hated you for so long, it feels strange being here with you."

"You can hate me... and still suck me."

She bit back a smile. "A hate suck it is, then."

She stroked his back with her fingers, then ran them over his shoulders and latched on to his triceps. "I've thought about blowing you for a while."

"One of my favorite Jack fantasies," he replied before kissing her.

The intensity of their embrace turned them into feral animals, but she broke the kiss. Gasping for air, she said, "Suck my tits."

When he captured her hard nib in his mouth, wetness seeped from his erect cock. The more he sucked, the grittier her sounds.

"Mmm, so good," she whispered. "Bite me."

He'd forgotten that she liked it rough.

"So, fucking good," she rasped, the huskiness in her voice catching his breath. "Time to get sucked."

She nudged him off her.

With a devilish gleam in her eyes, she repositioned between his legs. After tucking her hair behind her ears, she lowered her face and licked him like an ice cream cone. Pleasure flooded him, and he watched with total anticipation as she devoured him with her mouth.

She cradled his balls, massaging them while she worked him in and out of her mouth. She raked her teeth over his shaft, sucking hard on the head.

Euphoria pummeled him with hit after hit of sweet pleasure. Then, she slowly withdrew and started licking and sucking his balls. White-hot streaks of desire thrummed through him. She stroked his shaft, spreading the oozing wetness over him.

Then, she angled herself so she could see him and stared into his eyes. Jack was a dirty girl. She was uninhibited at the club, and he wanted all that wildness now. He wanted her to unleash her energy on his cock and suck him bone dry.

"You taste so good," she said. "I want you to come in my mouth."

Repositioning over his saluting boner, she devoured him in a low, raspy groan. She worked his shaft faster and faster, while taking him in until he banged against the back of her throat. He was a big boy and there was still plenty she couldn't suck, but her talented hands worked his entire shaft.

"Fuck, Jack, you feel so good. You're a naughty girl."

She increased her speed, bobbing over him, while sucking the pleasure from him. The orgasm started deep inside him, the waves of ecstasy taking hold.

"I'm gonna come so fucking hard."

She rolled her talented tongue around his head faster and faster, then slid him inside.

The release shot out of him so intensely, his body jerked like an earthquake, the pleasure pouring into her welcoming mouth.

When he stopped, she slowly pulled off and vanished into

his bathroom. He lay there boneless, yet eager for more. Time to take good, good care of her.

Seconds later, she crawled in next to him. With gentle fingers, she cradled his still hard shaft. Minty breath wafted in his direction.

He rolled toward her. "You're so fucking talented, and you were well worth the wait," he murmured.

Then, he pushed out of bed and returned with two neckties. "I know you like when I restrained you, so I'm going to bind your wrists together while I feast on your sexy pussy."

She released another lusty moan.

"Lay across the mattress," he commanded.

After knotting his ties together to make one long one, he bound her wrists and shoved the leftover material under his mattress to hold her in place.

Then, he leaned over her and kissed her.

"You could crawl over me for sixty-nine," she said.

"Next time." He walked around the bed and stared down at her. "You're trapped and I get to make you purr like the pussy you are."

"Yesss," she hissed. "I love when you eat me." She bent her knees, spread her legs wide.

Another hit of desire flowed through him. He planked over her, kissed her hard. She opened her mouth and thrust her tongue against his. Then, she bit his lip. Not hard, just enough pressure to let him know she wanted him to turn up the heat.

Leaning over her, he sucked her plump nipples. She started writhing beneath him, her hips coming off the bed while she arched her back, forcing her nib into his mouth. One of the things he loved about her was how responsive her nipples were every time they played. Doubling in size, they'd turn rock hard, and stay that way.

He ran his tongue down her tummy to the apex of her sex, her mostly hairless pussy inches away.

She started moving faster on the bed, so he lay his arm over her tummy to hold her in place. "Your pussy is mine," he growled. "Stop moving."

"I hate you," she whispered. "Hate that you were a fucking wrecking ball in my life."

"Hate me all you want," he bit out before placing his mouth over her pussy. He licked the hot folds, tasted her sweet clit. She was soaking wet and he gobbled her up like the treat that she was.

With his free hand, he slipped two fingers inside her, and she groaned.

"So good," she murmured.

Slowly, he started thrusting, while her insides expanded. Two fingers turned into three and she began moving on the bed again.

"Lie still," he hissed.

"Fuck you," she bit out. "I hate that you're making me feel so fucking good."

He withdrew, teased her soft folds with nimble fingers, then swirled them around her clit. Wild, feral sounds ripped through her. Leaning into her, he licked her sex, thrust his tongue inside.

Bringing her all the pleasure had turned him hard again. He loved how she was moving, despite his arm over her, but he needed both hands to take care of her.

While eating her, he caressed her asshole.

"Oh, fuck," she bleated.

He feasted on her like a wild beast, and she started bucking beneath him. Then, she started shaking and arching into his mouth.

"Coming," she murmured between jagged breaths.

She convulsed, hard, into his mouth, her sweet pussy juices covering his mouth and dripping down his chin while she groaned through her release.

When she finished, her tight muscles relaxed back into the mattress.

He moved away, but he didn't wipe her wetness off his mouth. He loved her juices, loved the way she smelled, the way she tasted. She'd been his dirty girl at Asylum and he was so fucking elated she was his dirty girl now too.

18

HERE COMES THE SUN

Jacqueline

Jacqueline wasn't surprised that the fire and passion they had at Asylum continued into his home... and his bed. It was becoming harder and harder to loathe a man with so many dirty talents. Now, with her pussy primed, she was desperate for more.

"Fuck me," she murmured. "And don't untie me. I want to feel every thrust, the full weight of you on me. Take me for your own pleasure."

Standing on the side of the bed, he peered down at her. All she could see was lust springing from his half-hooded eyes. His shoulders were rising and falling faster than normal, and he was sporting another impressive erection.

He opened a new box of condoms, rolled one on, and planked over her. His eyes, hungry with desire, were locked on hers.

"You fucked me good with your mouth, but that doesn't change anything," she whispered. "I still can't stand you."

He positioned his head at her opening. "You won't hate me for long," he said before thrusting inside.

The rapture spiraled through her as she wrapped her legs around him, lifting her ass off the mattress. Further in he slid, their collective moans a powerful aphrodisiac.

She loved being trapped, loved being imprisoned by someone she felt so completely safe with. Before meeting Mac, she'd never trusted another man to tie her up, but a few months after they started playing together, she asked him to restrain her. That orgasm had been as mind-blowing as the one she just had.

And she couldn't wait for her next one.

When it came to sex, she was greedy. "More" was always on the menu and Mac had always delivered.

They were moving as one, her like a bucking bronco, him driving himself inside her.

"I want to fuck you for hours and hours," she rasped.

He shifted so he could suck her nipple. With her hard nib in his mouth, she arched her back and sucked in a jagged breath. Hit after hit of pleasure pounded through her. He sucked her nipple, bit the other. She swallowed down the yelp, but couldn't stop bucking against him.

The intensity of their fucking was sending her hurtling toward another orgasm. In and out, he moved, his cock growing harder, her sensitive space expanding to accommodate his massive size.

"Flip me over," she said between breaths.

Slowly, he withdrew, but his mouth found hers and his kiss was hard and strong, just the way she liked them. The kiss ended. She flipped over, moved to the edge of the bed, so he could enter her from behind. He smacked her ass, the sting sending waves of painful delight through her.

Then, before she'd had a chance to recover, he plunged back inside her. Holding her hips, he thrust again and again, deeper and deeper. When he reached around and fingered her clit, the orgasm shattered her as he drove himself inside her faster and faster.

"Fuck, Jack, I'm coming."

When he finished, he stilled, his shaft still rooted inside her. She didn't want to move, didn't want him to leave. She just wanted more.

Slowly, he pulled out, untied her and kissed her wrists. "I haven't tied you up in a long time."

"I love being your prisoner. Love that you fuck me hard and show me no mercy."

"Jesus, you're gonna turn me hard again."

She got on her knees, wrapped her arms around his neck, letting her fingernails tickle his shoulders. "Good. I want to fuck until it's time to work. I need this escape. You need it. I don't want to think, I just want to feel."

"Lay down. I'll make you come with my hand." He went into his bathroom, leaving her alone in his bedroom.

From what she could see in the dimly lit room, it was large and similar to Ethan's room with grays and whites. But she wasn't there to decorate, she was there for the sexual release.

Relishing in the afterglow, she waited. *Nothing better than a sex high.*

Nothing.

A moment later, he lay beside her. There was no downtime with them, there was never a one-and-done.

"I don't want to stop," she murmured.

"Then, we won't."

One kiss turned into another passionate embrace. He made good on his promise when he slid his hand between her legs. Talented digits teased her sensitive skin until she clung to him and released another earth-shattering orgasm.

Snuggled against him, she caressed his heated chest. For

the moment, she was sated, but she was far from finished with him.

She loved the tender way he stroked her back. Gentle, light strokes that tickled and delighted her. They'd done some kinky things together, but they'd never once snuggled. Tonight was different in so many ways.

"I'm having the hardest time hating you," she whispered.

He tipped her chin toward him, dropped a tender kiss on her lips, but he said nothing.

"I should probably get outta here," she whispered. "I don't want Ethan to get confused or too attached to Loki."

He threw his massive thigh over her. "Stay with me."

She melted from his words, the possessive way he behaved. "What about Ethan?"

"He's afraid I'm going to leave him," Prescott said. "I think if he saw you here in the morning, he'd be so happy."

"Especially with Loki."

"He's not even four. He has no memory of his dad and now his mom is gone. I can't believe I'm admitting this to you, but I actually considered giving him up for adoption."

She pushed up, offered a comforting smile. "I get it. You weren't expecting to be responsible for a child. You've got a company, you've got your other life. I think you're doing a great job."

"Thank you. The realization hit me when I was talking to Z... *that little boy is mine.*" He shook his head. "I don't think I'm qualified—"

"Ethan feels safe and he feels loved. Seriously, you shouldn't be so hard on yourself." She ran her fingers through his thick hair. "You're so patient with him."

"We need to have sex every day. You're much sweeter after I've taken care of you."

She laughed, then her smile fell away. "Can I talk to you about something?"

He reached up, tucked her hair behind her ear. "Go 'head."

"There's this guy. I have the strangest feeling he's been following me."

Prescott pushed up on his elbows, his eyebrows jutting into his forehead. "What happened?"

"His name is Lou. I met him when I went to my sister's house. He's in some band and they're between tours, so he's staying with her. First, I ran into him at Asylum a couple of nights ago."

"I'm sorry about that, Jack."

"It's fine. Anyway, I was waiting in the bar and some guy started hitting on me, and this Lou guy stepped in. I was handling it, but he stood up for me. Then, yesterday, I stopped at the grocery store—the one near your house—to grab Loki's food, and he pulled up in line behind me."

"Where does your sister live?"

"Reston. He said he was heading to a band member's house for practice." She ran her fingers over his shoulder, then down his chest. She loved touching him, loved feeling the heat of his body on her fingers.

"I'll run a check on him. What's his last name?"

She shrugged. "I'll get it from my sister."

He leaned up, kissed her. "Let's make this simple. Move in here so I can make sure you're safe. You can sleep in the first-floor master suite or pick any bedroom up here, including mine, but I don't want to push you. Up until thirty minutes ago, you hated my guts."

"I've softened to a strong dislike," she teased.

Pausing, they stared into each other's eyes before he dropped a soft kiss on her mouth.

"I'm concerned Z's building isn't secure," he continued. "My brother sounds nothing like Philip Skye, but the guard wouldn't know that. Anyone could gain access to that building. If you won't move in here, I'll have Nicky install one of his security systems in the condo." Then, he collected her hand in his, kissed each one of her fingers. "Move in, Jack. It would be easier for us to work together, plus you'd be safe here by yourself."

Gazing into his eyes was the best medicine for her troubled soul.

That Lou guy creeped me out. Just do it.

"I'll move in, and I'll stay in the first-floor bedroom."

His smile sent a blast of heat through her. "We'll grab your things and get you in here tomorrow."

"Thank you for letting me stay here."

"I got you." His kiss made her traitorous heart soar. She had it so bad for this man. But she'd continue to play things chill, let him think she *didn't* like him.

As much as she wanted to stay in his bed, it was almost six in the morning. "I'm gonna get out of here before Ethan wakes up."

"The bathroom downstairs is fully stocked or you're welcome to shower with me." His lips curved into a tempting smile.

She kissed him, letting her lips linger on his. So much passion flowed between them, it was hard to separate.

After throwing on her clothes, she hurried downstairs, passing a conked-out Loki before entering the first-floor master suite. The bedroom was large, the king bed's luxurious gray comforter beckoning. But it was time to work, so she locked the door, stripped down, and walked into the spacious bathroom.

Her head was buzzing from being with Prescott. They vibed on a whole different level.

As the hot water sluiced her, she reminded herself to keep her emotions in check. Falling in love with him would be easy. It could also be a mistake. They had a job to do, and she couldn't allow her feelings to get in the way of that.

After she dried her hair, she pulled on yesterday's clothes, then found Prescott in the kitchen making a fresh pot of coffee. His hair was still wet and he'd dressed for work in black suit pants and a bright white shirt that made his tan pop.

Eye candy for days.

"Did you find what you need?" he asked.

"Absolutely. If I'm up before you in the morning, and I need to take Loki out—"

"I'll add you to my security system," he replied.

After taking her photo and uploading it, they recorded her voice, then he scanned her retina.

"You're all set," he explained.

Loki padded over, his tail swishing back and forth.

She knelt and rubbed him. "Loki, you did so good with Ethan, yesterday." After rising, she said, "Computer, turn off the security system."

"Good morning, Jacqueline, system is off," said the computer.

"Thank you for making me feel at home," she said to Prescott. "I'll take Loki out."

She hooked his leash, and outside they went. It was a beautiful morning, so she walked him down the quiet cul-de-sac and back. When she walked up Prescott's driveway, he was sitting on his front steps, sipping his coffee.

Her heart blossomed.

"Just making sure you're safe." He held out a small plastic baggie. "Do you need this for Loki?"

She took it. "He didn't poop, but he will."

"Hey, Loki." Prescott's deep rumbling voice thundered through her like an earthquake.

How could one man possess so much raw sex appeal?

He patted the frisky puppy, then pushed off the step. His penetrating gaze locked with hers and the familiar zoom of butterflies whirled in her tummy. It was exciting to be around him, thrilling to work with him, and downright terrifying to think that he could shatter her heart into a million pieces if his feelings didn't coincide with hers.

He shot her a smile, and her heart skipped a beat. "You ready to get to work, boss?"

"Time to catch a killer," she murmured as she stepped inside.

He shut the front door and flipped the deadbolt behind her. After unleashing Loki, she let her gaze drift to his. He was waiting.

He pulled her into his arms and kissed her. Just once, but his mouth lingered on hers. She could get so damn used to that kind of affection.

"I haven't pulled an all-nighter since college," he murmured. "And it was me pushing to finish a term paper that I'd waited too damn long to write. Staying up all night with you is something I'd do again and again and again."

Me, too, a hundred million times.

"Coffee?" His velvety voice caressed her ears.

There was a confidence in his timbre that instantly made her feel at ease, yet aroused her at the same time.

Snap out of it. You're losing it. He asked you if you want a cup of coffee. Coffee!!

"I'm telling Ethan that you and Loki are staying here with us." He filled two mugs and set them on the island. "I'm hoping he can roll with all these changes."

"I'm concerned it's too much for him."

"Having you here is good for *me*, Jack."

She melted from his words, the way he was peering into her eyes. She felt like the luckiest girl on earth, but she was getting way ahead of herself. They were working together and they were sleeping together. That was never a good combination. Someone could get hurt, and she had a pretty strong feeling it would be her.

"Maybe we should act like professionals while I'm here,"

she said, though she hated the words as they spilled from her tongue.

"What does that mean?"

"No fooling around."

His deep, sexy laugh sent a thrill skittering through her. It sounded like thunder, miles and miles away. "You think that's something you can do after what just happened? You love the way I touch you, how I take good care of you."

"Ohmygod, you are so arrogant. You think I won't be able to control myself around you? Let me tell you—"

He stopped her with a kiss. Then, a second, this one more urgent. His tongue pressed into her mouth and she groaned into his. Then, he ended it as quickly as he started it.

"I'm the one who's addicted to you," he said. "But, play hard to get if you want. I love a good challenge."

She stilled. Things were moving way too fast and her decisions were based purely on emotion. "You know, I don't think it's a good idea if I stay here."

His eyebrows slashed down. "Where the hell is this coming from?"

"We work together. We shouldn't be living together."

"Loki!" Ethan exclaimed as he padded into the room, still in his jammies.

The puppy bounded over to him while Ethan jumped up and down. "You came back, Jack! And you brought Loki! Hurray!! This is the best day ever."

Emotion surged to the surface and tears filled her eyes. She rarely cried, but this little boy had been through so much in his young life. The joy on his face had struck a chord in the deepest part of her soul.

She would risk her own heart, so she wouldn't break his.

Prescott

Prescott was busy fixing Ethan his breakfast while Jack fed Loki.

When she set the bowl of food on the kitchen floor, Ethan stood beside her and stared down at him. "What does he eat?"

"Meat and vegetables," she replied. "Same as us. Do you eat vegetables?"

"I like sugar."

She smiled. "Me, too, but you need less sugar and more meat and vegetables. That's what helps you grow strong."

Big brown eyes peered up at her. "Can I eat the dog food?"

"If you eat Loki's food, what will he eat?" she asked.

He started to reach toward Loki's bowl, but she pulled his hand away. "Since Loki is a baby, let's not put our fingers by his food when he's eating. I don't want him to get confused or angry and bite you, okay?"

She pretended to munch on his fingers and he giggled. "I'm being silly, but if he bit you, it would hurt, just like last night." She led him toward the table. "What are you having for breakfast?"

He climbed into his booster seat as Prescott set down a bowl of oatmeal along with a plate of scrambled eggs.

"Yucky." Ethan pushed the bowl away. "I want *my* cereal."

"Sorry, bud," Prescott said.

Ethan pursed his lips, narrowed his gaze, and sat there, his hands in two small fists.

"Do you like eggs?" Jack asked.

Ethan refused to answer.

She pulled Prescott aside. "I should probably mind my business—"

"And I should give him whatever the hell he wants, but he was eating junk."

"Do you have any brown sugar?" she murmured.

"No."

"Regular sugar?"

He shook his head.

"If you're okay with it, I'll pick up brown sugar on my way home—I mean—back here."

"I liked your first answer better," he said. "I get that there's a lot going on, but if you're here, we'll get a lot more work done."

"Yeah, that's what we're gonna do with our extra time."

He chuckled.

They returned to find Ethan had eaten the eggs, but not the oatmeal.

"You did a good job with your eggs, Ethan," Prescott said. "Let's get you dressed for school."

"I want to stay and play with Loki."

"Loki will be here when we come home, and you can play with him then."

Prescott waited while Ethan's expression morphed from frustration to acceptance. For someone who had little exposure to children, he was fascinated by the range of emotions that Ethan wrestled with on a second-by-second basis.

"Okay." He climbed down from the booster and headed toward the staircase. "Can Loki come upstairs with me?"

Prescott regarded Jack.

"It's okay with me, if Uncle Prescott doesn't mind him going upstairs."

"Whatever it takes to get this child out the door on time."

AN HOUR LATER, Prescott was saying goodbye to Ethan in his preschool classroom. "Have fun today, bud. I'll pick you up later."

Ethan peered at him. "Where do you go?"

He brought him to the window. "I work right there in that building on the top floor."

"Can I come see you?"

"Of course, but you have to ask Miss Nancy. You can't just leave."

A little boy ran over. "Come play with me, Ethan." Then, he eyed Prescott. "Are you his daddy?"

"I'm his uncle," Prescott replied.

Ethan flung his little arms around Prescott's legs. "Bye."

Warmth filled Prescott's chest and emotion gripped his throat. He rubbed Ethan's back and tousled his hair. "I'll see you later."

Ethan bolted toward the table with his friend.

As Prescott was leaving, Nancy stopped him. "Ethan's settling in really well. He asks me—a lot—where you are, so I thought it might be nice to set up a time when I can bring him by."

Like the other day, her cheeks flushed with color.

"Absolutely," Prescott replied. "I'll give you my assistant's contact info. She keeps my schedule and can set something up. Later in the day is better, in case Ethan wants to leave."

She nodded. "That's what I'll do."

He jotted down Francis's number and left.

As he rode the elevator to his office, the effects of getting no sleep started creeping in. He would have to kick up his energy with coffee until he could burn through the fogginess in his head.

The image of Jacqueline, naked and in his bed, popped into his thoughts. *That's not the kind of waking up I need right now.*

He stopped at his assistant's doorway. Francis was on her computer.

"Perfect timing," she said lifting her mug. "I'll grab a refill. You ready to get started?"

"Absolutely. Grab a mug for me."

"Always do." She jetted out, and he continued on to his office.

A few moments later, she returned, set down his coffee. After catching him up on everything he'd missed, she asked about Ethan.

"He's doing great," Prescott replied. "I have no idea how single parents do it."

"It's a lot of work, but it's all about time management." Though he knew she was a single parent, he'd never pried into her life beyond asking about her weekend or her holiday. Her three children were in college, with one about to graduate next week.

"How the hell do you get it all done?" he asked.

She chuckled. "I'm very organized, which you know, so I tried to do that with my kids, but I had to adapt my methods for each of them."

"Any advice for me?"

"Get very organized with your time... and pick your battles. Some aren't worth the time or the energy."

"Noted," he said. "Right now, I'm trying to get him to eat healthier."

"If mine didn't eat the food I prepared, they'd go hungry. My sister gave each of her kids whatever they wanted. I didn't have the time to be a short-order cook, plus I thought she was spoiling them." Francis shrugged. "Every parent or guardian has to find their own method or system. Children are a blessing, but they're also work."

While Prescott had always appreciated Francis, he had a newfound respect for her. He was having his challenges with one, but she had three.

Artemis strolled in. "Good morning, good morning." A big smile filled his uncle's face and he appeared to be touting an even darker tan, or maybe he'd whitened his teeth.

"Did you go somewhere warm for the weekend?" Prescott asked.

"No, why?" Artemis replied.

"You're super tan and it's only May. You been boating?"

He grinned. "Tanning bed. It's like the fountain of youth."

Though Francis stayed silent, she did a little shudder. Prescott bit back a smile. If Artemis got any tanner, he'd be a freakish shade of orange.

"What brings you by?" Prescott asked.

Artemis puffed out his chest. "The board approved my request for TopCon's rebranding campaign for the full one point five mil."

"Congrats," Prescott said. "Are you managing that project yourself?"

"At first, then the marketing director can handle it." He ran his hand through his hair. "I'm off to the doctor. Be back in an hour."

"Everything okay?" Prescott asked.

"I'm going for my fillers. Those injections take years off my face."

After he left, Prescott regarded his assistant. "He's an embarrassment to the company my great-grandparents started."

"I'm just grateful *I* don't have to work for him."

As she was leaving his office, he said, "Thanks for the advice about raising kids."

She turned back at his doorway. "Enjoy Ethan. They don't stay young for long. And not that it's any of my business, but I admire you for stepping up." With a smile she exited, leaving him alone with his thoughts.

He logged in to his computer and jumped to his calendar.

A moment later, Francis popped back in. "You've got a meeting in five."

"Yeah, I see that. Why am I meeting with Markesha?"

"She needs ten minutes, but she didn't want to discuss it with me," Francis said before jetting out.

Prescott scrolled through his unread email, skimming the

ones that needed his immediate attention. As he was replying to one, there was a knock on his open office door.

"Got a second?" Markesha asked.

Markesha was the marketing director. Though she reported to Lorenzo, the VP of marketing, Prescott had an open-door policy.

"Come on in," he gestured to his guest chairs.

To his surprise, she shut the door. Once seated, she placed her hands in her lap. "I've got an issue."

"What's going on?"

"I found out that one of my team's rebranding projects is being rolled out."

"I'm not following. Isn't that a good thing?"

"Three weeks ago, Artemis asked me to provide him with a high-level overview of our current projects. My team has been focused on two. The first is the rebranding of the sensitive skincare line and the second is a campaign for several new products in our Women of Color haircare line."

Prescott nodded. "Sounds great. I look forward to seeing those."

"I found out that the board approved Artemis's request to fund a product line he's outsourced to some consulting company."

"Right." Prescott sipped his coffee. "TopCon."

"Artemis presented *our* ideas for the sensitive skincare line to the board. They approved it, and TopCon is going to roll out the rebranding."

What the hell?

Why would his uncle lift an internal marketing campaign and present it as something the consultant created?

"My team has been very concerned that their jobs are in jeopardy because of this outside firm. Morale is in the toilet," Markesha continued. "One of my team leads quit. Another member has been calling in sick, but I think he's going on job interviews. Right now, my team does not feel valued because one of their ideas was stolen."

"Just to confirm, Artemis asked for an overview of your current rebranding projects, then presented the skincare rebranding to the board on behalf of TopCon. The board approved it and the consulting company will be managing the rollout."

"Right."

"But they don't have the full campaign?"

"No, but they could take the basics I provided Artemis and run with that."

"I'll look into it without mentioning you."

"Thank you." She showed herself out, leaving his office door open.

Prescott called Artemis's assistant and asked when he'd be back.

"He said an hour, but I'm guessing sometime after lunch," the assistant replied. "Do you want me to let him know you called?"

"Call or text me when he gets back. I'll swing by his office."

He hung up and grabbed his empty coffee mug. On his way to the break room, his phone rang.

"Armstrong," he answered.

"Mr. Armstrong, I'm a physician at St. Andrew's hospital and I'm calling with the results of Sally Sagall's autopsy report."

"Okay." He strode into the break room.

"You'll be receiving a copy in the mail, but I wanted to speak with you in advance."

This can't be good.

"She died of asphyxiation."

What?

"Did she choke on her vomit?"

"No, she was suffocated."

"That can't be right."

"I'm sorry, but that's the M.E.s findings. We're required to pass these results over to local law enforcement," the doctor continued. "Since you're listed as her next of kin, expect a call from someone."

Prescott gritted his teeth and stared out the break room window while the news sank in. Ethan's mom had been murdered. What in the hell had his sister done to deserve this? And who had killed her? Suffocation *wasn't* the MO of the ALPHA Killer.

He needed to take this one step at a time.

"Can you email me that report?" he asked.

"Sure." He confirmed Prescott's email address. "One more thing... did you know your sister was pregnant?"

19

BONDING

Jacqueline

After Prescott left for work with Ethan in tow, Jacqueline brought Loki out back to make sure his little bladder was empty. Then, she took him into the laundry room, where she had placed his doggie bed, a fresh bowl of water, and one of his toys.

"I'll be back soon."

First stop, Z's condo. While she loved the spectacular views of DC, she would sleep better in Prescott's home.

Well, maybe not, if last night was any indication.

After packing her clothes, toiletries, and what little food she'd bought, she left. Next stop, the grocery store. With that completed, she drove to Prescott's.

She loaded the food into his luxury-brand refrigerator and the pantry, left her suitcases in the first-floor bedroom. Then, she snuck into the laundry room to find Loki fast asleep. Pausing, she stared at his small body with those giant-sized paws.

He opened his eyes, stretched, yawned, and padded over to

her, tail-a-wagging. She gave him some kisses, then a quick rub behind his ears. "Who wants to go for a walk?"

When they returned, she grabbed a ball, took him out back, and tossed it. He was the cutest, fluffiest ball of fur she'd ever seen. After she exhausted her baby, they retreated inside, and she started working at the kitchen table.

Then, she spied Prescott's office. With her laptop in hand, she relocated there.

The bookcase held photos of Prescott with his family and several with his band of brothers. She wondered if she would fit into his world. Then, she spotted one of him and his friends on a boat.

No, that's a yacht.

Prescott was with the same group of friends, and there were women in the photo too. Addison and Addison's cousin, Liv, Emerson, and Danielle.

Loki wandered in, a toy in his mouth. He plopped down and started gnawing on it.

"Hey, sweet boy." She patted him, then opened her laptop and got to work. Today's goal? Could Gloria or Bert's spouses be suspects in the ALPHA Killer case?

After a thorough Internet search into Gloria's life, Jacqueline determined that her second husband—a widower—and his two sons were a happy, blended family. Gloria's first husband lived in Costa Rica and he hadn't been back to the area in years.

Jacqueline figured out how to run a report in ALPHA which showed Gloria's whereabouts over a period of time. There was no reason for Jacqueline to suspect either Gloria or her husband of having an extra-marital affair.

Time to move on to the second victim, Bert Grimes.

Her phone buzzed. Prescott's text made her heart skip a beat. "Can't stop thinking about you."

"What about me?" she texted back, then added a smiley emoji.

"Everything," he replied. "Making any progress?"

"Yes. How's your day going?"

"Are you a runner?"

"Depends on whether you're chasing me."

He sent a laugh emoji. "I need to go for a run after work, so I'm picking up a push stroller. Do you want to run with me?"

"I'm more of a jogger and a golfer. Do you want me to watch Ethan while you run?"

"YOU GOLF???"

"Yes. You?"

"Yes," he replied. "Come with us. I'll grab a stroller on the way home."

She sent a thumbs-up emoji.

"You want me to grab dinner for us?" he texted.

Her brain shorted as she stared at that message. Running together, dinner together. What was happening?

Stop reading anything into this. You eat. He eats. Ethan eats.

"Planned on grilling chicken or burgers. I'm making my homemade Jack's Fries, and a salad. Do you think E will eat any of this?"

"If he doesn't, he'll go hungry. See you tonight."

She turned her attention back to work.

Now, where was I?

Bert Grimes.

First, she checked to see if there was anything that pointed to him having an affair. The former Op was a straight shooter. He worked, went on missions, and he liked to fish with his brother and a couple of buddies. On occasion, he invited another ALPHA Operative.

Her phone rang from a blocked called.

She answered. "Hello."

"Hello, Jacqueline, it's Z. I'm checking in to see how you're doing."

"I've got a list of ten possible suspects and I'm vetting them now."

"I'm hoping you'll have a prime suspect soon."

Oh, boy. No pressure there.

"Me too. I should get back to work." She thanked him for the call and hung up.

Does no one in this organization understand how long it takes to find a killer?

Bert's wife had sent him a text the day he was murdered telling him she was having fun with her sister in Florida. After digging into his wife's travel plans, Jacqueline found pics she'd posted from that time frame. His wife had been on a Caribbean cruise.

And the plot thickens.

Jacqueline found a social media account where Bert's wife was using a different name. While he'd been burning the midnight oil and interviewing for a position with BLACK OPS, his wife had been on a cruise with her lover.

As she continued to research his wife, Jacqueline concluded that while she'd been cheating on Bert, there was nothing that would indicate his wife had murdered him.

I gotta take a break.

She made a sandwich, took Loki for a quick walk, then decided to take five minutes to start his training.

"Loki, sit." She gently pushed down on his backside. Loki sat, but before she could utter, "Good boy," he'd popped back up and grabbed a toy.

"You're so cute," she said. "Let's try this again." After taking the toy, she commanded him to sit and, again, gently pushed his rear down. "Good boy." She gave him a dog treat morsel.

After doing this several more times, slowly switching from the treats to praise, she finished with a belly rub. She concluded by telling him, "Free," then tossing his toy into the family room where he bounded after it.

She was ready to dive deeper into the six former ALPHA employees who worked there at the same time Gloria and Bert had. Because Prescott had taken out Terrence Maul, she started with the next person on her list.

If there was a killer in this group, she'd find them. And if none of these people panned out, she'd widen her search. Despite what might be perceived as a lack of progress, she had every confidence she'd unmask the evil lurking in the shadows.

∽

Prescott

Prescott spent the day powering through meetings, delegating tasks, and playing catch up. As he read through the autopsy report for the third time, he couldn't wrap his brain around the fact that his sister had been suffocated. Because of that, her death was now a homicide.

He had no idea she'd been in her first trimester. She hadn't even hinted at being pregnant. Did she know? And who was the father?

Was it the man Ethan was afraid of?

He had so many questions, but no answers.

He called the doctor back and asked how he could get a profile of the fetal DNA. After being transferred around, he spoke with someone in the coroner's office who could help him. Forms were emailed over. He completed them and sent them back.

At the end of the day, he drove around to daycare. After walking into the classroom, he scanned the room for his tiny target. Ethan was coloring with two girls.

"Hi, Mr. Armstrong," said one of the assistants.

Ethan flipped his attention to Prescott. "Uncle Prescott!" Ethan grabbed his paper and rushed over.

Ethan's big smile and enthusiastic greeting was fast becoming the highlight of Prescott's workday. He knelt just as Ethan flung his arms around him.

"Look what I made. It's for you."

Prescott took the piece of paper and admired the array of colors on the page. "This is great, Ethan. Thank you. I'll put it in my home office."

"I have to get my lunch box." Ethan bolted toward his cubby as Miss Nancy floated into view.

"Hello, Mr. Armstrong."

"How's it goin', Nancy?"

Her cheeks flushed with color. "I'm making headway potty training Ethan."

That snagged his full attention. "Really?"

"I told him we were low on training diapers, hoping he'd poop in the toilet."

"And?"

"He suggested I borrow one from someone else." She laughed. "He's a smart little boy, but we'll get this accomplished."

"Are you low on diapers?" Prescott asked.

"Oh, no, you gave us an entire box, but my goal is to get him fully trained by the time he turns four." She shot him a smile. "I'm sure I will."

Ethan ran back over and said goodbye to Miss Nancy. He clasped Prescott's hand and Prescott's heart softened. This little boy had become so important to him in such a short amount of time. As they walked to the car, Ethan chatted about his day. After Prescott buckled him in, he took off for the store.

Once in the parking lot, Ethan said, "I can't know. Why are we here?"

"I like to go running," Prescott explained as he carried him into the store.

"Me, too!" Ethan exclaimed.

Prescott found the push strollers. "I'm going to put you in this when I run."

"I want to run with you."

"We can do that, but when I run fast, I need to put you in here. It'll be fun, like a race car."

"Can Loki come?"

"Sure. We'll invite Jack and Loki."

He sat Ethan in one and pushed it around, then transferred him to another. He found a third and tried that. They all felt about the same, so he jumped online to check out the reviews.

When he finished reading a few, he glanced down. No Ethan. His heart slammed into his chest. "Ethan! Ethan, where are you?"

He took off down the aisle, calling out his name. No Ethan. He bolted toward a toy aisle shouting for his nephew.

Ethan wandered into view, a LEGO box in his hand, a gigantic smile on his face. "Can I have this?"

"Do not *ever* walk away from me in a store. Do you understand?"

Tears filled Ethan's eyes. "Uh-huh. Okay."

Prescott pulled him into his arms and hugged him. "You scared me. I want you safe. That means you stay with me. No running off, okay?"

He wiped his eyes. "Okay. Can I have this?"

And just like that, Ethan had moved on.

"Let's find one that's the right age for you." After a few minutes of searching, they found one. With a LEGO DUPLO box in hand, they returned to the strollers. Prescott pulled a box off the shelf and they checked out.

Fifteen minutes later, they were home. For a man who had excellent control over his emotions, Ethan had taught him a valuable lesson. Secure him in a shopping cart so he doesn't wander off.

Ethan waited for Prescott to unbuckle him, then beelined inside, calling for Loki the second he set foot in the house.

The first five minutes were utter chaos. Child and puppy fed off each other's energy, giggling and barking through the first floor like they were propelled by jet engines. Prescott and Jack stood in the foyer while the mayhem ensued.

"This is crazy," he murmured before dipping down and kissing her, then kissing her again.

Being around her grounded him, yet the second he touched her, the energy shifted. It palpitated through him while he peered into her eyes.

"I'll bet you never imagined this when you came back to town," he said.

"Hell, no," she replied.

"I like the mayhem... and the noise. It was too damn quiet."

"It's a big house for one person."

"It's a big house for ten people," he said.

She spied the stroller box. "You can take some alone time and go for that run, if you want."

"And leave you here with these two? I'm not doing that to you. I'll set it up later and use it tomorrow."

They took the wild ones out back to let them use up their energy.

When they returned to the kitchen, he inhaled the delicious aroma of homemade fries, baking in the oven. Burgers, waiting to be grilled, sat on a platter. Buns at the ready, a salad made, and carrot and celery sticks for Ethan.

Pulling her into his arms, he said, "Thank you for doing this."

She leaned up, dropped a soft kiss on his lips. "I love grilling in the summer, so I did this for me." Her adorable smile touched his heart.

Simply by existing, she'd become a top priority for him. "I couldn't wait to come home to you."

"I wish I knew the feeling," she said with a gleam in her eyes.

He chuffed out a laugh. "After you changed your mind this morning, I had my doubts you'd be here. Did you get moved okay?"

"No problem, and Loki did great in the mudroom."

"You belong here, with me, Jacqueline."

Smoldering eyes stared into his for an extra beat before she broke their steamy connection. "Can you show me how your grill works?"

"I want to take you upstairs," he murmured.

"Small, helpless creatures are waiting for us to feed them." She palmed his ass before sashaying toward the deck.

Two easy strides and he pulled up alongside her. Being around her changed *everything*. Every-fucking-thing was better because she was in his life. She grounded him, excited him, gave him something bigger than himself to live for. She'd left him once—because of him—but there was no way in hell he'd let that happen again.

Things were moving fast, but Prescott couldn't slow down his feelings, even if he'd wanted to. In a matter of weeks, so much had changed. This new normal felt so damn right.

At ten past eight—after dinner, playtime, a bath, and a bedtime story—Prescott tucked Ethan in, then found Jack working in his office. He loved that she'd made herself at home.

"Make any progress?" he asked, easing onto the love seat.

"I eliminated Bert's and Gloria's spouses from my suspect list."

"Nice."

"Looks like Bert's wife is having an affair. While her boyfriend had motive to kill Bert, he was out of town when Bert was shot, and I found no connection with the boyfriend and Gloria."

"Could Gloria have found out and confronted Bert's wife?" he asked.

"The boyfriend's body type was different from the man at the gas station. I haven't ruled out murder for hire, but I couldn't find anything that linked the wife and her lover to either murder."

"Gotcha."

"I'm tackling the former Ops next." Her gaze floated over his face. "How'd your day go?"

"I got the autopsy report for my sister, Sally. She didn't die of a blood clot. She was suffocated."

Jacqueline's eyes widened.

"And she was pregnant."

"Wow, okay. How far along was she?"

"Eleven weeks."

"That's even more tragic."

He nodded. "My gut's telling me that the person who shot her wanted her dead *because* she was pregnant. It had nothing to do with ALPHA, and Addison got caught in the crosshairs."

"When she didn't die, he went to the hospital to finish the job," she added. "I'll request Sally's phone log. What's her number?"

After rattling it off, Prescott growled. "I'm not interested in justice. I'm out for revenge."

Pushing away from the desk, she relocated on the love seat beside him. "I know that, and I will help you any way I can."

They stared into each other's eyes while the energy swirled around them. The pull was there, the need to touch her uncontrollable. He clasped her hand, caressed her soft skin.

"I didn't ask you to move in just because I want you safe," he continued. "I could have told Nicky to install a security system at Z's condo."

"I'm listening."

He could play this down, he could keep his emotional distance, but he wanted her to know the truth. "I'm falling in love with you."

Her eyes softened and the divot between her brows disappeared. "I like the sound of that."

"Don't feel like you have to—"

"I feel the same," she whispered, before they came together in a tender kiss. "And I love that feeling this way doesn't scare me. Being around you, Ethan too, is the most fun I've had in a long time. I work a lot—too much, really. I use work as an excuse to keep myself walled off."

He needed to know everything about her, so he pushed on. "Why?"

Her entire body went taut. "It's been a long a day." She rose, severing their connection. "I'm gonna say goodnight."

This should have been a special moment between them. They'd just shared a deeply romantic and soul-baring confession. The L-word wasn't something he uttered lightly, especially now, with Ethan in tow. But she meant so much to him and he wanted her to know.

He stood, wrapped her in his arms, and kissed her forehead. "I love having you here and I want you to feel safe. Does this have to do with the Winchester cult?"

"No," she replied, peering up at him. "It's about something that happened to me when I was in college."

20

SECRETS

Jacqueline

"Never talk about what happened" had become a mantra Jacqueline lived by, and she didn't want to relive the terrifying ordeal, not even with Prescott.

"I'm gonna call it. See you in the morning." She leaned up, kissed him.

The second her lips pressed against his, desire jumped to the forefront. She wanted to love him and fall asleep in his arms. But she'd already said too much.

Better to put a little space between us.

She broke away, but he clasped her hands, drawing her back to him. "If you change your mind, come upstairs." He tipped her chin. "I'll behave."

That made her laugh. "Where's the fun in that?"

She made her way, alone, into the first-floor bedroom suite. There, she got naked, went into the bathroom, and turned on the shower faucet. While the hot water beat down on her, she tried clearing her mind, then she did the breathing exercises her therapist had taught her.

Neither helped.

I'm just tired, she told herself, but that wasn't the real reason for her anxiety.

She shouldn't have pushed Prescott away, but that was her typical reaction whenever anyone tried to get close to her. The hot water soothed her, but being in Prescott's arms would work so much better. She dried off, pulled on a tank top, then brushed her teeth.

The king bed and modern furniture filled the large space, but she was drawn to the cozy sitting room with a comfy-looking chaise lounge and love seat, built-in bookshelves and gas fireplace. But she didn't need to read. She needed sleep.

After crawling between the most decadent sheets, she turned off the light, propped herself up on two pillows, and stared into the dark backyard.

The minutes ticked by but sleep wouldn't come.

Tap-tap-tap.

"Come in," she said.

The door opened and her heart skipped a beat. Prescott filled the doorway, dressed in nothing but a pair of shorts, his damp hair framing his handsome face. His massive chest and washboard abs sent a surge of adrenaline racing through her.

"I can't sleep if you're not okay."

She melted.

She turned on the table lamp. "You can come in."

He sat on the edge of her bed, collected her hand in his. "We just told each other we're falling in love, then you run away from me. If things are moving too fast, we can slow down. The last thing I want is for you to feel pressure from me."

"I don't." She ran the back of her fingers down his chiseled cheek. "I don't feel pressure and I don't want us to slow down."

With his gaze drilling into her, a growl rumbled from him. "I love your touch."

As she stared into his eyes, she started to shake. He pulled her into his arms and he held her. No words, no judgment. He just rocked her until his confidence seeped into her soul and she stopped trembling.

She didn't deserve to feel happy. She didn't deserve to feel his love.

"Is this really happening?" she whispered.

"What?"

"Us."

He dipped down, kissed her. "It is, for me."

"Will you hold me?"

He lay beside her, and she snuggled close. When he enveloped her in his strong, protective arms, she felt safe.

"I want to tell you why I put up a wall," she whispered.

"Okay."

The images of that terrifying night came rushing back and she shuddered in a shaky breath. "During my junior year at college, I was abducted."

"Jesus, Jack, I didn't know."

"Very few people do."

He kissed the top of her head, his tender touch urging her onward.

"My sorority sister, Janey, and I had been studying at the library. We left around ten to walk back to the sorority house, which took about twenty minutes. It was Thursday night, so the area near the library was pretty busy with students going to bars."

She inhaled a deep breath in the hopes of calming down, but she'd started trembling again.

"When we left the library it started raining, but about ten minutes in, it was pouring. An unmarked police cruiser pulled up, his rooftop beacon flashing. He asked where we were going and offered us a ride. We were soaked, so we jumped in."

"Okay."

"I got in the front, Janey got in the back. He was scolding us, in a nice way, about walking by ourselves at night."

"Why?" His deep voice rumbled through her.

"There had been five abductions around our campus and several more at a small college nearby. They'd named the perp the Campus Killer."

"Why were you out at night?"

"The library and town are highly trafficked areas. We thought we'd be safe together. We were stupid."

Her heart was thundering against her ribcage. She pushed onto her elbow, stared into his eyes. "I hate talking about this so much."

"I got you."

Shuddering in a shaky breath, she continued. "As the cop got closer to our sorority house, he was supposed to turn right at the street corner, but he went in the opposite direction. We told him, but he said he had a better route. That's when I realized he was lying. Even though I was freaking out, I stayed calm. I was able to sneak my arm behind the seat and grab Janey's knee, and she clasped my hand. I could tell he was headed away from campus, so at the next turn, I screamed for Janey to jump out of the car."

Jacqueline sat up and hugged herself while beads of sweat dotted her brow.

"I opened the door and rolled out. Everything happened so fast, but in slow-motion at the same time. I stopped rolling, jumped up, and looked for Janey." Emotion gripped her throat while tears clouded her eyes. "She hadn't been able to escape because there aren't any handles in the back of a police cruiser. I didn't know that."

Tears slid down her cheeks, and Prescott wiped them away.

"I'd hurt myself when I escaped, but I ran as fast as I could back to the sorority house—"

"Why didn't you use your cell phone?" he asked.

"He put our backpacks in the trunk because they were soaking wet." Jacqueline choked back a sob. "The Campus Killer was luring women into his car by impersonating a cop, but no one knew that."

He tightened his hold of her. "Monster."

She clung to him while the tsunami of emotions drowned her in grief, and pain, and guilt. She excused herself to the bathroom to dry her eyes and blow her nose. When she came back, he was sitting up in bed.

She crawled back in and leaned against the propped pillows. He entwined his fingers through hers. "I want to hear all of this, but not if it's going to wreck you."

"I can do it," she murmured. "I'm falling in love with you, too, and I think you should know I'm a mess." She shrugged. "I try to hide it, but I'm not okay. Not really."

"I'm sorry."

"When I had dinner with Addison, she told me hikers found Janey's remains in a wooded area. It was heart wrenching and terrifying."

"Did they catch him?"

She shook her head. "No, he vanished, probably because I could ID him. Or he moved to another part of the country and continued abducting and killing college women."

"Did they have any suspects?"

"Initially, they assumed he was a local police officer, but my description didn't match. Even though they widened the search to other counties, they didn't find anyone."

"He could have disguised himself," he said.

"I know, but all they had was a sketch, based on my description." After a beat, she said, "Ever since then, I haven't allowed myself to get close to a man."

"Are you afraid?"

"Not of men, in general, but I'm always looking over my shoulder, wondering if he's still out there. I blame myself for what happened to Janey. I wouldn't have escaped if I'd known she couldn't. I've always believed we could have overpowered him."

"Did he usually kidnap women who were alone?"

"Yeah, but he got bold with us, or he saw an opportunity he couldn't pass up. Two drenched women desperate to get out of the rain." She steeled her spine. "If the paranoia isn't bad enough, I have survivor guilt. I don't think I deserve to be happy."

"Oh, Jack, that's not true."

"I've heard that from my therapist, my family, my sorority sisters, including Addison. Logically, I understand, but emotionally, I can't get past it. When I saw you at Addison and Hawk's shower, I was so excited… until the guilt crept back in. Learning that you were the triggerman for the Winchester mission allowed me to push you away."

"But you're falling in love with me."

"I've been at war with myself ever since I found out we had to work together."

"What does your therapist tell you?"

"I haven't seen her in years, but she told me that Janey would want me to be happy. She asked me if the situation had been reversed, and Janey had gotten away, what would I want for her?"

"What *would* you want for her?"

"I'd want Janey live a full and happy life. I get it, but my heart is broken. That one incident changed me. While I'm proud to be a survivor, I'm also wrecked that she died at the hands of that monster."

He kissed her cheek. "I adore you, Jack. What can I do to help you to have that happy life?"

"Just accept me, and know I struggle with things that, maybe, other people don't."

He caressed her back before dropping a worshipful kiss on

her lips. "You're an amazing woman and I'll support you however I can."

Then, he stood and raked his hands through his hair. "Since we're being honest with each other, there's something I need to tell you."

Prescott

PRESCOTT HAD TOLD Jacqueline he was falling in love, but he'd already fallen.

Hard.

Knowing what he did about her, he was relieved he'd soft-pedaled his feelings.

After they moved to the love seat in the sitting room, he covered her with a throw, then held her trembling hand.

"I know you hated me for taking out the cult leader, but I didn't go rogue," he said. "I was following orders."

Her mouth dropped open and she bolted upright. "No, you went off script."

"That's what everyone was told to keep the truth from getting out. The command to take out the cult leader came from my boss who pulled me aside on day twenty-five of the standoff. The Director told him that if I got the leader in my scope, to take the shot. Then, the rest of HRT would get the cult members out."

"I had no idea," she murmured.

"Do you remember how the standoff started?" he asked.

"Yeah. A woman from the cult came into our office and told one of my agents that the leader was a sexual predator who was keeping everyone against their will."

"The night you were on the phone with him, he stepped in front of a backlit window. I took the shot."

"Why didn't your team get in there faster?"

"The place was wired to blow," he explained. "If HRT had gone in there, they would have died too."

"How do you know this?" she asked.

"Z."

"Why wasn't I informed?"

"I don't know," he replied. "The standoff was considered a total mission fail, but according to Z, the Director *hadn't* made that decision in a vacuum, so someone had to be the scapegoat. I was an easy target. I'd fired the kill shot, so they claimed I went rogue—"

"Why didn't you fight that?"

"My word against my superiors. They needed someone to take the fall." Prescott pointed at himself. "Yours truly got the honors."

"I'm so sorry," she murmured.

"I was forced to resign. My career was over. I was fortunate I had the family business, but I'd never planned on doing more than sit on the board. A month after I left the Bureau, Z asked me to complete a special assignment."

"Do you like what you're doing?"

"I like being a lone wolf. When all those cult members died, it broke me. I would never have taken out the leader if I'd known they were going to blow themselves up. I miss the team aspect, which is why I've done some ALPHA missions. Dakota invited me into his elite BLACK OPS team, but I said no."

Repositioning toward him, she tucked her legs under her. "Why?"

His stomach clenched. "If a BLACK OPS mission went sideways because I couldn't do my job—and my team died—that would kill me."

"You were following orders. You didn't have a choice. I understand what really happened, and I don't blame you." She kissed him, and the anger and guilt he carried around day in and day out lifted a little. "I'm sorry I was such a bitch."

"I hated me for what I did too."

"Even though you fly solo, you're handling Ethan well."

"Thank you," he said. "We gotta sleep, babe. I want you in my bed and in my arms all night long, but I will respect your decision if you want to stay down here."

"What about Ethan?"

"We can talk to him about us," Prescott said.

"My heart is telling me one thing, but I need to do what I think is right for him. I'm staying down here."

As much as he did *not* like hearing that, he appreciated that she was thinking of Ethan. "Why don't we tell him that you and Loki are moving in and leave it at that?"

"That's perfect."

"Knowing what you've been through, I admire you even more," he said pulling her into his arms and holding her close.

"And I respect you so much, now that I know the truth," she replied before marrying her lips to his.

He tucked her in, kissed her goodnight, and left. He hated that he couldn't hold her close all night, but he had every confidence they wouldn't be apart for much longer.

PRESCOTT WOKE, ready to take on the day. He worked out in his home gym, got ready for work, made Ethan's lunch, then swung back upstairs to wrestle the tyke awake.

Ethan was a ball of energy the second his feet hit the floor. He zoomed into the bathroom to pee and brush his teeth. Back in the bedroom, he selected his own T-shirt and shorts.

As Prescott helped him tug on his shirt, he said, "I've got a surprise for you."

Ethan's eye lit up. "Another LEGO?"

"Not today, bud," he replied. "Jacqueline and Loki are already here *and* they're going to be staying with us."

"Yay!! Loki is smart and fun to play with, but he's not very good to share."

Prescott laughed. "We can teach him. What doesn't he share?"

"He takes my blocks and he won't give them back, and he bites me a little when I take his rope toy."

"We'll tell Jack since he's her dog. What do you think about that?"

"I want to help train him," Ethan said.

Down the stairs and into the kitchen they went.

Jacqueline was scooping oatmeal into a small bowl. "Good morning, guys. Who wants oatmeal? I added blueberries and walnut pieces."

"Sounds great," Prescott replied.

"Ethan you want to try it?" she asked.

He ran over to Loki who was staring out the family room French doors. "Hi, Loki. Do you want to play?" He petted him while Loki's tail swished back and forth.

Prescott filled Ethan's cup with milk and poured two coffees. "Ethan, come on over."

After Ethan got into his booster chair, he took a spoonful of the warm cereal. Prescott bit back a smile as Ethan's face morphed into a grimace.

"Yucky."

Jacqueline had placed a small amount of brown sugar into a little bowl. "Let's add sugar."

He flicked his gaze to her. "Really?"

She spooned a little, then said, "Try this."

He opened his mouth and she fed him.

Ethan's eyes lit up. "Yummy!"

She sprinkled a little over his cereal. "Now, try it."

He scooped in a bite and swallowed. "I'll eat a *little* because Jack was sooooo nice and gave me sugar."

"Thank you, Ethan," she said. "Healthy cereal with a little sugar."

When she slid her gaze to Prescott, he mouthed, "Thank you."

She patted his back.

"I told Ethan that you and Loki are staying with us," Prescott began.

"Can I help train Loki?" Ethan asked her.

"Absolutely," she replied. "I'd love that. We can start after school."

"I don't want to go to school. I want to teach Loki."

"Today's Friday, bud," Prescott said. "One more day of school, then we'll have the entire weekend together. I thought it would be fun to see Nana and Papa, maybe even take a ride on my boat."

That got his nephew's full attention. "You have a boat?"

"I do." He pulled up a picture on his phone, and showed it to him.

"It's the biggest boat in the world!"

Prescott chuckled. "I want to take you and Jack for a ride."

"Loki too?" Ethan asked.

"Loki too."

Ethan's excitement propelled him to eat his oatmeal, then climb down. "Okay, let's go on the boat."

"That's tomorrow," Prescott explained. "Today is Friday and we've gotta finish the week strong. That means school for you and work for us."

"I thought it would be fun to try out your new stroller after work," Jack added. "And Loki and I will come with you."

Ethan looked from her to Prescott. "Is Jack your special friend?"

"What's a special friend?" Prescott asked.

"My mommy had a special friend. Mr. Man."

That's probably the father of Sally's baby. "What made him special?"

"Mommy let him stay with us, but I didn't like him."

"Because he scared you?" Jacqueline asked.

"Uh-huh, but I like Jack. She's nice to me, she gives me sugar, and she doesn't make scary faces."

"I like you a lot, Ethan, and I will never, ever make a scary face," she said. "I don't like them either. And I'm so happy you like Loki because I think you're his favorite person."

He grinned. "Really?"

"He always runs to you first and he likes playing with you best."

"He doesn't share."

Jacqueline smiled. "I can help with that. I'm happy to be here with you and Uncle Prescott. Can I give you a hug?"

"Uh-huh."

She folded her arms around him and gave him a gentle hug. "I hope you have a fun day at school." Then, her gaze fell on Prescott. "Can I give you a hug goodbye too?"

He folded her into his arms and held her there, then kissed the top of her head. "I'll see you later." Unable to resist, he dropped a light kiss on her lips.

On the way to his office, he called his mom, put the call on speaker.

His mom answered. "Hey, Scotty, Dad and I were just talking about you. How've things been?"

"The parental learning curve is steep," he said, and she laughed. "I've got Ethan with me and we're headed to school and work."

"Hey, Ethan," his dad said. "It's Nana and Papa!"

"Hi," Ethan called from the back seat. "I have a new puppy! It's Jack's, but she says he likes me best!"

"You got him a dog?" his mom asked.

"Not exactly," Prescott replied. "I'm taking the boat out tomorrow. Can you join us?"

"We've got something," his mom replied, "but we'll shift it to Sunday."

"That's great. I know Ethan would love to see you guys." He paused for a second. "I've recently reconnected with someone, and she'll be with us."

"Great," his dad replied.

"We look forward to meeting her," his mom added. "Why don't I put together a picnic?"

"You don't have to—"

"I have to run to the market anyway," his mom said. "What about nuggets?"

From the back seat, Ethan exclaimed, "I love chicken nuggets!"

"Nuggets are fine." Prescott pulled into the daycare parking lot. "Gotta run. See you tomorrow."

"Have fun at school, Ethan," his mom said.

"Bye, Nana and Papa," Ethan called out.

After situating Ethan in daycare, he drove to his office.

One of the first-floor receptionists flagged him down and handed him a business card. "A Detective Kealing is waiting in reception for you."

Several people were heads-down on their phones. As he made his way over, they all looked up. Some were seated on the sofas and chairs, while two stood near the floor-to-ceiling windows.

"Detective Kealing?" Prescott called out.

The woman near the window made her way over. "Mr. Armstrong, I'm Detective Kealing. I'm investigating the murder of your sister."

"Let's talk over here." He led her to the other side of the two-story atrium, where they'd have privacy.

"I'm sorry for your loss," she began. "Were you and your sister close?"

"We only met a few months ago."

"Why's that?" the detective asked.

"Her mom dated my dad. After they broke up, her mom found out she was pregnant, but never told him. My dad met and married my mom, but he died when I was a baby. After Sally's mom passed, she discovered we were related, and she contacted me."

"I see," Kealing said. "Did you know she was pregnant?"

"Not until the autopsy report," Prescott replied. "I requested the DNA profile of the fetus. I'm hoping to get that back soon."

"Was she seeing anyone?"

"She never mentioned it. But her three-year-old, Ethan—who's been living with me since she died—told me his mom had a special friend, but Ethan didn't like him because he made scary faces."

"Did he give you a name?"

"He called him Mr. Man."

"Who's Ethan's dad?"

"Also deceased."

"Wow, you have that in common with him."

"My dad had pancreatic cancer. I don't know how Ethan's dad died."

"Would you be willing to bring Ethan to the station so we can try to get a description of Mr. Man? I'll arrange to have a child therapist there as well."

Prescott nodded. "Whatever you need."

"I'll set something up for next week." She handed him her business card.

As Prescott escorted the detective out, Artemis pulled into his front-row parking spot.

He entered the building, phone to ear, a smile splitting his face. He hadn't seen his uncle this happy in a while. As he gave him the once-over, he realized he'd dropped at least thirty pounds.

Prescott wanted to follow up on Markesha's concern about TopCon's rebranding project.

"I'll talk to you later." Artemis hung up and regarded Prescott. "What exciting weekend plans do you have?"

"Taking the boat out. You?"

"Your aunt is flying to Manhattan for the weekend, so I'll be relaxing by the pool."

"How's the rebranding project with TopCon going?" Prescott began.

"Fantastic!" Artemis replied.

"What kind of time frame are we looking at?"

"I'm sure they'll turn it around ASAP."

"Did you see our in-house proposal for the sensitive skincare brand?" Prescott continued. "That campaign mirrored the one you presented by TopCon. That's some coincidence, huh?"

Artemis stepped close. "I showed our marketing team TopCon's rough mock up. Now, don't get me wrong, I am *not* pointing fingers, but I think they incorporated some of the consultant's ideas. And I get that. They're concerned about job security, but we're a three hundred-billion-dollar company with deep, deep pockets. A mil and a half for TopCon is a drop in the bucket." After patting Prescott on the back, like he was dismissing him, he said, "I wouldn't give it a second thought."

Artemis headed toward the elevator and Prescott fell in line with him.

"You've gotta run TopCon's campaign by the brand manager once it's finished."

Artemis stabbed at the elevator button. "Don't tell me how to run my own company."

"That's just it, Artemis, it's not *your* company. We're a publicly traded organization with a responsibility to our shareholders, our employees, and our consumers."

The elevator doors opened, but Artemis stood there glaring at Prescott. "When your beloved career came to an abrupt—and humiliating—end, who was there for you? I was! I step one toe out of line and hire a consulting company and you go ape shit! You should be kissing my ass, Prescott McCafferty Armstrong, for offering you a C-level position at a company where the only thing you ever did was keep a motherfucking seat warm on the board!"

Artemis stepped into the waiting cab, spun around, and said, "You should be ashamed of yourself for speaking to me like that!"

The elevator doors shut and Prescott's lips curved into a smile. That kind of outburst could only mean one thing. His uncle was guilty of something.

And Prescott was determined to find out what.

21

LOVE ME, LOVE YOU

Jacqueline

Jacqueline spent the morning doing a deep dive on the five former ALPHA Ops who'd worked with Gloria and Bert.

One had passed away, one had retired to Florida, and the third had moved to New Mexico. They had no motive to kill either Op, and she found nothing that indicated they'd returned to the area to take them out. The fourth had taken a job booking cruises at a travel agency. From the posted pics on her social media accounts, she spent a lot of time at sea. While she'd been in town the night Gloria had been murdered, Jacqueline had confirmed the travel agent had been working at her office, then driven straight home.

Frustration had her shoving out of the chair.

She was pushing hard to find something—*anything*—that would help move her case forward, but, so far, she'd come up with nothing.

She found Loki conked out in the middle of the family room. As she got closer, he opened his eyes and his tail started swooshing back and forth on the floor. She sat beside him and he rolled over for a belly rub.

"Hello, handsome. How's my boy doing?"

One rub later, he trotted toward the front door. She leashed him up, grabbed her sunglasses and a doggie waste bag, and left.

After pausing in front of the retina scanner, she said, "Computer, lock all exterior house doors."

"Doors secured, Jacqueline," replied the computer through the intercom.

The day was warm, the sun bright. She walked up the street, turning onto the next, then made her way down that short street. Rather than continue, she retraced her steps, and passed by Prescott's beautiful estate toward the cul-de-sac. Around it they walked, then back toward home.

The neighborhood was quiet, the homes pristine. As she got closer to the house, a gray sedan drove slowly toward her. She glanced through the windshield and her heart jumped into her throat. The driver was dressed as a clown—except this was the scariest, most freakish clown mask she'd ever seen.

Fear powered through her.

The car stopped, the driver unrolled the tinted window. The clown mask had oversized, shadowy eyes, and an open mouth with large, yellowed, fang-like teeth.

The clown lifted a costumed arm and waved at her, then continued driving.

She stood there, her feet cemented in place while dread filled her soul. She eyed the license plate. Maryland tags. She went to pull her phone from her pocket, but she'd left it at the house, so she kept repeating the combination of letters and numbers over and over.

"C'mon, Loki."

As she strode toward home, she glanced over her shoulder as the car continued toward the court.

With a mask that looked like that, there was no way he was headed to a children's party. She hurried up the driveway and over to the front door. As soon as the scanner cleared her to enter, she rushed inside, bolted the door, and activated the alarm.

With her heart pounding out of her chest, she rushed into the living room and waiting by the window for the car to drive past. When it didn't, she confirmed the front door was locked before bolting upstairs and into the spare bedroom with a side-facing window that offered a view down the street. The gray car was nowhere in sight.

Chills flew down her spine as she stood there waiting for that damn car. Loki came trotting in, dragging his still-attached leash, a toy in his mouth. She unleashed him, then continued staring down the street.

Normally, she wouldn't think twice about a car driving by in the middle of the day, but that mask was downright terrifying... and he'd stopped to single her out.

Her phone started ringing. Abandoning her post, she ran downstairs and into Prescott's office. The number was blocked, which meant it was probably Z.

"Hello," she answered.

No response. She tapped the mute button, put the call on speaker, and waited.

"I'm watching you." The line went dead.

Jacqueline hung up and called Prescott.

"Hey, there's my woman," he answered. "How's your day going?"

"Someone just called me from a blocked number and told me they're watching me."

"I'm on my way."

"There's more. Someone dressed as a scary clown is watching the house."

"Now?" he asked.

"Yeah." She told him what happened on her walk.

"Where's your gun?"

"In an overnight bag in the top of my closet."

"Get it. And alarm the house."

"Already did."

"I'd call someone in BLACK OPS to wait with you, but I'm probably closer than any of them."

The call waiting tone sounded. It was another call from a blocked number. "He's calling me again."

"Weapon up."

She bolted to the other side of the house and into the first-floor bedroom. After pulling down the bag, she put in the code to open the lock, but her fingers were shaking and she couldn't get the spinner to stop at the right combination. She finally got it, the lock opened, and she pulled out her Glock.

"Got it," she said to Prescott. "The other caller hung up."

Loki barked, and she hurried out. He was standing in the foyer, staring at the front door. With her heart pounding out a frantic rhythm, she peered through the peephole. No one was there. She hurried into the living room and glanced outside. The gray car wasn't out front.

"I have a safe room," Prescott said, his velvety voice a godsend. "Take Loki downstairs. Go into my theatre room. There's a door in the corner. Stand in front of the scanner. It should open for you. I gave you full-house access."

"Okay."

She grabbed a few dog treats from the kitchen and called for Loki. He came trotting in. She gave him one, then said, "Loki, come," and headed toward the basement.

Down the stairs they flew and into the theatre room. Now trembling, she stood in front of the scanner, the light stayed red. She moved away, returned to the scanner. No change.

"I'm at the scanner, but it's not giving me access."

"Fuck," he bit out. "Stay down there and away from the windows. I'm seven minutes out."

Prescott

PRESCOTT CRAVED CONTROL AND ORDER. At the moment, he had none. But that was about to change, one fucking problem at a time.

"How you doing?" he asked.

"I'm okay," she said. "But I'll feel better when you're here."

"I'm pulling into my neighborhood. What kind of car is he driving?"

"A gray, four-door sedan. Maryland tags, black tinted windows, except the windshield."

"I passed the house. I'm driving around the court and there's no gray car. I'll drive the neighborhood—"

"No, just come home. Please."

He pulled up to the garage, tapped the remote, the door rolled up. Once inside, he cut the engine, got out. "Computer, close the garage door."

"Welcome home, Prescott," said the computer.

He waited until it closed before he stood in front of the scanner. The light turned green and he stepped into the house.

Jack came rushing over, Loki bounding ahead of her, his tail sweeping the air at a rapid pace. She crashed into him and hugged him hard. Wrapping her in his arms, he held her tight.

She was safe, and he could breathe.

"I got you," he murmured.

"Thank you for coming home. I probably overreacted—"

"No, you did the right thing to call me."

He broke away, ran his hand down her back, then clasped her hand. She was trembling.

"Computer, did anyone approach the house this afternoon?"

"Checking." After a few seconds, the computer said, "Jacqueline Hartley exited through the front door at twelve-fifty pm. Jacqueline Hartley entered through the front door at one-oh-six pm. Prescott Armstrong entered through the garage door at one-seventeen pm."

Jacqueline broke away. "I'm sorry for asking you to come home. I feel like a baby, or worse, a helpless woman."

"Don't do that," he said. "You aren't helpless, and you don't need to deal with this alone."

"That's ironic coming from a lone wolf."

With his hand on the small of her back, he guided her into the kitchen. She set the gun on the counter. "Where can I keep this so it's out of Ethan's reach?"

"I've got a safe in my office and one in my safe room downstairs. I've never had to lock up a gun before." He glanced around the room. "We'll keep it in my office safe."

After filling a glass with water, he handed it to her. She took a few sips.

"Did you get the tag number?"

"Yeah." She shuddered in a shaky breath.

"Before we do that, let's make sure you have access to the safe room." Down the stairs they went.

She stood in front of the scanner. The light turned green.

"Computer, why couldn't Jacqueline access my safe room earlier?"

"One moment," the computer replied. "An unidentified individual attempted to enter the safe room at one-eleven pm. Retina scan failed due to excessive motion."

"I wasn't my most calm self," Jack murmured.

He stroked her back. "It's okay, babe. You're safe, now." Placing his hands on her shoulders, he peered into her eyes. "I will not let anything happen to you."

She nodded. "Thank you."

In his office, he logged into ALPHA. "Let's run the tags, then find a phone number to go with that blocked call." She rattled it off before collecting her laptop and sitting on the love seat.

"Give me your phone." He pulled a cord from his desk drawer, connecting her phone to his laptop.

Determination and fury fueled him. He would find the son of a bitch stalking her.

"It's gonna take a few minutes for the programs to run." He leaned back in the chair and studied her. *She's not okay.* "Going forward, we'll work together."

"Please check Ethan," she said.

He opened the daycare app. "There's the wild child." He showed her. "And he's okay. We'll pick him up together and I'll add you to the approved list."

Her heartfelt smile helped settle him down. "Thank you for trusting me with your child."

"My child. Still hard to wrap my brain around that."

She sat back down. "I need to get back to work. Z called me looking for results."

"Make any progress this morning?"

"I cleared four of the five former Ops," she said.

"That's good and bad."

"I know. It's not getting us any closer to finding the killer." She opened her laptop and resumed her search.

He called his assistant, Francis.

"Everything okay?" his assistant asked. "You ran out so fast."

"All good," he replied. "I'm going to be working remotely for the rest of the afternoon. I didn't see any meetings—"

"You're clear. Artemis stopped by and apologized for blowing up at you. He said he'd be happy to let the in-house marketing team roll out the sensitive skincare campaign."

That makes no sense. What the hell is TopCon doing for the million and a half?

"Thanks for the message." Prescott ended the call and made another.

His accounting director answered. "Hershel Jones."

"Hey, Hershel, it's Prescott. I need to know how much money was paid to TopCon."

"Got it," replied the director.

"And who signed off on those payments," Prescott added.

"When do you need this, and please don't say 'now'?"

"When can you get it to me?"

"Mid-week, next week," said the director.

"Keep this between us?"

"Of course," Hershel replied.

Prescott hung up, then slid his gaze to Jacqueline. She was reading something on her laptop.

Truth was, he was absolutely crazy about her. He always lived life on full thrusters, but the past several weeks had been total mayhem. And now, a fucking clown? He wasn't sure what to make of it. Jacqueline wasn't in ALPHA. Her life shouldn't be in danger, so was that drive-by unrelated? Or was it somehow connected to everything they were chasing?

BING!

The program had found a match. The gray vehicle was owned by a woman in Silver Spring, but her car had been reported stolen a week ago.

"Hey, babe," he said.

She flicked her gaze in his direction and smiled. "Am I your babe?"

"My babe," he confirmed.

"I love that so much. I've never been anyone's babe. Well, no one I cared this much about."

He pointed to himself. "Point goes to me."

She pushed off the sofa, sat in his lap, and dropped several doting kisses on his lips. "A zillion points." Her smile had him breathing easier. "What did you find?"

"The gray car was stolen. As much as I want to call the police, I think we're gonna let the clown think he's got the upper hand."

"Well, he kinda does."

Prescott flashed a devilish smile. "No, he doesn't. I'm a trained killer and I will do whatever it takes to keep you safe."

Her tight shoulders relaxed. "Oh, wow. Thank you."

"Computer, if a gray, four-door car with a Maryland license plate passes by the house, let me know."

"Yes, Prescott," replied the computer.

"Computer, if you see someone outside in a scary clown outfit, let me know."

"Yes, Prescott," the computer repeated.

"I haven't finished researching the final Op, but I don't think she's guilty of killing Gloria or Bert," Jack said. "I'll review the cases Gloria and Bert testified against. Hopefully, I'll have more luck."

"This is taking too fucking long."

She barked out a laugh. "Too long? I'm on my own. Usually, there are several others I can reach out to for help."

He released a growl. "We need a damn break. Just one. Something's gotta give."

She stood behind his chair, placed her hands on his shoulders and started kneading his muscles. "Whoa, you are tight."

After a few minutes of her massaging his traps, he inhaled deep. "That feels damn good."

He grew silent while she worked on him. As the tension started to melt away, he knew what he had to do. He needed to escape reality with Jacqueline for just a little while.

"Thank you," he said.

She leaned around and kissed his cheek. "I hope that helped."

"That felt amazing."

As she went to sit back down, he stood. "We're going upstairs to *really* relax. Just you and me. Now."

She cracked a smile. "You know you're insane, right?"

"For you, yes."

"With everything going on—"

"Sex is the great reset. Thirty minutes, that's all we need. My bed, or yours—"

"They're all your beds," she replied.

He slinked his arms around her, kissed her softly. "I need you, Jack. Everything else can wait. Every. Fucking. Thing."

Prescott's phone rang. He ignored it.

"It could be daycare," she said.

He glanced at his phone. "It's Cooper. I gotta take this." He answered, put the call on speaker. "Hey, Coop, what's going on?"

Jack loosened his tie and began unbuttoning his shirt while energy powered through him.

"I'm calling with good news," Cooper said.

He shoved down a moan as she pressed her lips against his chest and kissed him. "You caught the killer and my life can go back to normal," Prescott said.

"Life goes back to normal when *you* and *Jacqueline* catch the killer," Cooper continued.

With a gleam in her eyes, she removed his tie.

"I'm calling because we got the ballistics report back," Cooper said, but Prescott was only half listening.

Stunning green eyes drilled into his while she caressed his hardening shaft through his pants.

"I just sent it to you." Cooper continued. "The weapon that wounded your sister *wasn't* the same one that gunned down Gloria and Bert."

"Mmm," Prescott murmured, heat pounding his chest while blood rushed to his cock.

"Yeah, I thought the same thing," Cooper said, and Jack stifled a laugh.

Prescott muted the phone. "You're a naughty girl."

"You love it." She tugged down on his fly, slipped her hand inside, and extracted his hard shaft.

"Are you there?" Cooper asked.

Prescott unmuted. "Yeah, go 'head.'"

"Great idea," she whispered. "I think I will."

Kneeling at his feet, she caressed his penis. When she ran her tongue up his shaft like a lollypop, he growled.

"I know, this is frustrating as hell," Cooper said. "Are you looking at the report?"

Prescott was standing there with a boner shooting to the moon and the most gorgeous, naughty woman kneeling before him. He had no fucking idea what Cooper was talking about.

"Sorry, Coop, I'm not online."

"Hmm, the system shows you're logged on, otherwise I wouldn't have called."

Fuck.

He might not have a chip in his damn neck, but ALPHA tracked every fucking thing from the second they were online until the moment they logged off.

"Right, I am online, but I—"

Jack took him into her mouth, gobbling up his thick cock, her tongue swirling over his sensitive skin. He couldn't take his eyes off her. Sexy, stimulating as hell, and hauntingly beautiful, she had captured his complete attention.

"Whoa," he bit out.

"Yeah, it's crazy," Cooper said. "I couldn't believe it myself."

Jacqueline pulled him out, then slid him back into her warm, wet mouth. Seeing her suck him sent his blood whooshing through his veins. He couldn't think... could only feel. And she felt fucking fantastic.

"We've got a whole new set of problems on our hands."

Prescott gritted his teeth, then forced himself to speak. "I'm not looking at the report. I'll call you back in ten. No, twenty."

He hung up and roared, surrendering to the onslaught of pleasure. She was taking him into her mouth, sucking, licking, teasing his head with her talented tongue, then pulling him out and rolling her tongue over it. Every time wetness seeped out, she'd gobble it up on a long, ardent moan.

He sunk his fingers into her hair, closed his eyes while the euphoria thrummed through him. She was taking him higher and higher, turning him into a savage beast. He opened his eyes and watched her. Eyes closed, she was focused on him... just him. His pleasure, his happiness.

He'd been moaning, his voice sounding foreign, even to him. A deep, growl ripped through him as the orgasm shot out.

She could unravel him with very little effort, and each time she did, she owned a little more of him. As he stood there basking in the sweet, sweet release, he knew.

She's the one.

When she opened his eyes, they were black with lust, her luscious lips wet with his juices.

"You are So. Fucking. Sexy," he said as she left his office.

A moment later, as she sauntered in his direction, she stripped off her shirt. Then, she wiggled out of her yoga pants and fisted her hands on her hips.

Jack, in a black push-up bra and a black thong, was feminine perfection. Timeless beauty stared into his eyes while he appreciated her flushed cheeks and labored breathing.

The air crackled with wild energy while he soaked her up. But the pull was too strong. He went to her, snaked his arms around her bare waist, and kissed her. She moaned into his mouth, opened hers, and welcomed him inside. Grinding against him, she pushed onto her toes and bit his lip.

A flash of pain made him growl, then he collected a chunk

of her hair into a ponytail and tugged her head back. "You. Are. All. Mine."

A sliver of a smile lifted her lips. "Like a prisoner?"

The playfulness in her tone, coupled with the lust pouring from her eyes, had him capturing her face in his hands. "I am at your mercy." He wanted to pamper her, worship her, and bring her all the pleasure.

After moving their laptops, he pulled her close, peered into her eyes, then kissed her. The ferocity of their embrace had them raking their hands down each other's backs. He bit her chin, her earlobe.

"Yes," she cried out.

He unhooked her bra, tugged down her panties. "Lay on my desk. I'm going to make you scream my name when you come, baby."

Her breath caught, then a groan tore out of her, the desperation in her voice making his cock move.

"I need you naked," she said as she helped him out of his shirt, then worked fast to remove his pants.

Then, she laid across his desk, leaving her ass hanging off the edge. Heat charged through him while he regarded her naked form, but it was her jagged breathing and writhing hips that had him hitching a brow.

"I can't wait to eat you." Leaning over, he kissed her, letting his tongue sink into her mouth. The kiss continued while he teased her nipples, then pinched the nibs. She bit his tongue. He loved when she played rough.

"Behave," he warned before kneeling before her glistening sex.

She was stroking her clit, running her fingers over her opening. He collected her hand, sucked her fingers. "You taste good," he hissed. "So good."

He replaced her hand with his mouth, tonguing her sensitive flesh and teasing her clit.

"Yesssss, that feels amazing," she murmured as she pushed her pussy into his mouth.

He tongued her, fingered her, stroked her pussy with one hand, her anus with the other. Her sounds turned throaty, her cries urgent. She was bucking and thrusting against him so hard he threw his arm over her.

"You're greedy, Jack."

"Ohgod, you're making me crazy. I love how you fuck me with your mouth."

"If you behave, I can use both hands."

"I can't stop moving," she said. "It feels too good."

He released her so he could gently stroke her fleshy skin. Her moans turned to cries, she started moving faster, then she arched into his mouth. "Fuck me, Mac. You're making me come so good."

Her sweet juices oozed into his mouth, while he nursed her through her release. When she went boneless, he retreated into the bathroom, washed his hands, and returned. He scooped her off the desk and into his arms.

Her eyes fluttered open. "You are a perfect man."

He was so far from that, he couldn't even connect to her words, but he kissed her exposed neck before laying her on the throw rug. "Feel better?"

"I need you inside me. *Now*."

"I gotta grab a condom—"

"No. I'm on the pill, I'm clean, and I'm all yours... if you want me."

He wanted her until the end of time. He lay over her, dropping a soft kiss on her lips. "I'm clean, and I want you for-fucking-ever." Moving slowly, he pressed the head of his cock inside her heat.

Jacqueline

THROBBING NEED POUNDED THROUGH HER. She couldn't wait to take his naked cock inside her. Could. Not. Wait.

Arching up, she spread her legs wider, and relaxed, though she couldn't get her breathing under control. Her insides thrummed with an urgent desire to mate with him. Over and over, again and again. She was insatiable when it came to him, and she had been from the beginning. His power and charisma were a scorching-hot aphrodisiac.

He tunneled inside and she relished the intense, immediate shock of euphoria that ran wild through her. Nothing mattered —*nothing*—but the man inside her.

"I love being with you," she whispered. "Love how easy this is for us."

He stilled, his cock buried deep inside her.

"I love you, Jacqueline," he murmured.

While there was confidence in his tone, there was a vulnerability in his eyes that she'd never seen before.

She melted, the love washing over her, erasing all the bad. She had found her person. She knew in her heart that she had.

"I love you too." Jacqueline had fallen deeply in love with an assassin. Crazy, head-over-heels in love with someone she'd once loathed with a passion.

They stared into each other's eyes, soaking up the feeling. It was heady and amazing... and a little overwhelming.

Not because she felt that way, but because she'd been so willing to tell him. Being with him was different. Being with him mattered. His needs, his desires, his hopes were as important to her as her own.

He started moving inside her, the thrill snagging her attention while she ran her fingertips over his shoulders and down his back. Touching him, being touched by him, had her moving against his thrusts.

A simple repositioning and he ran his tongue over her nipple, sending skitters of excitement raining down on her. He nibbled, bit her. She yelped. Her reward. Bright eyes that drilled into her while a devilish smile danced on the corners of his mouth.

They moved as one, lost in each other and in the pleasures of the flesh.

He finished pampering one breast, returning to her mouth. "I can't get enough of you."

She reached over her head, resting her arms on the floor. "Hold me down."

A groan ripped from him as he held her wrists in his large hand. She arched up and started moving faster. His thrusts were harder, longer, and his cock expanded, growing thicker with each thrust.

Their sexy sounds filled her ears while her body bowed to his. Then, his growls turned feral while he fucked her faster and harder, the long strokes of his steel shaft taking her higher and higher.

And then, he sucked her other nipple, drawing the orgasm out of her. She started bucking beneath him and crying out.

"Me too, baby," he roared.

Blinding, deafening pleasure blanketed her in ecstasy. She opened her eyes to find his locked on hers.

They climaxed together, the spasms making her cry out and shake beneath him as her insides tightened around his massive cock.

Spent and sated, she lay there, unable to move, panting for breath, while beads of perspiration rolled between her breasts. This was the ultimate escape with the ultimate man.

They lay together in silence while they caressed each other. Tender strokes after hard and savage fucking, like wild animals, with no limits.

Still inside her, he rolled them over so she was laying on him. They shared a smile.

"I feel like I could take on the world right now," she murmured.

"We have to promise each other that no matter what life throws at us, we step away from the mayhem to have sex, make love, fuck. Pick one or all three. There's nothing better than being with you. *Nothing.*"

In that moment, her soul bound itself to his. She wanted to lay with him forever. Never move, never stray away. This was her happy place, and it had been from the moment they'd first gotten together.

"Have you forgiven me for the cult tragedy?" he asked.

"Forgiven." Pressing her lips to his, she kissed him. "As much as I'd rather stay here, we have to work." She pushed off him.

A short time later, they'd relocated onto the back porch, working side by side at the table.

Refreshed and energized, she said, "Your sister's cell phone log came back. After I finish researching the former ALPHA Op, I'll review it."

"I'll look over the ballistics report from Coop," Prescott said.

Thirty minutes later, she was convinced the former Operative had nothing to do with Gloria and Bert's murders. Forced to widen her search, she requested a report that listed every defendant Gloria and Bert had testified against.

As the computer compiled the data, she jumped to Sally's phone log, sorted it by numbers, and started scrolling. There were more texts than phone calls.

One incoming and one outgoing call caught her eye. Last month, an inbound call was recorded at four-forty in the morning. It lasted four minutes. Twenty minutes later, Sally called that same number. That call lasted almost three minutes.

In addition to those calls, there were two revealing texts between Sally and that same phone number.

She entered the number into the Bureau's database. While waiting for the request to process, she started sifting through Gloria and Bert's cases. There were eighteen cases where they both testified.

"This'll take forever," she grumbled.

Used to being alone in her cubicle, she flicked her attention to Prescott. He was so laser-focused, he hadn't heard her. Going forward, she'd have to keep her thoughts to herself. That was not something he needed to hear.

She sorted the cases by deceased, incarcerated, escaped, or released. Starting with the escaped convicts, she scrolled down the short list.

Prescott's raspy growl snagged her attention. His eyebrows were slashed down and a shadow had fallen over his eyes. After pushing away from the patio table, he made a call.

"I read the report." He listened, then said, "She's with me. I got this."

Prescott hung up, but he stood there staring out at his property. She couldn't take her eyes off his commanding presence. He inhaled a deep breath, his already expansive shoulders rising and falling. When he turned to face her, his narrowed gaze and flared nostrils said it all.

He was furious.

"Please don't tell me another Operative has been murdered," she said.

The angry energy billowing off him made her guts twist.

"I read the ballistics report Coop sent over," he began. "The gun used to kill Bert and Gloria was the same one used in the assassination attempt on Luther Warschak, but it *wasn't* the same one that wounded Addison and Sally."

That made total sense, since whoever had shot Sally had

gone to the hospital to finish the job. "No surprise there," she said.

"The bullet they removed from Sally matched the bullets recovered from the Campus Killer victims."

Jacqueline's heart rate surged into triple digits. She couldn't catch her breath, the shock sending fear pummeling through her.

"No, that can't be right," she whispered, not believing the news. "Ohgod, that clown. He found me. The Campus Killer found me."

22

THE BOAT RIDE

Jacqueline

The confidence Prescott wore like a second skin calmed Jaqueline, but his actions made her feel safe.

Being terrified wrecked her the most. Life was hard enough, but living in fear and looking over her shoulder was debilitating. Being around Prescott gave her hope that one day she could take back her life, fully and completely.

As the shock subsided and logic took hold, she said, "The person who shot Sally might *not* be the Campus Killer. It *has* been a decade. Guns travel. He could have given it to someone, ditched it, or sold it."

"We have to assume it *is* the Campus Killer," Prescott said. "And we have to assume you're not safe. If we don't, we're dumb as fuck."

"I know. I'm just surprised, that's all."

"You and me both, babe. Nothing will happen to you," he bit out. "Nothing."

She wrapped her arms around him. "Thank you."

He kissed her. "We've gotta pick Ethan up."

Back in the house, Prescott attached his ankle holster, slid his weapon inside, and concealed them beneath his pants. Jacqueline changed from her tight-fitting yoga pants to a regular pair where she could hide her weapon in the ankle holster.

Loki went outside to pee, then into the back of the SUV.

As they made their way through Prescott's neighborhood, Jacqueline searched for the gray sedan, but didn't see it. After he pulled onto the main road, she told him she'd gotten Sally's phone log back.

"Find anything?"

"She had multiple interactions with a number I couldn't ID. Last month, the person called her at four-forty in the morning. Twenty minutes later, she called that number back. Each call lasted less than five minutes. Then, two weeks ago, she got two texts from that same number. One said, 'I miss you' to which she replied with the same text, and the second text said, 'I love you'. She replied that she loved him. If we find the owner of that number, we find the baby daddy."

"Nice work." He wrapped his hand around her thigh.

His touch thrilled her, calmed her, and reminded her that she was his. That, she loved the most of all.

"If that's him, he misses her and he loves her, but did he kill her?" Prescott made a call, put it on speaker.

"Hey, bro," Stryker Truman answered. "Can Emerson and I can rejoin the human race?"

"Not yet. I need your hacking skills."

"Name it."

"Get me a copy of the surveillance video from the night my sister was in the hospital." He gave Stryker the date.

"You got it," Stryker said. "Do you have any suspects in the ALPHA case?"

"We're working on it."

"Sooner than later would be good."

"Just get me a copy of the video." Prescott hung up. "I feel like we're running in circles, going fucking nowhere fast."

This time, she set her hand on his thigh. "Things take longer than anyone wants. No one knows that better than me. I've been waiting ten years for law enforcement to find the Campus Killer."

Prescott pulled up to the security gate at Armstrong. He held his badge against the scanner, the light turned green, and he proceeded through.

"I had no idea this compound was back here," she said.

"Nine buildings, with three more in various stages of construction." He parked at the daycare center, and they got out.

She opened the liftgate and Loki jumped out without her help. "Good job, Loki!"

"You can't stay out here alone," he said.

"I can't go inside with a dog. As soon as you tell Ethan that Loki's here, he'll be out the door."

"Stay close to the entrance."

She offered a reassuring smile as her man disappeared into the building.

My man. I love that... and I love him.

She walked Loki into the nearby grass.

Despite the terrifying clown and threatening phone call, she'd bounced back pretty good. She might be scared of her own damn shadow, but she kept going. Ten long years of pushing herself out of her comfort zone, and she wasn't going to stop just because some nut job had freaked her the hell out.

The door to the building opened and Ethan came flying out. "Jack!"

As he beelined toward her, she knelt. He threw his arms around her and hugged her. Love filled her to the brim and she hugged him back. Loki jumped on them, almost knocking her over. Laughing, she stood.

"You brought Loki!" Ethan exclaimed "This is the best day ever!"

Prescott joined them. "Ethan, you're a ball of energy."

Ethan took her hand and started tugging her toward the building. "I want to show you my cubby, and my table, and where we sit for circle time, and I want Miss Nancy to see Loki."

"I would love to come inside, but Loki can't. Maybe Uncle Prescott can wait with Loki."

"Okay, hurry." Ethan took off toward the entrance.

"He's so sweet." She handed Prescott the leash.

"I added you to the drop-off and pick-up list," he said.

She dropped a quick peck on his lips before hurrying to catch up to Ethan, who waited by the entrance. She opened the door and he bolted inside. As she turned back toward Preston, he was watching her.

She held his gaze for an extra second, so much love flowing between them.

I lusted him, I hated him, and now I can't live without him.

Ethan showed her his cubby, his table, and where they sat for circle time. Ethan was pure energy... and pure light. His enthusiasm made her soul happy.

A young woman approached the table. "Hi, I'm Nancy. You must be Jack. Ethan talks about you and Loki all the time."

"I'm happy to hear that," Jacqueline replied.

"You're the envy of the entire school," Nancy whispered. "All the teachers have the biggest crush on Mr. Armstrong." Her cheeks pinked. "I probably shouldn't say anything, but mygod, he's so hot."

Jacqueline smiled, but didn't comment on the hot Mr. Prescott. Instead, she asked, "Did you want to come out and see Loki?"

"I'd love to, but I can't leave the classroom. Maybe another time."

She caught up with Ethan, who had pulled his lunch box from his cubby.

"Thank you for showing me your classroom." She extended her hand, though she wasn't sure he'd take it.

This time, instead of running off, he placed his small hand in hers, and her heart warmed.

Prescott waited in the grass, surrounded by a harem of moms and a gaggle of kids. She would bet her life savings those moms were *not* there for the dog.

As she made her way toward him, he turned, their eyes met and that familiar hit of adrenaline soared through her. She loved that she was his. Loved that they'd taken their intimacy to the next level. Loved that her heart felt so full when she was with him and Ethan.

"Hey, babe," he said once she was within earshot.

Every woman whipped her head in Jacqueline's direction. One glared at her, another snarled. These women were eager to sink their teeth or their talons into him. No doubt, he was a huge catch... but he was hers.

"Okay, kids, we're gonna take off," Prescott said. "Have a good evening." Prescott tucked Loki under his arm like a package.

With each step, her heart beat faster, color flooded her cheeks.

She petted Loki on his head. "How's my boy?" she asked him.

"I'm good," Prescott murmured. "Much better since you took *good* care of me."

They shared a smile before loading up their precious cargo. When they got home, Jacqueline suggested they put Ethan in the jogging stroller.

"And go for a run?" Prescott confirmed. "I don't think so."

"I won't let him turn us into prisoners, and I don't want him to know I'm scared. That gives him all the power."

"But you *are* scared."

"He doesn't know that. I held my ground when he stopped and waved. I *walked* back to the house. I didn't run."

Thirty minutes later, the newly assembled stroller was parked in the driveway, Ethan was strapped in, and they were ready to go.

"I want Loki to come with us," Ethan whined.

Jacqueline had been peering up and down the street in search of the gray sedan.

Ethan looked so cute tucked in, even his scowl was adorable. "He can next time. I need to make sure I can keep up before we bring Loki."

"You set the speed, babe," Prescott said. "And I'll try to keep up."

She chuffed out a laugh.

They started out slow, but twenty minutes in, she was pushing hard, though she didn't think Prescott was. At forty minutes, she got a runner's high, and she shot Prescott a smile. When they finished, they were drenched in sweat.

"That was fun," she said.

"I needed that," he replied.

"If that SOB is watching my every freakin' move, I just showed him who's boss," she murmured.

"Me," Prescott replied. "I'm the boss."

After dinner, Prescott told her that a homicide detective assigned to Sally's case wanted to talk to Ethan about his mom's boyfriend.

"I want to see what he remembers before I bring him in next week," Prescott said. "Any suggestions?"

She set a few coloring books, the stack of printer paper, and the large box of crayons on the kitchen table. "This might work."

Ethan had been playing in the family room.

"Hey, bud," Prescott said. "Do you want to color with Jack and me?"

As Jacqueline pulled up a chair, Ethan came walking over, climbed into his booster chair, and opened a coloring book. She and Prescott started drawing on the paper.

After a few minutes, Prescott said, "Ethan, do you remember telling us about Mommy's special friend?"

"I miss Mommy."

Her heart broke for him.

"I miss her too," Prescott said. "Do you like living with me?"

"Uh-huh. You play with me and you read me stories."

"Do you like that Jack and Loki are staying here with us?"

Ethan continued coloring, but didn't answer.

"Uh-huh," he said. "Is she your special friend?"

"She's definitely my friend," Prescott said. "And she's special to me, like you are. So, yes, she's my special friend."

Ethan's tongue has been sticking out as he continued coloring the picture.

"Do you remember your mom's special friend, Mr. Man?" Prescott asked.

Ethan stopped coloring and stared at Prescott. "I don't like him."

"Well, in order to make sure you're safe, I need to know what he looks like. Do you remember?"

Ethan went back to coloring, and a heavy silence fell over them.

"Did he have light hair or dark hair?" Prescott asked.

"I don't know."

"Do you remember if he was tall?" Prescott pushed.

More silence.

"He made scary faces and I told him no, but he just laughed at me." Ethan's tone had become indignant. "Mommy said the faces were funny, but I didn't like them."

The silence continued for a few more minutes.

"Ethan," Prescott said. "I'm sorry that he scared you. If you ever see him, you tell me right away and I will make sure he doesn't come near you, okay?"

"Okay."

Prescott's gaze slid to hers. She offered an encouraging smile.

Tossing a nod toward her picture, he asked, "Is that us?"

"Sure is," she replied. "That's Uncle Prescott and that's Ethan. That's me and this is Loki."

After studying her drawing, Ethan giggled. "Uncle Prescott is soooo big and Loki, he's tiny."

"That's how I see us," she said with a smile.

"We look like a happy family to me," Prescott said. "What do you think, Ethan?"

"My friends have a mommy and a daddy. A girl in my room has *two* mommies. I don't have a mommy *or* a daddy."

"Ohmygod," Jacqueline whispered.

"You do have a family," Prescott said. "You have me. You have Nana and Papa. You have Uncle Nicky and Aunt Addison, and Aunt Kerri and Uncle Lamar."

A tear streaked down Jacqueline's cheek. She had to do something to brighten the somber moment, so she extracted a large box from the coat closet, walked past them, and placed it on the throw rug in the family room.

"Hey, guys," she said. "Come check this out."

Loki zoomed over. She rubbed his ears, then told him to sit. Prescott eased onto the sofa, but Ethan stood beside her. After opening the shipping box, she smiled at him.

Ethan squealed with delight. "There is so many things!"

Even with Loki's face buried in the box, Ethan extracted three picture books, a backyard obstacle course designed for toddlers, and two doggie toys.

Ethan offered Loki the pull toy. He collected it in his mouth and trotted over to Prescott.

"Well, we know who Loki loves," Jacqueline said.

Jacqueline knew that "things" would never make up for the loss Ethan had endured, and that love would help him heal. But she wanted to move him past a scary memory. If anyone knew how paralyzing those were, it was her.

Ethan had pulled out the large obstacle course, still in its clear plastic packaging. "What's this?"

As Prescott explained it, Ethan started jumping up and down. Then, he ran over to Jacqueline and hugged her. "Fank you. Let's go outside and play!"

"I'm so happy you like it," she replied.

"How 'bout tomorrow when it's light outside?" Prescott asked.

Ethan stomped his foot. "I want to play *now*."

"I'm sorry," she said to Prescott.

"Hey, bud." Prescott held up one of the books. "Let's take it down a few."

As Ethan continued having his tantrum, Prescott said, "A book or you go right to bed. Your choice."

Ethan took the book and flung it on the floor. "I want to play."

"*Tomorrow*." Prescott's tone had become stern.

Ethan picked up the book and walked over to Jacqueline. "Will you read this to me, please?"

She did *not* want to get in the middle of this very classic triangulation, so she slid her gaze to Prescott.

"Ethan, we can disagree, but we always—*always*—have to be kind to each other," Prescott explained. "Do you understand?"

Ethan went to Prescott. "Okay."

"Thank you, Ethan. You did a good job calming down."

"Can you let Jack read me my new book?" Ethan asked.

Prescott bit back a smile. "That's up to Jack."

Ethan grinned at her.

"I would love to read to you, Ethan," Jacqueline offered.

She and Ethan sat together on the sofa, while Prescott sat on the floor with Loki. When she finished reading the picture book, she locked eyes with Prescott.

And her entire world fell into place.

When she'd come back to the area, she had no idea what to expect. Even in her wildest dreams, she never imagined falling head over heels in love with a man and his child.

This was where she was supposed to be. With the one man she'd hated with a vengeance. The one man who'd captured her body, her heart... and her soul.

She was his for as long as he would have her.

THE FOLLOWING MORNING, Prescott parked in the members-only yacht club lot. As Jaqueline eyed the massive vessels in their slips, there was no question she'd stepped into the lap of luxury. If his estate wasn't convincing enough, these boats certainly were.

Last night, after Ethan had gone to sleep, she'd told him that taking a day off felt like she was letting ALPHA down.

"They're counting on me—on us—to find the killer so they can resume their lives," she said.

"We deserve *one* day, so does Ethan," he'd pushed back. "There's no way I'm leaving you home alone, not after the shit that went down yesterday."

So, she decided to make the most of the day, then burn the midnight oil when they got back.

"Loki, heel," she said, keeping his leash taut. "Good boy."

"I'm in the boat slip at the end," Prescott said.

As they made their way down, a man and a woman stepped from a yacht onto the pier.

"It's Nana and Papa!"

When they pulled to a stop in front of them, Prescott's dad

lifted Ethan into his arms, then his mom kissed his pudgy cheek.

"Loki, sit," Jacqueline said, but he was too excited to pay attention to her. She repeated the command, yanking the slack on his leash. This time, Loki obeyed. "Good boy, Loki."

"Mom, Dad, this is Jacqueline," Prescott said.

"She's Uncle Prescott's friend," Ethan volunteered, "and Loki is her dog, but he's my best friend in the whole world."

"That's great, Ethan," Prescott's dad said.

"Hi Jacqueline, I'm Renée."

"I'm Mason," his dad said.

His dad was an older version of Hawk, with short, dark hair, graying temples, and bright blue eyes. Prescott definitely looked like his mom. She was a little shorter than Jacqueline with brown hair and a warm smile.

"This is Loki," Jacqueline said.

Mason set Ethan down before petting the pup. "He's a handsome guy." Then, he addressed his son. "Scotty, I readied her, so we're good to go."

"Everybody aboard," Prescott directed.

She spied the name of the yacht painted on the stern.

ARMSTRONG

That says it all.

As Prescott helped Jacqueline on, she said, "This is beautiful."

"It's a fifty-foot fly bridge Azimut," his dad offered. "Sleeps ten."

Jacqueline stepped into ultimate luxury. First class all the way with a large state room and generous-sized kitchen. On the bridge, were two large captain's chairs, and beyond that, an exterior sundeck for lounging. The décor was white with dark gray accents. Large windows on both sides of the vessel provided a great view from the interior of the craft.

"Wow, just wow," she said.

"It's a lot," his mom said.

She nodded. "It's... it's impressive." But that's how she felt about Prescott, so it shouldn't come as a surprise that his boat would be a reflection of him.

Despite his massive estate, she'd never given much thought to his wealth, but there was no denying that being an Armstrong had its perks.

Knowing she'd be on the water, she'd worn a white shirt and white gauze pants. With her hair pulled into a ponytail, she slipped on her visor.

Prescott went below, returning with lifejackets. After pulling one on, he handed them out.

"What's this for?" his dad asked.

Prescott tossed a nod at Ethan. "Safety, so we *all* have to wear one."

As everyone pulled on a vest, Prescott helped Ethan into his.

"Since it's calm, I can handle the lines by myself." Mason began removing one of the ropes from a cleat on the stern.

"Thanks, Dad. Ethan, you want to sit up there on the flybridge with me?"

"Okay. Can we go fast?"

"Absolutely. Jack, you with us?"

"I'll stay down here with Loki," she replied.

"We'll watch him," Renée said. "It's a lot of fun." With a kind smile, she said, "You should go."

"Thank you, Renée," Jacqueline said handing over Loki's leash.

"After you," Prescott said at the base of the ladder, then he dropped a light kiss on her lips. With a smile, she started climbing. He wasn't holding back around his mom and dad, and she liked that.

She liked that a lot.

With Ethan in his arms, Prescott said, "You ready, bud? We're climbing up there."

Ethan giggled. "This is soooo much fun!"

From the flybridge, she took in the sights. Two small captain's chairs sat beneath a white canopy. After she eased down, Prescott said, "Can you hang on to him?"

She patted her lap. "Absolutely. You ready for a boat ride, Ethan?"

His squeal of delight made her smile.

"Go fast," Ethan said.

"At first, we have to go very slowly," Prescott explained as he pulled out of the slip and motored toward open water. "That sign—" Prescott pointed— "says, 'No Wake Zone', which means we can't make big waves behind us."

A smile filled Ethan's face... and her heart. His wonderment made their outing that much more special.

She wrapped her arms around him.

"I'm not scared," he said.

"I know that, but I feel better holding onto you, in case we hit a big wave."

"I hope we go so fast we fly!"

Once out in the Potomac River, Prescott pushed the throttles forward and the yacht picked up speed, the vessel gliding effortlessly through the water.

"This is awesome." She glanced over at Prescott.

He stood at the helm, his hair blowing in the breeze, his white shirt unbuttoned, his tanned chest catching her eye. He was the epitome of style and grace. He was fearless and ruthless. A killer and a protector. He commanded the fifty-foot yacht like he commanded everything in his life. With total control and complete confidence.

He'd kicked off his shoes when he'd climbed aboard and, as her gaze floated past his strong hips and thighs, down past his muscular calves to his feet, she appreciated every magnificent inch of him.

He regarded her and his gaze softened. Then, he dipped down and kissed Ethan on the top of his head, then dropped a soft kiss on her mouth. "Love you guys."

Ohmygod.

Her heart was his.

"Ethan, are you having fun?" he asked.

"So fun! Can we go faster, pleeeeease?"

"Hold on." Prescott gave the throttles another thrust. The yacht lurched forward, then gradually got on plane, sending it skipping across the oncoming waves.

"Yaaaaaaay!!!" Ethan clapped.

She inhaled the fresh air, appreciated the sun's warmth on her skin. Then, the guilt crept in, as it always did. She was having fun. She was having an adventure with someone she'd fallen crazy in love with. Despite the mayhem, she was living her best life.

But Janey?

Janey's gone. Gone forever.

Her heart clenched, the familiar pang shot through her. While she'd told herself that she and Janey could have overpowered their abductor and escaped, she knew the serial killer would have murdered them both.

Emotion gripped her throat while tears pricked her eyes. The past had managed to creep into her perfect day, drowning her in sorrow and regret. Prescott slowed the yacht and she turned toward him.

His brows knitted together. "What's going on, babe?"

She pasted on a smile. "This is amazing."

"Talk to me," he said.

"Just thinking, but I'm fine, really."

"I want to see Loki and NanaPapa." Ethan started wriggling off her lap.

"Nice try." She tightened her grip on him. "We have to wait for Uncle Prescott before we climb down the ladder."

"No! You're a stupid buttweiner."

Prescott slowed the boat to an idle. "No name-calling Ethan."

"I want to go down."

"We do *not* talk to each other like that. What could you say to Jack that would be kind?"

"I want to see NanaPapa and Loki." He shot Prescott a big smile.

"What about please?" Prescott asked.

"Please," Ethan mimicked.

"What does buttweiner mean?" Prescott pressed.

"I can't know, but my friend says it."

"It's *not* a word we use, Ethan. Jack has been so nice to you. Do you think that was a kind thing to call her?"

"I want to get down," he repeated.

"Right, I got that," Prescott said. "No name calling. Do you understand?"

Ethan stared at him while another showdown of wills played out. After several seconds, Ethan turned to Jack. "You're nice."

"Thank you," she replied.

"When we say something that's mean, we can say 'I'm sorry' if we think we made a mistake."

"I'm sorry. Can I go down, please?"

"Absolutely." Jacqueline set him on his feet.

Prescott collected Ethan in his arms and retreated down the ladder. A few seconds later, he returned with Loki.

"I see the trade-off was a success," she said.

He set the dog on the floor and handed her the leash. "I won't tolerate disrespect. How'd I do, boss?"

She pushed out of the seat, kissed him. "You're incredible with Ethan." Then, she kissed him again. "With Loki, *and* with me."

He wrapped her in his arms and kissed her. One kiss that got heated pretty fast, but she slowed him down. "I'm definitely putting the brakes on a make-out scene thirty minutes after meeting your parents."

He chuffed out a laugh. "Fair enough, but you owe me one."

He resumed his spot at the helm, but instead of standing, he sat. "Get over here, woman." He pushed on the throttle and the boat picked up speed. "We're gonna continue down the river, then drop anchor and have lunch."

As she glanced at the other boats nearby, she couldn't help but wonder if the person in the creepy clown costume was watching their every move.

23

THE FAMILY OUTING

Prescott

Prescott loved boating, and he loved sharing it with Jack. Everything was better with her.

After lunch, where Ethan ate his entire plate of healthy food, he was inhaling Nana's homemade chocolate chip cookies.

As Prescott finished his third, he smiled at Ethan. "Nana's cookies are the best, aren't they?"

"The best cookies ever!" Ethan exclaimed. "I could eat them all!"

"Well, I made extra, so you can take them home with you," Nana said.

Ethan broke off a small piece and snuck it to Loki. Prescott caught Jacqueline's eye. "You okay with that?"

"Oh, sure," Jack replied. "We had dogs growing up, and I did that all the time, except not with cookies. I did it with broccoli."

"And they ate it?" Prescott asked.

"All, but one," she replied. "He couldn't stand it either."

"Ah, so you see what's happening under the table?" his mom asked.

Jack laughed. "He must really love Loki to share sugar."

Ethan giggled.

"How did you meet Jacqueline?" his mom asked.

"She was the agent in charge during the Winchester cult standoff."

"Are you still in Winchester?" his dad asked.

"I was transferred to San Francisco, but I'm back here working a case."

"Are you two working together?" his mom pressed.

"You know I don't work for the Bureau anymore," Prescott replied.

His mom held his gaze for a beat before addressing Ethan.

"Ethan, can Nana clean you up so you don't get chocolate all over the boat and we never get invited back?"

Her playful tone had Ethan smiling. "Okay, Nana. You have good cookies."

"I put a lot of love into them. Could you taste it?"

"I can't know. What does love taste like?"

Prescott's mom tickled him. "It tastes delicious."

Unless Prescott was completely missing something, he had definitely found his woman. But, once they solved the case—and he had every confidence they would—she would head back to California.

Not if I have anything to do with it, she won't.

THREE HOURS LATER, they were back in the slip. Ethan had fallen asleep on a king-sized bed in the lower level, and Prescott's mom must've checked on him twenty times. To say she was a doting Nana was an understatement. His dad was dozing on a cushion at the bow. Jack sat beside Prescott on the couch in the main cabin, Loki sleeping at her feet.

For the first time in as long as he could remember, he felt at peace. But the second he set foot on land, reality would slither back in and he'd be on the hunt for not one killer, but two.

Ethan emerged from the berth.

"Hey, bud," Prescott said, "You took a nap on a boat."

Ethan sat next to his mom on the sofa in the stern, and he and Jack joined them.

"Dad and I would love to take Ethan for a s-l-e-e-p-o-v-e-r," his mom said.

"That would be great," Prescott replied.

"Ethan, Papa and I want to invite you to a sleepover at our house tonight," his mom said. "Would you like to come?"

He glanced at Prescott. "Where will you be?"

"I'll be at our house," Prescott replied. "And I'll pick you up tomorrow."

"Can Loki come too?"

"Not this time," Prescott's mom replied. "I don't have any food for him."

"That's okay, Nana. He can eat my food."

The group laughed.

"Loki can spend the night next sleepover," his dad said.

"I bought Ethan a few outfits," his mom added. "And a toothbrush, and maybe even a toy or two."

"Toys?" Ethan asked.

"We're going to have the best time," his mom said to Ethan.

Twenty minutes later, Prescott was alone with Jacqueline. After walking Loki, they got comfortable on one of the sofas on the bow. Sitting side by side, their entwined fingers rested on her thigh, while they listened to the water lapping against the side of the craft.

"I could stay here forever," she said breaking the silence.

"I could, but only if you were with me," he replied.

She turned toward him, a smile lifting her lips. "I would be. Thank you for today. It was perfect." Then her smile was replaced with a sadness that touched her eyes. "It's hard for me to have fun."

"Why?"

"Because I lived," she replied.

He tucked a chunk of flyaway hairs behind her ear, leaned over and kissed her. "Babe, you can't spend your life punishing yourself for what happened."

"Yeah, I tell myself that, but I still struggle with survivor guilt."

He put his arm around her, caressed her bare shoulder. "You deserve to be happy, Jacqueline."

She nodded. "This has been an amazing day, and I'm so grateful I got to share it with you." Leaning up, she kissed him.

"There's no child here and I've got a large, very empty bed, down below. Who wants a tour of my ship?"

"I'll take one," she replied.

After a brief tour, he brought her into his stateroom. "You deserve to be loved."

"Are you the man to do it?"

"Yes. I. Am."

They helped each other strip out of their clothes, and they fell into bed. He took his time, appreciating her, arousing her, pleasuring her. They loved each other until the ecstasy reached its pinnacle, and they surrendered to the sweet, sweet relief.

In the afterglow, they lay curled around each other, safe in their cocoon. They'd traded the mayhem for one love-filled evening.

"I could love you for a long, long time," she murmured.

He kissed the tip of her nose. "I could love you forever."

She smiled. "If you're lucky, I'll let you."

Jacqueline

At nine o'clock, the following morning, Jacqueline eased down next to Prescott at the kitchen island, a mug of coffee in hand. She opened her laptop.

"You were right about yesterday," she said. "It was perfect. Thank you." She kissed his shoulder.

They'd returned home after dark, fed Loki, then retreated onto the dark screened-in porch where they made love under the stars. It was a perfect way to end a magical day.

"What time are you picking Ethan up?" she asked.

"My mom said he's having a blast, so we'll get him around one."

Her phone rang. "Hmm, it's my sister, Leslie." She answered. "Hello."

"Hey, Jacqueline it's Leslie's friend, Lou."

"Hang on one second." She tapped mute, then said to Prescott, "It's my sister's friend, the one I keep running into." She put the call on speaker, then unmuted. "What's going on?"

"Leslie wanted me to tell you she has the money she owes you. When can you swing by and pick it up?"

"Can I talk to her?"

"Sure."

"Hey," Leslie said. "What's up?"

"You've got my money?"

"How much do I owe you again?"

"Five thousand."

"You want me to leave it under the mat? Wait, hold on." Silence, then Leslie came back. "He told me not to do that. Just come by."

"I'll swing by today."

"Hey, how come you haven't followed me on social media?"

"I'm never on it."

"Well, just do it." Leslie hung up.

"What has happened to my sister?" Jacqueline muttered.

"Everything okay?" Prescott asked.

"Yeah," she replied.

"How many siblings do you have?" Prescott asked.

"Two. An older brother and sister."

"Are you tight with them?" He sipped his coffee.

"I'm close with Keith, closer with his wife, Naomi. Leslie and I used to be, but she's changed a lot since I've been gone."

"How?"

"She's become super obsessed with her looks and her Instagram modeling career. She's had a few plastic surgeries. You should come with me. If you're into humongous boobs, you'll love her."

"I love *your* boobs, and I *am* coming with you."

"Right." She sipped her coffee, pushed out of the chair. "This is cold. Can I heat yours?"

He handed her his mug. After heating both, she started working.

"I'm checking all the cases where Gloria and Bert testified against anyone they arrested while working at ALPHA."

Three hours later, she'd narrowed down the field from eighteen suspects to seven. "Terrence Maul came up again," she said. "What's his story?"

"He was in ALPHA—"

"You took out a former Operative?"

"Yeah," he replied. "Several years ago, he went on a mission with Bert and Gloria. From what I read about the case, they were supposed to take out six specific men and arrest anyone else in the house. He went crazy and killed *everyone*, including the women and children."

"Ohgod."

"It was a massacre. He got arrested. Bert and Gloria testified against him and he went to prison. He escaped last year and went missing for months until he surfaced in Fredericksburg. I was brought in to take him out."

"Which you did."

"I shot him, he fell into the river, but he hasn't washed up on shore yet."

"Gloria and Bert are dead, so Maul *definitely* goes back in the mix."

"You're wasting your time. He's dead." Prescott's phone vibrated with an incoming call. He answered on speaker, "Hey, Dad."

"Hey, Scotty. Ethan's been asking for you. What's your plan for picking him up?"

It was a little after noon. "We're swinging by around one. Everything okay?"

"He mentioned that his mommy didn't come back and he needs confirmation you are."

"Put him on."

"Ethan, I've got Uncle Prescott on the phone," his dad said. "Scotty, you're on speaker."

"Hey, bud," Prescott said. "Are you having fun with Nana and Papa?"

"Nana, she made me nuggets and she made them all by herself! They are soooo good. And they bought me presents that I get to play with when I'm here. When are you coming to get me?"

"I'll be there around one. Papa can show you on the clock."

"Okay, bye."

"We'll see you soon, son," his dad said before hanging up.

"Do we have time to swing by my sister's in Reston?" Jack asked.

"We'll stop by before we pick up Ethan," he replied.

In his office, Prescott slid his weapon inside his ankle holster. Then, he added his shoulder holster, covering the Glock with a lightweight jacket.

"Thank you for protecting me."

He kissed her. "Always."

Twenty minutes later, Prescott parked in Leslie's driveway. He lowered the windows for Loki, cut the engine, and got out.

As they made their way to the front door, Jack slid on her shades. "I've never had a bodyguard before. Are you round-the-clock?"

"Yes, ma'am."

"I'm going to take full advantage of my situation."

"I would expect nothing less." He palmed her ass. "But you gotta know, I'm a giver... and then I take."

She rang the doorbell. "I can't wait."

The door swung open and Lou stood there. Like every other time, he sported the knit cap, his long hair trailing down his chest. His gaze jumped from her to Prescott, then back to her.

"Hey, come on in," Lou said.

"Is Leslie here?" Jaqueline asked as she and Prescott stepped inside.

"She had to run out. You wanna wait?"

"I don't have time. Where's my money?"

He ambled toward the kitchen. "She couldn't find her checkbook, so she's gonna transfer the money."

She followed him, but Prescott pulled her to a stop in the foyer.

Lou was busy opening and closing kitchen drawers. "I'm looking for paper so you can write down your account number."

Yeah, like that's gonna happen.

"I'm not doing that," Jacqueline said.

"No problem. I'll call her." Lou pulled his phone from his pocket and dialed. While he waited, he tossed Prescott a nod. "You her boyfriend?"

To Jacqueline's surprise, Prescott didn't answer. She glanced up at him. His face gave away nothing, but his eyes were drilling into Lou.

Lou hung up. "She's not answering. Why don't you text her?"

Jacqueline typed a text. "I'm at your house. You're not. Where's my money???" She hit send.

No dots appeared.

Frustration tinged her mood. She should have figured Leslie wasn't good for it. "Let her know I stopped by."

Jacqueline was done. Initially, she believed her sister would pay her back, but now? No way. That money was gone, and she was done chasing it. Prescott said nothing as they made their way toward the front door.

"Hey, I'm leaving town," Lou said. "Our manager booked us a tour, so I'm taking off, tomorrow."

"For how long?" she asked.

"I'm a nomad. Gotta go where the gigs are. With any luck, we'll open for another band right after this tour ends."

"Who are you opening for?" she asked.

"Our manager said it's someone good. He's telling us tomorrow before we leave."

"Good luck with that." Jacqueline opened the door and stepped outside.

When Prescott exited, Lou shut the front door.

Prescott said nothing until he was backing out of the driveway. "I don't like him."

"Well, it's not like you'll ever see him again. He's leaving, and I'm not going back over there. My sister's never gonna pay me back."

"He was hoping you'd show alone."

"How do you know that?"

"I saw it on his face."

"Well, I'm never alone because I've got an *amazing* bodyguard."

"And I've got a *very* important client."

She leaned over, kissed him. "Thank you for keeping me safe."

He wrapped his hand around her thigh. "You can thank me later."

"Oh, I plan to," she replied.

Prescott drove into an older neighborhood with lovely homes and mature maple trees lining the streets. After pulling into a driveway, he killed the engine. "Ready for the mayhem?"

"Absolutely. I love Ethan and Loki's energy." She opened the liftgate. Instead of jumping down, Loki waited.

"Good boy." She grasped the leash. "Loki, out."

He hopped down.

Wagging his tail, he pulled her into the grass and started sniffing. One mini-pee later, and he was ready to head inside.

The two-story house was lived-in and comfortable. After hellos, she asked if his parents wanted her to put Loki out back.

"You can unleash him," Prescott's mom said. "He can run around with Ethan, if you can stay for a little while."

In their large family room, Ethan showed her and Prescott all the fun toys and educational books his Nana and Papa had bought for him. "But," he explained, "these are for here."

"You got some fun stuff here, bud," Prescott said.

"Nana and Papa bought me my own bedroom!" Ethan said.

"Why don't we go upstairs and show them?" Prescott's dad suggested.

Up the stairs they went, while Loki shoved his way through, determined to get to the top before anyone else.

Ethan proudly led the way into one of the bedrooms. "Nana said this used to be Uncle Prescott's." He pulled a framed photo off the night table, but instead of holding it out for everyone to see, he stared at it. "This is Nana and this is Papa. That's Uncle Prescott and Uncle Nicky. That's Aunt Kerri." He beamed at Prescott's mom. "I got everyone by myself, Nana!"

"You did a great job," his mom said.

He set down the frame, ran over to the toddler bed, and climbed on. "This is my big boy bed. Loki can stay here with me, and there's room for him!"

Jacqueline could not stop smiling. He was so happy. She believed he missed his mom, but he didn't dwell on the loss. Death was too complicated for a three-year-old to fully understand. Even so, he was managing far better than she was.

"Ethan mentioned that he sleeps in a crib," Prescott's mom said.

"Yeah, I've been meaning to buy him bedroom furniture," Prescott said before shifting toward Ethan. "How 'bout we go furniture shopping this afternoon and buy you a bedroom set?"

Ethan started jumping up and down on the bed. "Yay! Another present!"

Jacqueline laughed. "He's adorable."

"Ethan, do you want to shop with Uncle Prescott and Jacqueline or do you want to stay with us?" his mom asked.

Ethan stopped jumping and stared at her, then he regarded Prescott. He climbed down and slipped his small hand into Prescott's large one. Prescott picked him up and Ethan hugged him. "Nana and Papa, I'll come back and play with you another day."

"What do you say to them?" Prescott asked him.

"I can't know."

Prescott whispered in Ethan's ear. Jacqueline loved how patient he was with him. How everything was an opportunity to teach Ethan something new. For a man as ruthless as Prescott, she loved his softer side.

"Fank you for the sleepover, and for my toys, and my new room!"

His mom kissed Ethan on his cheek. "We loved having you. Next time, Loki can stay when you have another sleepover, if that's okay with Jacqueline."

"That's so nice," Jacqueline said, "and it's absolutely okay."

"Uncle Prescott and Jack can have a sleepover wif us too."

Prescott tickled Ethan and he started giggling.

"We can save you some time if you don't want to go to all the stores we went to," his dad said.

After his mom told him where they found the toddler bedroom set, they headed out, stopping at Prescott's to put Loki in the mudroom.

Back in the SUV, Prescott punched up Ethan's playlist as he drove to the upscale furniture store in Tysons. The oversized showroom was packed with shoppers hoping to grab a deal during the Memorial Day mega sale.

With Ethan in his arms, Prescott pulled to a stop inside the entrance. "Ethan, you have to hold my hand or Jack's hand while we shop. Do you understand?"

"Uh-huh, I won't go away."

As they were making their way through the large showroom toward children's furniture, Jacqueline glanced over at the home office sets. As her gaze floated over the shoppers, her brain shorted.

Her sister, Leslie, was shopping with the same man she'd been having dinner with at Carole Jean's.

Jacqueline pulled Prescott to a stop. "Look over my shoulder. There's a blonde with her back to us. She's with a tanned, older man. That's my sister."

He shifted his gaze past her. "No way," he murmured. "She's with my uncle."

24

I KNOW YOU TOO

Prescott

"What's my sister doing with your uncle?" Jack murmured.

"Can you put me down, pleeease?" Ethan asked.

"Not yet, buddy. I see my uncle over there. Let's go say hi." He clasped Jack's hand. "This'll be interesting."

Because the furniture was tightly packed in the showroom, Jack let go of his hand. He didn't like that she was behind him because he didn't have eyes on her, so he pulled over. "You gotta go first."

"Am I your shield?"

He chuckled. "I need eyes on you."

Her gaze softened, she leaned up, kissed his cheek. "Thank you."

Ethan giggled.

She gave Ethan's shoulder a gentle caress before continuing through the maze of furniture, Prescott close on her heels.

Artemis and Jacqueline's sister were staring at an office

furniture set, tucked in the corner. When Artemis glanced at them, his jaw became slack, his eyes grew large. He looked like he'd seen the devil himself.

"Hey, look who's here!" Artemis bellowed, his attention jumping to Ethan and Jacqueline. His eyebrows pinched together, before he gestured to the blonde. "You remember Leslie."

Leslie turned around and recoiled when her gaze met Jack's *That's the woman Artemis hired from TopCon.*

"Whoa," Leslie uttered. "What are you doing here?"

Jacqueline glared at her. "I swung by your house for my money, but you stiffed me."

Leslie barked out a laugh. "Relax. I just need your account number and that other number. Geez, don't pitch a fit." She flicked her gaze to Prescott, arched her back, and pasted on a big smile. "Hi, there, handsome. I remember you."

"What are you doing here?" Prescott asked his uncle.

"Window shopping," Artemis replied. "How 'bout you?"

"I'm buying Ethan bedroom furniture," Prescott said.

"Ethan?"

"My nephew. Sally's son."

"Whatever happened with that?" Artemis asked. "Did she get offered the job—"

"Hey, Ethan," Jack blurted. "Why don't we go check out the big boy furniture?"

Prescott waited until she'd taken Ethan out of earshot.

"Sally was murdered," Prescott said.

Artemis gasped. "Oh, how tragic. What happened?"

"She was shot," he said. "And now, Ethan has no family."

"That's so sad," Leslie said. "Poor little boy. Where's his dad?"

"Also gone," Prescott replied.

"Gone where?" Leslie asked.

"Gone, as in deceased," Prescott ground out.

"So, are you putting him in foster care, or what?" Artemis asked.

He glanced over at Jack. She and Ethan were examining a toddler bed.

"No, Ethan's living with me." Then, he shifted his gaze from his uncle to Leslie. "How's the marketing project coming along?"

"I finished it and gave it back to Artemis," Leslie proclaimed.

Prescott fought the urge to laugh. Rebranding a product line took months. Focus groups were brought in. Products were trialed in different-sized markets before rolling the brand out to the entire country. It was *not* something that could be completed in a month.

Prescott slid his gaze to his uncle, whose tanned cheeks had turned a bright orange.

What the hell are you up to?

He didn't have another second to waste on this shit show. "I'm taking off."

"*Great* seeing you," Leslie said.

Prescott regarded his uncle, before heading toward the children's section.

I'll deal with him later.

He scooped Ethan into his arms and soared him around like an airplane. Ethan started giggling.

"Look at you, Ethan," Jack said. "That looks so fun."

When Prescott set Ethan down, he showed Prescott the furniture Nana and Papa purchased for him. Jack caressed Prescott's back while they examined the other bedroom sets. Her soothing touch helped calm his mounting agitation.

"Ethan, what do you think of this one?" Jack eased down on a different toddler bed.

Ethan climbed on beside her.

"This is good, don't you think?" she asked.

"Uh-huh," he replied. "It's good!"

"Let's go pay for it, bud," Prescott said.

They stopped at a nearby sales desk to place their order. While Prescott was paying, Ethan asked how they were going to fit everything into the truck. Jacqueline explained that the furniture had to stay there, and that he was getting a brand-new bedroom set delivered to the house.

Ethan started crying. "I want to sleep in my new big-boy bed," he choked out between sobs.

"What about a slumber party in the family room tonight? We can play games and color, have a snack and watch a fun movie."

He stopped crying. "Loki too?"

She wiped his tears away. "Absolutely."

The sales associate said, "You're such a good mom. So patient."

To his surprise, Jack beamed. "Thank you."

There it is. She wants this.

And so do I.

On the way out, he picked Ethan up and put his arm around Jacqueline.

"You *are* a great mom," he said.

Her loving smile said it all.

As Prescott expected, mayhem ensued between boy and dog as soon as they got home.

"I never imagined this, but now I can't picture anything *but* this," she said. "I love this noise, the screaming, and the barking." She laughed. "They are pure energy feeding off each other."

He pulled her into his arms and bathed her in several doting kisses. "I adore you, Jacqueline Hartley, so fucking much."

"Lucky for you, I adore you back."

Later that evening, Ethan had fallen asleep on the family

room floor in a sleeping bag, an equally exhausted Loki conked out at his feet. Jack curled up on the sofa and patted the seat cushion next to her.

Instead of sitting beside her, Prescott sat on the opposite end. "How 'bout I give my amazing woman a foot rub?"

She placed her bare foot in his lap. "I'm at your mercy."

As he started massaging her soft skin, he said, "I've got a problem at work. Another cluster fuck, courtesy of my uncle."

"What's going on?"

"My uncle hired your sister as a marketing consultant to rebrand a skincare line."

She chuffed out a laugh. Prescott did not.

Her eyebrows crowded her forehead. "You're joking, right?"

"No, I'm not. Her company is TopCon."

"Leslie doesn't know the first thing about rebranding." She curled up beside him and showed him a photo of her and Leslie from a year ago. "My sister had gorgeous brown hair with beautiful chestnut highlights. She had a great figure too. Look how pretty she was."

"She doesn't look anything like that, now," he said. "Wow, look at you. You're a knock-out."

She kissed him. "Thank you, babe." She set her phone down. "I think the only one she's *conning* is your uncle."

"No, she isn't. He knows *exactly* what he's doing."

"Which is what, besides banging my sister?"

"Paying her for sex and disguising it as consulting services."

"That's not good." She resumed her spot on the other side of the sofa and laid her foot in his lap. "Last month, I was having dinner with Addison at Carole Jean's and saw her with your uncle, only I didn't know who he was. They looked pretty cozy. He gave her a diamond necklace."

"He's married."

"Okay, well, that means different things to different people. Maybe they're separated. Maybe they're married on-paper only.

Just to be clear, I'm *not* siding with my sister. I'm just pointing out that your idea of marriage might not be theirs."

"I love that you give people the benefit of the doubt," he said while massaging her heel. "What's *your* idea of marriage?"

"If the right man came along, I'd get married, but it has to be the right man because I'm getting married once. Just once. Hey, do you know anyone you can introduce me to?"

He squeezed her foot.

"Ouch," she said playfully. "What about you? What's in your future?"

"I've been thinking about adopting Ethan," he said. "I was going to talk to my dad about it, since he adopted me."

"That's wonderful. I'm sure Ethan would love that."

He could stop talking, and the conversation would end... or he could tell her how he was *really* feeling.

As he stared into her eyes, he needed her to know. "I found my person."

"Congrats," she said. "My condolences to your woman."

He laughed. "Why's that?"

"You're a handful, mister."

"She's amazing. I think you'd like her."

"What's she like?"

"Smart, gorgeous. She's funny and patient, and she's great with dogs and kids. She's fantastic in bed, and she's hard working. There's just one thing."

"What?"

"She's very hard on herself. She's been through something that left her scarred, but she never cuts herself any slack. She deserves to be happy and to have a fulfilling life. She deserves to be loved and to find her person. She deserves to have children, if she wants them. But she won't let herself be truly happy. Now, don't get me wrong. She's grateful, but she's holding back. I'm hoping that my love and support will help her to realize what an *amazing* person she is."

Tears filled her eyes. "Thank you," she whispered, "for loving me the way I am."

"Always." He pulled her into his lap and kissed her.

A single tear rolled down her cheek. "I found my person too."

Jacqueline

JACQUELINE WAS FLOATING on a fluffy cloud of love. She didn't want to think about the Campus Killer, or how she was going to ID the ALPHA Killer. She didn't want to go back to California and never see Prescott or Ethan ever again.

Life was perfect in Prescott's arms. She was safe and she felt deeply loved.

But, she'd been summoned home to do a job, so as much as she didn't want to leave his protective grip, she knew sleep wouldn't come with the case hanging over her head.

After withdrawing her foot, she kissed him, his moan streaking through her. But she ended it before she couldn't stop herself from more.

"I'm going to work."

"Now?" he murmured.

"Yeah." She kissed him again. "It's the right thing to do."

"It's the absolute wrong thing to do, but I give you props."

She retrieved her laptop, set up at the kitchen table. Seconds later, he set down his laptop and sat beside her.

"What are you working on?" she asked.

"I want to check out your sister's company," he said.

"I doubt you'll find one." His phone vibrated with an incoming call. "It's Stryker." He put the call on speaker. "Hey, bro, what's going on?"

"I sent you a copy of the surveillance video from the hallway outside your sister's hospital room."

"That didn't take long."

"You called the best... and the best delivered."

Prescott chuckled. "You are, and I'm glad you know it."

"Em and I are looking forward to seeing everyone at Hawk and Addison's wedding next weekend."

"Next weekend? I lost track of time."

"This lockdown has been great for us, but we're ready to get back to work." He started coughing.

After Stryker finished hocking up a lung, Prescott said, "That doesn't sound good."

"I'm coming down with something. How's the case going? You close to finding the killer?"

"Jacqueline's working it like a pro."

"Lemme know if you need anything else."

"Feel better." Prescott hung up, then hopped onto ALPHA's site, and over to his secure email.

The video started after Prescott left Sally's hospital room the evening she was admitted. Every few hours a nurse would enter. Five-to-seven minutes later, the nurse would exit. Some wore surgical masks, others did not.

Everything looked routine until four-forty-five in the morning, when a person in surgical scrubs, mask, and cap, walked head-down into Sally's room.

Fifteen minutes later, the person exited, again head-down, disappearing around the corner. Prescott fast forwarded to seven o'clock when a nurse entered the room. A moment later, she ran out. After that, it was mayhem. The last person on the video was Prescott as he made his way into his sister's hospital room.

Jesus, there it is.

Prescott called Stryker.

"Yo, baby," Stryker answered.

"Did you watch the video?" Prescott asked.

"No." Stryker coughed.

"Pull it up," Prescott replied.

A moment later, Stryker said, "Got it."

"Fast forward to four-forty-five AM, the person in scrubs."

"Got it."

"My sister died of asphyxiation, and I'm looking at the killer."

"Holy hell. Lemme see if I can get you a shot without his mask, or even a tag number from a car. It's gonna take me a little time to get that to you."

The call ended, and Prescott said, "I'm gonna find that son of a bitch and rip his fucking heart out."

"You're fearless," she said. "I admire that about you." She leaned close. "It's sexy."

He hitched a brow. "I like where this is going."

Steeling her spine, she said, "I've got all these cases to examine. I'm not doing anything here with Ethan in the room, and I'm not leaving him alone."

Prescott kissed her. "That sales clerk was right. You are a good mom."

"Work now, play later." She patted his thigh. "I'm requesting a background check on Leslie. The sister I knew is gone, and I want to know what's *really* going on with her."

"I need one too. Are you going through the Bureau?"

"Yeah."

"It's not related to the case, so it won't get approved. I'll request it through ALPHA and have the report sent to both of us."

Ethan started crying. He sat up and looked around, then started wailing. Prescott went to him, lifted him out of his sleeping bag, and held him.

"I'm right here." Prescott kissed the top of his head.

Jacqueline loved how much Prescott cared for a child he'd

just met, and taken on the role of father-figure without hesitation.

"I want my mommy," Ethan said between gasping sobs.

"Did you have a bad dream?" Prescott asked.

"Go away!" Ethan yelled. "You're not my mommy." When he started flailing and hitting Prescott, Prescott set him down on the sleeping bag. Ethan jumped up and ran toward Jacqueline.

She pushed out of the chair and scooped him into her arms. "I got you," she said.

A moment later, he calmed down.

After rocking him in her arms, she murmured, "How 'bout we have some of my special water we like so much?"

"Okay," he replied.

She carried him into the kitchen and filled two plastic toddler cups with some water.

When he drank that down, she offered him a little smile. "Feel better?"

"Uh-huh." Innocent, brown eyes stared into hers. "Will you be my mommy?"

She stilled, then her attention jumped to Prescott. She couldn't answer that question, so she searched his face for help.

In a few easy strides, Prescott joined them. "Would you like that, Ethan?"

"Uh-huh." He laid his head on her chest, and she rubbed his back, kissed the top of his head.

She'd fallen in love with both of them, and her heart was twice as full. But if things didn't work out, she wouldn't be the only one left with a broken heart.

This precious, innocent child would be broken hearted too.

∾

Prescott

MONDAY MORNING, while they were eating breakfast at the kitchen table, Jacqueline said, "I'm working here, today."

"That's not happening," Prescott replied.

"I can't leave Loki all day."

"We've got doggie daycare at Armstrong."

"Seriously?"

"There are four centers, two on each end of the compound. I called and they're expecting him. You aren't the only one who doesn't want to leave their pet all day."

She pushed out of her chair and threw her arms around him. "Thank you. You are the best."

He laughed. "That was easy."

"Does that mean Loki goes to school like me?" Ethan asked as he finished his cereal.

"Absolutely," Prescott replied. "He'll make friends, just like you."

"Yay!" Ethan said. "Can I visit him?"

"You can come with us when we pick him up," Prescott replied.

Ethan pushed his plate away. "I'm done. Can I get down please?"

"Yes," Prescott replied. "Can you brush your teeth or would you like some help?"

"Jack, can you help me?" He grinned at her.

"I'd be happy to." She set her plate in the sink.

"Ethan, instead of nap time, I'm taking you to a police station so you can meet a police officer," Prescott said.

"Okay," Ethan replied.

As they left the kitchen, Jack said to Ethan, "After dinner, let's teach Loki to stay. Would you like to help me?"

"Stay where?" he asked as they vanished up the stairs.

Fifteen minutes later, Prescott pulled into Armstrong Enterprises. First stop, Ethan's daycare. Second stop, doggie daycare where Jack registered Loki, answered a few questions, and left her pup.

Once inside his building, they rode the elevator to the top floor. En route to his office, he introduced her to Francis.

"Jacqueline's going to be working here for a few days," he told his assistant.

"Can I get you both coffee?" Francis asked.

He nodded. "Thanks."

"I'm good, thanks," Jack replied.

"When's my first meeting?" he asked Francis.

"In an hour."

After Francis headed toward the break room, Prescott brought Jacqueline into his office. "You good working at my conference table?"

She tucked her hair behind her ear. "If working on your lap isn't an option, I'll settle for the table."

"It's definitely an option, but we won't get any work done."

"Great office," she said as she eased into a chair, pulled out her laptop, and got to work.

He sat at his desk, unlocked his computer, and reviewed his schedule for the day. As he started scrolling through his unread emails, one from the coroner's office caught his eye.

The DNA profile on Sally's fetus had been completed. He clicked a link that took him to a secure site where he could download the digital profile. Then, he jumped online to a website the feds used for tracking criminals using DNA. After filling out the form, he uploaded the file, and paid extra to expedite the results. Then, he did the same thing with two commercial companies that linked people based on DNA.

Francis entered his office, set down his mug. "Hershel Jones wants a minute."

His accounting director stood in the doorway.

"Hershel, come on in." Prescott gestured to the guest chair.

Francis closed the door behind her as Hershel sat down.

"I have the information you asked for." Hershel glanced over at Jacqueline.

"It's okay," Prescott said. "What did you find?"

"Four months ago, TopCon was paid twenty-three thousand," Hershel began. "Two months later, thirty-five thousand. Last week, I got an invoice for two hundred thousand."

"Have you paid it?" Prescott asked.

"Not yet."

"Don't."

Hershel shifted in the leather chair. "It's a legit invoice."

"That can't get paid, but this needs to stay between us," Prescott said.

"Prescott, I need more than you telling me *not* to pay an invoice for a job that was approved by the board."

"Maybe not. Who approved the first two payments?"

"Artemis," Hershel replied. "He even came downstairs and signed off on the one for two hundred thousand. He told me to call him when the check has been cut and he'll see that it gets to the consultant."

Frustration made Prescott's blood boil. "Yeah, that doesn't surprise me. I can't say much yet, but TopCon isn't actually doing any work for us."

Hershel eyes grew large. "And you have proof?"

"I will," Prescott replied. "When's your department scheduled to cut the check?"

"In the next few days."

"I'll know sooner than that. If Artemis comes down looking for it, stall him."

"I do not want to lose my job by telling the CEO that he can't have the money to pay an invoice for a job that was approved by the board."

"You won't lose your job."

"Can I get that in writing?" Hershel stood. "I have a sick feeling about this."

"You're doing the right thing. Call me directly for any reason."

After Prescott gave Hershel his mobile number, he left.

Prescott did an Internet search for TopCon Consulting, but found nothing, so he searched the DC, Virginia, and Maryland business databases. Nothing in DC or Maryland, but he got a hit for TopCon in Virginia. After clicking on the business, he read through the information listed.

"Gotcha," he said.

TopCon was a DBA, owned by Artemis Armstrong.

He strode out of his office, stopping in Francis's doorway. "I need to call an emergency board meeting."

"For when?"

"Early afternoon," he replied. "I need Hershel Jones in the meeting. Tell him to bring everything he has for TopCon, and do *not*, under *any* circumstances, include Artemis."

25

YOU'RE FIRED

Jacqueline

Jacqueline opted to stay when Prescott and Ethan went to the police station. It took a little convincing, but she assured Prescott that she was safe behind the gated compound, hidden away on the executive floor of his office building. When she displayed her Glock tucked into the ankle holster under her pant suit, he finally agreed.

One kiss later, and he was out the door.

She was surprised he didn't lock her in when he left.

In truth, she was beyond frustrated with her lack of progress with the case. Rather than wait for Z to check in with her again, she decided to bring him up to speed. After a few rings, he answered.

"I'll call you back from a different number in two minutes." The line went dead.

She reviewed her summary page, pausing over the name Terrence Maul. Maul was in a class of his own. He'd been a respected ALPHA Operative who went way off script, losing his shit at the worst possible time.

Her phone rang with no caller ID.

"Hello," she answered.

"Hello, Jacqueline," Z replied. "I look forward to seeing you this weekend."

"Wow, Z, you never do small talk."

He chuckled. "It's not every day I have a daughter who's getting married. Are you looking forward to being in the wedding?"

"I love Addison so much, but I've become so obsessed with this case. I hope I can enjoy myself."

"Are you calling with an update?"

"Yes. I've reviewed every case Bert and Gloria worked together. Everyone they testified against is either in prison or deceased. My next step is to take a closer look at whether a prisoner is working with someone on the outside."

"I see," Z said.

"All my research points to one man, but Prescott said he's dead."

"Who?"

"Terrence Maul."

"His body hasn't surfaced, but they don't always."

"Or it won't because he's *not* dead. After he escaped prison, how did you track him down?"

"I had a team of agents hunting for him."

"My gut tells me that if we find Maul, we find the killer," she said. "If you send me over everything in his file, I'll track him down myself."

"You feel that strongly about it?"

"I do," she replied. "Someone has to get him off the street, and that someone is me."

Prescott

Prescott and Ethan waited for Detective Kealing in the lobby of the police station. Since he couldn't bring his weapon into the precinct, he'd left it in his office safe. Agitation had him biting back a growl.

How in the hell can I protect Jack and Ethan if I'm not armed?

Prescott didn't want to put his nephew through a police interrogation, but he was hoping they'd have more luck than he and Jack did. If anyone knew anything about Sally's boyfriend, it would be the little boy in his arms.

Detective Kealing entered the lobby, pasted on a friendly smile, and walked over. "Thanks for coming in, Mr. Armstrong." She addressed Ethan. "Hi, Ethan, I'm Detective Kealing. I'm a police officer."

As was the case when Ethan met strangers, he tightened his hold around Prescott's neck.

"I've got some cool markers," said Kealing. "Why don't you come back with me and we can hang out for a little while?"

"That sounds great," Prescott replied. "We like to color, don't we, Ethan?"

With Ethan in his arms, Prescott followed the detective to a room that housed a sofa, a round table with four chairs, and some age-appropriate toys in the corner. A stack of construction paper, coloring books, crayons and markers waited on the table.

Prescott set Ethan down, and Ethan clasped his hand. Prescott looked down at this small person and love filled his hardened hart.

"Ethan, do you like to draw?" Kealing asked.

"Are you staying?" Ethan asked Prescott.

"Absolutely," Prescott replied.

"We'd like to question him without—" Detective Kealing began.

"I stay," Prescott said.

Ethan sat at the table and the detective sat across from him while Prescott eased onto the sofa.

The detective offered Ethan several sheets of construction paper. He selected a light blue, and started scribbling with a marker.

A few moments later, a young man entered the room. "Hello, I'm Dr. Chan. I'm a child therapist who works with the detectives here." He shook Prescott's hand, smiled at Ethan. "Hi, Ethan. Can I sit with you?"

Ethan looked at Prescott, then back at the therapist. "Okay."

"I love to draw pictures." Dr. Chan drew a house with windows and a front door.

After a few moments of quiet drawing, Dr. Chan said, "That's good, Ethan. You're a good artist."

Ethan said nothing.

More silence until Dr. Chan said, "Ethan, do you remember your mommy's special friend?"

"My mommy died."

"I'm sorry that your mommy died," the doctor said.

No response from Ethan.

"I need your help, Ethan," Dr. Chan continued. "I want to find the person you called your mommy's special friend, and I was hoping you could help me with that."

"I don't like him. He's mean to me."

"That's very, very bad," Chan said. "What did he do to you?"

"Scary faces."

"Do you remember his name?"

"Mr. Man."

"Mr. Man?"

"Uh-huh," Ethan replied.

"What did he look like?"

Silence.

"Was he tall like your uncle or shorter like me?"

Ethan didn't answer.

"Ethan, I like your picture. Who are you drawing?"

"That's me and that's Uncle Prescott. That's Jack and Loki. We play together."

"That's wonderful," Chan said. "What a great drawing."

"Jack is nice to me. She reads to me and she brushes my teeth. She makes me good food and she does sleepovers. Everyone gets to sleep in a sleeping bag in the family room. I had a—" he looked at Prescott—"I was afraid one night and she held me and she gave me her special water."

Dr. Chan regarded Prescott. "Who is Jack?"

"My girlfriend, Jacqueline. She and Ethan have become close."

"She gives me sugar." Ethan grinned. "Just a little—" he indicated with his small fingers— "because Uncle Prescott says lots of sugar is bad."

Dr. Chan and the detective laughed.

"It sounds like you're a good eater, Ethan," said Chan.

"She has a puppy. His name is Loki. He's black and he's learning to share."

Dr. Chan nodded. "That's wonderful. Ethan, do you remember if your mommy's boyfriend had light hair or dark hair?"

Ethan looked at the therapist. "He has no hair—" Ethan put his hand on his head— "but he has hair on his face."

"That's very good, Ethan," said Dr. Chan. "Did he live with you and your mommy?"

"A little."

"Could you draw a picture of him?"

"I don't want to. I don't like him."

"Why?"

"He scared me."

"Is there anything about your mommy's friend that you remember?"

"He kissed my mommy."

The therapist had more questions for Ethan, but he'd grown silent.

"Thank you for talking to me, Ethan," Dr. Chan said. "Do you want to bring your artwork home?"

"Okay." Ethan went to the door, turned back to Prescott.

The detective escorted them to the lobby.

"I think he's blocking out the bad memories," the detective said.

"I'm hoping to replace those with good ones," Prescott replied. "Have you made any progress on the case?"

"We've gotten the hospital surveillance video and we did see someone enter your sister's room at around five in the morning."

"And?"

Kealing smiled at Ethan. "Mr. Armstrong, I'd be happy to discuss the case with you, but not in front of your nephew."

Prescott already knew what she'd seen on the video. "Understood."

With Ethan in his arms, he left the building, slipped on his sunglasses. "You did a good job, Ethan. I'm proud of you." He held up his hand and Ethan high-fived him.

After taking Ethan back to daycare, he returned to his office, stopping in Francis's to check in.

"Did you schedule the board meeting?"

"Today, at one-thirty," Francis replied. "Executive conference room. Not everyone could make it here, so I set up a video call."

"I'll email you over a link for TopCon. It's nothing more than a DBA held by Artemis." He growled. "He's paying the consultant for work she's not doing."

"Not true," Francis replied. "I'm guessing she's doing *all kinds* of work for him."

Despite the anger pounding through him, he chuffed out a laugh.

"Before I meet with the board, check with Hershel in accounting," he said. "He'll give you everything you need. One more thing... let security know. When Artemis gets back, have him held in the lobby. I'll go down and deal with him." Another growl shot out of him. "He's a disgrace to this company, and our family."

He returned to his office to find Jacqueline staring out the window. Her sweet smile assuaged his agitation.

"How'd it go?" she asked.

He made his way over to her, dipped down, and kissed her. "Ethan did great. He told them Mr. Man has no hair, but he's got facial hair. He said a lot of nice things about you."

"I love hearing that." Her smile faded. "I gave Z my list of suspects."

"Congratulations." He pulled his gun from his safe and slid it into the ankle holster. "He's probably got a team of agents working on that now."

"There is a team," she said, "and it's me. He's not assigning a team because he already did. Unfortunately, the suspect got away."

"Who are we talking about?"

"Maul," she replied. "Terrence Maul."

Prescott stared at her. "Maul's dead."

"No," she said, pushing back. "He is *not* dead. I'm going to find him, and when I do, you're going to finish him, for good."

Knock-knock.

Francis popped in. "It's time. Let's get you set up in the conference room."

Prescott eyed Jack. "This conversation is not over."

"Good luck."

With his laptop in hand, he strode out.

"Did you talk to Hershel?" Prescott asked Francis on the way to the conference room.

"Yes."

"Where's Artemis?" he asked.

"His assistant said he left at lunch and she doesn't expect him back for a few hours. Mel dialed in. Do you think she'll warn him?"

Mel—Artemis's daughter—headed up Armstrong's west coast division.

"Hard to say," Prescott replied.

"While you're meeting with the board, I'll loop in one of our in-house attorneys," Francis said.

They entered the conference room. The six people sitting around the table grew silent, as did the eight online. All eyes on him.

He sat at the head. "Thanks for being here on such short notice."

After Francis connected his laptop to the video projector, she left.

Steeling his spine, Prescott began. "As you know, Artemis hired TopCon to rebrand an outdated product line, and the board approved the million-dollar-plus project."

"The sensitive skincare line," added one of the board members.

"That's the one," Prescott replied. "After doing a little digging, I found out that TopCon isn't a real company. It's a DBA owned by Artemis. He's paying the consultant for work she's not doing." He pulled up Virginia's business registration website to show that Artemis owned TopCon.

"Our accounting director, Hershel Jones, has joined us today. Hershel has the paper trail of invoices from TopCon."

"Good afternoon," Hershel said. "Let me review those with you."

As Hershel went through the invoices, Prescott regarded everyone in the room, along with the members online. The press would pounce on this news, the story would go viral. He'd instruct the PR department to compose a brief statement expressing their regret in the matter, the company's commitment to excellence, and their promise to customers that the issue was a personal one and had nothing to do with the quality of the brands the public has come to expect. And they'd announce the acting CEO.

Prescott stilled. *Fuck. Fuck me.*

That's gonna be me.

As COO, he oversaw all departments. More importantly, he was the heir apparent. Of Artemis's two children, only his daughter worked for Armstrong. Years ago, she'd made it clear she loved living on the west coast, and wouldn't return to HQ.

Time to do what has to be done.

He'd stepped up for Ethan. He'd do it for his family's legacy.

"This is very disappointing," said one of the board members.

"And criminal," added another. "Armstrong built a company, one brand at a time... and they built it on trust."

"How do we deal with this?" asked an online board member.

"Artemis will pay back what he stole and be gone by the end of the day," Prescott replied, his tone filled with confidence.

"We need to vote Artemis out," said one of the board members in the room.

"Okay, then," Prescott said. "By show of hands, those in favor of Artemis Armstrong staying on as CEO of Armstrong Enterprises."

No hands went up, not even Artemis's daughter, Mel.

"Let the record show no hands were raised," said one of the members.

"Those in favor of dismissing Artemis Armstrong as CEO of Armstrong Enterprises, effective immediately," Prescott said.

Every hand—in person and on the call—went up.

The vote was unanimous. Artemis Armstrong was out as CEO.

"We need to nominate an interim CEO," his cousin, Mel, said, "and I nominate Prescott Armstrong."

Here we go.

"Thanks, Mel," he replied.

Someone seconded her nomination. Everyone voted and, just like that, Prescott sat at the helm of a three-hundred-billion-dollar empire.

"Thank you for your confidence," Prescott said. "There'll be some changes, but nothing in the immediate future. What questions do you have for me?"

"How are you handling Artemis?" Mel asked.

"By the book," Prescott replied, "and as low-key as possible. A press release will go out, but it'll be biz as usual."

Prescott answered a few more questions, expressed his appreciation to Hershel and Francis, and finished by thanking the board.

While the weight of Armstrong lay on his shoulders, he didn't have to carry it alone. He was surrounded by thousands of competent, honest employees who loved their jobs. It pained him to let his uncle go, but this was all on Artemis.

On the way back to his office, he called Detective Kealing. "Detective, it's Prescott Armstrong."

"Are you calling about an update on your sister's case?"

"No. I need to speak with a white-collar crime detective. Can you help get me to the right person?"

"What's going on?"

After he gave her the short version, she said, "Is your life always like this?"

He chuckled. "No, it's not."

"I'll find you someone." She put him on hold.

Prescott slowed at Francis's office. "What's the word?" he asked her.

"I spoke to one of our attorneys. She said she'd follow up with Hershel. Artemis is due back around four."

"Let me know when he gets here and have security hold him in the lobby," Prescott said.

"Mr. Armstrong," Detective Kealing said, "I'm going to transfer you to Detective Chavez."

"Thanks for your help," Prescott said.

"This is Detective Chavez. Is this Mr. Armstrong?"

"You got him," Prescott replied. "Let me bring you up to speed, Detective."

AT FOUR THIRTY, PRESCOTT got a call from reception. "Artemis is being held by security in the lobby."

"On my way." Prescott hung up.

"Babe," he said to Jack, "I'll be back."

She offered an encouraging smile. "You got this."

Frustration and disappointment coursed through him as he strode toward the elevator. He hated having to do this, but his uncle had left him no choice.

Thirty-minutes earlier, Detective Chavez and two plain-clothes officers had arrived at Armstrong. After setting Prescott up with a wire, they waited in the lobby for Artemis to return.

The elevator doors split open. Prescott heard his uncle ranting before he'd even exited the cab.

"You've got no right to keep me from going—" Artemis made eye contact with Prescott. "Oh, thank God. Security won't let me upstairs. What the hell is going on?"

"Let's talk over here," Prescott led Artemis to the far corner of the two-story lobby. He might be furious with him, but he wasn't going to humiliate him. His uncle had done that on his own.

Once out of earshot, Prescott said, "I know about TopCon."

A shadow fell over his uncle's face. "What do you mean?"

"TopCon is your company, and you've been paying Leslie for work she isn't doing."

Artemis got in his face and shoved a finger at him. "How dare you accuse me of that?"

"I know the truth," Prescott said devoid of any emotion. "You should be ashamed of yourself for committing fraud."

Artemis hung his head. "I knew it was a terrible idea, but she's incredible. I feel like I'm twenty-five around her."

"Why did you embezzle from the company?"

"I'd been giving her money from my personal account, but your aunt found out."

"How much?" Prescott asked.

"Over two hundred thousand." Artemis's shoulders dropped. "I bought her a house and a BMW, jewelry, so much clothing, acting lessons, photo shoots for her modeling career. Whatever she asked for."

"Jesus, this is fucked up."

"Look, Scotty, I'll just pay the company back. It'll be our little secret. I'll cut things off with her and never see her again."

"I'm sorry, Artemis. I can't do that. You committed fraud and you put the company in jeopardy."

Detective Chavez and two officers made their way over.

"Artemis Armstrong?" asked Chavez.

Artemis looked at them, then glared at Prescott. "I gave you a phenomenal job when *you* fucked up with the Bureau. And this is how you repay me!" Artemis shouted.

"I didn't fuck up," he rasped. "I was their scapegoat. It's two completely different things."

"You can't do this," Artemis screamed. "I'm the goddamn CEO!"

"Not anymore," Prescott replied. "I am."

26

HAWK AND ADDISON'S REHEARSAL DINNER

Jacqueline

Jacqueline had spent the last few days searching for Terrence Maul. Despite his getting shot and falling into the ice-cold Rappahannock River, she was *convinced* he'd survived.

And she was determined to find him.

She'd called the Fredericksburg hospital in search of a gunshot victim, but no one fitting Maul's description had shown up. Then, she widened her search.

Still, no luck... until today, when she called a hospital in Alexandria. A man with two gunshot wounds to the back had arrived hours after Prescott had shot Maul. He was alone, he had no ID, and he claimed he couldn't remember his own name. Once the surgeon had removed the bullets from "John Doe", he'd been kept overnight for observation. By the time police arrived to question the man, he'd skipped out.

Jacqueline needed access to the hospital's video surveillance, which meant she needed a search warrant.

Prescott came down the stairs, a just bathed Ethan in his

arms. He looked adorable in his jammies, his just-washed long brown hair neatly combed.

"I did a poopy in the toilet!" Ethan announced.

"Yay!" Jacqueline exclaimed. "Congratulations!"

Ethan beamed.

"We've come downstairs to give you a hug goodnight," Prescott said.

"Can Jack read me my bedtime story?" Ethan asked.

"I would love to," she replied. "Let's pick one with a happy ending. I could definitely use one of those."

Ethan chose his favorite picture book about a boy and his dog. After she sat on the sofa, he climbed up next to her and snuggled close. Her heart overflowed with love. With her arm around him, she started reading.

The book was funny and had a great life lesson about friendship. She loved how Ethan participated, pointing to the pictures and talking about how the boy and the dog were like him and Loki.

When she finished, he peered up at her. "You can tuck me in, if you want."

"I would love to." She rose and extended her hand. "What about Uncle Prescott?"

"He can come too."

"I love being an add-on," Prescott said.

As they climbed the stairs, with Prescott bringing up the rear, he caressed her ass. A hit of adrenaline charged through her. She needed him, but she'd become obsessed with tracking down Maul.

Since Ethan's new bedroom set wasn't going to be delivered for another two weeks, they'd pulled the double mattress from one of the spare bedrooms, and placed it on the floor in his bedroom.

"I like my new bed," Ethan said as he lay down. "It's so big and there's room for Loki too."

Loki hopped up and laid down. Ethan patted him. "It's time for sleep, Loki."

After kissing him goodnight, Jacqueline waited in the doorway for Prescott.

"Have a good sleep," Prescott said. "I love you, bud." He kissed Ethan's forehead and patted Loki.

She and Prescott returned to the first floor, and she eased onto a stool at the kitchen island.

"You've been working nonstop," Prescott said. "When are you going to give this Maul thing a rest?"

"When he's *really* dead," she replied. "I found a hospital in Alexandria that treated a John Doe with two gunshot wounds to his back. I reached out to two judges for search warrants, but I haven't heard back yet."

"I'm calling Stryker," Prescott said. "He owes me hospital surveillance from when Sally was killed."

He dialed, put the call on speaker.

"Hello," Stryker said, his voice hoarse.

"You don't sound good."

"I've been sick all week. I'm skipping the rehearsal dinner tomorrow night, so I can go to the wedding Saturday."

"Good call," Prescott said.

"I'm sorry I don't have any more surveillance for you. I can ask Danielle—"

"Just get better," Prescott said. "See you Saturday." He hung up and shook his head. "We are not getting a break. I'll see if Danielle can hack into the hospital's surveillance system."

Prescott sent Cooper a text. "I need Danielle's hacker help. If she's got time, have her text me."

Prescott's phone binged with a new email alert. "There's a DNA match for Sally's baby." As he read the email, the color in his face drained. "No fucking way."

"What?" she asked.

"The father of Sally's baby is Terrence Maul."

"*What?* That can't be right."

"Ninety-nine percent accuracy. It sure as fuck is."

"Ohmygod," Jacqueline blurted. "Maul is Mr. Man, the one who terrorized Ethan." Her frustration morphed into full-blown anger. "I hate him even more, if that's possible."

The anger rolling off him was palpable. The ALPHA Killer case had become personal for Prescott. Maul had escaped, met Sally, used her to help him stay hidden, then killed her when he learned she was carrying his child.

Jacqueline clicked on an open browser with Maul's mug shot. "I've had this page open for days. I'm grateful Ethan didn't see it."

"He's an escaped fugitive," Prescott bit out. "There's no way he looked like himself when he cozied up to my sister."

"He must be a real smooth talker. Sally actually loved that monster."

Prescott growled. "Now, we know who killed her."

"She moved up here for him."

"Or he lured her here, so he could kill her. I cannot fucking wait to take him out."

"Yeah, well, I gotta find him first." After a brief pause, she added, "Do you think Maul is the Campus Killer? I know I said that guns travel—and they do—but…"

"If he is, it's even more reason to take him out."

THE EVENING OF HAWK AND ADDISON's rehearsal dinner, Jaqueline found Prescott and Ethan playing a game in the family room.

"Wow, look how beautiful Jack looks," Prescott said as she made her way over to them.

As she modeled the black, halter-top dress, Prescott started clapping, so Ethan mimicked him.

"Thank you." Then, she realized the guys were dressed alike

in black shirts and black pants. "You both look so handsome. Let me put Loki in the laundry room and we can head out."

Prescott pushed off the floor. "Hawk said Loki can stay in the farmhouse since we'll be in the barn all evening. We'll put him in a bedroom upstairs."

"Thank you." She dropped a light kiss on his lips before addressing Ethan. "Are you excited to be in Uncle Hawk and Aunt Addison's wedding tomorrow?"

"Uh-huh," he replied. "Uncle Prescott said I get to walk down the aisle and carry rings. It's a very important job."

"Very important," Jacqueline agreed.

Prescott collected his sport coat off the sofa along with a jacket for Ethan. With a shawl and her clutch in hand, she grabbed Loki's leash and a small bag of his toys.

After everyone piled into the SUV, they took off toward Hawk and Addison's farmhouse.

Two armed guards were waiting when they pulled up to the private driveway. Prescott unrolled his window.

"Prescott Armstrong, Jacqueline Hartley, and Ethan Sagall."

One guard checked the list, while the second stood, a weapon in his hand, his arm by his side.

"You're clear to enter. Enjoy your evening."

As Prescott drove past the barn, Jaqueline glanced over. Both barn doors were wide open. Icicle lights dangled from the ceiling and tables had been set up on one side of the large space.

"So romantic," she said.

Prescott parked, got Ethan out of his car seat, while Jaqueline opened the liftgate. Loki waited for her command before jumping out, his tail wagging back and forth.

Inside the house, caterers bustled about in the kitchen, while Hawk, Addison, Prescott's mom, dad, and his grandparents all gathered in the front room.

"Loki, sit," Jaqueline said.

Loki did as he was told.

She patted his head. "Good job, Loki."

"There they are!" Granddad made his way over. "Good to see you, Scotty."

After hugging it out with his grandfather, Prescott introduced Jacqueline.

"She's much too pretty for you," his granddad said with a wink.

Addison hurried over and hugged her.

"You look beautiful," Jacqueline and Addison said in unison, then started laughing.

While getting ready, Jacqueline told herself she wouldn't let the frustration over the case ruin her evening... or anyone else's.

"Hi, Loki." Addison knelt to rub his head.

Despite Loki's wildly swooshing tail, he did not budge.

"Good boy, Loki," Jacqueline said.

Addison stood. "He's so well behaved. You can keep him in the barn with us."

"Thanks, but it'll be easier if I leave him in a room upstairs."

Addison stepped close. "How's the case going?"

"I've got a suspect, but he's been impossible to track down."

"You'll find him," Addison whispered. "I have complete confidence in you."

Uneasiness settled into Jacqueline's bones. The trail had gone ice cold.

Where are you hiding, Maul?

∽

Prescott

PRESCOTT CLASPED Jack's hand as they headed toward the barn. The sun was setting, the air crisp. A perfect May evening. With

Loki tucked away in a bedroom and Ethan being doted on by Prescott's parents, he finally had a moment alone with his woman. Despite the happy occasion, he couldn't miss the concern in her eyes.

The case was weighing on her. She'd been up half the night, tossing and turning. Even when he'd held her in his arms, she hadn't fallen back to sleep.

He knew, because he'd been awake himself. Even their middle-of-the-night lovemaking hadn't lulled them to sleep.

Maul was winning. And Prescott was so fucking angry, he could barely contain himself.

"Did you bring your weapon?" he murmured.

"Nowhere to hide it," she replied. "You?"

"Two."

"No confidence in the security guards at the bottom of the hill?"

"I don't know what to think anymore," he bit out. "My sister was with Maul. He killed her, along with Gloria and Bert. My uncle..." A long growl rolled out of him. "If you want to fuck around with a woman who's using you for your money, then leave your wife and retire with some damn dignity."

Jacqueline pulled him to a stop.

In his ear, she whispered, "You were destined to run Armstrong. The plan didn't go as expected, but it's always been your legacy. You'll surround yourself with brilliant, competent people so you can continue to work for Z. As far as Maul is concerned, I *will* find him."

"I'm so angry with myself."

She stared in to his eyes. "Why?"

"I didn't do my fucking job and good people have died because of it."

"You shoulder too much. If you won't be part of a team, you're vulnerable. When you went after Maul, you took out everyone by yourself. Anyone else would have gotten killed. I will find Maul, and you'll finish what you started."

He kissed her cheek.

"Your brother—your best friend—is marrying the love of his life, and one of my closest friends in the entire world," she continued.

"Nicky's not my best friend anymore," Prescott replied.

She laughed. "He got bumped? What happened?"

"You are." He kissed the top of her head. "Let's forget about the case for the next few hours."

"I'll try," she replied.

The rehearsal went off without a hitch. When it ended, everyone moved to the other end of the barn for a sit-down dinner.

"Can we check on Loki?" Ethan asked.

"That's a great idea," Jacqueline replied. "We'll be back in five."

"I'll go with you," Prescott said.

Loki was sprawled on the bed. After spending a few minutes with him, they left.

"We can check on him in a little while," Ethan said en route to the barn. "Do you think he's sad because he's alone?"

"I don't," Jacqueline replied. "He's with us all the time and I think he knows he's loved. What do you think?"

"I think he should come wif us to the barn."

"We can do that at the end of the party," Prescott explained.

Servers delivered chicken breast with a side of grilled vegetables and roasted parmesan potatoes. Jack started cutting Ethan's chicken, then sliced the potato into small pieces.

"This looks yucky," Ethan said.

Prescott whispered, "You have to try it so you don't hurt Uncle Nicky and Aunt Addison's feelings."

Jack sliced of a piece of the herb encrusted chicken. "Mmm. Almost as good as Nana's chicken nuggets."

Ethan picked up a piece with his fingers and put it in his mouth. "It's good."

Jacqueline bit back a smile as Ethan ignored the silverware.

"Ethan," Prescott began.

"Isn't he doing a great job?" Jack nodded.

Rather than tell Ethan to use his fork, Prescott praised him. "Super job, bud."

When dinner ended, coffee was served. Dessert stations were set up and the guests began migrating toward them.

"Sugar," Jacqueline said, and Ethan jerked his head in her direction.

"Can I have some?" the tyke asked.

Prescott laughed. "I'll get us something."

"Can I see?" Ethan asked.

"Absolutely," Prescott replied before addressing Jacqueline. "What can I get you, babe?"

"I'll have a bite of whatever you choose," she replied.

Ethan selected chocolate cake with chocolate frosting. Prescott, a piece of chocolate marble cheesecake. Returning to the table, he placed the dessert in front of her.

"I'll eat what you don't," Prescott said.

He situated Ethan, sat himself, and handed Ethan a fork. "You can't use your fingers, bud."

No argument from Ethan who forked the cake into his mouth. "Yummy," he said with a grin.

Jacqueline took two bites of the cheesecake, then passed it over.

"That's it?"

She nodded. "I'll have my own dessert at the wedding."

"Me, too!" Ethan exclaimed.

Once servers had finished pouring coffees and teas, Hawk and Addison stood.

"Thank you for being here with us," Hawk said. "We love you all."

Everyone paused to clink glasses, then Hawk and Addison shared a loving kiss.

"We want tomorrow to be just as relaxed and fun as tonight," Addison said. "This is a special weekend, and we're so happy to be sharing it with you."

Cheers and applause filled the room.

"Tomorrow, we've got a great band coming, but tonight we've got the best of Hawk's playlist," Addison continued. "Nicholas and I are dancing 'til dawn."

Prescott pushed out of his chair and raised his glass. "Here's to Nicky and Addison. Two people who were meant to be together from the moment they met. I love you both."

After everyone toasted the bride and groom, they sat back down.

"Who wants to dance with me?" Jacqueline asked.

"I definitely do," Prescott replied. "How 'bout you, Ethan?"

"No, fank you. I want to make sure Loki is okay."

"I'll take him." Jacqueline pushed out of her chair. "Save me that dance." She kissed Prescott, and held out her hand for Ethan.

Without question, he would save her that dance. And a million more.

27

THE KILL SHOT

Jacqueline

As Jacqueline and Ethan exited the barn and headed toward the house, Prescott's mom and dad pulled up alongside them. "Where are you two headed?" Prescott's dad asked.

"Loki is alone," Ethan explained. "And I want to make sure he's okay."

"That's very sweet, Ethan," Prescott's mom replied.

"Why don't we take you?" Prescott's dad asked.

"Okay," Ethan said. "We can play with Loki."

"You should take Prescott onto the dance floor," Prescott's mom said to her.

"I agree," Jacqueline replied.

A few of the catering staff passed them, each carrying a tray of dirty dishes, on their way to the house.

Renée and Mason each took Ethan by a hand and continued on, while Ethan chatted away. Jacqueline watched them before turning back toward the barn.

What a great family.

As she got closer to the entrance, one of the catering staff stepped out of the shadows. "Nice night for a party."

"Absolutely," she replied.

"Break time is over," he said. "Time to finish cleaning up."

He pulled up beside her. She glanced over as he shoved a gun in her face, threw his arm around her in a chokehold, and pulled her around to the side of the barn, obscured in darkness.

Adrenaline shot through her and her heart rate skyrocketed. He slammed her against the side of the building so fast, she hadn't fully processed what was happening.

Then, he pointed a Glock at her face.

"You scream, you're dead," he hissed.

Her thoughts were racing. Could she knee him in the groin before he had a chance to fire his weapon? Could she shove him and run? How could she warn everyone in the barn? She had no idea who she was dealing with, so she needed to get him talking.

"Got it," she said, trying to get her breathing under control.

"I've waited a long, long time for this day, Jaqueline Hartley," he said, his familiar voice catching her ear.

It was Lou, the musician who'd been living with her sister. Gone was the knit cap and long, dark hair. Either he'd shaved his head, or he'd been wearing a wig.

No longer clean shaven, Lou was sporting a beard and mustache. Dressed like the catering staff, he'd worn a white shirt, black vest, and black pants.

"What do you want with me, Lou?"

His eerie grin made her blood run cold.

"We met ten years ago," he continued. "It was a rainy night. You and Janey were headed back to your sorority house. I pulled over, gave you a ride."

Her racing heartbeat thrashed in her ears.

"Ohmygod," she blurted. "You're the Campus Killer."

"You were the one who got away. I've dreamed about this

day. Fantasized about it over and over and over, for years. But I never thought it would happen. I couldn't believe my luck when you walked back into my life. I was getting a do-over." His lips curled into another freakish smile. "I loved bumping into you, building trust, creating a bond. It was all gonna be over the day you stopped by for the money, but you brought that dude with you." He grunted. "Seeing him ruined my day."

Dread filled her soul.

She wanted to scream, she wanted to run, take her chances of getting shot in the back, but if she were shot in the back of the head...

"Do you know why no one ever found me?"

"No," she bit out.

"The police concluded the Campus Killer was impersonating a cop. I *was* a cop, and damn good with a disguise. I was having so much fun snatching up unsuspecting little girls and dropping their dead bodies into graves. My killing spree *should* have lasted forever—and it would have—if it weren't for you."

"You could have moved to a different town."

"No," he snarled. "You ruined it for me. I lost my confidence. I fucked up, fucked up big time. But now, you have a chance to make it up to me. You're going to die, and your friends are going to watch me kill you."

∼

Prescott

PRESCOTT AND HAWK were talking with Z in Hawk's newly finished loft above the barn entryway.

"The case is too much for Jacqueline to work on her own," Prescott said.

"I realized that, so I just assigned a team to find Maul," Z explained.

"I can't believe he killed Sally," Hawk said. "Do you think she knew he was a fugitive?"

"No," Prescott replied. "I don't think she would have let him near Ethan if she had."

"Why?" Z asked.

"Maul used to frighten him." Prescott glanced over the balcony in search of Jack and Ethan.

"Monster," Hawk bit out.

"Maul probably gave Sally a fake name," Z said. "Did Ethan talk about him?"

"No," Prescott said. "It scared him too much."

"Stop the fucking music and shut the fuck up!" shouted a man below.

Prescott whipped his head toward the sound. "Jesus, no," he whispered.

A man from the catering staff had Jack in a choke hold, a gun pointed at her head.

Addison killed the music. A hush fell over the group, all eyes on the stranger.

"That's better," the man bit out. "I just had the chance to get caught up with an old friend of mine. Jacqueline, why don't you tell everyone who I am?"

She said something, but Prescott couldn't hear her.

"If you try anything, I will kill you, then open fire on everyone here." The stranger yanked her head back. "Do you understand?"

Fury pounded through Prescott at a frenetic pace.

After Jack spoke, the assailant clamped his hand around the back of her neck while he shoved the barrel of the gun against her temple.

"This is the Campus Killer," Jacqueline announced.

Oh, Jesus.

Slowly, Prescott removed the Glock from the holster tucked under his arm, inside his sport coat. From his second-story position, Prescott was twenty feet away, but he didn't have a clean shot. Jacqueline's head was too close to the killer's. If he hit the motherfucker in the head, the bullet could pass through him and into her.

Fuck.

Then, Prescott removed the Glock from his ankle holster. Hawk held out his hand and Prescott gave him the second weapon.

"Tell everyone how we know each other," the killer shouted.

"He abducted me a decade ago, but I escaped," she said, her voice trembling. "I was the one who got away."

A terrifying hush fell over the room. Everyone was transfixed on them.

"Because of me, he stopped killing," she continued.

"That's only half the story," he continued. "Tell them my name, honey."

"Ouch," Jack said. "Stop squeezing my neck. His name is Lou."

"Lou's my nickname. What's my real name?"

"Luam."

"Spell it," Lou barked. "Backwards."

"M-a-u-l." Jacqueline turned in his direction.

"What the fuck are you looking at, bitch?" Maul slapped her face.

Jesus, this is bad.

"I've got a grudge to settle," Maul said. "Where's Luck?"

Both Sin and Dakota stepped forward.

"What the hell are you doing?" Dakota asked his twin.

"Saving your ass," Sin bit out.

"You're not helping," Dakota snapped.

"I'll take you both out if you don't shut the fuck up!" Maul screamed.

Prescott needed to move so he could get a better angle, but

he was concerned the floor would creak. If he fired his weapon now, he risked killing Jack.

Prescott took a step and stilled.

"I got you," Hawk whispered.

"Dakota, you and me, we used to be friends. We had each other's backs on missions."

"Until you shot up a houseful of innocents," Dakota growled.

"Then, you, Grimes, and Whelan all testified against me," Maul said. "I vowed to get my revenge. It's time to die."

Hawk flew down the stairs, the banging of his dress shoes against the wooden steps had Maul whipping his head toward the sound.

In that split-second, Prescott aimed the Glock, and opened fire.

BANG! BANG! BANG!

Maul dropped, blood gushing from the back of his head, his neck, and his back. Hawk kicked Maul's gun away and pointed his at Maul's head.

Prescott bolted down the stairs and pulled Jacqueline into his arms. "Talk to me. You okay?"

Though shaking, she murmured, "Ohmygod, that was intense."

They clung to each other while the heaviness of the situation took hold, the rush of adrenaline pounding through him. A long moment passed before she broke away.

"Check him," Prescott said.

Hawk felt his carotid. After several long seconds, he stood, "It's done, brother."

Addison rushed over and wrapped Jacqueline in her arms.

Dakota and Sin stepped forward, and Dakota extended his hand. "You saved all of us."

Prescott shook his hand while relief washed over him.

"I wasn't armed," Dakota said.

"Neither was I," Sin added.

Sin's wife, Evangeline, covered Maul with a black tablecloth.

"Prescott, you know what this means?" Dakota asked.

Prescott shook his head.

"You're joining BLACK OPS," Dakota replied.

"You're outta excuses, brother," Sin said. "Out of excuses. I'd want you on my team every single time."

Hawk squeezed Prescott's shoulder. "It's time. You've punished yourself long enough."

"I agree," Z said joining them.

Prescott peered down at the woman by his side.

"They're right," Jack said. "It's a perfect fit."

Prescott extended his hand toward Dakota, who pulled him in for a hug.

"Welcome to BLACK OPS, Armstrong," Dakota said.

"Ohgod, the security guards," Addison said.

Hawk and Addison hurried out of the barn.

"What's going on?" Prescott's dad's booming voice pierced the night. "We heard fireworks."

Prescott's mom, dad, and Ethan stood in the doorway.

Prescott and Jack hurried over.

"Hey, guys, we're moving the party up to the house," Prescott said.

"Ethan, did you get to play with Loki?" Jack asked.

Ethan yawned. "Uh-huh, we woke him and played with him, then we took him outside so he could go potty."

"You're holding a g-u-n," his mom said.

Prescott shoved the Glock into the shoulder holster before picking Ethan up. Snuggling close, Ethan slid his thumb into his mouth. Prescott hugged him. "Let's get outta here."

"Where were Nicky and Addison going in such a hurry?" his dad asked.

"They had to take care of something," Prescott replied

before addressing the guests. "We're moving to the house. Everyone is welcome, but if you've had enough excitement for one day, we'll see you tomorrow."

As the guests filed past, everyone stopped to thank Prescott.

Jericho pulled him in for a hug. "You did good, brother."

"Welcome to the team," Cooper said.

Hawk and Addison rushed back into the barn and over to them.

"He took out the guards," Hawk said breathing hard. "Police are on their way—"

His mom's eyes grew wide. "Nicky, you've got a g-u-n too. What is going on?"

Prescott passed Ethan to his dad. "Take Ethan to the house. We'll be there as soon as we can."

His family left, the guests vacated the building. Prescott regarded his brother and Addison, then peered at Jack. It was over. Finally, fucking over. And it had been much worse than anyone had realized.

A serial killer who had managed to trick so many people. Maul lived his life as a predator *and* as a civil servant, taking an oath to protect and defend. Terrence Maul was pure evil. The worst of the worst... and Prescott had taken him out for good.

The scream of sirens grew louder.

Hawk pulled him in for a hug. "You did good, Scotty."

Relief pounded through him. "You were right there with me, Nicky. Thanks for the assist."

When Hawk and Addison left to meet the police at the bottom of the driveway, Jack threw her arms around him, and he breathed easier.

"He was going to kill me," she said.

"Not on my watch, baby," Prescott said as he held her close, never, ever wanting to let her go.

Jacqueline

Jacqueline was going through the motions. First, she identified herself as a federal agent to local law enforcement. She gave a concise statement, provided her contact information, and waited while Prescott gave his own statement.

Truth was, she wasn't okay. She needed to process what had just happened and who this monster had been. Maul's lifelong path of destruction was overwhelming to take in, and it would take years for law enforcement to fully resolve, if they ever actually did. Based on what Maul had told her, there were probably more women who'd gone missing.

Maul was the devil. He was evil personified.

But he was gone. And she was free, for the first time in a decade. No more looking over her shoulder, no more sleepless nights, her weapon tucked under her pillow to ensure a few hours of uninterrupted rest.

A serial killer who hid behind his badge, he used his skills and expertise to trap the innocent. For the first time since she'd been abducted, she felt empowered. She could make a difference, for Janey's sake and for all the other women whose lives had been taken far too soon. She'd been a victim, then she'd been plagued by constant fear.

Time to step up and help others.

Z walked over. "Can I talk to you before I leave?"

"Of course," she replied.

"I'm sorry I put you in danger," Z began. "Are you okay?"

"I will be," she replied. "I'm amazed Maul was able to fool law enforcement for his entire career."

"Like a lot of serial killers, he was living a double life. He was good at covering his tracks, good at breaking the law while upholding it at the same time."

"My job here is done, so I'll have to return to the task force."

Z glanced at Prescott, then back to her. "Would you like to stay here?"

"Absolutely," she replied.

"I'll see what I can do. Are you open to change?"

"Depends on what it is," she replied.

"Understood," Z said. "I've had enough excitement for one night. I'll see you both tomorrow."

After the police left, and the coroner's office had removed Maul's body, she regarded Prescott. "Thank you for saving my life." She pulled him close and kissed him, letting her lips linger on his.

"Thank you for giving me mine back." He caressed her shoulders. "You stopped shaking."

She nodded. "You want to head up to the house?"

"What I want is to ask you to be my wife," he said. "Is that too crazy?"

She grinned up at him. "The only thing that would be too crazy is if you asked and I said no."

He got down on one knee. "You are the best part of my day and the best part of my life. I don't have a ring, I haven't even met your mom and dad, but I'm so in love with you, I can't think of a better way to turn this day around."

Leaning down, she kissed him. "I agree."

"Jacqueline Eleanor Hartley—my beautiful, brilliant Jack—spend the rest of your life with me. I will put you first, treasure you every single day, and love you forever. Will you marry me?"

She captured his face in her hands and kissed him. "Absolutely. I would love to be your wife. I would love to be Ethan's stepmom, and maybe even have a few more of our own."

"You are all in," he said with a smile.

"I love you Prescott McCafferty Armstrong, and I can't wait to go on a normal date with you."

On a laugh, they came together in a loving kiss. He swept her into his arms and strode out of the barn.

On the way toward the house, she said, "Should we tell your family or keep it a secret?"

"We gotta tell 'em. It's the good news everyone needs to hear right now."

After walking up the porch steps, he set her down. "Ready?"

She clasped his hand. "I'm ready for anything, as long as it's with you."

28

CLOSING THE CASE

Jacqueline

The following morning, while working in Prescott's home office, Jacqueline read through Terrence Maul's career history. He was a police officer with the Roanoke PD before moving on to Fredericksburg. From there, he was promoted to county SWAT. There were no complaints in his file, nothing negative that would ever lead law enforcement to suspect he was a cold-blooded killer.

Her mind was blown as she learned about the man who wreaked havoc on so many families, and preyed on trusting, young women.

But the killing spree stopped after Jacqueline escaped, and the case went cold.

After working with the SWAT team, Maul then earned a coveted spot as an ALPHA Operative. It was during a mission with Gloria Whelan and Bert Grimes that he lost it. Years of pent-up hostility, and the unrelenting urge to kill again, became too much and he unleashed his bloodlust on everyone in the house. A total of twenty-two women and children were savagely murdered.

From there, he was convicted and sentenced. Three years into a life sentence without the possibility of parole, he staged a prison riot, snatched a guard's gun, and shot his way out. From that point, he vanished, until he resurfaced with Sally, then posing as Lou, and finally at the rehearsal dinner.

Jacqueline pushed out of her chair and rubbed her aching shoulder. Tight muscles screamed back. As she made her way onto the back porch, Loki barked.

Outside, in the pool, Prescott was giving Ethan a swim lesson. Watching those two together made her heart happy. Loki, desperate to join the fun, was trotting around the pool in the hopes of being invited in.

She made her way down the stairs and into the backyard where she picked up one of Loki's toys and tossed it for him. Off he bolted, excited for the attention. Sitting at the edge, she dipped her bare legs into the heated water.

"Come on in, babe," Prescott called.

That morning, she'd put on her bathing suit, but had gotten diverted by work. She slid into the water and dropped below the surface. The water was heated to perfection, and she swam until she ran out of breath.

"Where've you been?" Prescott asked.

"Reviewing Maul's case."

"I'm taking an entire day off from reality," he said. "And we're going to have fun, right Ethan?"

"Jack, watch me," Ethan said.

After an adorable display of Ethan's ability to blow bubbles and float on his back while Prescott supported him, Jacqueline applauded his efforts.

"I'm going to swim," she said. "Are you guys staying in the pool?"

"Not going anywhere, " Prescott replied.

Jacqueline swam back and forth as she burned through her frustration. On one hand, she was ecstatic. The case had been solved, the killer eliminated. She'd fallen madly in love, gotten engaged, and might even get transferred back to the DC region.

Though she'd been more shaken than she'd let on, she didn't want to burden Prescott with her anxiety. If it turned into PTSD, especially when she walked back into the barn that evening for the wedding, she'd talk to a therapist.

She wanted to put the nightmare behind her and move forward with a sense of hope and excitement for the future. As if Prescott sensed her uneasiness, he waited for her to finish her laps before he asked her if she was okay.

"Still processing," she replied.

"Don't shut me out."

"I won't," she promised.

Prescott

Prescott was concerned about Jack, but he wanted to give her plenty of space to digest what had happened. Not wanting to pressure her, he kept the conversation light and the activities fun.

In the late afternoon, they left for the wedding.

Addison and her bridesmaids were upstairs in the master suite. Hawk and his groomsmen were getting ready in the newly-designed lower level in-law suite.

He spotted Stryker pulling his hair into a bun.

"Hey, bro, you made it," Prescott said.

Stryker pulled him in for a hand-clasp hug, then gave Ethan a high-five. "The guys have been filling me in. You kicked some serious you-know-what."

"I did what had to be done," Prescott replied.

First, Prescott helped Ethan into his white dress shirt and black pants, clipped on his black bow tie, and helped him into his jacket. "You're looking sharp. Go check yourself out," Prescott pointed Ethan toward a full-length mirror.

Prescott changed into his black tux while Stryker, Jericho, Cooper, and Rebel kept Ethan entertained.

When the guys were ready, Hawk presented Ethan with a kid-sized aluminum suitcase, the words RING SECURITY on the front and back.

"Ethan, you have a very important job," Hawk said, looking sharp in his black tux. "You have to carry this when you walk down the aisle." He offered it to Ethan.

"Fank you," Ethan said, taking it from him.

"Do you remember what to do?" Hawk asked.

"I walk down the aisle to Uncle Prescott."

"Good job, bud," Hawk said.

"What about the rings?" Rebel asked.

"I've got them," Prescott replied.

Knock-knock.

Prescott opened the door. "Hey, Mom, don't you look beautiful. You need Nicky?"

"Actually, can I borrow you for a minute?"

"Yo, Rebel, can you hang with Ethan?"

"I got you," Rebel replied.

Prescott pulled the door shut behind him, then joined his mom on a couch in the newly-designed rec room filled with light furniture, a billiard table and a ping pong table.

Like the bridesmaids, his mom wore a full-length black dress. Her hair had been styled by the pro Addison had hired, and she was wearing more makeup than usual.

"You look great, Mom."

She smiled. "Thanks, honey." I want you to have something that's been in our family for a long time." She pulled out a ring box, but she didn't open it. "When your dad—your biological dad—proposed to me, he gave me an engagement ring that had been handed down to him from his dad. The ring goes back four or five generations. When he passed away, I wore it until Dad and I started dating. It made me sad to take it off because I loved your father, but I knew that I had something very special with Mason." She opened the ring box.

Inside sat a large, emerald-cut diamond flanked by smaller emerald-cut stones, in an antique-looking setting.

"It's beautiful," he said.

"The stone is four carats, total carat weight is around five and a half. My feelings aren't hurt if you or Jacqueline don't like it. It's a family heirloom, and I was waiting for you to find your person." Her mom smiled. "I'm so happy you did, Scotty."

"Thanks, Mom. I would love for Jack to wear this, but it's up to her."

His mom handed him the box, then rose. "I'll see you out there."

After pushing off the couch, he hugged her. "Thank you for the ring."

She smiled at him. "I'm very proud of the man you've become, Prescott."

His mom vanished up the stairs, and Prescott slipped the box into his pocket. Time to get his brother married.

With the small suitcase clutched in Ethan's hands, Prescott lifted him into his arms. "You ready to get Uncle Nicky married?"

"This is soooo fun!"

Prescott smiled. "I think so too."

The guys made their way to the barn. Inside, over a hundred guests filled the rows of seats, the excitement palpable.

Pride filled Prescott's heart. Everyone was safe, in part because of him. Despite the relaxed and festive atmosphere, his Glock was secured inside his ankle holster.

He set Ethan down at the rear of the procession, then walked past his band of brothers—Stryker, Cooper, Jericho and Rebel—to his place at the front of the line. The bridesmaids entered, looking beautiful in their matching black dresses, smiles brightening their pretty faces.

For Prescott, only one woman stole his attention... and his heart. Jacqueline looked stunning in her black gown, her styled, auburn mane framing her beautiful face. Her gaze found his and her smile halted his breath.

When she came to a stop beside him, he offered his arm, and whispered, "You are gorgeous, and you're mine."

"All yours." She kissed his cheek. "You look amazing. So handsome."

As soon as the processional music started, he and Jack made their way down the aisle toward his brother, who waited alone. At the end, he kissed her cheek before taking his place by his brother's side.

Two at a time, the groomsmen and their bridesmaids made their way toward the alter.

Ethan, carrying the RING SECURITY case, grinned his way down the aisle, stealing the show. He waved at Jack before standing with Prescott.

Prescott rested his hand on Ethan's small shoulder, and Ethan grinned up at him. "You did a good job, Ethan."

When he peered across the aisle at Jacqueline, he knew they were meant to carve their own path and create a beautiful life together.

Then, Addison appeared, her dad by her side. Within seconds, she homed in on Nicky. They shared a smile before she set off toward him.

The wedding ceremony was low-key and filled with heartfelt love.

Even though the threat had been removed, Hawk and

Addison had hired a twelve-person security team from Maverick Hott's ThunderStrike organization.

Hawk had told his groomsmen, "We paid for it, and we're gonna ensure there are no more surprises."

During the reception, while Ethan was with Nana and Papa, Prescott invited Jack up to the loft. Earlier that day, Cooper and Jericho had carried up a sofa and a throw rug, so guests could check out the upper level. After she eased onto the cushion, he sat beside her, and clasped her hand.

"How are you doing?" he asked.

"Better," she replied. "Now that I'm no longer looking over my shoulder, I want to help others, but I don't know how."

"I'm here whenever you want to bounce ideas."

"Thank you," she said while caressing his hand.

Again, he got down on one knee, pulled out the box, and opened it. "Marry me, Jacqueline. Be my forever."

She stared at him, then at the ring, then back at him. "For real?"

"This is a family heirloom. My mom kept it for me, but we can go ring shop—"

She captured his face in her hands and kissed him. "It's stunning, and I would be honored. What matters most is us, together, for the rest of our lives."

He pulled out the ring and slipped it on her finger. He stood and she rose with him. Their kiss was filled with passion and love... and so much hope for the future.

The music stopped.

With a mic in hand, Hawk said, "Can I get your attention? Check out the loft. Looks like my brother has an announcement."

Prescott and Jacqueline peered down at the guests.

"She said yes!" Prescott hollered.

The guests cheered and clapped, but it was Ethan who yelled, "Hurray!"

Jacqueline beamed at Prescott. "Being with you makes me very, very happy."

"That's my goal," he replied. "Make Jack happy."

"What about the mayhem? Can we stop that?"

"Hell, no, but we can take a break for today."

She laughed. "I'm definitely gonna need more than a day."

The band started up again, and they hurried down the stairs and over to Ethan. "What do you think about including Jack in our family?" Prescott asked.

"Our family combine—combineded—with Jack and Loki. Loki will live with us forever! It's the best day ever!"

"You're right, Ethan," Prescott replied. "This *is* the best day ever."

Jacqueline

O<small>N</small> M<small>ONDAY MORNING</small>, Jacqueline opened the email regarding her sister's background check.

"Our apologies for the delay, but our servers crashed and we had a backlog."

She clicked on the attachment as Prescott walked into the house from the garage. Loki bounded over to greet him.

"Dogs are great," he said. "I was gone for twenty minutes and he's happy to see me." He kissed Jacqueline hello.

"I'm happy to see you too, babe. If I had a tail, it would be wagging just like his," she said.

"If you had a tail, I'm not sure how things would have gone down for us."

She laughed. "You'd love me, even with a tail, I'm sure of it."

He stole another kiss before pouring himself a mug of coffee. "Whatcha working on?"

"Leslie's background check came back."

He sat beside her at the island. "Ethan was telling everyone at daycare that he's going to have a daddy *and* a mommy... *and* he has a dog too."

Jacqueline smiled. "That makes my heart happy."

"We're taking a day, just the two of us," Prescott said, tucking a tendril behind her ear.

"I love that."

"We can spend the day boating, we can lounge by the pool, whatever you want." He kissed her again before turning his attention toward the background check. "Learn anything?"

"I haven't looked at it yet," she replied.

"What the hell?" Prescott blurted. "Look at her name."

Jacqueline read it and gasped. "No way. That can't be right."

Name: Leslie Hartley Maul

Seconds ticked by while she stared at the name, the harsh truth impossible to believe.

"She married that monster," Prescott said.

Jaqueline logged in to Instagram. After toggling around, she pulled up her sister's account. "She's not an Instagram star."

"How do you know?" He sipped the hot drink.

"She's got five hundred followers. That's not nearly enough to be an influencer. There were no modeling gigs. She was with your uncle." Jacqueline slid her gaze from the screen to Prescott. "More lies."

"Do you think your mom and dad know she got married?"

Jacqueline called her mom.

"Hi, honey," her mom answered. "Any chance you'd like to play a round with us tomorrow? I know you're working—"

"Sure, golf is great," Jacqueline interrupted. "Mom, I've got a crazy question. Did Leslie get married?"

"No," her mom replied. "Well, we haven't talked to her in a few months, so she might have."

"But not before that?"

"I think she would have said something, don't you?"

"The old Leslie, yeah, but not the new one," Jacqueline replied.

"Why are you asking?"

"I'll explain tomorrow at golf."

Jacqueline ended the call and said to Prescott, "My mom didn't know."

Prescott turned her laptop so she could see it. "They got married right before Maul went to prison."

"After he escaped, she was harboring a fugitive."

"She must've helped him once he got out." Prescott pulled out his cell phone, made a call.

"Hello, Prescott," Z answered. "Are you and Jacqueline taking the day off?"

"I need a warrant and I need it fast," Prescott replied.

AN HOUR AND A HALF LATER, Jacqueline and Prescott pulled up to Leslie's house. After parking in the driveway, Prescott said, "Babe, you ready to do this?"

"Absolutely."

They pulled on latex gloves and exited the SUV. With a plan in place, they made their way to the front door. Jacqueline rang the doorbell.

No answer, so she pounded on the front door. Still no response.

She texted Leslie. "I'm out front. Are you home?"

When no dots appeared and Leslie didn't respond, Jacqueline tried the knob. Locked. They walked around the house in search of an unlocked or open window on the first floor. When Jacqueline tried the sliding glass door on the back porch, it opened.

They drew their weapons.

"Leslie are you here?" Jacqueline called out.

No response. They went inside. Prescott opened the door leading to the garage.

"Empty."

"Do you think she moved out?" she asked.

"No idea. Let's clear the place."

They went through the first floor. No Leslie. Despite a few dishes in the sink, there were no signs of recent activity. The large, finished basement sat empty, the storage closets bare.

Up on the third floor, they cleared the master bedroom. Like the rest of the home, it looked unlived in.

Jacqueline checked the made bed. "There are sheets and a blanket under here."

In the bathroom were two toothbrushes and two bath towels.

"Leslie acted like she hardly knew Maul," Jacqueline murmured. "They barely talked to each other."

"Either he trained her well, or she was protecting him," Prescott replied.

The shower walls and glass door were still wet. One of the bath towels was damp. In the bedroom, Jacqueline opened the large walk-in closet.

Rows and rows of women's designer clothing hung neatly on hangers.

"Wow, this must've cost a fortune," she said. "Look at all these gowns. Half of these have the tags on them. This is a seventy-five-hundred-dollar dress."

"As the future Mrs. Armstrong, you'll need gowns."

"For what?"

"Charity and industry events." He pulled down a large box

from the closet shelf. "You want to check this while I search the dresser?"

He set it on the bedroom floor before he started opening dresser drawers and rummaging through them.

She eased down, opened the box. Inside sat a neatly folded white shirt, beneath that a pair of black dress pants. She moved them out of the way. A jewelry box sat on top of what looked like a scrapbook or photo album. After opening the jewelry box, she stared at the small, sealed plastic bags. There had to be dozens of them, each containing a single piece of jewelry.

She pulled out a bag and stared at the necklace.

Why does Leslie keep her jewelry in sealed plastic bags?

Jacqueline examined a pair of silver hoop earrings. Then, a bag with a ring. Dread sent shivers through her.

"Ohgod."

This wasn't Leslie's jewelry. These were keepsakes from Maul's killing sprees. She searched the bags until she found the necklace. The silver pendant had tarnished, but the Greek letters of her sorority were engraved on one side. With her heart thumping hard and fast, she turned the small bag over. Engraved on the other side was the message from Jacqueline.

Janey,
Friends Forever. Sisters Always.
In the Bonds, Jack

Fury and heartbreak, and a decade of loss, exploded out of her in a wail.

In seconds, Prescott was by her side, his gaze searching her face. She held up the small baggie. "This was Janey's necklace. A gift from me."

He regarded the jewelry, protected in tiny, plastic bags. Souvenirs to remind Maul of his heinous victories.

A growl ripped out of him. "I would kill him again, if I could."

She opened the book. Inside were neatly arranged newspaper clippings of all the women who'd gone missing or had been murdered by the Campus Killer. There was a list of names. Two columns that filled an entire notebook-lined piece of paper.

Maul's destruction had been way worse than anyone realized.

She set everything in the box.

"Looks like we found what we needed," Prescott bit out as he rose.

"He was pure evil." She stood. "Did you find anything?"

"Nothing," he replied.

Prescott set the evidence box in the hallway, and they moved on to the first spare bedroom. Like the basement, the room sat empty. They found nothing in the closet. When Jacqueline opened the door to the next bedroom, musty air filled her lungs, and she grimaced.

Dirty clothes were heaped on the sofa. Rather than do laundry, everything had been dumped in there. Empty beer bottles lay strewn on the carpet, empty soda cans thrown in the corner.

"What the hell?" she murmured.

"It's like we've pulled back the curtain in Oz," he said. "This is how they *really* lived."

Then, she spied the long-brown wig with the black knit cap. She hurried over and lifted it off the floor. They were sewn together. "Maul's disguise."

Prescott nodded, then opened the closet door, his weapon at the ready.

Piles of clothing lay wrinkled on the floor, the clothing on hangers was in a state of disarray. His shirts hung next to her dresses or pants. There was no organization whatsoever. Shoes strewn on the floor and tossed on the top shelf. Some in pairs, while singles sat with no mate.

"What a mess," he said.

On the shelf, a brightly-colored garment caught Jaqueline's eye. She moved the shoes out of the way and pulled it down.

"It's the clown costume," she said.

"You were right. Maul *was* stalking you." Prescott pulled down the horrifying clown mask. "Is this what you saw?"

A shiver charged through her. "That's the one."

Prescott set the mask down, then started shoving hangers aside, one after the next, his gaze laser-focused on the clothing. When he didn't find what he was looking for, he searched the layers of clothes strewn about the floor.

"What are you looking for?" she asked.

"The surgical gown he wore at the hospital when he killed Sally."

After rummaging through the clothes on the sofa, he pulled out a surgical shirt and pants.

Jacqueline started searching for the cap and mask. Together, they flung clothing out of the way as they dug through the mess.

"Got it." She lifted out the cap.

Seconds later, he found the mask.

She grabbed the shirt and checked the size. "It wasn't Maul who killed Sally," she bit out.

The floor creaked behind them and they spun around.

Leslie stood there, her eyes wild, a gun in her outstretched hands.

"Terr Bear didn't kill Sally," Leslie hissed. "I did."

29

YOU DID WHAT?

Prescott

Prescott needed to disarm Leslie, but he had to defuse the situation first.

Leslie—dressed in sweats, her hair pulled back in a ponytail—flicked her gaze from Jack to him, then back to her sister. "What the hell are you doing in my house?"

"We've got a search warrant," Prescott said.

She pointed the gun at him. "You need to shut the fuck up! SHUT UP!!! You took my sugar daddy away from me, and I'm about to get kicked out of my house!" Then, she glared at Jacqueline. "What's with the latex gloves? Jesus, are you here on FBI business?"

"Yes," Jack replied.

"You've got to be fucking kidding me!" Leslie screeched.

Jack stood her ground. "Put down the gun, Leslie."

"No, bitch, it doesn't work like that. I've got the gun, so I'm the boss. You do as I say and I don't blow his brains out."

"You need to take this down a few," Prescott said.

Leslie shoved the barrel of the gun under his chin. "I said

shut up or I'll shut you up with a bullet through your fucking brain."

Prescott could overpower her, no problem. But was he fast enough to do that before she pulled the trigger? He was about to find out.

"Jacqueline." Her name rumbled out of him, nice and slowly.

"I got you," she replied.

Silence.

"What's going on?" Leslie barked. "Is that code? What are you two—"

Prescott grabbed the weapon and pointed it toward the floor as Jacqueline pulled her Glock and pointed it at Leslie.

"AAAAAAEEEEEEEE!" Leslie screamed as she tried taking control of the weapon.

Prescott shoved her back, and she went flying into the pile of clothes on the sofa. In tandem, they aimed their weapons at her.

"Do. Not. Move," Jacqueline growled. "Leslie Hartley Maul, you're under arrest for the murder of Sally Sagall, for harboring a fugitive, and for assisting in a prison escape." She zip-tied Leslie's wrists and her ankles, then Mirandized her sister.

Prescott bagged Leslie's weapon. "This your gun?"

Leslie glared at him. "Fuck you."

"Answer. His. Question," Jacqueline said, her tone razor sharp.

"It was Terr Bear's. When he went to prison, he told me to keep it in a safe place." Her lips split into a sinister smile. "It came in handy when I needed it."

A growl ripped from Jack's throat. "Why did you kill Prescott's sister?"

Leslie glared at her. "I loved my husband. I helped him escape. I got him set up in Fredericksburg after he busted out. Do you know how that SOB thanked me?"

"How?" Jack asked.

"He met this Sally chick and fell-the-fuck in love with her! Then, he's over the goddamn moon 'cause this bitch is having his baby. He *hates* kids, but, I guess, since it was his, he was okay with it. Then, he tells me he's gonna leave me for her! I had to get that husband-stealing bitch out of the picture. I had already lost my husband to prison. I sure as fuck wasn't losing him to another woman!"

"You didn't have to kill her," Prescott growled.

"I was bankrolling Terr Bear and this is how he pays me back? He was gonna get with this bitch and dump me! So, yeah, I had to move her outta the way."

"Bankrolling what?" Jacqueline asked.

"He wanted to get revenge on the people who put him in prison, so I made sure he had money for his place, for food, for clothes, whatever he needed. Then, I got the surgeries and started posting. That's when I met Artemis. He was willing to pay me so I could live the luxury lifestyle, so I did whatever made him happy, which was screwing. Lots and lots of it. As soon as I got that million, me and Terr Bear were outta here. Poof! Gone."

Fuck. Artemis was funding Maul's ALPHA hits.

"Did Maul know about your affair?" Prescott asked.

"Nah, he thought I was going on all these modeling gigs," Leslie replied. "Then, he told me he met some woman and he became obsessed with her. Said he had to finish a job he started a decade ago. I had no idea what he was talking about—"

"That *job* was me," Jacqueline spat out. "He was the Campus Killer, Leslie! He was killing innocent women and I was the one who got away."

Leslie stilled. Several seconds passed while she gawked at Jacqueline.

"Bullshit. Terr Bear was just getting revenge on the jerks he worked with. They turned on him and put him in prison. I mean, the man was doing his job, for fuck's sake. He wasn't a serial killer."

"You married a monster, and somewhere along the way, you became one too." Jacqueline shook her head. "You make me sick."

"Fuck you."

"No, Leslie, fuck you."

"Is Terr Bear in jail?"

"No," Jacqueline replied. "He's not."

"Well, where the hell is he?" Leslie spat out.

Ignoring her question, Prescott pulled out his phone and called Cooper.

"Coop, I need backup. Jacqueline and I found Sally's killer. It's Maul's wife."

"Nice work," Cooper replied. "I'll send a team right over."

Prescott gave him the address and hung up, then shifted his sights to Leslie. "You're lucky I don't pump you with bullets, leave you here for the rats to eat, and go on with my day."

"You're gonna pay for this," Leslie threatened.

Jacqueline glared at her. "No, Leslie, you are."

THAT EVENING, after Ethan was tucked into his brand-new toddler bed and Loki was tucked into his *second* doggie bed in Ethan's bedroom, Jacqueline changed into a black, lace teddy. She needed alone time with her man, and she needed it now.

After slipping into a black, silk robe, she found Prescott relaxing on the sofa on the back porch, a snifter in his hand, a second on the coffee table.

"There's my beautiful fiancée," he said. "Come sit with me."

She curled up on his lap, lifted the glass, and smelled. "Mmmm, Grand Marnier." After tapping his glass with hers, she said, "Cheers to my hero."

"To us for getting the job done."

"I need you," she said caressing his thigh.

He dipped down, kissed her. "I'm all yours, baby, all night long."

"Listen." she said.

"I don't hear anything."

She smiled. "Exactly. No mayhem."

He shot her a smile. "Not until we work our next case together."

"What does that mean?"

"Z called you, but you were reading Ethan a bedtime story, so he called me."

"And?" She held her breath.

"Babe, don't you want Z to tell you?"

She kissed him. "No, I want to hear it from my man."

"You can relocate with the Bureau to the DC office or—"

"Or?"

"You can join ALPHA as an Operative, which means, we'd partner on some missions."

Excitement soared through her. "Well, that's a no-brainer. I'd get to work with Addison too. I can start in a week."

"I'm sure you could ask for two."

"What would I do with all that extra time?"

He set down their glasses, cradled her in his arms, and rose off the sofa. "Me," he replied. "You'd do me."

"Yes," she whispered before nibbling his ear.

He carried her into their bedroom and locked the door. After she stripped him naked, he untied her robe, slid his hands under the silky material, and pushed it off her shoulders.

Then, he stepped back and gave her a once-over. "Wow, you are sexy." After kissing her, he said. "You look fantastic, baby."

Together, they tumbled into bed. Her lips found his, her kisses turning ardent. She was finally free. Free from looking over her shoulder, no longer terrified that Maul would find her.

Jacqueline loved Prescott with a fervor that left them both breathless. He was hers... all hers, for the rest of her life.

In the afterglow of lovemaking, as he held her in his arms, she asked him if he wanted more children. Lifting her head off his chest, she peered into his eyes.

"Before Ethan, I didn't think about kids," he said. "My career and the company were my life." He entwined his fingers through hers and kissed her warm skin.

"What about now that you've got a child?"

"I'd have a whole litter of them, but that's just because I have an amazing woman to raise them with."

"I love that our story is different, that we became a family in our own way."

"Me, too, babe," he replied. "Do *you* want children?"

"Absolutely. I would love for Ethan to have siblings, but there's a lot of other things that I want to happen first."

"Like?"

"Well, I need to move back east, start my new job, get married."

"In that order?"

She laughed. "That *would* be the most organized, but then, where's the mayhem?"

"Where *is* the mayhem?"

"Right around the corner," she replied. "I'm sure of it."

EPILOGUE

Six months later, Thanksgiving Day

Jacqueline

Prescott and Jacqueline's families were camped out in their family room, everyone too full to move.

Rebel, sitting on the floor with Loki, patted his stomach. "I ate enough for three people. Dinner was *that* good."

"I agree," Jacqueline's sister-in-law, Naomi, said. "Jacqueline, that was the best stuffing I have ever had."

"It was," Prescott's mom added.

"Thank you," Jacqueline replied. "Is it too soon for dessert?"

Moans filled the room, and she laughed.

"Babe, I can't eat another bite," Prescott replied.

She smiled. "We've got plenty of time for dessert and coffee. You'll make room for Naomi's homemade blueberry pie. I've been looking forward to that all day."

"Same," her brother, Keith, added.

"I'm ready to head to the basement for some putting," Jacqueline's mom said. "Ethan, are you with me?"

Ethan had been playing a card game at the kitchen table with his Papa and Jacqueline's dad, who he called Gramps.

"Okay," Ethan replied as he climbed out of the booster seat. "Everybody should come downstairs!"

With Loki bounding down the stairs first, the family made their way into the basement. When Jacqueline's mom and dad had bought Ethan a starter golf club set, he'd taken to the sport so much so that Prescott converted the spacious game room into a putting green.

With clubs in hand, they watched as Ethan set up his shot. As the putting got underway, Jacqueline's mom pulled her aside.

"We visited Leslie this week," her mom murmured.

Leslie was in jail, awaiting her trial date.

Jacqueline had *not* visited her, and had no intention of doing so. Instead, she'd spent the last six months working through the wreckage Leslie had left because of the horrible choices she had made.

"How'd that go?" Jaqueline asked.

"Well, she actually saw us, this time, but she was pretty angry."

"At herself?" Jacqueline asked.

"No. She's angry at *you* for arresting her. She blames us for not helping her out more financially. We gave her twenty thousand, but even that—which we considered a lot—wasn't enough. She's angry with her husband for lying to her about, pretty much, everything. She felt used by him. It's sad, really."

Jacqueline put her arm around her mom. "I'm sorry. If she hadn't helped her monster husband, things would be different."

Her mom squared her shoulders. "Very."

"Yay!" Ethan ran around giving everyone high-fives.

"He sunk one from fifteen feet," Prescott said.

"Nice, Ethan!" Jacqueline called out to him.

When Ethan returned to the putting green, Jacqueline said, "I'm headed to Tech next week to talk to the sorority."

"That's wonderful, honey. Is Prescott going with you?"

She glanced over at him. He was helping Ethan with his stance. "He is," she replied. "He's been so supportive."

Her mom ran her fingers down Jacqueline's long hair. "I'm not surprised. Do you need us to watch Ethan?"

"His mom and dad are watching him, but we're heading to two different colleges next month. If you and Dad are available, we'd love the help."

"Count us in," her mom replied.

After much thought, and several conversations with Prescott, Jacqueline had put together a presentation about campus safety for women. She wanted to share her survivor story with others so what happened to her wouldn't happen to anyone else.

When she reached out to her sorority, they were interested. Word had spread, so she was speaking to several campus-related groups while there.

The doorbell rang.

"That must be Hawk and Addison," she said. "Be right back."

On her way to the front door, she asked, "Computer, who's out front?"

"Nicholas Hawk, Addison Skye Hawk, Z, and an unknown female," answered the computer.

She swung the door wide. "Happy Thanksgiving!"

"I hope it's okay that I'm crashing the party," Addison's sister, Brit said.

"Absolutely." After shutting the front door, Jacqueline hugged her. "It's great to see you. It's been way too long."

She brought them into the living area.

"I thought everyone would be too stuffed to move," Hawk said. "Where are they?"

"Putting in the basement," she replied.

"Baby, I'm going downstairs." Hawk kissed his wife's cheek. "Z, you with me?"

After the men went downstairs, Jacqueline said, "Coffee?"

"None for me, thanks," Brit said.

"I'd love some," Addison replied.

While Jacqueline made a fresh pot, she said, "Britain, you look phenomenal."

"That's exactly what I told her," Addison added. "She's glowing. I asked her if she was pregnant."

"Definitely not pregnant," Brit replied.

"You got a new hairstyle, and I love the highlights," Jacqueline said.

"Sis, make a muscle," Addison said.

"Stop," Brit said with a smile. "You're embarrassing me."

"I thought *I* had muscles, but my baby sis has been working out like a beast," Addison said.

Brit shrugged. "I've got a trainer who shows me *no* mercy."

Rebel moseyed upstairs.

After hugging Addison hello, Rebel extended his hand to Britain. "Joaquin Dillinger, my friends call me Rebel. How's it goin'?"

"Hey, Joaquin." She shook his hand. "Britain Skye. My friends call me Brit, but you can call me Britain."

"*Brit*," Addison scolded, but Rebel chuckled.

"That's cool," Rebel replied.

"Your home is beautiful," Britain said. "I'd love a tour."

"I'll take her on one, if you're down with that," Rebel offered.

"Go for it," Jacqueline said.

As soon as they were out of earshot, Addison said, "I want to talk to you about something."

After filling two coffee cups, she sat beside Addison at the kitchen island. "What's going on?"

"I'm leading a mission in two weeks, and I want you to come with us," Addison said.

Excitement pulsed through her. "You think I'm ready?"

"You've been ready," Addison replied, "but I've been waiting for the right job."

Jacqueline loved her job at ALPHA, and she had a *great* mentor in Addison.

Ethan and Loki came bounding into the room. "Uncle Nicky got a hole in one!"

"That's great," Addison exclaimed.

"Are you done golfing?" Jacqueline asked.

"Nuh-uh," Ethan replied. "Aunt Naomi would like you to pleeease put her pie in the oven."

Jacqueline mussed Ethan's hair, then pulled him close, and kissed his cheek. "Are you having fun?" She turned on the oven.

"So much fun!" Ethan exclaimed. "Uncle Prescott said we can play golf on the big grass tomorrow. He got us a tee time and everything!"

Ethan walked toward the basement, then stopped. "Loki, come."

With a rope toy in his mouth, Loki bounded over. "Good boy. Loki, sit."

After the dog sat, Ethan patted his head. "Good job. Let's go to the basement."

Ethan headed downstairs, but Loki didn't move.

"Don't forget Loki," Jacqueline called out.

He came rushing back upstairs. "Loki, free."

Loki took off toward the basement and Ethan went running after him.

"They're adorable," Addison said.

Jacqueline smiled. "I love them both so much."

"Are you golfing with them tomorrow?" Addison asked.

"Absolutely," Jacqueline replied. "Prescott and I have a running competition. Winner gets sex of their choice."

Addison laughed. "No losers there!"

Jacqueline pulled Naomi's pie from the refrigerator, uncovered it, and set it on the counter.

"Definitely no losers, but Prescott is so competitive, he's become a scratch golfer. I'm convinced if he wasn't running Armstrong, and if he wasn't in BLACK OPS, he'd try to qualify for the PGA Tour."

"We need him too much in BLACK OPS," Addison whispered, then she eyed Jacqueline's bracelet. "You're wearing Janey's pendant."

"I bought a charm bracelet so I'll always have her with me."

Addison put her arm around her. "I love what you're doing to keep her memory alive. When are you going to Tech?"

"Next week," Jacqueline replied.

"You'll do great." Then, Addison glanced over her shoulder. "Should we wait for Rebel and Brit?"

"They'll find us."

As they walked downstairs, Jacqueline glanced at the pendant dangling from the bracelet, the one she gave Janey all those years ago.

Love you, Janey. Miss you so much.

Prescott

PRESCOTT HAD BEEN LOOKING FORWARD to the holiday all month. He'd always loved Thanksgiving, always loved that everything came to a halt so family could come together and be grateful.

He hated that Sally was gone, and he hated that he couldn't change that, but he would do everything he could to ensure her son had every opportunity in life.

For Prescott, family was everything, and he wanted to instill his loyalty and commitment into his child. He wanted Ethan to feel like he belonged, so he'd done what he could to show Ethan how much he meant to him... how much he would always mean.

After golfing, they returned to the family room. Conversations resumed, while a few turned their attention to the football game on TV.

Before everyone filled up on pie, Prescott wanted to share his big news. "Family, can I get your attention?"

They grew silent, his dad muted the television. Prescott pushed off the sofa and stood in front of the gas fireplace, the heat warming his legs.

"Ethan, do you remember we talked about adoption?"

Ethan was sitting on the floor, next to Loki. "Uh-huh, it's when you become my daddy."

Prescott grinned. "Guess who's been adopted?"

Ethan popped up. "Me?"

"That's right! You're officially my son, Ethan Armstrong. What do you think about that?"

Ethan started jumping up and down, which triggered Loki jumping up and barking. The family started clapping and cheering. Ethan ran over to Prescott, and he lifted him into his arms. Ethan had grown so much in the past six months. He'd gone from a toddler to a little boy, and Prescott couldn't imagine his life without this amazing person.

"That was quick," Hawk said.

"Kinship adoptions can move fast," Prescott replied.

"You're my daddy?" Ethan asked.

"I'm your dad." He hugged Ethan.

"Hurray! I have a daddy!" Then, he asked, "What about Jack? Is she and Loki in our family too?"

"Of course," Prescott explained. "Do you remember what we talked about?"

"As soon as you and Jack get married, she can get her permission to be my second mommy."

"Tell everyone what you're going to call me?" Jacqueline prodded.

He grinned at her. "Mama Jack, so we always remember my first mommy."

Jacqueline smiled. "That's right."

"I have a daddy and two mommies!"

More happy applause and cheers from the fam as Rebel and Brit walked into the room.

"Hi," Brit said to everyone.

"This is my sister, Britain," Addison announced as she put her arm around her younger sister.

"What'd we miss?" Rebel asked.

"Uncle Prescott is my daddy!" Ethan announced.

Rebel high-fived Ethan. "That's great, bud."

Ethan beamed. "This is the best day ever!"

Prescott set him down, and he ran over to play with his toys. The chatter resumed, the television was unmuted, and happy sounds filled Prescott's once too-quiet home.

Prescott asked Rebel, "Did you take my bike out?"

"No. Addison's sister wanted a house tour, so I gave her one."

Prescott chuckled. "It must have been *some* tour."

"Why's that?"

"You got bed head."

Rebel raked his hands through his long hair. "You still sellin' your motorcycle?"

"It's yours, if you want it." Prescott squeezed Rebel's shoulders. "When shit went down during the cult mission, you were there for me."

"Goes both ways. I got my ass outta there in time, 'cause of you." He turned toward the group. "I'm taking Prescott's motorcycle for a trial run. Anyone want a ride?"

Britain stepped forward. "I'll go with you."

"I don't think so," Z said.

Britain laughed, then kissed her dad on the cheek. "I love you, Daddy."

"Does that mean you're *not* getting on the motorcycle?" Z asked.

"Uh-huh," Brit replied with a gleam in her eyes.

"You got extra helmets?" Rebel confirmed.

Prescott nodded before Rebel and Britain exited into the garage, shutting the door behind them.

"Britain *never* listens to me," Z said.

"She's a carefree spirit," Addison replied. "Always has been."

"I didn't know they knew each other," Prescott said.

"They just met," Jacqueline said.

"They got friendly fast," Hawk added.

"Looks that way," Prescott replied.

IT WAS AFTER MIDNIGHT when he and Jacqueline tucked an exhausted Ethan into his bed, then returned to the family room.

The house was quiet, the dancing flames in the fireplace cast a warm glow across the room. Prescott sat on the sofa while Jacqueline started cleaning up the glasses, mugs, and dessert dishes.

"Babe, we can do that in the morning. Come sit with me, honey."

She curled up beside him and ran her soft fingers through his hair. "Today was fun, don't you think?"

"It was great."

"Tell me we don't have an early tee time tomorrow."

"Eleven. I put us down for eighteen, but we might stop after nine. We've got a full day tomorrow."

Jacqueline smiled. "When don't we? What else did you have in mind after I whip your ass on the course?"

"You won't win, but I'm more than happy to pay up, if you

do." He kissed her, letting his lips linger on hers. "I thought we'd go Christmas tree shopping."

"Are we cutting one down?"

"Hell, yeah."

She smiled. "That'll be fun."

"I heard from my cousin, Mel," Prescott said. "Her mom is divorcing Artemis."

"No surprise there," she replied. "Oh, that reminds me."

She vanished into their home office, returning with papers. "For you."

He read the first line and laughed. "What the hell? Is this a joke?"

"No, it's a prenup."

He stared at her. "Why?"

"I thought you'd want one. Your company is worth billions."

He tore the sheets in half and set them on the side table. "We're not getting a divorce—"

"I *know* we're soulmates, but I figured—"

"No, Jacqueline, no prenup." He tipped her chin toward him and kissed her again. "On this day of thanks, I want you to know how much I appreciate you, and how much I love you."

"I do know," she replied wrapping her arm around his shoulders. "You show me every single day."

He extracted a small jewelry box tucked between the sofa cushions and held it out to her. "For you."

"You bought me a present?"

"Yeah, and you handed me a prenup."

She laughed. "I was doing that for you."

"You, woman, are stuck with me. I'm a one-and-done man and you're going to be my only wife."

"Thank you." She opened the small box "Oh, wow. I love these."

Inside were three diamond charms. A dog paw-print, a diamond heart, and a golf bag filled with tiny golf clubs.

One at a time, she pulled them out, examined them, then kissed him. "Thank you, these are beautiful."

"Not as beautiful as you, babe," He captured her face in his hands and kissed her.

When the kiss ended, she straddled him. "Listen," she said.

"I don't hear anything."

"Exactly." She kissed him again. "I'd love to pay up on my golf debt. Are you interested, Mac?"

"There's nothing I love more than loving my woman," he replied.

"And there's nothing I love more than loving my man back," she replied with a smile.

Another Happily Ever After by Stoni Alexander

A Note from Stoni

THANKS so much for reading BROKEN! I hope my novel was a fun, exciting escape for you. Writing is my passion, and I'm so grateful you've chosen to read my story.

I loved getting to know Prescott in the previous story, WRECKED. Of all his qualities, his loyalty stood out to me the most, and I wanted to write something where he felt *compelled* to work alone, then put him in situations where he'd be forced into relationships where people depended on him.

Turns out, my muse did me one better. In the end, his entire company depended on him, as did the guests at the rehearsal dinner. No pressure there! Ha!

While I adore my badass heroines, I wanted Jacqueline to have a wound so deep that everyday life was a challenge. I loved her tender side, how she took to Ethan right away, how she struggled to reconcile her feelings for Mac with her feelings for Prescott. The more emotionally complicated my heroines are, the happier I am!

I also loved creating a story about three broken people who become a close-knit family and heal from the immense power of love.

Now, it's time to turn my attention to what I think is going to be the sixth and final story in my Vigilantes series... Rebel and Britain's story.

And you know, being Z's daughter, Brit will be a major kick-ass woman. My muse is ready to dive in and start creating, so off I go again! And Rebel wasn't given that nickname... he earned it. I'm excited to see where their journey takes them!

Please join my Inner Circle to find out when my next book is releasing or if I'm having a Kindle e-book sale. Once you sign up, you'll receive METRO MAN, a short story about a man, a woman, and a steamy subway ride. Go to StoniAlexander.com.

As I've said for years, I have the best readers. If I'm a new-to-you author or you've been a loyal reader for a while... thank you so much for stepping into my imagination. I love hearing from you, so drop me a note at Contact@StoniAlexander.com.

All my books are available exclusively on Amazon, and you can read them free with a Kindle Unlimited subscription.

The Touch Series is also available on Audible and Apple Books! I loved hearing my stories brought to life... it's a dream come true.

Thank you for spending time in Prescott and Jacqueline's world. Walking away from these two is hard, but it's time to shift my focus to Prescott's ruggedly handsome friend, Rebel, and Addison's super-secretive sister, Britain.

Be well. Be happy.
Cheers to Romance,

Stoni Alexander

Coming Next

THE VIGILANTES, Book Six - Romantic Suspense

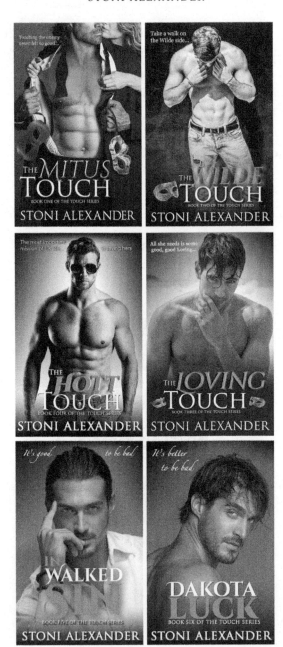

THE TOUCH SERIES - Romantic Suspense

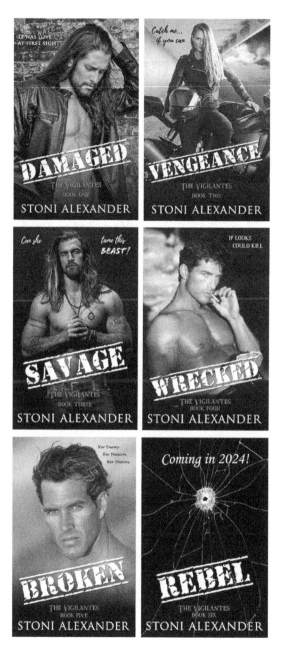

THE VIGILANTES - Romantic Suspense

LOOKING FOR A SEXY STANDALONE?

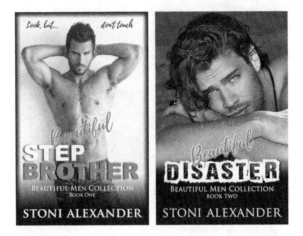

BEAUTIFUL MEN COLLECTION - *Contemporary Romance*

Buy them on Amazon or Read FREE with Kindle Unlimited!

ABOUT THE AUTHOR

Stoni Alexander writes sexy romantic suspense and contemporary romance about tortured alpha males and independent, strong-willed females. Her passion is creating love stories where the hero and heroine help each other through a crisis so that, in the end, they're equal partners in more ways than love alone. The heat level is high, the romance is forever, and the suspense keeps readers guessing until the very end.

Visit Stoni's website:
StoniAlexander.com

Sign up for Stoni's newsletter on her website and she'll gift you a free steamy short story, only available to her Inner Circle.

Here's where you can follow Stoni online. She looks forward to connecting with you!

- amazon.com/author/stonialexander
- bookbub.com/authors/stoni-alexander
- facebook.com/StoniBooks
- goodreads.com/stonialexander
- instagram.com/stonialexander

Made in the USA
Monee, IL
01 September 2023